D1053653

WILDBOUND

Books by ELAYNE AUDREY BECKER

Forestborn
Wildbound

WILDBOUND

ELAYNE AUDREY BECKER

A TOM DOHERTY ASSOCIATES BOOK
NEW YORK

WILDBOUND

Copyright © 2022 by Elayne Audrey Becker

Map by Rhys Davies

A Tor Teen Book
Published by Tom Doherty Associates
120 Broadway
New York, NY 10271

www.tor-forge.com

Tor® is a registered trademark of Macmillan Publishing Group, LLC.

Library of Congress Cataloging-in-Publication Data

Names: Becker, Elayne Audrey, author.
Title: Wildbound / Elayne Audrey Becker.
Description: First edition. | New York : Tor Teen/Tom Doherty Associates,
    2022. | Series: Forestborn ; 2
Identifiers: LCCN 2022008278 (print) | LCCN 2022008279 (ebook) |
    ISBN 9781250752246 (hardcover) | ISBN 9781250752239 (ebook)
Subjects: CYAC: Magic—Fiction. | Shapeshifting—Fiction. | Fantasy. |
    LCGFT: Fantasy fiction.
Classification: LCC PZ7.1.B434746 Wi 2022 (print) | LCC PZ7.1.B434746
    (ebook) | DDC [Fic]—dc23
LC record available at https://lccn.loc.gov/2022008278
LC ebook record available at https://lccn.loc.gov/2022008279

Our books may be purchased in bulk for promotional, educational,
or business use. Please contact your local bookseller or the Macmillan
Corporate and Premium Sales Department at 1-800-221-7945, extension 5442,
or by email at MacmillanSpecialMarkets@macmillan.com.

First Edition: 2022

Printed in the United States of America

0 9 8 7 6 5 4 3 2 1

For my brother, Sam.
We go together, always.

Map of
ALEMARA

Oraes

The Decani Mountains

ERADAIN

Elrin Sea

Caela Ridge

WESTERN VALE

Niav

GLENWEIL

The Purple Mountains

Grovewood

Land of
Giants

The Old
Forest

Roanin

Briarwend

TELYAN

*Fendolyn's
Keep*

Elrin Sea

Poldat

ONE

HELOS

Four words have haunted each step, every dawn, any long silence or starless night.

For weeks, they have settled beneath my skin like a curse, worming their way into my thoughts. Worse than a prison sentence, harder to bear than a life with no sun.

The answer is no.

"Astra!" Weslyn calls, shading his forehead as his wiry deer-hound tears past the trees at the meadow's edge. "Come on, girl."

The ragged hound bounds out of the hickory woods, a gray smear streaking frost across the ankle-high grass. When her speed renders her invisible, I only roll my eyes and continue marching for the forested hills lining the horizon. Lately Weslyn talks more to his dog than he does to me, and thank fortune for that, because if I have to respond to another word from his infuriating mouth, I might just pummel him instead.

Beyond the meadow, hickory, oak, and river birch are only just beginning to turn; this early into the autumn season, green leaves still far outnumber the smattering of red and gold. I lead us determinedly past the tree line, mindful of the clouds hanging low just behind and having no desire to sleep unsheltered in a downpour. Weslyn clears his throat and branches off farther west, invalidating the course I've set with a single, subtle frown.

I swat at Astra when she hovers too close, my jaw clenching. I'm trying to give him a pass, since his castle was empty and his people are missing and he's only just learned his father is dead. But every time I look at his stony countenance and broad, soldier-fit figure, every time I'm forced to listen to his stupid, lilting voice, all I can think about is that he's one half of a pair of brothers, and he's the wrong one.

It's been five miserable days since we set out from Roanin. The city that once felt vibrant and bursting with life had sat alarmingly silent in its abandonment. The absence of people unnerved me more than I cared to admit, and I'd scoured the apothecary shop and the stairs to my shabby apartment for any message Bren and Tomas might have set out for me, some clue as to why the entire capital cleared out without apparent warning. But my bosses left no note. After my disappearance stretched longer than I'd promised it would, I wonder if they stopped expecting me to return altogether.

Though afternoon heat still clings to my limbs like a second skin, the nights are growing cool enough to cause discomfort. Even so, we carry on after the sliver of sun has taken refuge beneath the horizon. Weslyn is convinced that his sister, the crown princess Violet—*Queen* Violet now, I suppose—would have taken their people to Fendolyn's Keep in a crisis, and it's difficult to say which of us has been pushing harder to reach it. We're both desperate to find the historic garrison buried among southern Telyan's endless hills within the next couple of days. Well, if Weslyn's charged silences and half-vacant expressions can rightly be called desperation. Truly, the man's as emotive as a brick.

"Your dog is flagging," I announce, when at last it's grown so dark the thought of continuing is laughable. It's a joke, really, considering she's half a dozen paces ahead of me.

Weslyn halts and backtracks at once, throwing himself down and checking her paw pads for scratches for the fourth time today. His breath is coming more quickly than the situation warrants, and maybe I should pretend not to notice, but too late, I'm already staring. Anything not to look too long at the woods huddling close in the gathering darkness, their branches interlaced like cobwebs, cold and conspiring.

Old enemies.

"We'll stop here, then," Weslyn says at last. He catches me rolling my ankle. "You're hurt?"

"No."

"You're squinting."

I raise a palm in his direction. "Just tend to your dog, okay?"

After studying me another weighted moment, Weslyn orders Astra to stay and goes in search of firewood, since it's his night to.

Finally, some peace. I loosen my laces and pull my foot from the worn boot, wincing as my ankle scrapes the sides. Beneath my torn-up sock, the skin is puffy and tender. It was careless of me to pick a fight with a coyote yesterday while hunting in fox form.

Astra sidles closer when I pull the jerky from my pack, sniffing hopefully at my closed fist. I lift it high and look her in the eye until she turns away. Since I'm trying hard to ignore the scrabbling sounds of Weslyn gathering twigs nearby, for a while, I let my mind paint a better picture. One, not of loose brown curls and a beard in need of a trim, but of rose-tinted white skin and golden hair and eyes the color of a clear summer sky. *Finley.* But Weslyn has spoiled that for me, as well, and all too soon the perfect features melt into decay, sunken cheeks and heavy lids. Throat tightening, I shake the image clean away, salvaging what I can of the meat pulverized against my palm.

Weslyn sets down his bundle of sticks and leaves, carving a hole into the earth and building the fire just like I taught him. Back when our journey still held the hope of success. When my sister, Rora, was here to bridge the gap between us, the glue that came to hold our group of three in place. Now there's only the two of us, divided by our differences and the mutual understanding that I would have been willing to trade his life for his brother's.

By the river, I am tired of walking.

"We might reach it tomorrow, if you can maintain this pace," Weslyn says, gaze flitting to my feet as he sits by the flames.

"Have I slowed you down yet?" I demand.

He doesn't rise to the provocation, only assesses me with an indeterminate expression before pulling out his waterskin. Astra yawns and flops down at his side. The flames sizzle and pop.

"He's still alive, Helos," Weslyn murmurs, his tanned white skin flickering orange in the firelight.

My muscles lock up. It's the forbidden subject, the one we've been avoiding since that day on the riverbank. The nightmare of water pounding and Rora falling and Weslyn lying broken and then not broken on the bank.

"There could be time to—"

"To what?" I reply bitterly. "We have nothing that could help him. Thanks to you."

Weslyn's fingers must have tightened around the curls in Astra's coat, because the hound raises her head in my direction, a low growl rumbling through her teeth.

Whatever. I tear the remains of my dinner apart piece by piece, chewing forcefully. If Rora were here, no doubt she would give me that singular frown of hers—part wounded, part indignant. But I let her go. Alone, after we promised we'd go together, always. And I still can't get over the waste of it all.

Four weeks journeying into the Vale and back, that wretched magical wilderness with its shifting terrain and perilous unpredictability. Bartering with giants, fleeing from Eradain soldiers, and that evil—that—no, don't go there. I brush my nose hastily. All to obtain the stardust that could have cured Finley, and anyone else afflicted with the Fallow Throes rampaging the three realms east of the river, killing humans at random. To think that we'd actually managed to do it, secured enough stardust to *cure them all*—until Weslyn fell into the river and nearly drowned.

The monstrous current from which Rora saved him had ruined most of the stardust, but there had been a little left. Enough for one.

And she used it on him.

In the present, Weslyn's still staring at the fire, not having touched a scrap of food.

He checks Astra's paws again.

I didn't want him to die. I can admit that. But with Fin— No, just . . . just lock it away. That's what's best—pushed to the far recesses of my mind before the weight of it can drown me, too.

I force down a few drops of water, mostly just to give myself something to do, then lay out my bedroll on the other side of the fire, bored. In my weaker moments, I suppose I can understand what Rora sees in him—both so serious, so exasperatingly stubborn and stuck on doing what's right. And I'm not exactly blind to the strong jawline shrouded in stubble, the way the rolled shirtsleeves fit just so around the forearms.

But still. Weslyn is broad strokes of gray, the whole package too noble and intense and quiet and *predictable*.

Finley is a portrait in iridescence. He's the sudden break in rain in the middle of a downpour, the kind of unexpected gift that makes your breath catch before you run out to meet it. Finley is the boy who snorts when you kiss him softly, unsure, then grabs you by the shirt and pulls you close to do it properly.

He's like a hummingbird, flitting from one topic, any given pursuit, to another. A sketch in constant motion, as easygoing as he is easily distracted. Curious, quick to laugh, lazy at times, eager to grab hold of any loose thread that might lead to an adventure.

The answer is no.

Stomach sinking, I try to count the objects around us. The flames arcing high, the wolf-sized dog. Rough bark, a mossy stone, a— No, it's useless. It's one of the tricks Rora employs to calm herself down, but when I try, the anger only tightens its grip in response. This torturous ire that has lodged inside my chest like a bramble, its thorny edges oozing poison, puncturing any moments of levity that dare to raise a challenge.

I used to be better at this.

I look again at Weslyn, on his back now with a hand behind his head, staring at the sky. I wonder if he's still seeing his father's head mounted on the post. I see the dead king's vacant stare behind closed lids more often than I'd like, a horrible sight that I wouldn't wish on anyone, no matter how much they get under my skin. But since I don't know how to ask, and I don't think he'd tell me even if

I did, all I do is follow his lead and rest my head on top of my pack. Our usual arrangement.

Maybe Rora's right, and reawakening the land as she's off trying to do will free the dwindling magic from its fear of extinction. Maybe she'll succeed, and the Fallow Throes will loosen its hold on human hosts whose bodies can no longer tolerate magic or offer the sanctuary it's seeking.

But every time I allow myself to hope, I remember that her strategy could take weeks, months maybe, and even then it's still only a guess. Finley could be long gone by then.

Tomorrow. Let us find him tomorrow. Alive.

The fire burns lower as Weslyn rolls over, away from the flames. After another quick glance in his direction, I remove my pack from under my head and set it down by my feet, resting my swollen ankle on top of it.

The rain begins to fall.

Silence hangs heavy as we break down our tiny camp at dawn. Silver mist snakes through the deciduous woods, as it seems to most mornings in these parts. The Smoky Rise, the Telyans call this stretch of hills, and though I suppose it's pretty enough, I can't help but wish I were back in Roanin. It's irreplaceable, to wake with four walls around you, no matter that the paint is flaking, the glass a little smudged. To hear windows creaking open and rubber soles striking cobblestone and know you're safely inside, yet decidedly not alone.

After Weslyn checks his map against the sun's position, he launches forward with his hands closed tight around the straps of his pack. Astra keeps pace with him as I follow shortly behind, just grateful my ankle feels less tender today.

By the time we reach an old stone road that seems to appear out of nowhere, winding between the forested slopes rising on either side, the dense brown hair that falls midway between my jaw and shoulders has dampened with sweat.

"Do we take it or skirt around?" I ask. The question has divided us every time we hit signs of civilization—two towns and a handful of streets in the days since leaving Roanin, all of which appeared empty from a distance. Weslyn wants to find people to question. I've argued we should travel in stealth until we know what's what.

He shades his forehead with a hand, examining the road until it disappears round the bend ahead. I can tell by the grim set of his mouth that he resents feeling uneasy in his own kingdom, but I have no intention of dying for the sake of his pride.

"Take it," he decides, like an idiot, stepping onto the road with purpose. "We're getting close. The valley that hides the Keep should be just around those hills."

The forested hills ahead that, like all the rest, hide potential adversaries from view. Anyone who travels this road is locked in between them and utterly exposed.

"It's too open," I insist.

"It's ours," he replies, meaning Telyan's, but what if it's not?

"So was Roanin." I grind a heel into the ground.

"So *is* Roanin. It's been evacuated, not lost. Come on."

Doubt flaring, I fall into step beside him, keeping an eye on the patchy woods. Perfect coverage for an ambush. I can't help but study the shadows within as Weslyn plows ahead.

I swear by the river, one of them shifts.

"Weslyn."

"Relax, Helos. I know where we are."

"So will anyone scouting these hills," I tell him, nervous now. "We should get off the road."

"Despite what you seem determined to believe, I'm not stupid," he says, rather shortly. "I don't doubt we're being watched. But our soldiers are not trained to kill on sight, and in any case, they will recognize me."

Astra's tail stiffens as she keeps to Weslyn's side, either picking up on my own misgivings or sensing something else amiss. My heart rate kicks up as we walk another thirty paces or so. Far up and to our left, a shadow shifts again.

"Get back here," Weslyn calls, but I don't take orders from him

and am already climbing the slope. It doesn't seem to have oc-
curred to him that the people in these hills might not be Telyans.
My hands curl into fists at my side, weaponless, but there's always
the elk. Sharp antlers and powerful hooves.

I melt into the coverage of low-hanging elms and adjust my gait
until my footfalls could passably sound like a small animal rustling
the undergrowth. I hope. Sure enough, I spot a sky-blue shirt and
black trousers moving through the trees, the stranger facing away
from me, a knife at his side. His proximity is a bit of a shock, really, considering I haven't seen another person aside from Weslyn
in almost a week. A soldier from the Keep—or an Eradain scout,
perhaps?

Remembered fear flutters in my chest, but it's best to take no
chances. Besides, if Rora were here, she wouldn't hesitate. *Lock it
away.* I creep up behind him—the fool doesn't even turn, thank
fortune—and disarm him clumsily but successfully. Ignoring his
stuttered cry, I grab his slender shoulders and slam him against the
nearest trunk, raising a hand to his throat.

At the sight of his face, the air rushes from my lungs.

Messy blond waves. Crystal-blue eyes. Hollowed cheeks and a
small, bewildered smile stretching across his narrow face.

"Hello," says Finley.

TWO

RORA

I hold my body as still as I can, scanning the surrounding trees for any signs of movement.

It's chilly up here at higher elevation. A sharp breeze teases a few tresses of hair, the mountain air crisp against my skin and carrying the heady scent of cedar. I breathe it in deep, willing my pent-up nerves to unfurl a little in response.

He's late.

Perched on a large, slanted rock face hidden among the creaking spruce pines, I roll my neck in an attempt to release some of the tension. These conifer woods end a mere two dozen paces ahead, old forest and birdsong giving way to barren, brown plains beyond, which means I should be near enough to the tree line to spot an approaching uniform with ease. Frustratingly, there are none.

Perhaps he decided it wasn't worth the risk of getting caught. Or perhaps they've forced the truth from his traitorous mouth already.

I glance again at the sun poking out from its nest of drifting clouds. Midday. Soon it will sink into afternoon, and our carefully orchestrated window will be gone.

When wings flutter past my ear, I twist to see a black-tipped caw alight on a nearby branch, his razor-sharp feathers carving shallow lines into the spindly wood. The magical raven lurks too close to my face for comfort, but he only tilts his glossy head, sizing me up through beady chestnut eyes.

"My friends have a saying, you know."

The lithe boy who speaks steps onto the base of my rock, his caribran-hide boots unnervingly quiet.

Cursed fortune. I need to pay better attention.

"Studying a bud does not make it bloom," he goes on, sounding faintly amused. Silver eyes gleam bright beneath thick lashes and above long features etched into a rich brown face.

"Maybe not," I reply, the sudden tension easing as I brush a pine needle from my dark cotton shirt. "But better to arrive early for the moment than to miss it entirely."

Peridon smiles as he nods in the direction I've been monitoring. "Still no sign?"

My lips press into a thin line.

"Coda," he murmurs. Heartbeats later, the black-tipped caw perches on his narrow shoulder, inky talons pressed into the moss-green cloth; somehow, the bladed feathers never seem to graze Peridon's skin. The rest of his command is inaudible to me, spoken mind-to-mind, and Coda flies away.

Removing the bow slung over his back, Peridon sets the weapon on the rock face and takes a seat beside me. A few strands of silver-and gold-streaked hair have tugged free of the leather band knotting the rest behind his head, and six golden rings are spaced evenly across his left forearm like a second skin. One appeared for each animal species he learned to compel, he explained the first time he caught me staring, all requiring different levels of mastery. He'd looked prepared to offer more if I'd asked. I hadn't.

With Finley ill, Telyan's leadership unknown, and Eradain's thirst for violence sweeping the realms, each sunrise feels precious, every day without progress a waste. Yet even pushing hard, it took me two days to trek back through Telyan and across the tree bridge, into the Western Vale, and another three still to track down Peridon amidst the sprawling, changeable wilderness where most magical people and creatures now reside—or did, before Eradain began capturing and slaughtering them. The whisperers here are nomadic, annoyingly adept at covering their tracks, and the only other time I'd spoken with Peridon was the day I tried to persuade his circle of friends to help me infiltrate the prison compound I've returned to destroy.

Of the whisperers I'd entreated, only he had been eager to help—except his clan leader, Feren, forbade it.

This time, I made sure to catch him alone.

"Rora."

Peridon and I push to our feet as Coda lands on a nearby tree, scarcely any time since setting off.

"He's coming," Peridon says, voice grim.

Two figures appear in the distance. We split up, positioning ourselves among the low-hanging branches to either side of the boulder. Our plan for dismantling the prison feels simple enough—in broad strokes, at least. Break in and blend until nightfall. Dismantle the watchtower guards and steal the master key. Free the prisoners, like Peridon's cousin. Flee. The tricky parts lay in the details, and most of all, in securing the aid of the Eradain soldier I've managed to turn.

Low, angry words ride the breeze to our hiding place, discordant among the chirping jays and rustling vegetation. Peridon and I exchange a glance as pinecones crackle beneath heavy boots. These humans travel as loudly as timber bears.

"—in a bind. I told him all he needs is one good scuffle in the woods."

The response is too quiet to make out.

"Please. He's about as tough as a sack of grain, and just as smart, too."

"He's the commander's nephew."

"As I said."

The voices are much louder now; the men can't be more than a few steps away. Peridon tosses a stone, which clatters against the boulder.

"Did you hear that?" says the reedier voice.

"Bloody ends, man. Loosen up." A sword scrapes free of its sheath, and a burly soldier saunters around the rock face, blade raised. "There's nothing to—"

He chokes on the rest of his bluster when I slam my boot into the back of his knee, then my fist into his temple. The soldier collapses, limbs splayed like a stack of firewood dropped on the ground.

"His voice could wake the dead," Peridon observes, stepping out from behind his tree.

The second man rubs his arms, fitted in the red-trimmed navy uniform that marks him a soldier of Eradain. His dark brown hair is cropped short, his nose bent in the middle as if formerly broken, his white skin marble-smooth. He looks young.

"You're late," I tell him, massaging my knuckles.

A lump bobs in his throat. Beside me, Peridon fiddles with his bow, muscular arms taut.

"I came as soon as I could," the soldier insists, any stab at authority belied by the waver in his voice.

"Are there any more?"

He shakes his head.

"Good."

With another glance at his comrade, I focus on the place in my core and pull matter from the air around me, heat rushing through my tingling body as my spine lengthens and my neck grows wider, my arms and legs broader and hairier. My nut-brown waves that usually fall just below my shoulders shorten to raven-black strands close to my scalp. A scraggly beard hugs the sides of my face uncomfortably, and the olive skin that Helos and I share morphs into a paler shade of white. Disconcertingly, his eyes were already the same dark brown as my own.

The conscious soldier gawks. "You look just like him."

"Yes, and I can keep the façade only as long as you keep yours." I strip the fallen soldier and pull on his uniform, my skin crawling as the borrowed clothes settle against it. The threat is merely bluster; I can hold this form for two days if I have to. But I need to make sure he's with us. "Let me remind you that if we're found out, I'll take you down, too, which would make you as good as dead."

"Your name?" Peridon prompts.

"Gerig," I answer for him, my voice deep and gravelly thanks to my newly thickened vocal cords. "We had the pleasure of meeting several weeks ago."

When he watched his comrade kill a caegar and fire a crossbow at my chest, then made his own half-hearted attempt to catch me before I clawed free of his grasp.

Gerig shuffles a little, composure wavering.

Not for the first time, I wish Weslyn were here. He's the more effective negotiator between us, and no doubt he could stoke this turncoat's loyalty on logic alone, without issuing threats. My chest heats at the thought. Unfortunately, I really don't have his patience.

Besides, Gerig's presence carries too many grim associations. The metal cages where they keep their magical prisoners and, once, held my brother. King Jol's systematic efforts to eliminate every magical being from Alemara, in a misguided attempt to prevent another Rupturing that could break the continent apart. Each heavy, ashen wall that shields the room in which they imprisoned me from prying eyes. That horrible shed, its darkness swollen with discarded, empty bodies, the stench of death hanging nearly thick enough to taste.

The base of my throat tightens, and I clench my fists, shrugging away the ghost sensations of rolling corpses and rotting limbs.

"Are you ready, Gerig?" Peridon asks.

Gerig lifts his chin. "I'm here, aren't I?"

Endeavoring to tamp down the fear, I force myself to focus on more practical memories instead. The time Gerig sat silently in a recreation room, separate from his chattering comrades, staring at nothing. When the caegar had paralyzed me with her hypnotic gaze, and Gerig had tried to tug me to my feet. To save me. "You are," I say, and hold out a hand.

He hesitates a moment, then takes it.

"The next burning is scheduled for tomorrow morning," he says, his voice coming out a little stronger. "So it'll have to be today."

"Tonight," I amend. Though Peridon and I have only been reunited for two days, neither of us feel we can delay further. "Human eyesight is weaker in the dark." I mean it as fact, not as insult, and

Gerig seems to take it as such. "Remember, the watchtower first. Then we get the key." I tuck my stolen shirt into my pants and nod to Peridon.

He pulls a knife from his boot and slits the naked soldier's throat in one smooth motion.

"What was that for?" Gerig cries, falling back a step.

My stomach churns at the blood spilling onto the earth, but I swallow and force myself to look Gerig straight in the eye. "It had to be done. We can't have him waking up and stumbling back to the prison before we're through."

Gerig begins to gag. Hardly the stomach to be a soldier—which is why I chose him. "Why not kill him first then, instead of knocking him out?"

I tug on the soldier's navy shirt hugging my frame. "I can't walk in with all that blood on my clothes."

He frowns, unimpressed by this level-headed assessment. I know how callous it sounds, and discomfort gnaws at my core. But it really is the only logical way.

"Ready?" Peridon asks, wiping the blade clean and returning it to his boot. He appears fairly uncomfortable himself.

I look to Gerig. "You brought the rope?" When he holds it up, I position myself opposite Peridon and take a breath. "Make it look real."

Peridon raises a hand, then hesitates. I roll my eyes and punch him in the face.

"*Shit*," he swears, doubling over at the waist. He spits a wad of saliva and blood onto the grass.

"Now is not the time to be polite," I remind him, stumbling back when he rams a fist into my cheek. Tears spring to my eyes at the white-hot pain singeing my face.

Gerig clears his throat. "Is this really—"

I slam my borrowed body into Peridon and pin him to the ground, trying to get his shirt to stain. "The rope," I instruct, holding out a hand. Gerig drops it into my palm, and I make sure to bind Peridon's wrists tight before helping him to his feet.

"Blood?" Peridon suggests through swelling lips, nodding to the corpse.

Now it's my turn to hesitate, and in the end, Gerig is the one who dabs his blade against the crimson throat and smears it along Peridon's side. He rips a hole in the fabric for good measure.

We're all silent a moment.

"Well?" Peridon says at last, looking down at his disheveled state. "Do I look like a prisoner?"

I wonder what his family would think if they knew what he was doing. Helos would undoubtedly object in horror, but my brother, my only family, is all the way east of the river, days away. "You look like you lost."

Well, not my only family.

"And you're sure about this?" Peridon asks, watching me closely. Unbidden, Weslyn's face floats to the surface again, the morning after Helos's capture, when we uncovered the trap door hidden in the earth. *Are you sure you want to go in there?*

What is it with boys and asking me if I want to go through with my own plans? "Of course I'm sure," I reply, a bit impatiently. Trying, with only a small measure of success, to turn my thoughts away from missing Wes once more.

The curling hair. His gentle smile.

"It's just, you look—"

"Yes?"

"Concerned."

I fold my arms, feeling the bulky biceps constrict. "I was thinking about something else," I say truthfully. "Worry about your own nerve, not mine."

He adopts a slightly wounded look, but I do my best to shrug off the prickle of guilt as Gerig pulls the body beneath a tree—whether to hide it or offer a shred of dignity in death, I don't know. Peridon and I may have built up a rapport these last two days, and I'm glad he's here, but I know better than to entrust him with the *concern* that thoughts of family evoked. Anyway, I've no doubt he would abandon the mission the moment he knew.

That Jol Holworth, Eradain's beloved king orchestrating this mass slaughter, the one whose prison we're setting out to destroy— he's my half brother.

Try as I have to cast aside the note he left for Helos and me, pinned to one of the thrones to either side of King Gerar's mounted head, the poisonous words are never far from the surface, demanding attention.

> *To Mariella's children,*
>   *Yes, I know that's what you are. We did not meet or part on friendly terms, but I would like to rectify that. If you should return to Roanin and see this, I ask that you come to Oraes, so that we might better understand one another. There is much I'd have you tell me, and much that you should know.*
>   *-J. Holworth*

"Okay," Gerig says, emerging from where he's stowed the body and wiping his hands on the grass. "They'll be expecting Karlog and me to reappear within the hour. We should move."

Come to Oraes, Jol requested.

With one last glance at the sky, I steady my racing heart. Oraes, Eradain's capital—I'll be there soon enough. But first things first.

"All right," I say, uncrossing my arms. "Let's go."

THREE

HELOS

It takes several long moments for words to come, and when they do, all I can manage is Finley's name. I stumble back a fraction, feeling dazed and off guard and entirely overwhelmed by the sudden nearness of him.

His face. Have his eyes always been that vivid? Has he always been this tall, the top of his head nearly level with my jaw? I see my own shock reflected in his delicate features, sandy eyebrows lifted to the sky.

Fin's lips part as he leans toward me, that disbelieving smile drawing me in like a parched man to water, and for a wild moment I wonder if I've imagined it all. The weeks of distance prior to the Vale, the message he left for me. Those four aching words. Before I can stop myself, I cup his face between my hands.

His smile slips at my touch.

"Helos," he warns, straightening abruptly in the manner of one having struggled against some impulse and come out the stronger. I register the shift like all the warmth has been sucked from the air.

I drop my hands.

Finley starts to say more—and collapses.

"*Fin!*"

Muscled arms barrel me off to the side, and suddenly Weslyn is there, dropping to his knees and gripping Finley by the shoulders. "What is it? What's wrong?" he demands, heaving for breath as he scours his younger brother's body. Frantic energy laps off of him in waves, but Astra's tail wags like mad as she licks Finley's face.

"You're here," Fin says, laughing as he pushes the dog's head away. He shuts his eyes and rests his head against the trunk. "You came back."

"Of course I did!" Weslyn exclaims. "Are you okay? Where is Violet? We returned to Roanin and—" His voice catches.

The whole display is slightly bewildering to me, considering his usual stoicism. I've only ever seen him this undone once before— the day I escaped that prison compound, when he realized Rora stayed behind.

Where is she? Helos, is she—

"Do you have it? The stardust?" Finley asks, opening his eyes.

Somehow it's only now that I realize how utterly silent it is apart from our voices. All the surrounding sounds have been snuffed out like a candle. And the trees, each bending toward him in a twisted mockery of deference. The sway and the silence.

Stomach prickling, I join them on the leafy ground, noting Finley's tensed posture and the flush rising to his cheeks.

What feels like an eternity later, Weslyn shakes his head.

Finley just blinks at him. This new silence spears my heart on the edge of a knife. After a long while, he nods and ducks his chin, as if it doesn't matter, the unforgivable loss of this thing he's spent the last few weeks hoping to receive. "Ah, well," he murmurs, attempting a smile that doesn't reach his eyes. He shrugs, stroking Astra's back when she flops down by his side. "It was worth a try."

A muscle works in Weslyn's jaw. "Fin, I—"

"We left, to answer your question." Finley exhales slowly. "Roanin is empty. Violet evacuated the city after Father . . ." His gaze flicks to me before surveying Weslyn's face. "Wes," he says, quiet. He rests a hand over his brother's. "Something has happened."

Finley chews his bottom lip, panic blossoming in his gaze, as if the sentence was out before he fully thought it through. The long pause after those ominous words is only making things worse, but it's clear he does not want to continue.

Maybe Weslyn senses this, too, because he soon rescues Fin. "I

know about Father already. I went home before coming here—
that's how I knew where to find you."

"Oh," Finley says, glancing at the trees. "So you . . . You got
my message, then? Vi said we couldn't write anything down, but I
thought—well, maybe it wasn't clear enough, but I thought it was
worth a shot, in case you—"

Weslyn pulls a notched wooden disk from his pocket, which I
didn't even know he'd kept—the strange calendar he claimed Fin
had left for him to find. "It wasn't very difficult," he says with a
touch of amusement, dropping it gently into Finley's palm.

Finley laughs once, a rather strained sound as he peers down at
the disk. "Yes, yes, you're the smart one, no need to brag." He's still
nervous, which isn't like him at all. Whatever Weslyn is doing to
cause this, I'm desperate to make it stop. "So you—you're okay?"
Finley asks, searching his brother's face.

"Don't worry about me, Fin," says Weslyn. "Where is Violet? Did
she—"

"You're hurting him," I interrupt, catching Finley's subtle
wince with alarm.

A crease appears in Finley's forehead. "Helos—"

"You're hurting him. Let go," I command, ignoring his protest.

Weslyn releases Finley's other shoulder, eyes wide. "I'm—
sorry, Fin, I didn't—"

"Oh, you know Helos," Finley remarks. "He likes to fret."
Weslyn and I avoid each other's gaze. "Now someone help me
up."

Weslyn rises and holds out his hands, but I offer my arm, thinking that might be easier on Finley's sore shoulders than yanking.
After a brief hesitation, Finley uses me to boost himself up, sweat
beading along his forehead. "Hand me that, will you?"

Weslyn retrieves the wooden walking stick and brown satchel
resting against a nearby trunk. He opens the bag's flap. "Are you
gathering herbs? Do you need help?"

"Did you come here alone?" I ask more quietly.

"By the river, will you *shut* it?" Finley snaps, snatching the
walking stick from his brother. "A couple of nursemaids, the pair

of you. I have enough of those in the Keep already. Stop trying to be my healers."

"I *am* a healer," I remind him, just as Weslyn asks, "You're staying in the Keep, then?"

"Me and Vi, among others." Finley walks toward the forest's edge, leaving us to follow. Weslyn slings the satchel over his shoulder. "The rest are set up in tents around the base. Violet ordered evacuations in all . . ." He trails off, halting abruptly. "Where's Rora?"

Weslyn's jaw clamps shut.

"Helos?"

I sigh. "It's a long story."

"Where is she?" he demands, hastening toward me.

Something twists inside my gut at his raised voice and panicked expression. "She's fine, don't worry," I assure him, hoping to all the world that's true. "She returned to Roanin with us, but she's gone back to the Vale."

Finley's mouth drops open. When I don't offer more, he turns to Weslyn, who's studying the ground.

"You let her go back there again?" he asks. "Alone?"

His accusation evokes unwelcome images. Rora attacked. Rora screaming. Rora lying injured, covered in blood.

I've seen the way he acts around you, she'd said of Finley with a smile, the last conversation we had before she left. *Like he never wants to look anywhere else.*

I push the hair back from my face. *Rora, if you could see him now.* "It was her choice," I say, taking a step toward him. "I'll explain everything when we get to Fendolyn's Keep. She's tough, Fin. She can take care of herself."

The words ring false in my heart against a lifetime of fighting to keep her safe.

Stormy emotion flickers through Finley's eyes as they sweep over my face.

I don't know what I expected our reunion to be like. Most of my fantasies were limited, built on the merest hope of his survival and little more. Others reached farther, idealistic even for my dreaming mind. Finley laughing like he used to, unburdened and unconstrained, buzzing with energy. Realizing he made a mistake and pulling me close and kissing away the rejection. Maybe more.

The Finley before me seems different, and it's not just the illness.

"I'll hold you to that," he says, looking away. "Let's go."

We reach the edge of the forest, and the land opens up into a sprawling green valley, mostly treeless, with two small lakes stacked like the number eight. The ridge we're on appears to be part of a ring of hills half-encircling the valley, forming a shield that would make it difficult to spot the Keep from the other side. Many are sharp-tipped, more like small mountains, with rocky, inhospitable-looking slopes that may have boasted trees before the land began to weaken. Our road appears to be the main route in or out.

After hooking around our ridge and across the valley floor, the pavement climbs all the way up a great slab of land maybe half the height of the surrounding hills. A massive rectangular fort with rounded corners commands the plateau—Fendolyn's Keep, I'm guessing. Part military academy, part active garrison. Even from this distance, I can spot three pairs of towers built into the rampart, and crowded within, a collection of long buildings arranged at right angles. A huge spread of tents, hundreds at least, are sprawled around the plateau's base and along the lake shores.

"How many cities has Violet evacuated?" Weslyn asks, assessing the scene before us like pieces on a game board.

"All those in the far north. Roanin, Grovewood. The scattered villages," says Fin.

We descend into the valley.

The trek toward the Keep drags painfully slow. The farther we walk, the more Finley steps as though there are needles affixed to the bottoms of his feet, a constant series of minute hesitations between setting his heel on the ground and letting that impact extend to his soles. His face grows drawn and haggard, forehead coated in sweat, his hand white-knuckled where it grips the walking stick.

Magic swirls uneasily in my core. On Finley's other side, Weslyn appears ready to jump out of his skin. Sensing the desperation to help, to get Fin to safety, elk instincts prod the corners of my mind. A pair of pressure points juts up against my skull, antlers endeavoring to cleave through.

"Should I shift?" I ask.

Finley glances at me sidelong before following my gaze to his feet. The offer to carry him the rest of the way clicks—he knows my forms—and his back straightens indignantly as he replies, rather roughly, "Never mind that."

We failed him. The refrain spirals over and over in my head as I nudge the antlers back. *He's going to die. We failed.* If Rora were here, she'd tell me not to be ridiculous, that our new plan could work. And I'm trying to hold onto the hope, I am. But it's hard to pull from that well when the fear speaks so much louder.

We're halfway to the mass of tents when four riders emerge from the makeshift village, driving their horses toward us with obvious urgency. My pace falters a little.

"Your Royal Highness! Prince Finley!" one shouts, dressed in the starched gray uniform of Castle Roanin's Royal Guard. She raises her fist in some kind of signal, and the other three guards fan out to surround us. One has a fifth horse tethered to his with no rider in its saddle. "Sir, we expected you some time ago. Her Majesty left instruction t—" Her voice breaks off, and she pulls her horse to a stop, dismounting and approaching Weslyn with a baffled expression.

"Your Royal Highness?" she says, taking in Weslyn's travel-worn clothing and untrimmed beard. "You're back!" She slams a fist against her heart and bows at the waist.

"Broden," Weslyn calls without pause, extending an arm to the rider with the spare mount. "The gelding. Now."

The young, ruddy-cheeked man called Broden dismounts, unknotting the spare horse's tether and leading him forward with a curious glance my way. The roan horse snorts and tosses his head, ears pinned back.

"Cascade!" Finley exclaims, while Broden pulls on the lead. The horse whinnies and rears a little, and I fumble backward.

"Give him to me," Weslyn says, shouldering Broden aside and

ignoring Fin's indignant remarks about being able to tend to his own horse. "Step away, Helos," he adds without looking back.

The guards appraise me with open suspicion as I retreat further, upwind of the panicked animal. I scratch the back of my head and return their stares pointedly while Weslyn shortens Cascade's lead in increments, patting the broad neck and murmuring words too low for me to make out. Eventually, the horse calms.

Peace restored, Weslyn hands Finley's walking stick to the closest guard and lifts his protesting brother by the waist. After setting him into the saddle, Weslyn pulls himself up and grabs the reins, his arms around Fin like a shield.

"What about Helos?" Finley asks. He bites his lip when our gazes connect, but we both know no horse will bear a shifter as a rider.

Weslyn studies me through narrowed eyes, trying to hold the horse steady as it dances sideways a couple of steps. "I'm sorry," he says at last. "Can you walk?"

I'm sure he's as intent on getting Finley back as I am, so for once, we're in agreement. "Go," I say, smiling at Finley to reassure him. "I'll catch up."

Finley opens his mouth to say more, but Weslyn urges the horse forward, and the group tears toward the garrison.

I sink to the ground and bury my face in my hands.

Eerie quiet envelops the tents stretching out from the plateau's base.

The road looping through the encampment is largely deserted, and the few people I encounter only nod in greeting or pass me over with indifference. It's hard to determine whether the cream-colored tents were arranged with any attempt at organization; the clusters appear haphazard, like paint thrown at a wall. As I walk, I spot evidence of impromptu gathering places sprinkled throughout: pots with bowls stacked perilously high, a threadbare purple rug spread over the ground, wooden beams marking the floor plan for some future design, fire pits still smoking with no one around. Many of the items appear worn or secondhand, and I've no doubt

I'm seeing the mark of three years spent sacrificing income to King Gerar's military tax.

I wonder if these people will be thankful for his efforts to bolster Telyan's army in recent years, given the burgeoning war. Then again, gratitude can only go so far toward amending empty bellies. I know hunger's gnawing power better than most.

At one point, a group of young children dart across the road and flit down a narrow channel, like caged birds searching the gaps between bars. The last girl follows more slowly, a young forest walker with needlelike green hair and gray-brown skin, and frustration churns at the distance the rest have put between themselves and her. I'm tempted to follow, to see if she's okay and maybe even search for Bren and Tomas. But thoughts of Finley pull my feet through the grounds and up the hill.

A massive gate slashed into the rampart marks one entrance to Fendolyn's Keep, flanked by stout, rounded towers built from the same thick slabs of dark stone as the wall. It's old architecture, remnants of the fighting that spurred Alemara's first queen to divide her single realm into three. Well, four, if counting the Vale. Threading that nearly eight-hundred-year-old past through to today, Telyan's standard flies at the top—a green oak encased in a purple mountain, both stitched across a huge cut of gray cloth.

To my relief, a familiar face is waiting for me where the arched wooden doors spanning the gate have been propped wide. His purple-accented, light gray uniform jacket hugs the top of long slacks, which in turn are tucked into boots. Naethan—one of the four Royal Guards who accompanied us to the river in summer. The one who became my friend.

"Looking a bit worse for the wear," Naethan says, with the beginnings of a grin. He always was more pleasant than his older counterparts—well, once he got over his obvious skepticism of traveling with two shifters.

"Wish I could say the same for you," I reply, shaking his out-stretched hand. I've never quite forgotten the day Finley teasingly listed the boys he found handsome throughout the estate. Naethan, with his lean, toned figure, close-cropped hair, deep brown skin, and a brow usually bent in thought, was one of them. Though he was, of course, *quite off-limits, being Wes's friend and all.*

Apparently, my jealousy was "cute."

"That's sweet of you, Helos." Naethan's smile widens. "But I'm afraid I'm taken."

"Don't flatter yourself. Finally bared your heart to Ansley, then, did you?" I ask, falling into step beside him. Ansley was another of the four Royal Guards, a slender young woman with a long tangle of flaming red curls crowning a freckled white face. Quiet, polite, handy with a sword. By the time our group had reached Niav, his and Ansley's continued reluctance to voice their obvious feelings out loud had begun driving me mad. "And where are we going?"

"I might have, and Wes's orders," he replies. "I'm to take you directly to the Officers' Hall."

My eyebrows shoot up. "Am I under arrest?"

"Arrest?" he echoes. "No. The Officers' Hall is where the Family lives."

The Family. Maybe that's where I'll find Fin. "Lead the way."

Naethan steers me down the road that cuts a straight line through the garrison, chatting as we go. Since Violet ordered Grovewood residents to evacuate, his family has set up in the valley below. The southern villages and towns, however, will not clear out unless Eradain's fleet takes to the sea, which means several families—Ansley's included—had better hope for poor sailing weather.

Though I'm eager for the news, it's difficult to focus amidst the sudden inundation of sights and sounds. While the valley below felt sedated, Fendolyn's Keep is a flurry of activity. Cadets travel the grounds in twos and threes, chatting animatedly, while a woman's voice barks orders somewhere out of sight. On my request, Naethan identifies each building we pass—to our left, the pair of barracks that house the academy students, an academic hall, and a paved practice yard. To our right, a granary and an enormous cistern for storing fresh water. Since the Keep functions as both academy and active army base, its grounds are divided in two: soldiers-in-training on this end; career soldiers, or "careers," on the opposite.

Naethan takes the forked road left, past a long, rectangular mess hall and another practice yard, until we reach a squat, brick build-ing he dubs the hospital.

I plant my heels. Finally, my terrain.

"Are any of the valley folks treated here as well?" I ask, strain-ing for a vantage point inside. The windows are too high up to see through, even for me. "Thinking of Fi—the Fallow Throes. Do you see many instances of it here?"

Naethan runs a hand over his head. "I'm never really in there," he mutters. "But it's getting worse, or so I hear. Come on," he adds, before I can open the door.

After cutting across a small courtyard neatly decorated with benches and potted flowers, we arrive at a square building four sto-ries tall. Our footsteps echo loudly in the long, oil-lamplit corridors as we climb another set of stairs and veer into an unmarked room.

Weslyn is standing there, along with two others I don't know.

The wrong brother. Again.

"Thanks, Naet," he says, indicating the door. Maps hang along the wood-paneled walls, illuminated by oil lamps and the sunlight sifting in through iron-barred windows. A few desks are scattered around the periphery, miniatures of the central table that spans a third of the room.

"Sir." Naethan dips his head and leaves.

"Helos." Weslyn circles the table and extends an arm behind my back, as if to guide me. "This is Ursa, the Royal Treasurer, and Gen-eral Powell, the Academy Master." They both nod courteously. "Helos aided me in my recent business for the crown."

"Ah," General Powell says, offering a hand. He's a tall, sturdy man with a bald head, thin-rimmed glasses, and deep brown skin. "I don't recognize you from the Guard."

"I'm not in the Guard," I reply.

General Powell's chin juts up. "I see. You have a soldier's build. Did you attend the academy?"

"Actually, I'm a—"

"My sister is away on a scouting mission," Weslyn interrupts. "We'll wait here until she returns."

While the three of them resume their quiet conversation, I set my pack against a wall and pace to a window overlooking several rows of cadets running drills in a practice yard. I don't know why I have to be here. I'm itching to find Fin, torn between a desire to demand answers and to let him rest. *He's alive,* I remind myself over and over. *He's alive, and that's all that matters.*

My hands tighten around the sill.

When the door bangs open at last, the captain of the Royal Guard steps over the threshold—Torres, I think her name is—followed by two gray-clad guards who cross to the windows to either side of me.

Boxed in.

At once, my feet are moving, heart hammering, pushing toward the safety of an unoccupied wall. Expecting pursuit, my neck tenses as I glance behind, prepared to—

The guards don't seem to care.

Weslyn is watching me, his brow furrowed.

Releasing a breath, I do my best to glare back.

Violet sweeps in next, looking every inch the monarch, despite the fact that her charcoal riding jacket and dark green breeches are smattered with dust. Quickly scanning the room's occupants, she spears me with the briefest of glances before asking Ursa, General Powell, and the two more junior-ranking guards to leave. Which is the signal I need. I make my bid for freedom and Fin as the others bow at the waist, but Violet adds to me, "You stay."

My fingers begin to tick against my leg.

Once the door has shut behind them, she circumvents the massive table and hugs Weslyn tight.

Just like that, impatience ebbs into discomfort, watching the siblings reunite. I twist a hand through my hair, feeling Rora's absence more keenly than ever. She should be here for—whatever this is—instead of off by herself, in fortune knows what kind of danger. Glancing away, I lock eyes with Captain Torres, a formidable woman with broad shoulders, bronze skin, and a knack for giving the impression that she knows more than anyone reasonably should. She nods my way, the gesture more warning than welcome. Undoubtedly, she's contemplating the cursed Prediction that has plagued Rora and me for all four years we've lived in Telyan. The one that warns of *two shifters* and *death*.

It doesn't help that the last time I saw her, she was seeing us off for the Vale alongside King Gerar. And now the king is dead.

We weren't even there, I want to scream.

At last, Violet pulls back and grasps Weslyn's shoulders, exactly the way Weslyn held Fin. The eldest of the three Danofers, she stands a full head taller than he but shares the same thick brows, weather-worn complexion, and dark brown hair—hers is cropped in a severe line midway down her slender neck. Her frame, however, is lithe like Finley's, with the same pronounced cheekbones and a small nose turned up a little at the end.

"Wes," she says, her tone grim. "This ought to be done in private, but I don't want you to hear it from anyone else first if you haven't already. Father is dead. I'm sorry."

She says it gently, but without hesitation, which I don't know I'd be brave enough to do. Weslyn swallows, appearing less composed than he did earlier with Fin.

"I know." He blinks rather rapidly. "We saw him."

Violet has been searching her brother's face, perhaps looking for whatever it was Finley feared to find, but at that, her eyes narrow. "What do you mean, you saw *him*?"

"When we returned to Roanin, Father's h—" Weslyn clenches his hands and takes a breath. "His head was mounted on a post in the throne room."

"*What?*" The word is ice itself.

"It was Jol. He left this as well." Weslyn pulls a folded parchment from his back pocket. I know it must be the one in which Jol absurdly justified murdering King Gerar by accusing him of treason, because I fed Jol's other message to the fire before leaving Roanin. The one asking Rora and me to meet him in Oraes.

By the river, our newfound brother is an ass.

Violet grabs the notice and reads quickly before passing it to Captain Torres. "Father was walking the streets greeting the people when he was murdered," she explains. "An arrow to the heart. We couldn't save him, Wes. But we did bury him." She folds her arms tightly across her chest. "They must have returned and dug him out."

Weslyn blanches. "Did you manage to find the person who did it?" he asks, as Captain Torres's features pinch in fury.

"An assassin from Eradain. Ansley tracked her down. Speaking of whom, she, Naethan, and Dom returned from their journey without Carolette, and none of them are able to account for why she disappeared in Niav." Her brow arches meaningfully, and Weslyn and I exchange a glance.

"Helos," Violet says. "Welcome back. Where is Rora?"

Weslyn clears his throat. "She stayed behind."

She's just outside, he might have said. *She has brown hair. She takes her tea black.* So evenly does he speak. But maybe Violet hears something I don't, because she peers at him curiously.

"Stayed where?"

"She's gone back to the Vale," I cut in. "Which we can explain, but first you should know that Carolette is a traitor."

Captain Torres frowns at me.

"Your Majesty," I add belatedly.

Violet drums her fingers above the crease in her arm. "That was clear to me already."

"It was?"

"Carolette disappeared near the border with Eradain, and shortly after, my father was murdered. So, yes, Helos. It was."

My leg starts bouncing.

"Is Rora's absence connected to the fact that you don't have the stardust?" she continues.

Now my pulse is racing, too.

Weslyn seems to shrink ever so slightly. "How do you know?"

"It is written on your faces," she replies, not unkindly. "And if you had it, I think you would have said so already."

Weslyn bows his head, gaze dropping to the floor. Suddenly he looks ancient, weighed down beyond his years.

Then again, aren't we all?

"I'm sorry," he says quietly.

That's it. No explanation, no excuses. I could jump in and offer a fuller account, but really, does it matter? We failed. We'll lose Finley. Unless—

"You came back safe," Violet says. "And that's important. There will be time for the full story, but first, tell me why Rora has gone back."

The silence stretches on. When I make no move to fill it, Weslyn tells her about the prison compound. It's secondhand information since he's never been himself, and he glances my way more than once, clearly hoping I'll fill in the gaps. But I don't want to talk about that place or my time there, so I studiously look elsewhere until he closes with, "She's going to destroy it."

Violet's eyebrows arch. "By herself?"

It's difficult to say whether she's impressed by this plan or skeptical of it, but regardless, Weslyn only nods. "It wasn't my place to try to stop her."

"It was," Violet says.

"It wasn't."

The two of them stare at one another, Violet looking exasperated, Weslyn simply stubborn. At last, Violet shakes her head. "Her intention is noble, I grant you, but to attempt an operation of that scale on her own is—"

"After she destroys it," Weslyn presses on, apparently unwilling to entertain doubts, "she's going north to Oraes to spy. Like you wanted."

Violet considers this a moment, then smiles. "Good."

"Good?" I demand, indignant.

"Good," she repeats, growing cross. "Rora works for me now, and I'll thank you to remember that." She appraises me a while. "You haven't said much, I notice."

Blood rushes to my face. The observation is simple enough, but the way she says it—it's as if she's peeling back the skin and seeing straight into my soul, the guilt and doubt and fear within all warring for prominence.

I don't know what she wants to hear. That I may have been mistaken to let Rora risk her life alone instead of going with her. That I didn't argue when she told me I was needed here instead, because truthfully I'm the selfish one, nothing but a hopeless, lovesick fool, and likely a coward besides.

The longer the silence stretches on, the more agitated I become.

"Did your father know the truth about us?" I blurt. "About our mother?"

"Mind your tone," Captain Torres snaps. "You're speaking to the queen."

I'm tempted to ask if weeks spent traveling with one Danofer brother and months spent sleeping with the other earns me enough familiarity to treat Violet as their sister and not my sovereign, but I bite the question back. "Forgive me." I force the rest out. "Ma'am."

Part of me is hoping Violet will say I can drop the title, as Weslyn once did.

She does not.

"To which truth are you referring?" she asks.

My attention darts to Captain Torres. "May we discuss it in private?"

"No."

Violet holds me in her gaze until I feel compelled to speak the rest. "Our mother was Queen Mariella of the north. King Daymon's wife."

Tension descends upon the room.

Weslyn is watching for Violet's reaction, while Captain Torres stares like I've grown a second head. Violet hasn't so much as flinched; only her eyes tell the full story. She didn't know.

"If he suspected this," she answers slowly, "he did not share it with me. How long have you known?"

"About two weeks."

To my resentment, Violet glances at Weslyn as if for confirmation. He nods.

"I see," she says, considering some more. "And what do you plan to do about it?"

It takes me a while to realize what she's driving at. "I don't know yet."

And I don't. The one time Rora and I discussed this, I as good as told her one of us should make a bid for the throne. But they were brave words, spoken in the heat of the moment and out of desperation for *some* semblance of power after that horrible place. Earnest, too, I admit, because I really do want to mend the wounds Jol is inflicting. But I'm no politician, only a healer, and now that I've gotten some distance . . . Besides, back in Telyan with Finley only a stone's throw away, how could I leave him?

"And Rora?" Violet presses. "Is this inheritance part of why she's going to Eradain?"

Behind her, Weslyn fidgets a little.

"No," I reply. "She doesn't want a crown."

Violet holds my gaze, marking the word I didn't say: *either.* Because on this matter, Rora's mind is made up. Mine is not.

Which is unfortunate, because as Violet has made so painfully clear, my sister is the one who's gone north while I retreated south. Rora has always been the brave one. Not me.

I swallow.

"The longer you take to decide, the longer he remains in power, unchallenged," she says at last. The implications of this don't need to be spoken aloud. "You will have to decide, Helos, and soon. We will speak on this again when you've had time to reflect."

Leg bouncing again, I open my mouth to respond, but she's already pivoting into an account of what's happened here in Telyan while we've been away.

In the nearly two weeks since Jol struck Glenweil, Violet has sent troops to aid in her neighbor's defense; while it holds, Glenweil remains a barrier between Telyan and the north. Meanwhile, she and her councilors agreed that King Gerar's assassination amounted to a declaration of war on Telyan. Jol's army has not yet attempted to make landfall here, but she doesn't expect this grace period to last.

"We have been watching the ports for any sign of an invasion by sea," she tells a somber Weslyn. "Eradain will come. The question is when."

"And the Fallow Throes?" Weslyn asks.

She presses her lips together. "Still spreading. Our healers are no closer to finding a cure."

At this, Weslyn explains our theory that Eradain's efforts to expel magic from Alemara have prompted magic to create tiny explosion events—the crack in the mountain overlooking Eradain's prison compound, the tree which fell across the gorge. All part of magic's fight to survive, miniature versions of the Rupturing that broke the continent apart—only this time, the fragments of magic upended by these events are imbedding themselves in humans and animals whose bodies are no longer compatible.

The Fallow Throes.

"Is there a way to make magic feel less threatened?" Captain Torres muses.

"Rora has an idea," I put in.

Violet frowns. "Speak plainly."

"She wants to wake up the land."

This time, the silence stretches even deeper than when I revealed our newfound lineage.

"It could save Finley," I remind a skeptical-looking Violet.

"His Royal Highness," Captain Torres reminds me.

"Or," Violet says, "it could awaken the land and have no impact on the Throes." She holds up a hand when Weslyn looks ready to argue. "I'll make no promises either way. I need to think on this more. For now, you must be tired from your journey. You and I will speak more later," she adds to Weslyn. "In the meantime, the Guard will find you both quarters here in the Officers' Hall."

Captain Torres raises her eyebrows.

"Helos's lineage puts him at risk," Violet goes on, seeing this. "We don't know who else outside of this room might know the truth. And Jol has already managed to get an assassin through our defenses once." Captain Torres opens her mouth, but Violet's already halfway to the door. "He stays here. See to it, please, Captain. Oh, and Helos, you worked as a healer, correct? Go to the hospital and make yourself useful. You'll find they could use the help."

She's gone before I can thank her.

"The guards waiting just outside will escort you, when you're ready," says Captain Torres. Then she, too, leaves.

Now only Weslyn and I remain in the room. Our traveling

partnership, thankfully, at an end. Determined to check on Finley at last before following Violet's order, I grab my pack from its place by the window without a word.

Weslyn intercepts me at the door, grabbing my arm.

"What are you—"

"Listen," he says, his voice low. "I can guess where you're headed. I know you and Finley have a history."

I fight to keep my expression calm. Finley always swore we were a secret.

"I also know he asked you to stay away," Weslyn continues, looking infuriatingly unruffled. Try as I might to rip free from his hold, his grip is too strong.

"Let go of me!"

"Don't make things worse for him. He needs to focus on getting better."

The words plunge my heart-rate into a treacherous spiral. Blood roars in my head, and it's all I can do not to punch him in his royal face. "Getting better?" I practically shout, laughing without humor. "Getting *better*?"

At last, some of Weslyn's control shatters. He releases a breath, only a small one, and drops my arm. Then he walks from the room.

FOUR

RORA

It's a long walk across the open land.

Gerig has taken up a position in front, while Peridon and I trail close behind. By now, blood has dripped down Peridon's chin from the split lip I gave him, and half of his tricolored waves have pulled free of their knot. He smiles when he catches me staring, and the expression reminds me so much of Helos that I have to look away.

The clouds have parted to reveal a vibrant, unbroken blue sky, and far ahead, the swaying aspens blanketing the Decani Mountains have started to turn with the season. Yellow and sunset orange blend into a golden haze, far brighter than the evergreen woods we've left behind. In contrast, the torn-up turf spread before us offers few signs of life, just the occasional tree stump scattered among half-hearted patches of grass. The first time I crossed this expanse was on wings, and it's a different experience entirely to see the ancient growth reduced to mere specters in my sight line, to feel my borrowed shoes' rubber soles pressing brittle stalks into the wounded ground. Grazing land now shrunken to a shadow of itself, as if the prison is a parasite, sucking the earth dry.

At the base of the range, the compound looms as heavy and dark as I remember. A long, rectangular building with slits for windows dominates much of the site, with the wooden watchtower I infiltrated on my first visit brooding close behind. To the right, the first row of sickening cages is just discernible in the glaring sunlight.

Two months ago, I would have done everything in my power to stay east of the river forever. Prior to our journey west, Helos and I had spent so many years fighting to survive the Vale that even the thought of returning made my muscles lock up and my lungs struggle for air. Today, I keep my boots fixed on course. Only a fool would feel no fear, but beside the fear, there is also hope. Somehow my heart is learning to make space for both.

We're nearly across the plain when the ground rumbles beneath our feet. Crows erupt from the swaying trees with grating cries, and Peridon, Gerig, and I fight for balance as the sudden earthquake rattles our bones.

"Careful," Peridon warns, as if there's anything we could do but wait for it to pass. A loud crack arcs through the cacophony behind, and I twist in time to watch the two trees fall.

The shaking rolls to a stop.

"The Vale seems active," I observe, eyeing one of the peaks in the range ahead. A huge fissure splits its stormy face in two, and a jumble of dislodged stones has cascaded down the middle, filling the gap like a rockslide frozen in time.

"More so lately than it's been in a while," Peridon replies. "I cannot explain the sudden change."

Because the magic is fracturing, I almost tell him. *Just like the eruption that split the land so many thousands of years ago, except this time the cracks are smaller, and there are many.* Wary of Gerig's presence and how little I know Peridon, I keep my theory to myself.

"It's time," Gerig says, when we're maybe fifty paces from the prison grounds.

I slide behind Peridon to grab his bound wrists. He assumes the role of struggling captive, and we walk the rest of the way to the cages in a staged battle of wills.

"Ho there, Karlog," someone hails from up ahead. "Caught yourself a fish?"

Peridon attempts to twist free, and I knee him lightly in the back. "A slippery one," I call back, mimicking the accent as best I can.

A handful of uniformed people meet us at the first line of cages.

They're like pillars of stone, wide-shouldered and broad-armed, with boots that look heavy enough to snap bones and navy shirts tucked lazily into pronounced, muscular belt lines. Next to them, slight Gerig appears as out of place as a moth among hornets.

Our conversationalist saunters forward from the chattering group, nursing a thin chewing stick between his teeth. The blood-stains blotching the shaving towel slung over his shoulder are red enough to be fresh, and his pale hair has been greased to an ugly shine where it flops across his white forehead. His eyes are clouded amber.

"A trout, eh?" he says, pulling the stick from his mouth. He grabs Peridon's face, hard enough his nail beds redden. "Just a baby," he adds, turning it this way and that.

Peridon yanks free, and my stomach clenches.

"We should put him in a cell," Gerig says. "The rest of the drug will wear off soon."

Drug? An image in my mind, then, of a sweet-smelling cloth cast over my once fleeing figure before everything darkened. I shift my weight and focus on counting buttons on their uniform shirts.

"The mouse was your second?" asks the man with the stick, leaning back with exaggerated wonder. "This *is* a miracle catch. Next time, he'd serve you better as bait."

"I'll use you as bait if you don't get out of my way," I say, shoving Peridon forward a step.

The remaining onlookers fall silent.

The man studies me a moment, then steps forward—one, two—close enough I can smell the remnants of ash on his yellow teeth. "Is that so?"

Nerves flutter in my chest, suggesting wings and flight and escape. I turn my thoughts to the prisoners, the bodies they'll burn at dawn, and the fear slides into steely rage. Numbness spirals through my limbs at the new emotional response. *Jaws. Claws. Tear. Maim.*

"Did I stutter?" I demand.

Peridon stands rigid beneath my grip. The man stares me down, unblinking. Probably for the best, his lips curve into a smile, and he returns the stick between his teeth.

"I think I do not want to fight you today, my friend." He steps back and gestures toward the cages with a mocking bow, laughing with the others. "For your trout."

I force a half smile, like it's a joke between friends, and push Peridon toward the second row. Gerig runs inside to grab a key, and together we walk the line to a space near the end.

Various magical beings fill the cages along the aisle, and the sight only fuels my anger. Timber bears with their limbs bound tight. Widow bats hanging upside down from the top of their cage like rows of teeth. Gemstone beavers whose iridescent tails look dull enough to suggest they've been away from water for a while. Black nightwings curled up together as if for warmth. And, as was the case before, there are people here, too—forest walkers and whisperers, primarily.

Helos's old cell—my cell—is now occupied by a pair of changeling wolves pacing the length with quick strides. The sight makes my gut constrict. As we draw near, their coats ripple to match the cement floor and the crosshatched wire fencing, rendering them invisible to my eye.

When I was here about two weeks ago, Peridon's cousin Andie was imprisoned in the same row, two cages down. She's still there, her curvy figure looking drawn in the pounding sunlight, her silver- and gold-streaked, curly brown locks falling across her shoulder blades and over her rich brown skin in tangled clumps. She scrambles to her feet when she spots us.

"Peridon," she says, clutching the fence. Black grease streaks across the long-sleeved, cream-colored shirt that reaches halfway down her thighs.

Peridon meets her stare and looses a breath. "You're alive."

"How did they catch—"

"You're alive," he repeats, sounding relieved beyond measure.

The back of my neck prickles with the sensation of being watched, so I knock his head with my hand for the sake of the charade. "Time enough for chatter later," I say, ushering him through the cage doors that Gerig has opened opposite the changeling wolves.

Andie spits a string of curses my way, each more vile than the last. She doesn't know this is a ruse, only sees her battered cousin with his scrapes and bloody shirt, and the role-play makes me feel rather sick. I slam Peridon's cage doors shut—both the inner one made from crosshatched wire and the outer one lined with vertical black bars—and grab the key from Gerig to make a show of locking them. I leave them unlocked.

"How do I look?" I ask Gerig in an undertone, steeling myself against Andie's continued vitriol.

His eyes sweep my face, which aches where Peridon's fist connected. "Starting to bruise."

"Good."

Though it feels wrong, we leave Peridon without a backward glance.

Walking through the main building's double doors is like stepping back into a nightmare, the suffocating feeling of close walls and being closed in. The corridors are mostly bare, save for pockets of oil lamplight suspended amidst the shadows, and I shudder to imagine what they've witnessed even as I will my feet forward. Deep voices seep from the adjoining rooms, and my skin shivers at the sharp smell, the kind of clean only chemicals can produce.

Gerig and I head straight for the office at the end of the hall. My first time here, I slipped under the door as a mouse. This time, I knock.

"Enter."

The long-faced commander is seated behind an imposing wooden desk, leafing through a stack of papers. His brown hair is oil-slick and carefully parted, the buckles and badges studded along his navy jacket polished to a shine. A portrait of control, or at least a dogged attempt at it.

I can still feel his iron fist sinking into my stomach, his mocking breath hot in my ear. *Don't forget, shifter, I have plenty of techniques at my disposal. A finger broken, perhaps, or a toenail removed. Don't worry. None of it would kill you.*

"What is it?" he drawls without looking up. His sun-darkened white skin is drawn tight over high cheekbones and around a mouth that appears too wide for his face.

"Sir," Gerig replies, "We caught something on patrol."

The commander lifts his head abruptly. He appraises us through narrowed eyes, pinching his lips together before removing his reading glasses and leaning back in the upholstered chair. "Shut the door."

Gerig complies while I cross to the center of the room, trying to restrain the rage bubbling up my throat. The memories run thick and fast—the commander's morbid delight at casting me inside the shed full of corpses, and his visible disappointment when Jol specified, *alive*. I'd like to meet his piercing gaze with a harsher response—a dagger through one of his limbs, perhaps, or even my hands around his throat, if the thought of touching him didn't repulse me so. Instead, I salute the way Gerig taught me. "Sir."

"What about this catch?"

I turn to Gerig, who steps forward. The commander raises an eyebrow.

"It was a whisperer, sir. A young one."

"Was or is?"

"Is, sir. We put him in a cell."

"A joint effort, I trust." The commander eyes my face.

"It was Gerig who spotted him," I put in.

The commander's expression suggests this was the wrong thing to say.

"I seem to recall you telling me a dog would make a better partner than Tanburn just this morning," he observes mildly.

I shrug, neck tensing. "Turns out he's got some bite."

The commander sets his hands on the table, studying Gerig with new interest. "Very well. Tanburn can be the one to question it."

Gerig lifts his chin a little. "Sir."

"Not today." The commander rises from his chair and smooths his jacket at the sides. "Give it until tomorrow afternoon. No food or water." He circles around to the front of the desk and leans against it. "You know, Tanburn, I had my doubts about your commitment. You have done well."

"Thank you, sir." Gerig keeps his gaze straight ahead.

"Dismissed."

Neither of us speak again until we're on the second level, in a corridor almost identical to the one below; apparently pairs who work double patrols are rewarded with a break afterward. Gerig nods to Karlog's room before disappearing into his own, and I breathe a sigh of relief. The first phase of the plan was a success.

Now we wait.

It seems to take years for evening to arrive. Watching the clouds roll back in throughout the afternoon, I wonder if we'll have to do this all in the rain. I plead illness and do not go down for dinner, behavior that Gerig warned me could invite suspicion. I don't think it will matter in a couple of hours.

The long wait in Karlog's room is incredibly dull, but I don't rifle through his drawers. I'm somewhat apprehensive as to what manner of things I might uncover, and in any case, it feels wrong to uproot the belongings of a man whose bleeding throat still haunts my mind. I don't envy Peridon having to wear the scarlet-soaked shirt.

Instead, I divert my attention with happier thoughts, memories I haven't allowed myself to dwell on since reuniting with Peridon. The giants' peaceful home, stardust shimmering down, and Helos circling the grassy clearing, tugging down vines that fell on his face. Finley challenging Helos to a race across the castle grounds, then accusing my brother of letting him win, which was definitely true. The feeling of flying far above the treetops on a clear night overrun with twinkling stars.

My hands curl into fists. I am dancing around thoughts of him, even in my own mind.

I shoot from the bed and begin to pace, checking the sky through the slitted window far more frequently than is practical. I catch my borrowed reflection in the small, dirty mirror, then wish I hadn't. When I run out of ideas, I relent at last and unlock the gate I've built in my mind. The one that keeps Wes at bay.

His face appears with startling clarity, thick hair and honeyed eyes and a smile. That quiet, subtle grin that is so distinctly his. His sleek collared shirts, with the sleeves always rolled just below the elbow. The way his voice sounds in the morning, when he hasn't used it for hours. The heady grip of his hands holding my waist. My name on his lips and his lips on my neck and his fingers brushing a few strands of hair off my face, the morning we said goodbye.

I don't know what's wrong with me. Why it suddenly feels a little harder to breathe, why my chest feels like it's tethered to a rope, and that rope is pulling out and away. Now that we're not on the journey anymore, it's easier to see the impossibility of a future together. He asked me to come back to him, but surely things are more complicated than that. I had a choice between saving Finley or him, and I chose him. Besides, would he actually wait? I can't predict how long I'll be away; perhaps his feelings will have changed. Perhaps I'm opening myself up to hope, only to have farther to fall when things inevitably fall through.

In any case, royal relationships are based on advantage, not on romance. Our worlds are different, despite—despite what he said to me on the riverbank.

I shake my head, my throat rather tight.

It doesn't matter, because surely what he feels most right now is grief. He didn't share the details of the years following his mother's death, but I can read between the lines. Things got dark. Now he's lost his father, too, he is hurting, and I'm not there to share his pain. Worry and guilt mingle with renewed fury that Jol could be so cruel.

By the time the sky dims to inky coal, a steady ache has permeated my limbs. My body is beginning to feel the strain of holding this form, even though I can hold it all through tomorrow if I have to. This time I force my gaze to linger on the reflection in the mirror, just to reassure myself of my disguise, before I step out into the night.

Early autumn's chill has sharpened the air. I keep my head down as I walk the aisle to Peridon's cell, strong gusts skimming my skin. A faint light filters down from the watchtower above—my first target. But for the most part, the cages are dark as the sky above.

Peridon grunts when I whisper his name.

"I can detect a good number in one of the caves on the mountain side," he murmurs. "It's a fair distance, but I'll call down as many as I can. Give it a count of eighty."

"What about Andie?" I ask. "Will she help?"

There's a small silence. "She will try. She's very weak."

"All right, I'm going. Listen for my signal."

I steal up the watchtower's wooden stairs as quietly as I can. Though it's difficult to hear much over the wind, muffled voices filter unmistakably through the tower door. The last time I was here, I managed to take out three guards on my own, but one had come dangerously close to triggering an alarm. Tonight there are six, the commander clearly having expanded the watch force in the wake of my previous escape, and that's far too many for me to handle alone.

I whistle a low note and begin to count.

Eighty passes, then ninety. I fold my arms across my chest and work to steady my racing heart. One hundred. A band of laughter erupts from the other side of the door, and whiskers nearly poke through my skin at the shock.

I get as far as one hundred and eighteen before I detect the flutter of wingbeats.

The colony approaches like a cloud of death stretching its hand across the sky. Widow bats, enough to cover a small cave ceiling in its entirety. My body locks up. When hunting or feeling threatened, they spin their toxic saliva into webs that are lethal to the touch; I've seen them take out a timber bear within the span of twenty heartbeats. This flock looks blacker than the surrounding darkness, and it's moving fast.

Goshawk instincts yank on my core, urging me to fly away. Peridon assured me he could compel them to pass me by, but right now it feels like madness to stand in their path. *Stay back,* I beg the numbness seeping through my limbs. Peridon wants to see the prisoners freed, same as I. I can trust him. I think. Wings are threatening to poke through my shoulder blades, but I need my hands to open the door, so I try and try to focus on happier thoughts. Calmer ones. Strong hands and a subtle smile.

When the wingbeats roar like thunder in my ears, I hunch my aching limbs, duck my head, and throw open the door.

The colony blazes past in furious motion, the seemingly endless mass of bodies so close that their flight lifts the hair from my shoulders. Clinging to the knob, I press my body as close to the wood as I can and squeeze my eyelids shut. My heart slams against my rib cage at every brush of wings against my fingers, once or twice across the back of my neck, but when the air around me stills, I have the presence of mind to shut the door on the guards' anguished screams.

The barrier does little to mask the sound. If other soldiers leave the compound for a patrol, we'll be in trouble. I brace the door with my back, expecting an escape attempt at any moment, but the only jolts are tiny—presumably the bats rebounding in the tiny space.

It's awful to hear the guards die. To stand on the other side of the door and do nothing but will them to die faster. I know they could very well have stood in my position countless times after depositing magical beings in the shed, but that knowledge isn't enough to loosen the harsh netting in my abdomen, the nausea coating my tongue. The pressure around my neck.

A whistle arcs through the night, the higher harmony to my own.

I don't let go of the door. I simply press harder.

The bats are bumping the wood more purposefully, growing agitated, impatient. The whistle sounds again, but my muscles refuse to obey. He promised they would ignore me, but they're wild animals and have a taste for it now. He told me himself he hasn't yet mastered the art of compelling larger creatures, only smaller ones—birds and bats, rodents and hares. If they spot me again, could he really hold them back?

The next time they slam against the door, the force of it knocks me to the side. The slat hits my back, hard, pinning me against the wooden railing as the bats funnel through the opening and make as one for the mountain.

I'm still alive.

Behind me, the tower is silent. Breathing deep, I ball my trembling hands into fists and maneuver around the door.

Milky white gossamer threads are strung from end to end, wall to floor, more scattershot than a spider's web and thicker stranded, too. All six guards lay dead on the ground, their limbs arranged haphazardly and half covered in webs. A sickening spectacle, whatever they've done. Lines of welts trail across their skin and through their torn clothing where the venom made contact, and their open-mouthed expressions and gaping eyes make it clear they did not die peacefully.

Shadows converge around the room, half of the oil lamps having been extinguished in the scrabble. It's a miracle none of the flames were knocked loose. I shut the door on the tomb and tread down the stairs as lightly as I can. Luckily, the tower stands tall enough that from the ground, I can only just spot some of the wreckage through the window.

The main building's long corridor is empty when I step back inside; most of its residents will have gone to bed by now. According to Gerig, the commander alone has a master key, so I make my way to the office at the end of the ghostly hall. To my surprise, the handle twists easily under my grip.

The door swings open, and the commander looks up from his desk.

"Wahters," he says, rising abruptly.

I shut the door behind me, fighting to master my nerves. I really had hoped he wouldn't be here.

"What are you doing?" He pulls a knife belted at his side and raises his arm, and the action triggers something in me. Something violent. Something vengeful. Heedless of the knife, I grab his wrist with a meaty hand and slam him back against the wall, my other palm squeezing his throat. Beneath my bulky arms, his squirming is nothing but a fish between the jaws of a bear.

"This prison is closed," I say, pulling his shirt and slamming him back against the wall. His head rebounds against the plaster with a painful sound. He tries to speak but can't muster enough air through the force of my grasp. "What was that?" I ask with mock politeness, releasing my hold a touch.

"You'll hang for this," he puffs out.

"No," I tell him. "I won't."

I knock his head against the wall again, and his body goes limp beneath my hands. Letting him drop to the floor, I press two fingers against his neck. A pulse still drums, stubbornly.

I find the key in one of his pockets and straighten above him, considering.

I could kill him now. It would be easy enough, and knowing his crimes, I feel certain he would deserve it.

There's also the matter of security. A dead commander cannot create as much trouble for us going forward as a living one.

I see the choice laid before me—Karlog and now the commander. Continue taking life after life until it ceases to give me pause. Or choose mercy. The commander is sprawled across the ground, powerless to stop me.

I walk away. Not for his sake, but for mine.

Gerig emerges from the recreation room and meets me halfway down the hall. "I heard the door," he whispers, nodding behind me. "Well?"

I reveal the key in my palm and watch his eyes widen.

"Did you—"

"Supply room," I interrupt.

Gerig leads me to the closet and throws open the doors, which creak loudly in the empty hallway. I bite my tongue to stay focused on the array of tools before me. Weaponry, netting, rods, ropes—Gerig and I each sling a bow and a quiver full of arrows over our shoulders. Gritting my teeth against the noise, I lock the doors with the master key.

There's a thump on the ceiling.

"If you betray us," I warn in an undertone, fisting Gerig's collar and yanking him toward me, "You will die. Slowly." He opens his mouth to respond, but I release him with a small shove. "Let's go."

Gerig and I each grab a lamp from the wall. Though we try to keep our footsteps quiet, there's nothing we can do to silence the groan of the double doors. Our small flames cut through the charcoal night as we hasten over to Peridon's cage.

"There's a light coming from the second floor," Peridon says urgently. He opens the doors and grabs the bow and quiver he requested from me, then nocks an arrow and nods to Andie's cage. "Hurry."

After setting my lamp on the ground, it takes me a few moments to unlock his cousin's doors. Andie stands on the other side, small hands clutching the metal crosshatching.

As soon as I open the doors, she pushes past, the wind whipping her long shirt and tangle of curls around her like a cyclone. Peridon steps forward as if to embrace her, but she marches straight for an occupied cage five doors down. "This one next," she says, her voice deep and raspy.

The wildcat inside is enormous, and like nothing I've seen before. Slightly lower to the ground than a caegar, but broad-shouldered and easily twice as muscular as my lynx form. With my lamp's flickering light, I can just make out the dark spots dappling its thick orange coat. I hesitate at the doors.

"Open it now," Andie hisses. The wildcat watches me, un-blinking.

"What is it?" I ask, slightly hoarse.

"You've never seen a jaguar before?" Andie rips the key from my grasp and wrenches open the doors. The cat glides past and vanishes into the dark. "Did you bring another bow?" she asks, then frowns and drops the key into my hand. "Open the rest. Hurry."

Peridon flanks me as I make the rounds, arrow nocked and ready. Andie has disappeared and I can't find Gerig, but there's no time to worry about that now. Each lock gives beautifully under the master key, and most of the occupants flee into the night with-out a backward glance. Some seem too weak to move, but I leave them to figure it out while I hasten on to the next. Three other whisperers are imprisoned here, each in the next row over from Andie's, and they exchange hurried words with Peridon.

A high-pitched sound screeches in the darkness, causing feathers

to jut up against my skin. Lights appear in the compound windows, one after the other.

"They must have found the commander," I shout over the
alarm, struggling to open the next cage with shaking hands. Two
of the rows are done, but we still have the third left.

"Where's Gerig?" Peridon says, voicing the other possibility.

"Come on!" I urge, starting on the final row. A pair of nightwings are crouched low inside, staring at me with wide, frightened
eyes.

Raised voices sound from somewhere nearby.

"We're running out of time!" I say, pulling open the nightwings' doors. The little black foxes wait until I've shuffled to the
side before streaking out and away.

"We should douse the light," Peridon yells back. "We're a sitting
target with it!"

"I locked the supply room—"

"They may have more!"

"I won't be able to see in the dark unless I shift, and if I shift, I
can't open the doors!" I release a roost of two-headed snakes.

"Give me the key," Andie demands, materializing out of nowhere. The other three whisperers are by her side. One fixes the
tangled snakes with a look, and they slither out of the cage and
toward the watchtower.

"They will burn it," he says.

Andie stamps her foot. "Give me the key!"

The double doors to the compound burst open.

Dozens of soldiers burst forth, too many to count. Numbness
sweeps my limbs as they hasten toward us, swords and torches in
hand, while the light streams out from behind. Peridon starts firing arrows. The massive jaguar leaps out of the shadows and brings
two soldiers to the ground. That's all I see before someone snatches
the key from my hand, blows the lamp out, and casts us into the
dark.

FIVE

HELOS

"Come on, Fin," I murmur, keeping my mouth close to the door. "I know you're in there. I can hear you moving around."

I knock a third time, but he seems determined not to answer. At the end of the empty hall, a single window casts the corridor into a filmy, cloud-like haze.

"Fin," I say again.

There's a noncommittal thump from the other side.

I exhale slowly, hunching my shoulders against the draft sweeping the back of my neck. What started out as a particularly warm day has grown chilly and gray with early evening's onset. "All right. I'm going out."

Wrapping my dark red jacket around me, I make my way alone through the corridor, down the echoing stairs, and out beneath the overcast sky. Fog is rolling across the surrounding hillsides, obscuring most of the peaks from sight. My boots crunch loudly on the graveled paths. Violet said to make myself useful, and I will.

Sundown at Fendolyn's Keep seems to be an orderly thing. Smoke still curls through the forge's chimney, while cadets and careers saunter by in packs, their cheerful voices a welcome alternative to silence. Before I head for the hospital as ordered, I grab a plate of rationed potatoes and vegetables in the densely packed mess hall, finding the portions are slightly smaller than what I could afford on my salary back in Roanin. My stomach hollows in recognition of the hunger to come. But I lift my fork without complaint; I can't begin to work out how they plan to feed this many people for weeks or more.

Which is probably the kind of thing I'd *have* to work out if I wore a crown.

I shove the thought aside, choosing to ignore that nagging dilemma just as I'm ignoring the way my skin is prickling amidst this sea of uniforms. The windows in here are scarcely more than slits.

"Thought you might like some company."

The boy who slips onto the bench across from mine looks rather young for his Royal Guard uniform, despite his bulk. Wide, red mouth, brown hair cut short on the sides. His pale complexion is a couple of shades lighter than my olive tones, more like Finley's, though with decidedly ruddier cheeks.

I set my fork down. "Do I know you?"

"You were with the princes this morning," he says instead, lacing his fingers together on the tabletop. "But they rode back without you."

Now I recognize him—the one with the spare horse. I shove a forkful of orange squash into my mouth. "Broden, was it?"

He just continues to study me.

"Let me guess," I say, nodding at his uniform. "Someone asked you to keep an eye on me."

Broden shrugs, his mouth curving a little. "I wasn't told why."

Again, he drops this fact somewhat expectantly, but I make no move to hazard a guess. Because of my relation to Jol, perhaps, unless someone wants to be notified if I look in on Finley again. "I should tell you, Broden. I'm not accustomed to having a watchdog." I note that he hasn't specified who exactly asked him to tail me.

"But I am accustomed to watching," he says.

"Watching, or interfering?"

He considers. "Whichever the situation requires."

"I see. And is there anything you're to stop me from doing?"

"That depends on what you intend to do."

I appraise him a moment longer and polish off the last few bites. "I hope you have a strong stomach, then."

Broden frowns. "What do you—"

I rise from the bench before he can finish, walking the plate to a dirty stack and heading for the door. Broden catches up quick, but as soon as we reach the hospital entrance, he hesitates.

"Is there a problem?" I ask, wrapping my fingers around the handle.

He eyes the door uneasily. The squeamish type—that will make my life more difficult. "No."

"Good. After you." The heavy sliding door groans open, and I gesture for Broden to step inside.

Back in Roanin, my apprenticeship under Bren and Tomas was largely confined to their apothecary shop, with the occasional house visit folded in. Here, it looks as if I'll be working on a larger scale. Row after row of low-seated cots span the length of the long ward, many of them occupied, arranged in three columns to either side of the center aisle with a small dresser next to each. The gray light filters in through iron-barred windows situated high on both walls, and healers mill about in long purple shirts.

One of them, a heavyset white woman with dark, plaited hair and an array of freckles, comes to greet us. "Can I help you?" she asks, wiping her hands on her shirt.

"I'm a healer. Helos," I reply. "The queen thought I might be of some assistance to you, if you'll have me."

She raises her eyebrows and appears to take in Broden's uniform for the first time. "Is that so?" she says, uncrossing her arms. "Well, you won't be working anywhere until we've spoken further. Follow me."

Mahree, as she introduces herself, leads Broden and me down the center aisle. She asks several questions about my training and background against the din of quiet words, rasping breath, metal striking trays, and crinkling, starched sheets. I mention my old bosses and attempt to skirt the rest by asking after her patients' current states. They're divided into two sections—one for those with the Fallow Throes, the other for everyone else. Since no one here knows how to cure the Throes entirely, most of the healing work has been concentrated on treating the symptoms.

They bury the bodies at the base of the hill.

Behind the large hall, there's a smaller ward sectioned off with a similar setup. Before I can ask after its purpose, Mahree steps into a side room and quirks her head. I give a bracing pat on the back to a very sallow-faced Broden before following.

The side room turns out to be a supply room, rather small and cramped, yet functional nonetheless. Shelves of jars, boxes, bags, and tools span two of the windowless walls. There are books, too, some bearing cracked spines and paper pulling free of the binding, others more polished in appearance, encyclopedic sets spanning several volumes. Against the other walls and scattered throughout, wooden crates are stacked either individually or several boxes high, with amber-colored bottles peeking through some of the slats. A small sink sits in the corner.

"You haven't answered many of my questions," Mahree points out as I examine the shelves in greater detail. Her gaze darts to Broden, who has entered somewhat reluctantly.

"Which questions?" I ask, distracted. They look well-stocked, though there are some labels and tools I haven't encountered before.

"Where do you come from, exactly?"

"Roanin," I remind her.

"You didn't arrive with the rest of us." She folds her arms. "You said you trained under Bren and Tomas?"

"Their shop is off of Briar Street."

"I know it," she replies, a bit impatiently. "I've just never seen—"

"Helos!"

Heart leaping, I swivel round to find Bren's wide frame towering in the doorway, a delighted smile lighting his bronze face. His dark hair has grown out enough to part to one side, and the beginnings of a beard shadow his usually clean-shaven chin. Other than that and the purple shirt, he's the same as he was before, down to the soft manner in which he speaks. I grin in return as he crosses the room in a few long strides.

"When did you get here?" he asks, slapping my shoulder fondly.

"We waited as long as we could, but the queen evacuated the city before you returned."

Mahree's eyes narrow suspiciously, but I don't care. By the river, it's good to see his face!

"It took longer than I predicted, but I'm back now," I say simply. Bren and his husband knew I was away on royal business, but I was instructed not to give specifics.

"Good. We could use the extra set of hands."

"You're certain he's old enough to be tending to patients?" Mahree asks, peering up at me with thinly veiled skepticism.

Indignation swirls to the surface. Before I can ask whether Broden looks old enough to handle a sword, Bren places a hand on my shoulder.

"Mahree worked in Castle Roanin," he says. "She's used to do-ing things a bit differently." To Mahree, he adds, "Helos is the best apprentice I've ever had. He's plenty capable. Tomas and I will su-pervise, as we have before."

His praise warms my core.

"So why is he under guard?" she asks, eyeing Broden.

"I'm not under guard," I reply, just as Broden says, "Dom's orders."

I face him abruptly, a hot flush of adrenaline overpowering the warmth. *Dom*? That stuck-up bastard who accompanied us to the river and threatened to kill Rora in Niav? "On what grounds?" I demand. And to think, I thought the tail might have been for my protection.

Broden shrugs. "Just said you needed watching."

Ah. So Dom thinks people need protection from *me*. "Because I'm a shifter," I say dryly.

Silence stretches thin between us.

"You're a shifter?" Broden echoes, forehead wrinkled.

Bren looks at me, a question in his eyes.

It's true that back in Roanin, I asked him and Tomas not to share that detail with customers. Not because I've ever been ashamed, but because it always just seemed easier, given the Prediction.

After everything I went through these last few weeks, however, I'm rather less inclined to pretend.

"Is that a problem?" I ask, resisting the urge to curl my hands into fists. Strange—I never used to have to do that before. Lately, though, this newfound anger is always lurking just beneath the surface, pulsing with a heartbeat of its own.

Broden's expression curdles, his former tranquility dropped away.

"Young man," Bren says, sounding uncharacteristically stern. I'm relieved to see he's speaking to Broden, not to me. "I will not have you harassing my apprentice at his place of work."

"My orders were clear," Broden replies, looking offended at being called young.

"The queen herself gave me permission to be here," I say, somewhat loudly. "If you have a problem, take it up with her. Either get out, or let me get on with my job."

Broden steps toward me.

"None of that," Mahree says, cutting between us. "I won't have you agitating my patients. Helos, you may stay if Bren is willing to vouch for you. But I would ask you not to tell the other staff you're a shifter. Particularly with the Prediction . . . now is not the time for internal rifts."

Bren starts to argue with Mahree, but I barely hear the words.

My stomach is prickling. My face burning. I force myself to breathe through the rising discomfort, in and out until the hurt recedes. Why should I care if my being a shifter bothers other people?

Lock it away, I tell myself, batting aside the emotions and the sound of Mahree's voice. *With Finley and Rora and Father and all the rest. You don't have time for this.*

Rora's rejoinder from the Vale rings out. *You can't just shut every bad thought into a box and throw away the key.*

Watch me.

I flinch from the pressure on my arm, but it's only Bren.

"You look like you could use some air," he says, watching me carefully.

Nodding, I let him usher me outdoors, trying to ignore the

way Broden follows doggedly. Dom or no Dom, shifter or not, I've gotten myself a job. A way to help. This, at least, is something I can control.

A short time later, Bren reunites me with Tomas, who welcomes me back with his usual practical haste before introducing me to the rest of the hospital staff. All of them are older than I am save for one. The women roll their shoulders back and the men stroke their beards, clearly having decided my youth renders me useless.

The rest of that day and all the next, I make an effort to speak with every patient hospitalized for the Throes. As usual, there is no pattern to the afflicted, no hereditary transfer or transmission through contact we can trace. Many are also undernourished thanks to Telyan's increasingly poor harvests, which certainly doesn't help their bodies fight. It's frustrating.

From Roanin's city center, I exchange words with a gray-capped miller from Oak Lane, a weaver from Southend, a baker who stocked the royal kitchens with loaves and cakes, a sums teacher from the school on Fairbanks. A leather worker, a bank teller. Farmers and loggers from the city's outskirts are here as well, but I sense some intangible tension between them and those from Roanin proper. Occasionally, I have trouble understanding the stocky, cynical laborers and slow-speaking fishermen from northern Telyan's farther corners, as their accents are stronger than the lilting intonations to which I've grown accustomed.

Few seem enthusiastic at the prospect of talking with me, but their reticence increases severalfold when they feel Broden's tight-lipped presence bearing down on them. After the conversation with Mahree, he's latched onto me like a foul shadow.

"Don't mind him," I tell each patient in turn. "Her Majesty just wants to get to the bottom of this. Any piece of information might help."

When I invoke Violet's title, most acquiesce, though they sound more resigned than hopeful. Those in the illness's early stages speak of their reduced appetites, of the nausea and roaming pains that keep them up at night, despite their general fatigue. Those farther along, whose symptoms have become overtly magical, describe the fright of experiencing the sway and the silence, the embarrassment of lapsing into an episode of delirium among strangers and friends, and the difficulty of having one's vision and hearing and sensitivity to touch heighten many times beyond ordinary human capabilities.

Eventually, I reach patients who complain of incessant headaches and the fact that their voices have changed into a stranger's. These, I find most difficult to receive with a neutral healer's countenance, as the voice change typically signals the beginning of the end. It might take weeks, or only days, but soon enough they'll lose the power of language, so that they can't shape sounds into words no matter how hard they try.

Most tell me they do not want to die.

With each new conversation, I feel another shred of agitation and sorrow settling beneath my skin, weaving a sticky web around the pain already there. When the helplessness grows overwhelming, fox instincts tug on my core, gently urging the solution that worked in the Vale when young Rora was severely ill and I couldn't find her herbs in human form. I force myself to breathe deep, in and out, until the suggestion of whiskers, fur, and tail recedes.

By the end of the second day, my emotions are just about spent. Trying to ignore Broden's presence, I leave the hospital and am surprised to find Weslyn standing near one of the practice yards, dressed in a long navy coat. He's staring at the sky, his breath clouding in the crisp evening air.

My feet slow to a stop. I have a mind to break our silent stalemate and request a new babysitter, or better yet, none at all. Weslyn and I might not see eye to eye very often, but surely even he could empathize in this. Particularly if I suggest that Broden is interfering with civilians' well-being. Deciding it's at least worth a try, I pivot toward him—but at the sound of our boots on the gravel, Weslyn walks away without turning.

I swear I can feel Broden's breath on my neck.

"Stop clinging to me like a spider," I snap, whirling around and sending granite pebbles flying. "I can't focus with your constant hovering. If I have to spend another day with you intimidating my patients, I'll go mad."

"*Your* patients," he says.

"Yes, my patients."

"What difference does it make? I'm there to protect them."

I don't know how Rora could have withstood this for years. For me, it's only been two days. "Protect them from what? My teeth? You sound like a child spinning bedtime tales."

Broden's hand drifts to his sword hilt. Subtle. "My duty is to the crown and my queendom. Not you."

My fingers ball into fists. But since my patients are the priority here, I inhale slowly. Work to keep my tone civil. "Then serve the crown. It's difficult to gain anyone's trust with a Royal Guard looming at their bedside, watching in silence. Surely you can understand that. You might at least tell them something reassuring."

"What reassurance is there to give?" he counters. "They are all going to die. They would know it for a lie."

So much for keeping calm—the blood begins roaring between my ears. "There can be kindness in honesty, even if the words are harsh. You make the problem worse."

"I make it worse? That *thing* that sustains you is what's killing them all. Are you sure you aren't drawing more of it to them like a magnet?"

"That's not how it works," I grit out. "And in any case, I'm there to help them, not hurt them."

"No one can help them," Broden replies, though at least he has the decency to sound sorry about it. "The people in that room, Prince Finley—all of them will die because of magic and people like you."

My fist strikes his nose before he has time to raise his own. It hurts, but instead of backing down, I drive my knee between his legs, then pin his curling form against the wall.

"Do you know what?" I huff, my face close enough to see the tears glistening through slitted eyes. "I've changed my mind. You talk too much." He twists in my grasp, red-faced and panting, and I use the momentum to swing him onto the gravel. "I'll say it one more time. Stay out of my way."

"Forest scum," he mutters, spitting the blood that streams from his nose as he regains his feet. "The queen's mercy will not last forever. The day the young prince dies is the day you—"

He dodges my next punch and catches me on the cheek, rattling my vision momentarily. I twist to avoid his second attempt and slam a boot into his left side, right above the liver. He goes down. I don't stop.

My sore fist cracks against his face, grinding his head into the gravel. Again. Again. He raises no defense. He can't; I chose my target with care. My body sings with every impact to my arm, craving the release, relishing the pain in my hand. In a softer voice, a whisper of bruised awareness curls beneath the surface, lodged inside and out of reach. Something gone wrong. Something broken. And deep in my core, in the place that grounds the magic, there is a tendril of response.

It feels like writhing worms. Or bees. Or the head of a pestle milling herbs in the mortar, twisting, crushing—

Arms hook beneath my shoulders, yanking me up, away from Broden. I thrash against the hold and find myself trapped up against someone, my wrists pinned firmly across my abdomen.

"This won't help, Helos." Weslyn's voice is close to my ear, his arms wrapped tight around me. I writhe to break free of his grip, to bring him down with me. He doesn't budge.

"Get off of me!"

"He would not want this."

At the words, some of the fire leaves my veins. My gaze falls to Broden, who is a scarlet mess at my feet. Dimly, it occurs to me—as my heaving breath slows, while the pressure in my bubbling core recedes—that a handful of onlookers has gathered at the nearby practice yard. A steely-eyed officer beside some open-mouthed cadets.

I imagine one of them is Rora.

My arms go slack. Weslyn releases me and kneels at Broden's side, verifying he's still hanging onto consciousness.

"He—" I take a shuddering breath. "I don't . . . I didn't—"

"Take a walk, Helos."

There is blood on my hands. Blood on Weslyn's navy coat. The officer has come forward to help. I step backward on the stones, away from the trio, from the force of Weslyn's quiet fury. The students follow my retreat with wide eyes, mostly shock with a tinge of fear. They're not much younger than I am. Broden is not much older.

I turn and circle hastily round the Officers' Hall, hot shame scalding my stomach. The buildings encircling me, so often a comfort in their solidity, begin to feel like they're closing in. Out through the north gate, then, and down the grassy hill. One foot before the other. The way here is steeper and laden with switchbacks, but my feet careen down it as if it were flat.

By the time I reach the bottom several minutes later, I have admitted to myself what that twisting sensation in my core was. It doesn't matter that I've felt it only twice before, both several years in the past. The knowledge is certain as breathing.

I sink into the grass a good distance from the hill, completely alone this far from the lakes and surrounding encampment. The wind buffets my hair as I study my aching, blood-caked hands. I want to wash them clean. There is nowhere to do it.

So close. My body came so close to shifting. A third and final animal form, born at last—from violence.

I don't know what's happening to me. Ever since that day by the river—no, ever since the Vale—it feels as if someone's untying the strings around my heart, one by one. Every time I try to grab the loose ends, another knot pulls free. It feels—

Stop. Please stop.

It feels like I'm *unraveling,* a ball of yarn bouncing down an infinite staircase, unable to stop the course, to slow the descent, the core of it shrinking smaller and smaller as the light at the top recedes from view. I reach for the start, but a palm presses against my chest, pushing me further into the blackness. A place that is hollow, and echoing, and empty. No one's here to hold me, to distract from the pain—only voices breathing desperation, the hands of my past pulling at my hair, the ones I have failed grasping tight to my clothes, the shreds of a once-sought future shrouded by the midnight-woven certainty of failure. And then it is silent. Vast, empty silence.

I realize I am crying. I am bent at the waist, my forehead on the ground. A person Rora would no longer recognize. Do I? No wonder Finley's keeping me away.

Between the dandelion heads and blades of calf-high grass, I grind my palms against my ears and scream into the dirt. The cold, black silence is the hardest part of all.

SIX

RORA

I shift to lynx. I have no choice. My clothing rips as my body shrinks and stretches, and suddenly the noise is loud as thunder to my tufted ears.

Soldiers spill like ghosts into the broken darkness, pale gray shapes with spiraling limbs and flaring torchlight. Beside me, Peridon fires arrow after arrow, his whisperer eyes apparently as sharp as my feline ones. Further afield, the jaguar has wrapped its jaws around someone's neck.

The soldiers stumble toward us more hesitantly now, no doubt blinded by the pitch darkness beyond their sphere of light, the line of arrows singing toward them visible only when they hit their marks. Ordering myself to get moving, I jolt forward and swipe unsheathed claws along one's knees. She buckles with a cry, silenced when my fangs sink into her throat.

It's like air released from a long-held breath. Or the moment a candle's flame dissipates, just like that, into smoke. That is the way this woman's life seeps from her body. To the lynx part of my brain, there's a calm familiarity with this sensation, the twitching growing scarce and the warm blood filling my mouth. The way prey has felt between the lynx's jaws since time began. I focus on those instincts, trying to let them drown out the human thoughts reaching for the surface. Those comprise a different reaction entirely.

I release her throat, feel the moment she sags to the ground ripple through my paws, and reassess. A whisperer with an age-lined face disarms a soldier with a kick-and-hit combination, grabbing his bow and firing stolen arrows into the chaos. The other two whisperers we freed are flanking Andie in the last row as she opens the cages with her back to the fray.

As I race over to where the fighting is thickest, in the strip of land between the cages and the light-filled double doors, various creatures flee in the opposite direction: caribran sprouting grass underfoot; loropins flying up and away; a pair of blinded caegars creeping slow, working hard to make sense of their surroundings. Determined to guard their escape, I skirt around a marrow sheep felled in the crossfire and position myself at the darkness's edge, a whiff of smoke sharpening the air.

A soldier advances with a torch in one hand and a sword in another. My body pressed low to the ground, ears laid flat, I leap from the night's protective black and into the fire's circle of light, pinning him down. He doesn't cry out, simply abandons the torch and rolls out from under me, swinging his sword. Pain sears my shoulder as the blade tears skin, and I flinch back, scouring wildly for a way to approach.

Focus is fleeting. My hypersensitive ears, made for picking up the slightest scrabbling of prey hundreds of paces away, are inundated with the sounds of chaos: people shouting, animals screaming, arrows thudding into flesh. Torch flames snapping, metal scraping from sheaths, starched uniforms crackling. Fleeing paws striking earth, dying soldiers gasping, spitting blood. It's far too much, and I shake my head, trying to parse the torrent, to blot out the pain. I need to heal the shoulder wound. I need—

But suddenly I'm turning, twisting around before my brain has even caught up with the noise that propelled my feet: a second soldier, scarcely an arm's length behind, buckling to the ground facedown. Her outstretched sword falls where I stood a moment before. Black fletching lines the arrow shaft protruding from her back.

The body on the ground. The black-fletched arrow. I have lived this scene before, but this time, it isn't Father bleeding onto the ground. This time, I can see who fired the killing shot: wide-eyed Gerig, bow still raised, little more than a stone's throw away.

There is no time to thank him for saving me. My original opponent appears distracted by the flames licking out from the fallen torch, and I take advantage of the lapse, rolling onto my back and kicking hard with my hind legs.

The soldier stumbles right onto the fire. He screams as the flames climb his calves like ivy, but I only draw matter from the ground and direct it to my shoulder until the torn flesh knits back together—a temporary fix, but it will have to do. By the time I've darted back to Gerig, my eyes are watering in the smoky air.

"We're losing," he says, face flickering in the firelight. "We should leave now. There are too many!"

He's right. One whisperer still encircles Andie like a shield as she works through the final few cages, but the other is on the ground, bent at an odd angle. Though many of the soldiers have been felled by arrows, there must be thirty more slowly encroaching upon the smoldering darkness, and surely our stolen arrow supply is nearly spent.

Discouragement deepens when I realize it's not just my wildcat vision allowing me to see in the dark. The night is actually growing lighter; more fallen torches have kindled the grass, and flames are crawling up the wooden watchtower, striking the air with ferocious jabs. My stomach plunges. Without the cover of darkness to shield them, Peridon and the rest won't stand a chance. But if we leave now, the remaining prisoners will burn in their cages.

We can't stop yet. Not when we're so close.

Coldness shrouds my bones and numbs my core as my legs stretch into wings. In goshawk form, I fly toward the soldiers with the steady purpose of a hunter. Despite the fierce stinging in my throat, I use the low-hanging smoke as cover, alternating between evading blade tips with a goshawk's grace and dragging my talons across shoulders or skulls.

The crowd shuffles uneasily, caught between the arrows below and talons above. Their world going up in flames. Several point to the fire devouring the grass.

That's when the widow bats return.

"Rora!" Peridon shouts, barely audible between the blazing watchtower and the chirping bats now loosing their venom on the soldiers below. Andie has finished with the cages.

I fly over to the remaining group of former prisoners, all of whom are desperately making for the safety of the forest across the barren plains—forest walkers, the jaguar, a pair of black-tipped caws, and only one whisperer besides Peridon and Andie. Gerig brings up the rear, casting several glances over his shoulder.

We are maybe a fourth of the way over the plains when the watchtower collapses behind us, crashing to the ground in a fiery tomb. Flames have nearly engulfed the vile compound.

"Faster," Peridon urges, but the forest walkers have been imprisoned for who knows how long, and their progress is slow and stumbling. When one with a nearly translucent frame collapses, I drop to the earth and shift to lynx, two taloned feet giving way to four massive paws. She blinks up at me, uncomprehending in her exhaustion, and I touch my nose to her bark-patterned palm. She braces her hands on my back, rising.

Halfway to the woods. Behind us, the wildfire is catching, spreading, down to the mountains' base and over toward us. Heat presses in like hands on our backs, urging us on, warning of worse to come. Peridon looks at me, then the blaze, but I don't know how to stop the encroaching fire any more than he. If it reaches the forest, the entire Vale could burn.

We are nearly at the tree line, the flames no more than a caegar's leap away, when the ground begins to rumble.

Not again! The forest walker by my side falls upon the shuddering earth, wheezing as she presses her forehead to the ground. At her other shoulder, Gerig rubs his arms with obvious hesitance before offering his hands. The forest walker peels her eyes open and recoils.

Once the others have cleared the trees, Peridon races toward us, stumbling several times as the earthquake strengthens. I can feel the heat from the fire singeing my fur, my body vibrating at the shifting terrain, terror strengthening its hold. My body shifts to goshawk of its own accord, begging me to flee, and still the forest walker does not rise.

The ground opens up behind us.

Gerig cries out as the earth cracks and groans, splitting into a cavernous hole. Like a changeling wolf prying open its jaws in a yawn, the shadowed gap stretches left and right, carving a ravine across the plain. Relief cascades over me, strong as a waterfall. The fire hugs the edge opposite us, but it cannot jump the gap.

It's trapped.

I'm the first to recover, and I fly a tight circle around Peridon until, shaking himself, he bends and offers the forest walker his arm. It takes an agonizingly long time for her to pull herself up. But she does.

The moment we cross the tree line, some of the color returns to her skin. Like an artist filling in the lines of a sketch, her features become clearer, more solid. She inhales deeply, as if she is breathing the forest inside of her.

To my surprise, many of the forest walkers we saved have remained among the firs, their faces glowing in the firelight. Two clasp their friend's upper arms, offering quiet words of thanks. A short distance away, Andie sits panting softly, her hand clutching that of the whisperer beside her—a wispy figure maybe twice her age. The older is crying.

Leaving Peridon to catch his breath, I fly to the boulder where I left my pack only hours before, then shift to human and tug out clothes and a bandage. My fingers are shaking from the shock of death's close call, and I can't help but think of the last time I escaped that evil place—Helos's face alarmingly serious as he held my own and asked if anyone had hurt me. Wes holding back my hair while I gagged and draping his cloak around my shoulders when my body began to tremble even more violently than it does now. For a moment, the strength of missing them nearly overwhelms me, and I have to distract myself by releasing my hold on the borrowed matter stitching together my shoulder.

The sword wound splits open, pulsing angrily. Tonight, there's no Helos to bind my damaged skin with a healer's efficient touch.

No Wes to wrap an arm around my waist in case my own strength gives out. I have only myself, gritting my teeth against the sharp sting as I bandage my shoulder as best I can. Fighting to stop the trembling as I sit alone in the darkened wood.

Well, not quite alone.

When I return to the forest's edge, the survivors remain gathered where I left them. Peridon lifts his chin but remains with his cousin, while Gerig slouches a short distance away, apparently trying to ignore the prisoners' accusatory glances. I pick my way over to his side.

"Thanks for your help back there," I mutter.

Gerig shrugs but uncrosses his arms, staring at the ruined compound with an air of mild disbelief. "The land," he says. "It saved us."

"More likely it saved itself," I point out. "Magic always fights to survive. It must have sensed the fire nearly reaching the trees. We're lucky we were as close to them as we were."

We both twist at the soft thump behind. The jaguar has laid down by Andie's side.

"It's gone," Gerig whispers, turning back to the fiery blaze.

I search his tone for remorse and find just a little. "It's only one part of the problem," I reply, pressing tight against my bandaged shoulder. "But yes. It's gone."

A short time later, the clouds from earlier break. In the shadows of the forest, the glow lighting our faces slowly fades as we watch the rain douse the wildfire and wash the flames away.

/EVEN

HELOS

By my fourth morning at Fendolyn's Keep, I don't expect a response when I knock on Finley's door. I rap my knuckles against the wood anyway, and to my surprise, it swings open.

Finley hovers by the door, fingers grazing the handle. There's a bit more color in his face this morning, or maybe I'm imagining it. He's dressed for going out.

"You're later than usual today," he remarks, eyebrows raised.

It's true. I woke feeling depleted, like the sleep had done me less good than I'd hoped for. "You answered," I reply, rather simply.

"I wanted to see the evidence for myself." With a small step, he reaches for my hand and turns it this way and that, scrutinizing the purple bruises. The feel of his touch is so familiar, it seems to call a part of me back to myself. "Helos the fighter," he says, sounding confused, and drops my hand.

I scrape a foot along the floor, guilt squeezing my throat. "Weslyn told you?"

"Torres brought it up with Violet while I was in the room. I'm afraid you have rather lost a fan in her." He leans against the doorframe.

"Violet?"

"Torres." Finley rubs his cheek. "Vi is reserving judgment."

"I'm sorry," I murmur. "It had been a long day, and he baited me."

"Don't apologize to me," he says. "Save it for Broden. Maybe you can stop by his cot during today's hospital rounds."

I'm not sure how to respond, so I wait for him to soften the words with his usual humor.

He doesn't.

"I learned something else in Violet's company," he says after the silence grows strained. "Yesterday a bird arrived bearing a message. One of her spies in Oraes reported seeing smoke in the west, probably from two nights before. A lot of it." He bites his lip. "They said it looked like there had been a fire across the river."

My heart rattles against my ribs. "A wildfire? Did it reach the trees? Is the forest burning?"

Fin shakes his head, his expression serious. "We're not sure."

Spinning. My vision is spinning, it's shaking, my chest surely on the verge of collapse. Rora's there. To spot the fire that far north, where she intended to go—it had to be her. Somehow, I'm sure of it. And if the flames reached the trees? She could never outrun them, though maybe with wings . . . I place a hand on the wall, breathing fast. Like the fool I am, I let her go alone. I watched her walk away. I let her.

"*Helos,*" Finley says again, grabbing my arm and tugging me inside. "Calm down. It's all right. Sit here."

Blinking rapidly, I perch on the edge of his bed and touch my cheeks, where whiskers have broken through. The fox recognizing the terror, my desperation—the need to find a better path than the one laid before my feet. My skin prickles with unease. I used to be better at containing these instincts.

I draw air into my lungs until it hurts, sending the whiskers away. When my head clears, I realize Finley's hand is still clutching my arm.

He lets go when he sees me looking.

"Don't jump to conclusions," he says while scraping a hand through his hair, his voice oddly tight. Leaving the door open, he sinks into an upholstered chair near the window. "You realize a fire might mean Rora succeeded?"

I glance at him sharply.

"Wes told me what she intends to do. And—her theory about reawakening the land. That it might work in place of stardust." Fin's face brightens a touch, the first hint of joy I've seen in him today. Out of habit, I feel my own brushing off the dust and reaching to meet it, like a candle to flame. "Remember what you told me, Helos. If anyone can take care of herself, it's Rora."

Wrong, my heart cries, another habit teased forth. *I was wrong. She needs my help.*

I squeeze my temples between my fingertips.

Gradually, as my heart rate slows, Finley's room slides into focus. The layout is similar to mine, despite our difference in station—a curved, wooden headboard crowning the bed, a beige rug softening the slatted floor. Stark, bare walls devoid of color and the maps he prized in Roanin. Gauzy curtains, polished shoes by the door, a sleep shirt rumpled on the ground, and a dresser with half-open drawers. And in one of those drawers, a brown book with a faded spine, one I recognize because I bought it for him in the antiquarian shop owned by Naethan's father, Feryn. A memoir of a man who climbed every mountain in the Purple range. Finley kept it.

The answer is no, his voice rings in my head, pitiless.

"Why did you open the door today?" I ask quietly.

Finley massages the soles of his feet. "I told you, I wanted to see the proof for myself." After a beat, he drags a pair of shoes before him and stands. "And I was on my way out, in any case. Now I'm late."

"For what?" I ask, startled. I can't remember the last time Finley cared about keeping to a schedule.

He checks his pale green shirt in the mirror and re-tucks the part that's come loose, and now I'm fully staring. "I've been taking a horse down to the valley most days. Mainly to speak with people in the encampment. Make sure they don't feel forgotten, promise to relay their concerns to Violet. You know." Satisfied with his neat reflection, he reaches for a long black coat and glances my way, head tilting back at the sight. "What?"

I run a hand over the back of my neck. "Nothing. You just sound—" I realize I don't know how to finish that sentence, so I pivot. "It sounds like you enjoy this."

"I do," he agrees, though he fidgets a little.

That's usually a sign that he's struggling against saying more, like he's trying to rein in his words. It's an impulse I've always found strange, considering I could spend hours listening to him talk about nothing at all. "And?" I prompt.

After wrestling with himself another moment, Fin grabs his walking stick and perches back on the chair. "Before my father . . . well, before," he murmurs, looking away. "He always meant for me to have a public-facing role. Something with people, boring things like officiating ceremonies or standing in at diplomatic functions, because he thought—" Again, Finley trails off, but I can guess why King Gerar would have wanted his youngest son among the people. Fin brings the sun. He always has. "He meant well," he continues. "But I fought him on it, a lot. I made his life difficult, and I didn't care. But I know I can do better, Helos. I want to make good on his wishes. I owe it to him. And to— Well, it's the least I can do."

I nod, struck by the sobriety in his manner. Wondering at how much could have changed in the weeks I've been away, and the month of forced separation before that. He seems older than just sixteen, weighed down by burdens I'm having to hear about secondhand rather than experiencing alongside him, and all I can think is how badly I want him to take me with him in this next step rather than leaving me behind.

"I think it suits you, Fin," I say honestly. "But you don't need to be better. You're fine just as you are." *Fine* feels woefully inadequate, but I need to start respecting the line he set between us, however much it hurts.

Finley's hands still where they've been drumming the chair's arms. I start to worry I've said something wrong, even more when his eyes flit to the ground.

"Did I—"

"What about you, Helos? It seems you have an unexpected inheritance of your own." He leans forward in his chair. The directness in his gaze sharpens into the sort of intensity I'd expect from his brother, but not from him. "What are you going to do with it?"

That hushes me. In the days since my conversation with Violet, I'd all but pushed the question out of my mind. I scratch my head, slightly annoyed he didn't learn this information from me. "You and Weslyn sure covered a lot."

Fin doesn't take the bait. He just waits.

The truth is, I don't know what to tell him, any more than I had his sister. The hours I've spent at the hospital have been hard, but they've also felt like coming home, settling back into comfortable routine after weeks of maddening uncertainty. Bren said I have a knack for healer's work, and I like to think he's right, but it's more than that. For me, this work is like breathing. It just feels right.

The more I immerse myself in this world, the less certain I become as to whether I could really give it up for a role that's unlike any I've known before, for a kingdom I've never even been to. Of course, perhaps in another life, my mother would have raised me there—but the subject of my mother is not one on which I care to dwell.

"I don't know," I say at last. "Maybe it's too much for me. Too big a charge. I wouldn't even know how to claim a throne, let alone rule." *And it would take me far from you.*

"You could learn," Fin offers quietly, undeterred.

Mild irritation sparks, unfamiliar and biting. I know what kind of people I'd be dealing with in Eradain, better than he. I know what hangs in the balance if I choose not to pursue the throne; I have the scars to prove it. I don't need a lecture or added pressure in this, least of all from him. "I'd think you of all people should understand avoiding responsibility."

Finley looks taken aback. Even I could hear the strange bitterness in my tone, but I can't bring myself to break the silence that follows.

Eventually, he forces a laugh.

"Well done, Helos," he says, as if impressed. "I didn't know you had it in you." He's striving for humor, but I can hear the strain in his effort.

I've hurt him.

All those things he said about his father, and I said *that*.

"Fin, I'm sorry, I don't know what came over me," I say, getting to my feet, but he waves me off as he, too, stands.

"Don't be. I mean it," he stresses, when I start toward him. "You're right. I would have thought that way, once." He checks his reflection again in the mirror. Smooths his collar. Then his eyes find mine in the glass, and he turns. "But my father is dead, Helos. War is coming. More people are going to die." His voice shakes on the last. "Violet shouldn't have to be queen this young, but she is. Wes shouldn't have to risk his life in battle, least of all to spare me. But he will."

I start to object to this self-deprecation, but he cuts me off.

"I don't know what you should do about the crown, Helos. Honest. All I know is that our old life is gone. We no longer have the luxury of indifference." With that, he crosses to the doorway, smiling a bit when he sees my hesitation, our brief fight forgiven. "Are you coming?" he asks.

Hope rises, because this, at least, feels like familiar ground— Finley blazing a trail ahead and glancing behind, hoping I'll follow. I always will.

"Can I make one suggestion?" I say. "For your trip down the hill."

Fingers on the handle, he lifts his eyebrows expectantly.

I gesture to his messy hair. "Maybe you should try a comb."

Finley looks aghast at the idea, which tugs a grin from me at last.

That's the Finley I know.

"Helos," he says sternly, "I'm trying to look more responsible. Not *ridiculous*."

It's a vastly different experience to walk the Keep with Finley. I feel acutely aware of almost everything about him: his blond hair lifted by the cool morning breeze, his freckled nose somewhat pink, the way he carries his weight unevenly while his walking stick swings ahead. He seems to breathe a little deeper outside the Officers' Hall, and I try to notice it all without him noticing me.

"This is my stop," I tell him somewhat reluctantly when we reach the hospital doors.

Finley glances farther down the path, appearing to waver. "Maybe I should stop in for a bit, before my rounds."

"I thought you were running late."

"Well, yes," he admits.

I wait. He doesn't move.

"Come on, then," I say, opening the door and following him inside.

Most of the ward is laid out as it has been before. Patients on or milling about their beds, dust swirling in the light filtering through the glass. But the hall hangs eerily quiet save for an argument breaking out on the far end. Most heads are turned in that direction.

Unease pricks my spine. "Maybe you should—"

Finley's already making for the other side.

In the uncharacteristic hush, the snap of his walking stick against the stone floor draws dozens of eyes his way. Many people straighten in surprise, and several hurry to their feet. A protest rises to the tip of my tongue, to tell them to stop, to rest, but Finley says nothing. Just strides firmly down the center aisle.

"Your Royal Highness," says Rian, a lanky healer with a grizzled beard. He steps toward Finley as if to block the view of the cot behind, ignoring me entirely. "We were not expecting a visit."

"Is that a problem?" Finley asks, navigating around him. "Is there something you don't wish me to see?"

Rian starts to protest, but Finley holds up a hand and steps to the bed's end.

On the cot, a woman bends over a piece of parchment, writing slowly. My throat pinches at the sweat beading along her sickly pallor, the wads of cotton stuffed into her ears to provide relief from the worst of the heightened hearing. I remember her case. A couple of weeks after her voice changed, she lost the ability to communicate through speech. She doesn't have long.

When she spots Finley, she beckons him over urgently, wide-eyed.

Fin ignores Rian's objection and circles round to her side. Sinking onto the bed, he reads the passage to which she's pointing. "Where is her family?" he asks, looking up. "Should they not be here now?"

I lift my gaze from the pair to find Mahree leaning against the wall with her arms folded tightly across her chest. She's watching me with a grim expression.

"We thought not, sir," Rian says. "The patient, her behavior—"

"What is your name?" Finley asks the woman in a kind voice, holding up a hand when the man tries to answer. *Lyra,* I think. It takes a while for her to get it down on the page, but she does. "This is Lyra," Fin tells Rian. "Not 'the patient.' Understand?"

I have to stop myself from throwing my arms around him then and there.

"Sir," Rian says, apparently less enthralled, "Lyra might be clear now, but in an hour, she won't be. We feel it would be most distressing for her family. She will hardly recognize they're here."

"Do not say 'we,' like this is a joint decision," Mahree cuts in. "I told you last night to send someone down the hill. Her family should be notified."

Lyra clutches the back of Finley's hand.

"You didn't send one yourself?" Finley challenges.

Mahree's eyes flash. "I do not delegate tasks just to hear myself speak, sir. My order should have been enough. There is much to do."

"And now Lyra has spent another night alone." Finley straightens, though he doesn't withdraw his hand from underneath Lyra's. "From now on, you call their families here. You *call* them," he repeats, pivoting between Rian and Mahree. "I don't care who gives the order or what state the patient is in. Issue a runner and bring them here. You can start with Lyra; go ahead and send for hers. I'll wait."

Rian's forehead wrinkles. "Sir—"

"Now."

Rian does as ordered, and Fin remains where he is while Bren pulls me away to begin my shift. Half an hour later, Lyra's three children arrive.

"Open a window," Fin tells the closest healer, rising to leave. "The air is stale in here."

Vaguely in awe, I mumble excuses and follow him out of the ward.

Once outside, Finley crosses to a set of wooden crates stacked against the armory wall and rolls his ankle, grimacing a little. His eyes are bright. "I'm glad I went inside," he tells me, looking earnestly to where I hover a couple of paces away. "I'll add it to my rotation. Maybe there's more I can do."

My heart lifts at the thought of Finley coming around more often. Still, I'm struggling to focus on much beyond the tenderness in his movements and the obvious toll this morning's work has already taken. Magic has never been predictable, and the duration of each person's illness is impossible to predict. It took Lyra four months to reach the point of losing her speech, whereas I've seen others reach that stage in three weeks. Thank fortune Finley's course appears to be progressing more slowly than Rora and I feared, but even so—

"Are you still going down the hill?"

"Of course," he answers, sounding surprised. "Just—in a moment."

I chew the inside of my cheek. "Maybe you should rest instead."

"I know my own strength, Helos," he says sharply.

"I know, but—"

"You don't, actually. Let me make my own decisions."

Finley turns away rather pointedly, switching to the other foot. Figuring this might be the opening for which I've been waiting, I sink onto the crate next to his, weighing my words with care. "Like pushing me away?"

That pulls him back. "What?"

I study the hollow planes of his face, undeterred by his subtle nerves. "You sent Rora with a message," I remind him. "Tell me why. Please."

He swallows, as if wishing he could avoid the question. "You asked for the impossible."

"I didn't," I reply, trying not to allow the blow to land. "I asked for the truth."

"The truth," he echoes faintly, his attention flicking to four careers walking nearby, enmeshed in some lively debate. Donned in the green-accented gray uniforms of Telyan's army, they brighten when they spot Finley.

"Good to see you out, Your Royal Highness," says a handsome one with green eyes and loose brown curls. All four of them raise their fists against their hearts.

"I'm not an officer, you fools." Finley rolls his eyes fondly.

"You still outrank us, sir."

"True. And isn't that awful?" he says cheerfully.

To my surprise, the group only grins. It's hard to miss the way the one with green eyes sweeps his gaze over my body before rounding the corner with the rest, but I shrug off the invitation in favor of Fin. If the answer is going to remain no, I at least deserve to know why.

Finley watches them go and shrugs. "It helps to remind them we're human, too," he tells me. "Give them someone to joke around with. Fortune knows that won't be Wes."

"I suppose," I reply, not really in the mood for him to change the subject.

Perhaps he senses this, because his expression sobers in the quiet that follows. "The truth, Helos, is that you've always given too much of yourself to me. Whereas I," he murmurs, bending to rest his arms flat across his legs. "I just take."

"How can you say that?"

"Because it's the truth," he says firmly. "I took my father's peace of mind, and now he's gone. I took my brother's future. I took your—" Finley breaks off, and for a moment, I catch the torrent of emotions sweeping his face. Fear. Guilt. Anguish. Longing.

My hand strikes out with a will of its own, settling over his. Fin just looks at it, shoulders slumping.

"It was hard for me, when you left for the Vale. I didn't know if I'd ever see you again. And it made me realize—" He pauses to gather himself, breathing deep. I squeeze his hand, but he pulls away. "No, what I want no longer matters," he says, more quietly still. "You're the best of us, Helos. You deserve more than what I can give you."

Adrenaline heats my core, my mind stuck on the words *what I want,* the truth he isn't saying. "What *do* you want?"

"Haven't you heard what I just said? You cannot tie yourself to me, Helos. I see that now." His mouth pinches tight. "Especially now."

Anger flares behind my eyes. "What makes you think it's a choice?"

"Because love is a choice!" He straightens abruptly, looking me in the eyes. "It's always a choice. You truly think I'm the only one in this entire world who could ever make you happy?"

For a while, I'm unable to summon a response. We just sit there, studying each other. Closer than we've been in weeks, yet in some ways, farther apart than ever. His eyes search my face, and I find myself wanting desperately for him to read it all, like I've read him. My sorrow, my uncertainty. This interminable anger that's clawing me apart. Read it and take it away, say the words that will make it stop hurting so much. I want him to fix me. By the river, I want him to *touch* me.

Finley bites his lip and turns away. "I saw my father in the years after my mother died. I watched the grief chip away at his heart." He releases a long breath. "He lost himself, Helos. I won't let you do the same. I wouldn't before these fortune-forsaken Throes, and I certainly won't now. You deserve better than that."

"Then why did you answer the door?" I ask again. This time, the question comes out barbed.

"Because I thought we could still be friends." He pushes to his feet. "In any case, we're burning daylight. Aren't you meant to be working a shift? And I should be getting on."

"That's it, then?" I ask, throwing my hands up. "That's all you have to say?"

Fin rubs the back of his neck. "That's it."

Disappointment lodges in my stomach, thick as mortar. I shake my head at him. "You should be resting instead."

His attempt at restoring ease between us deflates in a rush. "You cannot be serious."

"Oh, I am," I assure him, getting to my feet, my face close to his. The only way I know to push back. "You shouldn't overdo it, Fin."

Finley's face flushes red as he opens his mouth to retort, then shuts it again. Without another word, he walks in the direction of the stables.

I remain there long after he disappears from view. Unsure how we got here, after nearly two blissful years of talking and laughing and kissing and arguing and spending the nights in his bed. After I told him I loved him, so certain he would say it back, and asked him to be with me for real. Publicly this time. No more sneaking around to avoid the added attention his status and the Prediction's warning bring, no going back. Only forward, together, all of me in. Was he?

My fingertips mash against the sides of my skull.

I will never stop reliving that night behind closed lids. The soft press of silk upon my bare chest as I curled my arms beneath the pillow, contentment drifting into sleep. Once the candles burned low, waking in the best way—to fingers brushing the planes of my back, along my shoulder blades and down the valley carved between them. The utter certainty I felt as I shifted to rest my head on my hand, my elbow on the pillow, and began. *Finley. I want to tell you something.*

It still keeps me up at night—the panic in his eyes, just enough light left to see. The entirely wrong reaction, suddenly not himself at all. He'd thrown off the sheets and begun to pace, clutching his head as if it hurt. And to think, I was so sure King Gerar was to blame, some conversation about royal obligations I wasn't there to observe.

I swear this rift inside my chest is growing claws, snapping the threads around me one by one.

When I feel myself starting to slip back into that place, I push to my feet and shove my hands into my pockets. Abruptly itching to move, to do *something* other than sit here drowning in my own thoughts. No one tries to talk to me as I make my way to westgate, hospital shift forgotten, but a few cadets stare, while others actively avert their gaze. Word of my attack on Broden must have spread.

I ignore them all and march through the gate, but I only make it a short way down the hill when a commotion breaks out behind me.

One of the careers atop the rampart shouts an order and hands her spyglass to the woman beside her. I squint back out at the valley below.

The horse and rider tearing across the open expanse look little larger than a boulder from this distance. I watch until they've skirted the farther lake and nearby tents before hurrying back up the slope and into the Keep.

To my surprise, Violet waits just inside, her eyes slightly narrowed and her arms folded loose across her chest. Her cream-colored sweater, long green skirt, and boots are elevated variations on the careers' uniform—the cream a bit brighter than the standard gray, the dark green slightly richer. Captain Torres, General Powell, and another person in uniform I don't recognize stand at attention just behind her, along with a particularly somber-looking Weslyn. But it's regal Violet, her stillness, who somehow draws my gaze like a physical force.

"What's happening?" I ask, approaching without thought. "Is something wrong?"

Captain Torres snaps a few words about propriety and formal address, while General Powell looks slightly shocked. Violet doesn't even spare me a glance.

"I saw a—"

"Your observations have no part in this," says Captain Torres. "Leave us."

I consider appealing to Weslyn, but he meets my gaze and shakes his head, just once from side to side.

"Return to the hospital, Helos," Violet says in a level voice. Her attention remains fixed on the gate.

Biting back a reply, I make my way down the main road. When I reach the granary, the first building to my right, I duck around it and wedge myself in the gap between the stone and the Keep's outer wall.

The horse canters through the gate a short time later, its hooves clattering across the pavement.

"Your Majesty," huffs the rider, tugging on the reins. The mare dances in place, frothing around the bit, her broad neck coated in sweat. "Eradain soldiers are approaching Briarwend. We estimate their numbers at three hundred strong, all on foot, enough to challenge the units stationed there. General Wahlen calls for re-inforcement."

"She will have it," Violet promises, uncrossing her arms. "General. Your recommendation?"

"Mounted unit, a hundred-band," says General Powell. "If they take the pass, they can be there in just over an hour."

"An hour may be too late. Make it half that, three-quarters if you must. And send riders to scout the hills in all directions; this may be a diversion, and I do not want us caught unaware. Go."

"I will join them," Weslyn says, stepping up as General Powell and the other uniform run away.

Violet holds his gaze a long moment, then nods. "Bring Naethan. Don't do anything foolish."

Weslyn hurries toward the stables.

"And me," I call, stepping out from my hiding place. "They will need someone to tend the wounded." At last, something tangible to grab hold of, a way to flatten the inner turmoil into a steady line.

Captain Torres starts to object, but Violet raises a hand. "Helos," she says. "I thought Rora might have explained to you how protocol works in this court."

"She explained plenty."

"Then you make your case worse. Having a disregard for the rules is a poorer defense than ignorance of them."

"I want to help!"

"Tell me, since you seem so eager to rush off: how will you get there in a timely manner if you cannot go by horse?"

I close my mouth.

Violet lets us stand in silence for a time. A low-pitched horn bellows in the Keep, and the air carries the soft-edged murmur of a crowd gathering out of sight. I think she might genuinely be waiting for an answer, but between my prickling skin and churning gut, my mind is struggling to focus.

"You take a cart," she supplies, "and fill it with herbs. Pungent ones. Maybe rub some on yourself as well. Find a driver and sit in the back. It might work. Or it might not." She takes a step closer. "I do not employ reckless people, Helos. You would do well to learn to control your emotions."

Blood rushes to my face.

"They will need a healer," she concedes at last. "Go to the hospital and find another to travel with you. There are carts near the stable. If the draft horses spook, you will not slow the party. You will stay here and send them on. Understood?"

"Yes," I reply, vaguely breathless. "Yes. Thank you."

"Do not thank me. Learn from me. Now go."

I don't hesitate. I turn toward the hospital and run.

EIGHT

RORA

The ceaseless pulse in my shoulder tugs me awake.

Rubbing my tired eyes, I force myself upright and ignore the way my muscles groan at the movement, stiff and sore after yesterday's fight. Acrid ash mingles with the sweet scent of gardenias in the hazy morning air.

I reach for my waterskin, attempting to soothe my raw throat, which aches all the more for the smoke that has drifted south overnight. That isn't the only change—the conical firs that sheltered me the previous evening stretch taller now, at least five times my height, with pine needles sharp and shiny enough they glint like crystals in the light. Unexpectedly moved, I watch the teal-striped hummingbirds darting among the wildflowers and drag a hand along the bumpy ground. Acorn tops, the hummingbirds' fallen crowns.

I shouldn't linger. But with sleep-driven memories fresh in my mind, I can't help but take my time pulling on a gray, long-sleeved shirt that reminds me of tanned arms and soft-spoken words, kisses on a riverbank and sodden clothes sticking to skin. Out here, it feels easier to pretend. I shut my eyes and breathe in slow, imagining the brushed cotton settled against my waist belongs to him.

Get moving, Rora.

Peridon is in the small dip of earth where I left him, cradling his head on the crook of his arm. Andie is sleeping, too, face twitching restlessly, her stout form curled tight like a crescent moon. When I approach, a low growl rumbles overhead.

I freeze, fingers stretching into claws at my side. From his perch atop a gnarled branch, Andie's jaguar peers at me with wary yellow eyes, his tail lashing in agitation. I've no doubt he could pin me to the ground in one quick pounce.

"I have to wake them," I mumble, blinking slowly up at the wildcat to show I'm a friend. He remains unmoved, unwilling to grant me the trust of closing his eyes in my presence, and a chill trembles up my spine. "Peridon," I say, loudly.

Peridon and Andie jerk awake, Andie's hand going to the broad-bladed dagger she lifted off someone last night. She relaxes when she spots me, but only a little.

"There you are," says Peridon, giving me the once-over. "You could have stayed with us."

I shrug, faintly uncomfortable, while he ties his brown hair into a fresh knot. One of the jaguar's ears is bent in Andie's direction.

"Wasn't there another person with you?" I ask, recalling the older whisperer who had been crying.

Andie's forehead creases.

"Lona," Peridon says, getting to his feet. "Her husband was killed in the battle. She's been keeping vigil."

"Oh." I fold my arms across my chest. "I'm sorry."

"She will meet us at the dell," he says, watching Andie toy with the long sleeves encircling her wrists. "Let's go."

Though last night's escapees all spent the night in different wooded corners, some agreed to convene this morning after sunrise. I'd detected an unspoken web threading between us as we scattered into the wild—ties that bound us together as survivors of a shared horror.

I'm hoping they will have felt the connection, too. I may be used to working solo, but reawakening the land—I can't do that alone.

We wind through cottonwoods that trace the outskirts of a jagged stream, gray-barked and huge, with slender leaves fluttering among branches wider than my hips. When Peridon and Andie stoop to

freshen their faces in the bubbling stream, I sink my hands beneath
the sun-streaked water and brace myself against the sharp slap of cold
against my skin, listening to the gentle ripples down tiny waterfalls
and over mossy stones. Sometimes, a forest just needs to be felt.

Despite the jaguar prowling protectively a short distance away,
Andie moves with a decidedly edged gait, fingers always clasped
around the hilt belted to her waist. Through the corner of my eye,
I watch her attention fluctuate between dazed and hyper-alert, as
if she's struggling to settle back into the person she was prior to
imprisonment.

My nerves had felt wrung-out by the end of just two days beneath the mountain's shadow. I have no idea how long the soldiers
held her there.

The designated meeting place is a secluded, grassy hollow
stretched like a river between slender aspens. The far end of the dell
rises into a ridge, which should effectively hide us from intruding
eyes. Following my gaze, Andie inclines her head, and the jaguar
climbs the slope a moment later. To keep watch, no doubt.

"You're back," Gerig says with obvious relief, clamoring to his
feet a few paces away. He decided to sleep here alone, convinced he
would never find his way back if he left.

I appraise the soldier critically. He looks rough after a night
with no walls, his movements stiff, the red-trimmed uniform rumpled. Beyond his bow and quiver, he hasn't brought a pack or any
supplies. That will make things difficult.

"We're back," I agree.

"When will—"

Andie throws the dagger directly at his head.

"Don't!" I shout, too late, my heartbeat skidding as Gerig
throws himself to the side. The dagger thumps to the ground, and
Gerig stumbles back, clutching a bloody ear.

Andie frowns. "I'm out of practice."

"What did you do that for?" I exclaim, marching to retrieve the
weapon before she can.

She looks at me like I have completely lost my mind. "He is a
murderer."

"He has information we need."

"We need *nothing* from him. He's one of them. How many for-estborn have you tortured or killed?" She directs the last part at Gerig, who shakes his head, sputtering.

"They told us—"

"*No,*" she spits, pounding toward him.

I intercept her with outstretched hands. A short distance behind, Peridon simply watches, a conflicted expression pinching his face.

"You make excuses for your crimes before you even confess them!" Andie levels over my shoulder.

"I never killed or tortured anyone." Gerig's voice breaks on the words, and I turn in time to see tears rimming his eyes. "I only en-listed a couple of months ago. He said our homes were at risk, that rooting out magic was the best way to protect ourselves, to stop the Silent End . . . but I thought we'd go to war, I never signed up for—"

"Who said?" Andie presses, just as I ask, "The silent what?"

"Silent End," Gerig says, voice lowering. "A—a terrible illness. Magical," he adds, casting a fearful look at us. "And always fatal."

I smooth my features into neutrality.

So the Throes has spread to Eradain, too. It's not a surprise, nor is his apparent belief that eliminating magic might cure it; Telyans have come close to that troubling conviction often enough, with their mistrust of magic growing in time with the Throes. But only one realm built the prison, and I keep my mask firmly in place, devoid of recognition. The less any soldier of Eradain knows of Telyan's vulnerable points, the better.

Andie places her hands upon her hips.

"Look, I helped you, didn't I?" he asks, wiping at his cheeks. Either he's a convincing performer, or his guilt is genuine.

Still—

"One good deed does not make up for months of poor ones," I say after a beat, conceding that that much, at least, is true. "You chose to enlist. You may not have done the killing, but did you ever stop the others from doing so?"

He hesitates, his hand painted scarlet against his ear.

I twist back to Andie, who has venom in her eyes. "He is not a good man, but he has knowledge about Eradain that we could use. We should reserve sentencing until then."

"You're going to use me and then *dispose* of me?" Gerig asks, voice reedy.

"I didn't say dispose of you," I reply, again speaking at the same time as Andie, who says, "It's no more than you deserve."

I truly don't know which of us is right.

With a grating call, Peridon's black-tipped caw cuts across the dell and alights on his shoulder.

"The clan will be here soon," he says, stroking Coda's feathers.

Something like fear flashes across Andie's face, there and gone before I can interpret it.

Sure enough, several whisperers are emerging from the trees, their silver eyes gleaming in faces topped with silver- and gold-streaked hair. Lona travels with them, running a scraped hand over her head while her hollow gaze traces the perimeter with disinterest. Most wear forest-colored shirts with the sleeves cut short enough to display the golden rings imprinted on their left arms, and two have rings extending all the way from wrist to shoulder. I glance at Andie standing nearby. Her sleeves fall past her wrists.

"Andie!" exclaims a man with a partially shaved head, long-legged with a narrow frame like Peridon's. With a jolt, I realize I've met him before, back when he and his friends briefly held Wes and me captive. He approaches Andie with open arms, not paying me any heed. "Merciful fortune, it's good to see your face."

Andie's mouth pinches tight. "You could have seen it sooner, had you come after me like Peridon."

"You're angry." He flinches as she slaps his hand away. The new-comers exchange uneasy looks, and I, too, have the uncomfortable feeling I'm intruding on something private. "You're right to be."

"That was never in question, *Father*." She says the last word as if it's a joke. "I don't require your validation."

"Andie—"

"No," she says, with one firm shake of the head. "Don't speak to me as if you care."

"Take the circle, both of you," orders an older woman, short-statured with a sizable waist, her warm beige face etched with quiet authority. Thin brows, soft jaw, broad nose. A rowan bow hangs from her back beside a long plait of raven hair.

Feren. Another whisperer I met on my last trip to the Vale. The one who learned I survived the massacre at Caela Ridge and called me a ghost. Once father and daughter have sunk to the grass, Andie turning away from the face now folded in pain, Feren's attention slides to me.

Recognition kindles in her gaze, along with anger.

"You enlisted Peridon's help after I forbade it," she says. When she flicks two fingers, the remaining whisperers join the others on the ground in a loose circle. All except for Peridon, who sends Coda fluttering away, as though sensing trouble to come. "You made a loyal clansman disobey direct orders."

"Rora didn't make me do anything," Peridon objects, stepping to my side. "My decisions are my own."

"And now you both bring this filth into our council," she goes on, gesturing to Gerig, who cowers across the dell. "Have you no shame?"

"We *brought* you two people who would have otherwise continued to suffer, and would probably have died," I retaliate, indignation churning in my gut. "We did what should have been done a long time ago."

Peridon places a hand on my shoulder. "No, I feel no shame," he says more quietly, meeting Feren's gaze directly. "Only regret for those who didn't make it out."

From the circle, Lona gasps, as if discovering her loss all over again. The whisperer at her side puts a hand on her knee.

Feren weighs Peridon's response before she offers him a tiny nod and steps toward me. "It is not for you to decide what my clan should or should not do. That is human arrogance speaking through you, no doubt the influence of that young man you were traveling with. Where is he now?" Feren reaches for the bow across her back.

My throat tightens abruptly at the painful awareness that I have no idea where Weslyn is. Or Helos. The two of them were planning to travel to Fendolyn's Keep, but more than a week has passed since I saw them last. "He's east of the river," I tell her, when I find my voice. "He's in Telyan."

"He has left you, then." Feren sounds unsurprised.

"No." I draw myself up to my full height, easily two heads taller than her. "He's doing what he needs to do."

Out of the corner of my eye, I can sense Peridon watching me, as if this might be the moment he gets answers at last. My usual guardedness mingles with guilt. He's asked about my life in Telyan more than once since reconnecting, but in truth, I've gone so long having attempts at friendship thrown back in my face that trying to respond was like reaching for a flame that has burned me before. I no longer really know where to start, how to go about trying—or if it's even worth the risk when I have no intention of sticking around.

"And your brother? Did you free him?" Feren asks, her manner softening.

Tears prick my eyes, unexpected and unwelcome. I blink them away hastily, even as I reach for the pebble safely stored in my pocket. The one Helos tossed to me the morning I left Roanin alone, the only remnant of him I have. "Yes. He's east of the river, too. He's safe now." *I hope.*

"Yet you're here."

The observation floats in from behind, and I whip my head around, alarmed that I hadn't noticed anyone's approach.

A forest walker melts out of the trees, a wide figure with blue-green, bark-like skin and needle-sharp hair threaded with silver, features mimicking the blue spruce that must be his home tree. "I have come as promised," he says, glancing my way. "And I sense a story there." His voice is cool and crisp, like moving water.

"Torac," Feren says, inclining her head before I can answer him. "Please, take the circle."

Clearly, she expects to lead these proceedings. I bristle at her presumption, but Torac folds onto the ground without complaint.

More forest walkers arrive. First a lodgepole pine, reed-thin with olive eyes and hair that bunches around her shoulders like cones. Then a ponderosa, I think, all leaf-green hair and patterned, red-brown skin. When he steps into the dell, thick roots rumble beneath the ground and burst forth to capture Gerig in a rigid hold. It takes several anxious moments for me to convince him to release Gerig, and his mouth twists in distaste.

Next comes a more faded forest walker whose figure mimics a tree I've never seen. Her limbs are long and knobby, her posture crooked, and a squirrel clings to a pinkish shoulder which looks tough and plated as armored scales. When she greets us, her voice rasps like the wind.

Last is the forest walker who was almost too weak to make it out last night. In the firelight, her wasted figure had looked nearly translucent. Now her skin shines gray like a sky promising rain, her hair an autumn palette of red, orange, green, and gold. Wordlessly, she steps into the dell and takes a seat in the loose circle. Aspen, it seems.

"Is this all of us?" Feren asks. Only she and I remain standing.

"Not quite."

Two more people step into the dell, both the kind of bony thin that comes from long deprivation. They're human by all appearances—but then, so am I. They must be shifters.

"Hala," Feren greets, sounding surprised. "I thought you weren't coming."

"I changed my mind," Hala replies, a washed-out figure of smooth white skin and pale blond, shoulder-length hair. She and her companion sit.

Feren fixes me with a stern expression. "Take the circle, Rora."

"Together," I suggest, gesturing to the wide ring of magical folk courteously. We're all forestborn here, and I don't answer to her.

After a pause that stretches painfully long, she seats herself by Andie's father. A red fox has come to rest at Andie's feet, eyes blinking sleepily as she curls her fingers into his fluffy fur. Has she released the jaguar, or is she holding them both?

I circle round and sit in a wide gap at Peridon's side.

"What of the soldier?" asks the more faded forest walker. The squirrel on her shoulder burrows into her leafy hair.

Everyone stares at Gerig, who still hovers several paces away. He twitches uneasily.

"He helped me and Peridon enact the plan that freed your kin." My voice comes out shakier than intended in the presence of so many people, and I fold my arms across my chest. "I think he has information we could use."

"For what? He should not be here."

"Please. Let me explain."

The pause that follows is laced with doubt, but no one interrupts.

"There is a sickness east of the river," I begin, realizing I'm going to have to reveal Telyan's secrets in front of Gerig, after all. "It's infecting humans and animals, warping their senses, changing their bodies. Most of the time, it kills them. On rare occasions, they survive—with small changes. Fading outlines, streaks of silver or gold in their hair, the ability to change their eyes. All tiny fragments of things we've seen before." I uncross my arms. "Magic."

One of the whisperers snorts. "Affecting humans? I doubt that."

"It is," I insist. "I could smell it in animal form. The magic is breaking itself apart like it did after the Rupturing, only this time, the hosts are no longer compatible."

"Even if you're right, why should we care?" Feren says.

My fingers curl into fists. *Keep going.* I have to get them on my side; Finley's relying on it. "Because it's a symptom of a larger problem, one that affects us all. Magic feels threatened; Eradain pushed us into the Vale, and then—well, you know the prison."

At that, the shifter Hala presses her hands into her forehead.

"With fewer forestborn walking the continent, the magic in the land is receding. It's dying. If we let it die completely, people like us will eventually die, too."

"Who told you this?" asks a whisperer who looks around Violet's age, her nose sitting prominently between sunken cheeks. Her posture is ramrod straight.

"The giants."

"You spoke with the giants," Feren says, skeptical.

"They said that people like us—people and animals both— keep the land from becoming dormant," I continue, undeterred. "As long as we walk the earth in sufficient numbers, the continent will remain active. Otherwise . . ." I trail off.

"You are planting many seeds with no water," says Torac, scratching at his skin. "Speak plainly. Why do you mention these things? What are you asking us to do?"

I force my breathing to remain even as I meet his shrewd gaze and deliver the words I practiced last night. "I want to drive magical creatures east of the river and revive the land there. I want to reclaim the lives that we lost. I want to take back the east."

Silence. Nothing but the aspens fluttering softly in the breeze and the birds around us chirping a staccato rhythm; for them, this is a morning like any other. Half the circle, however, is staring in astonishment.

"Are you mad?" Andie's father demands. "You would be driving them to the slaughter. The human realms are no longer safe. They'd be hunted."

"If we can remove the threat to magic, it might stop seeking refuge in nonmagical beings. We could end the illness and revive the land, both," I reply. "Now is the right time. The humans are preoccupied, not just with the sickness I mentioned. The king of Eradain has razed Niav and beheaded King Gerar in the south. There will be war." I swallow, thinking of Minister Mereth's flaming city. "There is already."

"Then you *are* mad," he persists. "That is all the more reason to stay away."

"It's an opportunity," I argue, staring him down. "Telyan will not yield to Eradain without a fight, and I imagine Glenweil won't, either. If reviving magic in the east puts an end to this sickness, their people will be better able to beat Eradain back."

"At the expense of magical creatures' lives."

My mouth flattens into a thin line. "Eradain's defeat would benefit us all. If they win the war, they will come for us next. Better to fight in numbers than alone."

"Are you asking us to reawaken the land there, or to fight?" Feren says. "Make up your mind."

"They amount to the same thing, if reawakening the land hastens Eradain's defeat. Do it for yourselves, if nothing else. As I said, the weaker magic grows, the more doubtful our survival."

"I don't like it." Andie's father sits rigid as a board as his gaze moves around the circle.

"I do," Andie cuts in unexpectedly. "Reviving the land would show the humans that magic can't be rooted out. That we won't remain invisible forever. We'd be restoring Alemara to the way it ought to be."

Her father turns to her, gaze growing wary. "You are speaking reactively, not rationally."

"They are the same. I have spent enough time in a prison cell. I'm tired of inaction." Andie looks at me. "I will help you with this."

"You do not have the authority to make that call," Feren speaks over my surprise. "I am still in charge of this clan. *Your* clan."

"Where was my clan when those soldiers were starving me, or degrading me, or beating me?" Andie's words spew forth like flames. "You are not my clan any longer."

Her father flinches back as if struck.

"I will help as well," says Torac. "The land is crying. I can feel it in the trees and the soil. If the magic fades away, so will we."

The one who resembles a ponderosa nods, the movement creaking. "Me too."

I glance at Peridon, a question in my eyes.

After holding my gaze thoughtfully for a long while, he says, "So will I."

"There's a bridge that spans the river," Gerig offers, drawing all attention to him. "My kinsmen built it east of the compound to connect the Vale to Eradain. There's a watch on it, but—" He pauses. "If you overpower them, you could use the bridge to drive the animals across."

A bridge. That explains how those soldiers have been crossing into the Vale without anyone noticing.

"Why should we trust a word you say?" asks the forest walker who resembles an aspen. Despite her desperate, semi-conscious flight from the compound just last night, her high-pitched, bell-like voice rings out quite steadily.

"I helped—" Gerig falls silent, likely remembering this argument already proved ineffective with me and Andie. "I made a mistake. Many mistakes. I—want to help. Please let me help."

"I intend to," I tell him, coming to another decision. "After this, I have business in Oraes. You're going to show me the way."

Hala studies me with suspicion. "What business?"

I raise my chin a little, doubt flickering. "My own."

In truth, I'm beginning to wonder if I was wrong when I told Wes it's my responsibility to turn Jol's people against him. Sitting here in this hollow, with the peril of last night's battle fresh in my mind, my bold plan feels altogether too big for me to tackle alone.

Regardless—I can at least gather information like Violet wanted. That, after all, is a job I already know how to do.

Gerig shifts his weight from side to side, alternating between straightening his shoulders in tight resolve and bending beneath the strain of cowardice. I don't know if I'm looking for good in him where there is none. Perhaps that hope is merely a fiction born of necessity and nothing more.

"We will make no promises," Feren says at last, speaking for her clan. Her eyes narrow meaningfully when they connect with Andie's. "But we are here, so we'll listen." My heart leaps as she beckons Gerig closer. "Tell us what you know of this bridge."

I struggle to determine how long Gerig and I have been stationed in this shamble of a hideout a few dozen paces from the bridge, under cover of night, waiting for the whisperers to do their work. An hour, at least. Our sanctuary is nothing but a shallow dip in the open land, one side rimmed with two twisting, knobby roots that grew rapidly and artificially under Torac's influence. Beneath an almost full moon, the cover is just enough to hide us from sight if we lie flat on our stomachs beneath the roots—and if no one comes bearing torches within a few paces of our spot.

Through unspoken agreement, Gerig and I have spaced ourselves as far apart as possible within the little bowl. Which means my left side is scarcely more than an arm's length away from his right. The closeness makes my skin crawl, and my nose wrinkles at the barest remains of aftershave, mingled with the sticky scent of sweat.

"What if the stampede isn't enough of a distraction?" Gerig frets.

Digging a hand into the soft earth, I bite back the first retort that springs to mind. "Then we'll try something else."

"And if they find us first?"

This time, I don't bother answering.

Loath though I am to find any commonality with his former comrades, I'm beginning to understand why the man with the chewing stick called him "mouse." Gerig startles at the slightest disturbances—a bird overhead, a leaf blown into our hiding place. A rogue gust of wind is enough to unhinge him. Worse, every few minutes, he's taken to voicing another part of our plan that could go wrong. What if Andie, Feren, and the rest betray our trust? A day has passed since the council; they could have changed their minds. What if the bridge breaks before we can cross into Eradain?

What if, what if, what if?

The onslaught is relentless, and enough to drive anyone mad. I don't know how I'm going to make it all the way to Oraes with his constant mewling. But I need him. Once we get across the bridge, Gerig is my key to reaching Oraes and navigating the city undetected.

"You think they'll find us," Gerig continues, as if my silence has confirmed his greatest fears.

I twist my head toward him, gaze flitting to the ugly pink scars scraped across his forearm. My doing, that day with the captured caegar. "I think you should shut up."

He closes his mouth, not a drop of defiance in him, and it's easy for me to understand his particular brand of complicity.

In the end, Peridon and Andie agreed to accompany us into Eradain, to receive the animals that other whisperers drive east and compel some south toward Telyan. Once we reach the capital, Gerig and I will be on our own. First, though, we need to secure a way to get the animals across the river, beginning with the whisperers' first offering—a herd of caribran.

Fortunately, Eradain was kind enough to provide.

"That's the signal," I say, when a whistle arcs through the darkness.

Gerig tenses, but this time, I have no intention of hesitating at Peridon's cue. Ignoring Gerig's objection, I lift my head enough to see over the rim.

The trembling in the earth drums like rainfall at first, quiet, before growing rough enough to shake my bones. The caribran herd is approaching fast, a dark jumble of antlers and long necks and *hooves,* dozens of hooves kicking up clouds of dust that float eerily in the moonlight. Patches of grass spring up underfoot, trailing green in their wake.

Gerig and I exchange a glance. As he can't fly across the river like I can, and I'd rather not lose my pack, that herd is more than Andie's and Peridon's first mission. It's also our cover.

We take off from the bowl as one, feet pounding hard.

My lungs are on fire, legs screaming as I push them almost beyond endurance, straining not to lose the safety of the herd. Between the stampede's thunderous clamor and my own ragged breathing, I can't hear much of what's happening at the bridge. But I can see several figures riding amidst the caribran, and farther ahead, soldiers are streaming inland from the river. Defenseless against so great a tide, they're moving out of the stampede's path— but not out of range.

The whisperers astride the caribran begin firing arrows, felling the soldiers like plucking berries from the vine. For every one that drops, I imagine the corpses in the shed, Lona's husband, the fleeing caegar run through with a knife. Every ancient pine and elm and oak murdered with an Eradain axe. My father, facedown with an arrow in his back. I'm not sure when it happened, when for every one of them we kill, I stopped seeing *their* blood spilling onto the earth, and instead see the innocent blood that came before. I'm not sure when *I* became *we,* but I know I spoke the truth to Helos that day on the riverbank. This is now bigger than either of us. Than myself.

Packed earth turns to wooden slats underfoot—thank fortune. Gerig and I have reached the bridge. The voices I can make out are indecipherable, so I keep my eyes on the caribran clattering across the wood and fanning out onto the opposite shore. Eradain, no more than twenty paces away.

Gerig makes an odd noise just behind.

"What's wrong?" I demand, twisting to meet his wide gaze.

He doesn't reply, only sways on the spot. Blood dribbles out of his mouth and down his chin.

I say his name, but he's already falling, over the railing and into the midnight water. Angry as always, the river churns around the black-fletched arrow protruding from his back as the current carries him away.

Another arrow sinks into the railing beside me with a thud, and I'm running again, no time to think or question whether I should mourn. Swerving to make a more difficult target, I nearly collide with a caribran heading in the wrong direction. Back toward the Vale. Astride the stag, Andie fires two arrows in rapid succession before she reaches down and grabs my arm.

She nearly wrenches my shoulder from its socket as she pulls me onto the caribran. Maybe she's had practice at this, but I haven't, and I cling to her waist in desperation, legs pressed to the caribran's sides so hard they ache.

On the shore, Peridon's caribran circles in place; neither he nor Andie ride with any kind of tack. "Come on!" he shouts, firing the last of his arrows over my shoulder.

Andie spurs the caribran forward, and the three of us tear into Eradain and across the dusty plain. When I last look behind, I can just make out the vengeful roots tearing out of the ground, strands of ivy wrapping around the bridge's railing. Turac's doing. On and on, until it's difficult to discern any wooden slats beneath the green.

NINE

HELOS

The horse-drawn cart rattles and bumps on every notch in the road, making my skin feel ready to vibrate off my body. Save for a semicircular opening in the canvas in back, the covered carriage is dark and filled with the heady scent of herbs. I feel utterly ridiculous, stuffed in among the crates of bandages and tinkling medicine jars like a sack of turnips. But at least it seems to be working.

Tomas and the other healer who volunteered are driving the horses fast, hoping to arrive in Briarwend not too long after the mounted unit; those soldiers had gathered and departed with astonishing speed. I've grown restless beneath the anticipation jittering throughout my body. The nettle-sharp nerves. I have never witnessed a battle on this scale, nor have I treated soldiers fresh off the field, and imagined injuries are cycling through my thoughts at a dizzying rate.

Fortune's sake, I cannot stand this part. The waiting. In here, there's nothing to do, no task on which to focus aside from studying the light filtering through the gap. When that fails, I try to ground myself in a series of counted breaths—one, two—searching for the patience I had in droves not all that long ago. The patience which seems to slip a little further from my grasp with every passing day. No, even that's no good; by the time I reach ten, my eyelashes have grown wet.

I force myself to wait another three before wiping the tears away. I don't know why this keeps happening. Why anytime I stop to think for more than half a minute, I feel I'll start crying instead.

Stop, I order myself. *You can't do your job if you're too busy weeping.* I scrub my face and pivot toward happier thoughts. Finley tugging my arm to show me—no, maybe not that one. A tiny Rora grinning in triumph when she caught her first fish, the sadness lifting from her face for the first time in days. Much better. The way she doubled over when I watched this transformation and decided to accidentally fall into the stream. I'd bruised both my knees, but for once her stomach had ached with laughter instead of hunger, and what's a tiny trickle of blood compared to that?

Unbidden, the images start to change. The river claims Finley's cure without care, rendering the stardust useless. A holly hare sinks its razored teeth into my leg when I try to grab it because we are starving. I limp for a week.

The fleeting smile fades from my face.

A younger me forces my tears to fall in silence, watching Rora fever without a clue what to do. I wake to peppervine wrapped around my neck, and Rora frantically trying to saw it off with a sharpened rock. I wake to navy uniforms and windowless walls. Pain.

"Stop," I murmur, ramming the heels of my palms into my eyes. My stomach cramps so fiercely, I think I might be sick. It doesn't help to remember. All it does is hurt. And I don't even know why it *should* still hurt, when so much time has passed. Years, in fact. I'm not the one dying from the Fallow Throes.

The cart shudders violently, and I bite my tongue hard enough to draw blood. Enough of this. Using the crates for balance, I push to my feet and stick my head through the canvas's half-moon opening.

The hills encircling Fendolyn's Keep stagger across the gray horizon like crooked teeth. To either side of the rough-paved road we've been traveling, stone walls half a man in height bar the way to sprawling farmland and the wooden mills beyond. The farmers closer to the road watch our cart pass with shrunken figures, though surely we must be a less agitating presence than that of the mounted hundred-band we're chasing. Given how long the king-dom has been at peace, I imagine the sight of cavalry on the move was as new to them as it was to me.

As far as the eye can see, tidy rows of hard-won wheat and corn mingle with long patches of bare earth. In the latter, good soil has dried to dirt, useless and infertile. My grip tightens on the canvas window. Receding magic makes the land more comfortable for a time, but even I'm beginning to recognize that as a bad bargain. These humans can continue to work the ground and till the earth until they've sucked every usable corner dry, but still the land will die and so will they until someone agrees to compromise. No one's starving, not yet. But it isn't difficult to imagine a day far in the future, when people come seeking remedies for malnutrition and there's nothing I can do.

Rora, I hope your plan works.

In time, the hum of distant commotion drifts nearer on the breeze. When that murmur hardens to a sharpened peak—metal striking metal, people shouting, horses whinnying—I abandon all thoughts save the present.

This must be Briarwend. On the map, a small farming town abutting the river, where one of Rora's almost-friends, Seraline, lives. In person, it appears little more than one-story homes, linens draped across gardens to dry, and patches of grass sticking out from cracking, old stone roads. People are hastening past our cart, head-ing in the opposite direction.

"Come along!" urges a woman with long, blond hair, grasping an elderly man's arm in one hand and a kitchen knife in the other. Many residents are making the same frantic escape, clutching wool caps and billowing skirts, spare hands laden with makeshift weap-ons, dusty books, even a cat twisting madly to get free. I don't see how heading for the fields will help; surely walls offer better protection than corn?

We hook around a corner and stop.

"Grab the bandages," says Tomas amidst the din, as soon as he's thrown open the canvas flaps. My second boss, a middle-aged man with golden spectacles and black stubble lining his narrow, deep brown face, has always taken a no-nonsense approach to both his healing work and the business of training me. More brusque than his husband's softer edges, though not unkind. I pass him a crate as the third healer, a relative stranger named Cara, climbs up beside me.

"Essentials next," Tomas instructs, tilting his head for me to jump down once I've secured the next case. When two younger townspeople shuffle over to help, Cara issues orders with clipped efficiency.

Arms aching under the crate's weight, I follow Tomas inside a brick building topped with a miniature clock tower. The corridor connects to a dark, broad hall with tables along the back and rows of chairs facing a platform up front. Behind the platform, narrow windows admit half-hearted light and—

"Merciful fortune," I breathe.

Small as they are, the panes of glass stretch wide enough to offer glimpses of the chaos reigning just outside. Horses blur past, swords slash in frenzied motion—

"We'll set up here," Tomas says, undeterred, setting his crate onto the platform. "There's a door out back; we'll get the wounded through there."

He doesn't even glance behind him.

"Bring that here and help me move the chairs," he adds, spurring me back into action. "Then we'll need the tables. Quickly now."

We stack the slatted chairs in messy piles along the sides, clearing half the hall by the time Cara and her volunteers appear with the remaining supply crates. Our group has grown to eight or nine at a glance, most of the faces looking scared but alert.

"What are you doing?" a towering man exclaims, stumbling into the hall and running a hand through his frizzing hair. "Didn't you hear the bell? That means evacuate."

In fact, I never heard any bell, even standing just beneath the tower. Either the noise outside is too great, or they long since stopped ringing it.

"We've come to tend to the wounded," Tomas replies, pointing to the purple healer's band wrapped around his upper arm. He gave me a matching one to wear. "Help us move the tables."

"You can't stay here."

"Help us or get out."

Wooden boards bend underfoot as we hurry toward the tables lining the wall opposite the platform.

"Jonah, are you mad?" Still lingering by the entryway, the man clutches the sides of his long, woolen coat. "Get to—"

"I'm staying," says a boy who's built like a bear. Round face, thick neck, muscled arms. He rolls his sleeves to the elbow and gestures for me to grab the table's other end.

Together, we carry it to the foot of the platform, where Cara has two of the volunteers unpacking the crates. The protesting man sways on his feet before he shoves his hands into his pockets and flees the hall.

"My uncle," Jonah explains, looking grim.

We've barely had time to arrange the tables into rows when a pair of women in civilian clothing appear in the doorway touting a rough-hewn slab of wood that might be a door. The soldier lying across it is screaming.

"Here!" Cara shouts, gesturing to a table close by. Jonah and I watch them transfer the soldier onto the hard surface, the metal bands meant to shield her shins all dented and wrong, her mangled legs beneath gushing blood onto the floor. Jonah looks like he might be sick.

"What can I do?" I ask, striding over. Our makeshift hospital—rigid tables, brick walls, improper lighting, and chilly air. I suppose it'll have to do.

Cara's pressing cloth onto the wounds and assessing the damage simultaneously. She meets my gaze with a sorrowful glint in her eye. "She's losing blood too quickly."

"I have to go," the soldier says, eyes unfocused. "They're attacking—Briar—"

"You went already," Cara replies, her hands reddening as the cloth soaks through. "You fought bravely. Look for others," she adds to me. "You can do no more here."

Grabbing several bandage strips and the bloody door—there's no way we'll be able to keep this vessel clean—I beckon Jonah with a tilt of my head. "Come on."

But Jonah's acting sheepish now, his face flushed with shock, feet rooted to the floor. "I—"

"Fine." I begin dragging the door toward the back entrance on my own. One of the women who carried the soldier in lifts the other end, and soon we're through the dimly lit corridor and into the open air.

With a feeling in my stomach like writhing worms, I pause alongside my partner just beyond the threshold, trying to evaluate our next steps. It's difficult to plan much of anything, though, given the scene playing out before us. Telyan's mounted hundred-band sweeps through the field of invading infantry in brutal lines, dropping enemy foot soldiers with a blow from their horse or a downward thrust of the spear. The din is so loud—cries of command and pain, blades thumping shields, hoofbeats drumming across the quivering earth—that I would have to shout to be heard, and even then it might not be enough.

I have no idea what's going on. Why they're fighting here or how to read the strategy in their movements. I know nothing of warfare, can only smell the heavy, metallic notes of death and see a tangled mass of dust and confusion, and bodies strewn among them like boulders.

"How are we supposed to get to anyone?" I yell.

My partner leans over the door to hear. "I don't know. The one we brought—she was right by the entrance. She must have dragged herself."

Up close, this woman looks much younger than I'd originally thought, hardly older than Rora. Her heart-shaped, warm beige face is smooth, her figure soft, and she's knotted her long black hair behind her head. She looks back at me with steady purpose.

"Do we go in there?" she wonders aloud.

I glance back at the town hall's threshold, but no one older is coming to help.

"Maybe we try that stretch," I say at last, gesturing toward a hoard of fallen soldiers lying a couple of arrow-lengths away. Walking into that mess might mean death, but if we wait for the battle to end, that could be too late. And we're here to heal people, aren't we? "The fighting seems to have moved further afield."

With a nod, the girl adjusts her grip on the door so that she's holding it behind her. "I'm Lilyn, by the way," she calls over her shoulder.

I call back, "Helos."

It's awkward carrying the door between us, Lilyn being much shorter than I, both of us trying not to trip over churned earth. The clotted blood from the door's prior load smears my fingers red.

Underfoot, the bodies coalesce in varying degrees of recognition. Dirt and grime coat metal breastplates and bruised hands alike. Broken limbs are bent from horses' hooves, and open eyes stare at nothing. My nose wrinkles of its own accord.

"What if we—"

My suggestion slips into a curse when something catches my ankle, driving my knees into the pliant earth.

"My legs," someone rasps close to my ear. I wrench my leg free from the hand grasping it, my chest heaving. "Please—"

"Leave her," Lilyn says firmly. "She's one of theirs."

"She needs our help." Regaining my voice, I crane my neck to assess this soldier's wounds. Her accent, the way she clips her vowels short, tugs at the reddened scars across my shoulders. Windowless walls. Cruel fists and jagged bars.

"Not ours," Lilyn insists, tugging the door's other end for emphasis.

"I'm a healer," I remind her, blinking rather rapidly.

Lilyn yanks the door right out of my hands. "And my sister's in the army. *Our* army."

Knowing it for a lost cause, I push to my feet and grab the door's other end. The soldier's grip remains an echo around my ankle, but without supplies or time I can only glance back at her, uncertainty fisting my heart. Her people have hurt so many. She would likely hurt me if she knew what I am. But beneath the curtain of bleak ideologies, she bleeds the same as any.

We reach another segment where the bodies lay thick, this stretch demarcated by a fallen horse. Lilyn loses her balance on the rumbling earth more than once; the fighting can't be more than thirty paces away.

"Here!" she calls, circling around the horse. One of our hundred-band is struggling to free his foot from beneath the gelding's flank.

"Can you move it?" he shouts, grabbing at his thigh. Blood trickles beneath his helmet and down the back of his neck.

"Not the horse," I reply, coming up behind him. Lilyn breaks into a coughing fit as a dusty gale sweeps through, her fingers turning white where they clutch the door. "This will hurt. I'm sorry."

I bring my arms beneath his shoulders and *yank,* heart hammering at the strangled noise that erupts from his mouth. The wound beneath his helmet is still flowing.

"We've got to—"

"*Helos!*"

Still supporting the soldier's weight, I swivel at Lilyn's shriek to find an Eradain soldier not more than ten steps away, coming fast with sword and shield. Lilyn scours the ground for a weapon, but I feel frozen in place, keenly aware that I have never even lifted a blade.

Numbness seeps from my core to my extremities, pressure knifing through my skull, urging the elk. But would Lilyn and the soldier climb aboard if they saw? Would they balk at the shift if the alternative were certain death?

Time's up. The man in navy swings his sword into position—and drops flat on his face, his neck spurting scarlet. Lilyn screams.

I spot the protruding hilt of a dagger as a pair of enormous warhorses pound to a halt before us, the gray one's helmeted rider slowing him into a bouncy circle-in-place.

"What are you doing here?" he demands.

The river take me.

"Looking for the wounded," I retort as the numbness recedes. To my right, Lilyn drops into a startled bow.

"Get inside, both of you," says Weslyn, just as the second rider shouts, "Sir!"

"We're fine, we can—"

"That's an order. Go."

Both riders spur their horses back into the fray.

"Are you mad?" Lilyn rounds on me, shaking her head. "Do you know who you were arguing with?"

I bend to collect the foot-crushed soldier who now looks close to fainting. "Trust me, I'm well aware."

When we return to the makeshift hospital with the soldier on the door, Tomas rushes over and echoes Lilyn's sentiments. "I thought you were smarter than that. You could have been killed."

"This man needs help." I speak through gritted teeth, helping a rejuvenated Jonah shift the soldier onto a table. A second one groans from another surface nearby, while two more lay against a far wall, unmoving.

"You're not ready to take the field," Tomas continues. "You have no training." His hands are moving over the man as he speaks, gently removing the helmet, then pressing the back of the head with cloth. When he glances up at me next, his gaze softens a touch. "You did well to bring him here; I'm sure his family will be very grateful. Now fetch the disinfectant and a clean wrap. Hurry."

As I rifle through the crates, I steal a glimpse of Cara, who tends to the second patient without looking up. Per Mahree's request, I still haven't told the staff I'm a shifter. She'd have no reason to want me hurt. Would she?

The battle is over by the next strike of the clock tower, audible now. Tomas bids me put on a purple smock from the cart, which stains to a grisly red-brown within minutes. Though the consensus holds that Eradain suffered three losses to each one of Telyan's, I quickly lose count of the patients that soldiers and volunteers tote in. Hour after hour passes in a haze of urgent motion—cauterizing wounds, setting broken bones, distributing poppy to ease agony, fighting to stave off infection. I hold eleven people's hands so that they will not die alone, and I can feel the ghost sensations of each weakening grip long after I let go.

I'm trying not to look too long at the bodies lining the wall.

I'm trying to view my work as a chance to save some, and not as moments spent living in a future others no longer get to see. Focus on the dozens of eyes watching me, scared or expectant or hopeful, because that means they're alive. Feel the warmth still radiating from slick, grimy skin. A hallowed heat. I've seen death, of course, but not at this scale, one after another and another and another. I experienced the violence of Jol's leadership firsthand, but it's harder to shove aside thoughts of more to come when the *now* is pulsing between my hands, spilling onto the floor, and stinking up a dimly lit hall.

As I had in the days following Rora's rescue, with the prison's horror freshly stamped upon my mind, I can feel my flight instincts pivoting toward a more unflinching course. A desire to intercede. Not so much to gain the power, more to remove it from such abusive hands. But how? Even if I wanted it—and in this moment, I do want it—I don't know how I could hope to hold a throne in Eradain when I'm prohibited from revealing I'm a shifter at my own place of work.

The burning in my chest grows near-scalding when Weslyn appears, supporting an armored young man I recognize. Naethan.

"Put him here," I instruct, looping my arm around Naethan's waist and forcing myself to *breathe* because my friend is on his feet, surely he's not bound for the wall.

"Helos," Naethan greets, clutching at his gaping upper arm. Volunteers have been scrubbing the tables between uses, but the oak has darkened several shades beyond its natural hue. "It's just a cut," he adds, when he sees where I'm looking.

"Helos will determine that," says Weslyn. He, at least, appears physically well despite the grim set of his mouth.

Naethan lifts his eyes to the ceiling. "It'll heal on its own."

"Don't be a hero," I say sharply, though my hands remain steady as I unstrap the light metal breastplate. Weslyn removes the guards from Naethan's forearms, and my quick examination of the oozing tear near his shoulder tells me all I need to know.

"You've got something lodged in there," I tell him. "A shaft of wood, maybe. Jonah!" I wave the boy over; he doesn't even seem to notice Weslyn. "Get me disinfectant, a towel, and a haymark bandage. It will be about the width of your hand."

"We're running out of disinfectant, sir. Cara says so."

"Cara says so, or you've seen it yourself?" I press. Ever since I snapped into healer mode, Jonah has taken to calling me "sir." Weslyn's eyebrows arch, but I feel no need to correct him.

"I've seen it, sir. We're down to four bottles."

Cursed fortune. We started with twenty.

"Change of plans," I say, assessing quickly. "I'll fetch the cloth. You go gather garlic from people's homes, as much as you can carry. Have someone else collect honey. Whisky, too."

"Why the whisky?" Naethan asks, a touch apprehensive.

I pat his unharmed shoulder. "Because this is going to hurt."

By the time Jonah returns with the bottle and a basket of garlic bulbs, Naethan has lost some of his bravado. His mouth pinches at the sight of the metal tongs I've laid across the bandages.

"Drink," I instruct, handing him the uncapped bottle. "And start crushing the garlic into a paste," I add to Jonah, who seems to have finally registered that the grimy young man hovering nearby is a prince. "That will be our disinfectant."

"*Garlic,* sir?" Jonah says, tearing his gawking gaze from Weslyn. "What about the whisky?"

"Do as I say. Did you send someone for honey?"

"Bonnie is asking around. It isn't easy, sir. Most folk are still in the fields."

Well. I'll use the whisky if it comes to it, but we're nearly out of the poppy we've been using for pain. If the liquor goes as well, the wounded will just have to bear the discomfort.

When the paste is ready, I grab the bottle from a reluctant Naethan and set it on the floor, then turn to Weslyn, who has been tracking my movements in silence. "Try to keep him still."

"Very reassuring," Naethan grumbles, but Weslyn braces a shoulder and a knee nonetheless.

Keeping an ear to Naethan's breathing, I try to do as little digging around as I can. His groans are proof there's only so much I can do. I guide the tongs in farther, not wanting to risk splintering the wood from too top-heavy a hold, until I extract what might be a javelin shard.

In the end, Naethan handles the procedure far better than Jonah, who had to wander away midway through in search of a bucket.

"Hand me a bandage, would you?" I ask Weslyn when I've washed the wound and am nearly finished applying the paste.

Weslyn has been staring at the hole in Naethan's arm, as if caught in a trance—or lost to memory. I snap my fingers close to his face, impatient, and he startles a bit before doing as I ask.

"Thanks," Naethan mutters, his own gaze growing distant once the wound is securely wrapped.

"Find me tomorrow so I can change the dressing." After a brief hesitation, I thrust the whisky back into his hand. "Another swig for luck and then off you go."

Weslyn glances at me curiously.

I shrug, wiping my sticky hands on a towel. "I figure he's seen enough today he'd rather forget."

Weslyn surprises me with half a smile. He surprises me still further when he grabs the bottle from Naethan and drinks from it deeply himself.

TEN

RORA

For two days, we work our way toward Oraes, unchallenged.

At least, I hope we're heading for Oraes. I know that it's to the north, along the coast, and I know that a river cuts through it. If we find the river, we should find the capital. In theory. But it's rudimentary information, pulled from the maps I studied back in Castle Roanin. Maps I saw no point in carrying with me, because they offered little more than simple overviews. I feel the loss of Gerig's expertise more keenly with each passing hour.

After our flight from the bridge, we had watched the stampede wander east into the night to make their new home this side of the river. Between the cousins, only Andie is adept at compelling mammals as large as caribran, and she released the two we rode soon after we crossed. Excitement mingled with nerves in my core as they returned to their herd. I can only hope the rate of repopulation will outpace Eradain's hunting laws.

Since then, Peridon and Andie have stayed by my side to get a lay of the land. "Marrow sheep would do well here," Peridon observed on the first afternoon, while Coda perched on his shoulder. And later to Andie, once we reached saffron prairie wide as the sea, "Peeku, maybe?"

I'm grateful for their company. It's nerve-racking to walk the sloping plains.

Just over the river, spiraling clay towers and sprawling rock formations streaked with yellow, orange, and gray sedimentary bands, like a washed-out sunset, provided at least a semblance of coverage in which to take comfort. But those monoliths receded the farther east we trekked. Here, the land is so *open,* scratchy green-and-gold grass that alternates between reaching my ankles and tickling my waist, swaying with goldenrods in autumn bloom. Few trees stand to intercept the brutal winds, only rippling streams and the occasional pointed spires of silver-green sagebrush.

Tension weaves among the three of us, each more accustomed to life in the woods. I am constantly on alert, scanning the unbroken horizon for civilians and soldiers alike, and my body aches from the exhaustion of continued hyper-vigilance.

By the second night, I can feel the cousins' departure drawing near. Andie is growing restless, seeming content only when another animal comes into view—prairie dogs with quivering noses, small tawny deer with two pronged horns curving inward like pincers. Rattlesnakes sunning on the rocks. Yellow-bellied meadowlarks and falcons that swoop and swerve over the prairie, even little brown owls that burrow underground. I realize, unexpectedly, that I don't want them to leave.

The three of us make camp in the high grass with nothing more than our travel packs and the darkness to shield us from sight. No other choice. Given our exposed position in enemy territory, we decide against risking a fire, and I clutch my gray woolen cloak tighter against the evening's chill. Overhead, a brilliant array of stars stretches across the cloudless sky. It takes me back to another place, a different night. To him.

You love the stars.

"I'll refill that, if you like."

Shaken from memories before they have time to fully settle, I find Peridon crouched beside me, seemingly indifferent to the cool air grazing his bare arms. He nods to the waterskin clutched tight in my hand.

"We can do it ourselves," Andie points out, when I hand over the waterskin with a smile.

Peridon's already walking away.

Huffing a breath, she watches him go and shrugs. "He always was nicer than me."

I glance at her curiously. That's the kind of thing I would have said once about Helos, only Andie's assessment carries no hint of guilt. Simply fact.

The faint levity fades from her tone as she meets my gaze. "We're leaving tomorrow."

"I know." My attention falls to Coda, foraging for insects among the grass with a series of small hops. I've grown rather fond of the magical raven myself.

Maybe Andie heard the disappointment in my voice, because she goes on. "Thank you, by the way. For helping Peri get me out of there."

She waits until I see her nod, brow line straight and severe as Violet's, before turning away. As if she's made good on a debt, and that's that.

Moonlight skims the gently rippling grass like a dusting of snow, casting the prairie into a pale silvery glow.

"When my brother was captured, and I took his place in the cage," I respond, remembering how she watched in muted shock before warning us about the dogs, "thank you for not telling the soldiers."

Andie's forehead creases. "That was you."

Once again, I'm angry at my past self for not thinking to grab her key along with Helos's. Two weeks passed before I returned with Peridon to finish the job.

A lot can happen in two weeks.

"How long were you there for?" I ask, to blot out Jol's mockery of a warning, the bloodless pallor of King Gerar's mounted head.

Andie's features close in on themselves, lips pinching in her heart-shaped face. "Don't," she says.

"Don't what?"

"This is a business relationship, okay?" She separates a chunk of hair from the rest and starts to work out the tangles. "We came to do a job and we'll do it. Let's keep it that way." When I start to object, she cuts me off. "Why are you risking your life going to Oraes? Why you?"

I can't bring myself to reply.

"As I said," Andie continues, her silver eyes nearly sparkling in the starlight. "Let's keep it that way."

Before, her words were a variation on the way I once viewed my brother in relation to myself. Now they are an echo, giving shape to my unspoken stance when I first enlisted Peridon's help and deflected his more personal questions. The guarded sentiment feels wrong, though, hearing it spoken out loud. Too much like the wariness tossed my way all those years in Castle Roanin.

"It's more than business," I murmur slowly, as if testing the words on my tongue. "Peridon is my friend." *Or at least, he's tried to be.*

"Peri?" Andie rolls her eyes, though the gesture holds humor. "My cousin is easy to please. Give him a smile, and he's got a close friend. Give him his birds and his river, a family, and he's got a full life. He's happy." Her voice wavers the barest touch on the words. "I am not Peridon."

Her fingers work through the knotted curls with more bite than before.

I think she may have meant to insult me, but truthfully, her blunt words aren't hurtful. It's the silence that makes me sad, this tension threaded between a couple of girls who have been stretched too thin, too young. Finding it difficult to trust after the world took what was rightfully ours. I don't know her, but I recognize myself in her, and that makes me want to try harder.

I don't want them to win.

"I'm going to Oraes to gather information and send it south," I admit. "Anything that might help Telyan win the war. I work for the queen."

Please, let Violet be alive. Say that she's queen.

Andie studies me a long while, her thick hair billowing in the evening breeze. "You're like Peri," she says at last. "I can tell. You still see the good in other people."

I blink at her, uncertain how to respond.

Seeing this, Andie nods once and turns away. "I have no interest in looking for goodness. Not anymore."

Sorrow tightens its well-worn fist around my heart, rendering me quiet in the face of her bitter distrust. Rather than prodding further, though, I leave her to her thoughts. In time, Peridon appears in the distance, his lean torso and corded forearms poking above the tall grass.

"Rora, I was thinking," he says, distributing full waterskins into our outstretched hands. "Are you sure you'll be okay in Oraes on your own? Maybe Andie and I should see you inside, now that Gerig is gone."

Behind, Andie lifts her brows at me. Expectant, but I don't need her to tell me this is one generous offer I can't accept.

"The city is too dangerous for you," I remind him, pulling the thin bedroll from my pack. My eyelids are growing heavy. "I can change my form. You can't. I'll be okay."

"Still not without risk, even for you," he replies, taking a seat in our loose circle.

"No," I agree, more quietly. "But I have to go there, all the same."

Peridon must have spoken with his bird mind to mind, or maybe the black-tipped caw has simply grown fond of his adopted companion, because Coda flutters onto Peridon's shoulder and nips his shirt collar affectionately.

"If you're certain." Peridon strokes the inky feathers above their blade-sharp tips. "I'll send Coda to check on you sometime, in any case. Andie and I can always spring you from the city if needed."

His smile is so warm and open, I can't help but return it. Finally, I see what I've missed here, an offer of friendship I've been too busy, too jaded, to invest in. Andie has a right to her silence—fortune knows I've been there often enough. But tonight, I think I'm ready to move forward.

"Will you tell me about them?" I say, gesturing to his left arm. "The animals you can compel."

Peridon leans back on his hands and raises a knee. "Well," he begins, looking pleased. "Falcons were the first."

As we sit there talking quietly late into the night, Andie cloaked in silence nearby, my thoughts drift absently to Castle Roanin.

Afternoons spent among the hickory grove or the old carriage house, listening to Helos and Finley's steady chatter grow bright enough to keep the darkness at bay. My knotted insides unwind. Maybe this time, while Andie holds her shadows close, Peridon and I can be the ones who offer the light.

When I bid farewell to Peridon and Andie, and Eradain's capital comes into view at last, the first thing I see is the sunlit wall.

It's not a particularly tall structure. One story high, maybe two. When I move close enough through the gathering crowd to see the underside of a wide archway cut into the brown stone blocks, I can tell it's not particularly wide, either. At most, three or four paces deep. But it's a barrier where Roanin and Niav have none, marking the boundary between here and there, us and them. It startles me.

The people amassed in a loose line awaiting entry to Oraes remind me vaguely of the crowds that flock to Roanin for the annual Prediction reading. Here, however, there's no charged anticipation or travelers jostling for better positions, simply quiet conversation and calf-high boots scraping idly across the stone road. A handful of uniformed men and women stand beneath the archway, questioning individuals as they enter, and all together, their routine calm forms a decided contrast to my wildly beating heart.

I've borrowed a stranger's form for this pivotal test—shorter and skinnier, with long, doe-like lashes, a stick-straight bob brushing the back of my neck, and a nearly flat chest. My muted Telyan clothes are cut tighter than the wind-beaten coats and wide-legged trousers I keep seeing ahead and behind, but what feels like a blinding disparity isn't drawing any added attention, so I keep my expression carefully blank.

By the time I reach the entrance, I have my story ready.

"What's your business in Oraes?" asks a listless guard. Eradain's symbol, a gold crown encased in a scarlet sun with five rays, parades in bold stitches across her navy jacket.

"A short trip to visit family," I reply in the northern accent. I've been practicing. "I received an invitation."

Which is, strictly speaking, true.

The guard doesn't question the vague story. Assuming, I'm sure, that anyone magical in these parts would be trying to *escape* the city, not enter through the front door. She waves me by, and I walk confidently under the archway and into a paved public square.

Into my mother's city.

Throughout the journey here, I've pictured Oraes as a city whose appearance matched its government's vile practices—stiflingly close and unwelcoming, with dirty streets, foul air, and crumbling façades. The section before me, however, is clean and open. Low buildings made of sun-dried bricks line the bustling plaza, a cobbled expanse which narrows into roads at each of its four rounded corners. Though the ocean remains out of sight, pearly seagulls are squabbling over roofline perches with grating calls, and whispers of seawater salt the air.

The discovery gives me pause. But years of traveling Telyan in different guises have taught me not to linger near entry points, lest I look like the outsider I am, so I choose a street at random in the city that wants me dead and walk the merchant-lined road like I've done it a thousand times before.

After Roanin's slopes and gentle curves, Eradain's capital lays uncomfortably flat. Oraes seems a city of earth and wood combined, the buildings either red-toned brick or covered with whitewashed timber—Telyan wood, I'm sure, given Eradain's limited access to homegrown trees. The thought of our resources bolstering this city's infrastructure makes me feel faintly ill.

Nobody pays me any heed. Few are even around to, likely still at work or the schoolhouse. Regardless, my chest grows heavy as a rock, my stomach swirling like worms, with each new person I pass shifting crates or shining shoes or hawking local leaflets bearing news. The threat of discovery looms, should my emotions get the better of me, as does the painful awareness that any one of these people could actually condone Jol's violence and hate-filled rhetoric and vision of a so-called better future built upon the bodies of others. His subjects bought into the fear and now I'm afraid of them, a poisoned well we seem destined to draw from forever.

"Do you need help?" asks an older man with glasses and a cattle-hide coat. He's smoking a pipe beside the door to a butcher shop, eyeing me.

I shake my head firmly and focus on the narrow side streets branching off the wide road like tributaries, considering which to choose. There's one with a tawny cat sitting on a cellar door built into the ground, one that dead-ends between blackened buildings suggesting fire damage, one which rings with the laughter of a small group gathered on a wraparound porch. The sudden outburst among this section's low hum feels as jarring as a clock tower tolling the hour, and I quicken my pace, pivoting toward an alley with only a child tugging a scruffy dog on a lead.

My feet grind to a halt.

A cat has crouched beneath the shadow of an awning straight ahead, its coat distinct enough to be unmistakably the same animal I saw a few streets back—bushy, orange-brown fur, black paws, and a series of stripes ringing its feathery tail.

It's very clearly watching me.

The cat twists its head as if—well, as if to check for any onlookers—before it pads over, pauses a beat, and heads down the nearest side street.

That's when I know.

Skin prickling, I follow the cat down a series of roads whose smooth pavement gleams almost silver in the sun. Another shifter, right in the heart of Jol's domain! It seems a miracle, too intriguing not to see where this thread leads, but I keep my guard up nonetheless. By now, I've learned the potential danger of apparent coincidence.

That flicker of suspicion, that I should have gotten this lucky so soon, only strengthens when the cat stops outside of a shabby-looking shop.

The façade has a dilapidated air, unswept dirt sprinkled before the door and a couple of windows smudged with grime. A sign droops from the awning, painted with words too chipped and flaking to make out, while another posted in one of the windows claims the shop is open. An uninviting prospect, but when the cat looks up at me pointedly, I turn the handle.

Inside is not much better than out. The tepid space forms a spectrum of grays and browns, thick dust hanging limply in scattered shreds of sunlight. The timber shelves spanning half the room hold a mismatched assortment of metal tools and trinkets, spools of thread and wooden horses that might be toys, and the occasional mounted ink drawing styled to attract those who can't afford to buy better. All in all, the kind of general store one might step into if they had nothing better to do.

There's no one inside.

The cat streaks ahead and disappears around a corner near the back. In its absence, the empty store takes on an unnerving quality. What if my suspicions are merited, and this is a trap? I'm edging toward the door, uncertain, but just as my fingertips graze the handle, a girl in a rich brown woolen dress rounds the corner.

"Don't go, please!" she says, crossing the room with her palms up in a placating gesture. She's maybe a year or two younger than I am, with bronze skin, a broad nose, and thick brown hair that curves at the ends, just beneath prominent shoulder blades. The kind of thinness that speaks to malnourishment, judging by the way her eyes sit a little too large in her sunken face, and the fact that her dress's waist hangs loose where it's clearly designed to be fitted. "It isn't safe."

I say nothing, my body still angled toward the door.

"I have no reason to betray you. I'm like you, see?" In the span of two heartbeats, her features morph into those of a person I don't recognize—taller and broader, better fed—before returning to her natural form.

So long has passed since I've seen someone other than Helos shift, I'd almost forgotten how it feels. Like a candle kindling in a window across the lane. A small tether tying her world to mine.

The suspicion loosens its grip, just a bit. "Why did you bring me here?"

"You were wandering the city in broad daylight." She sounds nervous that I'd even have to ask. "You could have been caught."

"And here, I won't be?"

She quirks her head behind her. "In the back, it's safe. Quickly, or someone might see."

Through those grimy windows? Unlikely. I want to trust her, but that answer's not good enough, and I stay put.

"There's a place for people with—you know." Though the girl has dropped her voice to a whisper, she still won't say it aloud, as if the walls themselves have ears.

Magic. The word hangs heavy in the dusty air.

"Safe," she repeats, like I don't understand, as if everyone in Alemara doesn't speak the same language. "Here, I'll go first. You can follow."

She disappears around the corner in back, and I trail her wordlessly into a windowless side room lined with mostly empty shelves. Without a lamp, it's scarcely bright enough to see, but I hear the scrape of stone against stone as her shadowy form bends toward the floor. I keep my back against the wall.

"This is the way," she says.

As my eyes adjust to the gloom, I make out the thick tile she's lifted to the side, as well as the yawning blackness carved into the floor. A hole.

Unease drips down my spine. I do not fear the dark, but I can't make my feet move, all the same. Maybe the girl senses this, because she says, "Wait here," and disappears inside.

I note the close sound of her footsteps, muffled strikes against stone that suggest the passage isn't wide enough to echo. When the noise fades entirely, I crouch down and breathe the draft in deep, scouring for any notes in the air that might hint at what's down there. The musty scent gives no clues.

The last time I was facing a hole in the ground, it was back in the Vale, tracking the soldiers who stole Helos. Weslyn had looked between the passage and me, his dark honeyed eyes creased in concern.

In the solitude, I allow myself to sink into the scene, reaching for its warmth even as other memories jostle for prominence—the surprising strength of his hard-won laughter, the leather-bound book filled with notes and illustrations documenting our journey through the wild. I move to the riverbank, as I always do, trying to conjure the ghost sensations of sturdy arms and wandering hands and mouth against mine. Being held and feeling wanted, feeling safe. Seen.

My eyes drift shut, present fears giving way to better thoughts.

For so long, nightmares plagued my sleep, but lately my dreams have moved in an altogether different direction. An insistent collage of clasped hands building into tangled limbs and fabric giving way to bare skin. I wake to pulsing heat, the breath heavy in my chest, surprise and disappointment merging into determination for all the things I aim to do when we're together again.

If I can work up the nerve.

If he's waiting.

The distant footsteps return and I shake the images away, frustrated. Wishing I could afford to lose myself in memories for more than a handful of heartbeats.

I can't.

I'm back against the wall when my guide pokes her head out of the hole once more. Next to her, a second, round-faced girl pops up with a tiny glass lantern, the candle's flame illuminating deep brown skin set against brilliant silver eyes and plaited hair streaked with silver and gold.

"It's all right," the newcomer says in a kind voice. "I know the tunnel looks frightening, but it leads to safety. My name is Gemma. This is Merisol."

Though I've drawn myself up at the implication of being scared, the appearance of yet another magical person reassures me. When Gemma holds out a second glass lantern about the size of two stacked fists, I take it.

"Follow me," she says.

In the lantern's soft glow, I can just make out a set of stone stairs descending into the passage. They look ancient, the landings shallow and pockmarked with age; when I lower myself in, my foot nearly slips on the first rounded step. Even with my heel braced against the back, the toe of my boot still hangs over the edge.

"Watch your step," Merisol warns from behind, belatedly. After dragging the slab back into place overhead, she offers a reassuring smile and brushes past me to slide in behind Gemma.

The feeling of entrapment settles over my bones like a shroud. The air down here is close, and cold, and misgivings shiver across my skin like spider silk. It takes all of ten steps for the urge to race back up and out to grow nearly unbearable, but I'm determined to see this through now that I've begun.

I swear as my forehead scrapes the passageway's rough ceiling and refocus on not sliding down the steep descent.

After maybe forty or fifty steps, the stairs flatten out into a corridor narrow enough that I can't extend my arms fully to either side. The candlelight trails along large, empty shelves built into the walls. I don't understand. An old silver mine, perhaps? Gemma takes us around one corner, then another, and the next corridor's walls are lined with—

Cursed fortune.

"It's a tomb," Gemma supplies, sounding unbothered by the hundreds of human skulls set into the walls like gemstones. "We think it dates back to Eradain's foundation, around the war. These could be some of the fallen."

Save us. If she's right, that would make this underground maze nearly seven and a half centuries old.

I imagine the ceiling crumbling overhead. Feathers jut up against my skin. "Who else knows about it?" I force out, my breath fogging in the lantern light.

Gemma rounds another bend. "Just us, we think."

Before I can question who exactly *us* comprises, the path opens up into a cavernous hall.

Mounted wood torches and oil lamps cast the chamber into warm light. Chairs, dusty cushions, and tables are spread between walls mercifully devoid of skulls, and scattered among them all—people. Maybe two or three dozen, heads tilting up at our approach. A few get to their feet upon spotting us, but most don't bother.

I freeze.

"Who have you brought us, Merisol? Shifter or human?"

I can't locate the source of the voice in the crowd. Everyone either looks human or has whisperer gold and silver etched into their features; I'm guessing the former are shifters, though I can't be sure in this form. Like Merisol, many wear shirts, dresses, and trousers that appear too large for their frames; at least two have wound rope around their waists like belts.

"Shifter. She was in the Red District," Merisol replies before smiling at me. "You never mentioned your name."

I keep my expression neutral, trying to decide if I should lie. Jol knows my name and may have put it out into the city, along with some reward for Helos's and my capture. If so, someone here could offer me as collateral in exchange for lenience, perhaps, or let it slip aboveground on accident. Then again, would Jol risk drawing the city's attention to finding us, if he fears someone spotting the resemblance? And that's another problem, because I can only hold this borrowed form until tomorrow night.

"If you're a shifter, that must be a disguise."

That voice again. Back tensing, I attempt to sound indifferent. "Why would you say that?"

"Because you'd never walk the city in your natural form if you had any other choice." The speaker has stepped forward—a whisperer who looks middle-aged or slightly older, with light brown skin, metallic-streaked curls cut short, and horn-rimmed glasses set over pale silver eyes. The muscles in his arms are pronounced. "And that's no northern accent," he adds.

The river take me. It worked well enough in the past.

"What is this place?" I ask, dropping the accent. No point to it now. "Are you all in hiding?"

"Telyan," the man pronounces. Which is a surprise—I didn't realize the years there had started to show in my voice.

Inexplicably, it pleases me.

There's some shuffling at one end of the group.

The man doesn't answer my questions, simply waits, and under the scrutiny of so many eyes, the brief flare of satisfaction snuffs out. Giving away my southern identity is one thing, but relinquishing my disguise . . . Any one of these people could be a spy for Jol.

I hear Helos's voice in my head, telling me that sometimes, you just have to trust people.

And so, despite my better judgment, I release my hold on the borrowed matter and regain my natural form.

For a long while, there's no audible reaction. Then a voice calls, loudly, "What are you playing at?"

The group parts around a woman striding toward the front. She's a blend of severity and softness—thick, dark brows bent critically over tanned white skin, doughy arms and hands that curl into ready fists. Dense brown hair brushes her wide shoulders, and wrinkles play at the corners of her mouth.

I cross my arms. "I don't know what you mean."

When the woman closes the distance between us, lynx instincts prod the edges of my mind. I feel the slight pressure in my fingertips that precedes claws and clasp my hands behind my back.

"Either you are Queen Mariella back from the dead," she says, "Or you are the king's blood."

"I'm neither."

"Don't lie to me," she snarls. "I have not come this far to be thwarted by another Holworth brat." Out of nowhere, a knife is out and driving toward my chest.

I manage to dodge the blade, barely, goshawk feathers shooting through my skin. I send them back and allow the claws to come forth, bracing for a fight.

"Penelope, wait," says a new voice. "I've seen her before."

The speaker is seated at one of the tables, tall and slender with a jaw cut from glass, androgynous with deep brown skin and hair cropped close to their scalp. "You're Rora," they continue. "You worked for King Gerar."

Another secret forced from my arsenal. Uncertain whether I should be annoyed at their announcement or grateful for the interference, I scour my memory for any recollection of this person and come up short. "I don't remember you."

"You wouldn't. I've been here a while," they reply, expression indecipherable. "Queen Violet's eyes and ears, you might say."

No one else looks shaken by this news.

Queen Violet. *She's alive.*

I swallow. "And, are you—"

"Human," they interrupt with a slight smile. "Not all of us buy into the fear. Welcome to the resistance."

The resistance. Functioning right in Eradain's capital! I feel the beginnings of a grin stretch across my face.

"What are you doing here?"

"Viol—Queen Violet asked me to come." I reason that's at least somewhat true, since according to Wes, she advocated sending me north long before the onset of war. "I'm here to gather information that could help Telyan."

"Solet is already doing that," Penelope says with a wave in their general direction, other hand still fisting the knife. "And you haven't explained your resemblance to Mariella."

"I can't explain that, because as I told you, she's no relation of mine," I insist. "A lot of people look alike. As for the other, I plan to go where a human could not. I'm going to infiltrate Jol's court."

Merisol fixes me with an incredulous glance, while Solet's eyebrows merely raise in interest.

Penelope looks deeply unimpressed.

"Listen," I say, growing impatient with this interrogation. "I'm heading there with or without your approval. But I'm not your enemy. If anything, it sounds to me like we have the same one." Penelope's fingers loosen a bit on the knife, and I reach a decision. "If you want, I can share my findings with you."

"What's the catch?" she asks, sounding interested despite herself.

"No catch," I assure her. "I want the Holworth reign brought down, same as you."

And if there's a chance, any at all, I might uncover something that could stop this war from marching to my friends' doorstep, I have to take it.

"You don't understand," the man with glasses says softly. "We've tried what you suggest with another. He— It didn't end well."

"He was caught?" I ask.

The man pauses. "He was killed."

"He was *tortured,* Horan. You know he would have been." The reed-thin boy who speaks has a shock of spiky hair as red as Ansley's, but he's far younger than she, maybe fourteen, fifteen at most. He folds his arms and drums a shoe against the ground, filled with a restless energy that instantly reminds me of Helos when his emotions run high. "He didn't talk, though," the boy adds, a challenge in his blue gaze, like it's important I get this straight. "He could have told them where we're hiding, but he didn't. Otherwise, they would have found us by now."

The allusion to torture makes my skin crawl. I may be good in a fight, but that would be a different kind of battle, one I don't think I'd be able to withstand.

And yet, I didn't come all this way to fail.

"I can do it," I insist. "I just need to study someone long enough to take their place. If you help me, I'll share my information with you. Take it or leave it."

Penelope exchanges an endless look with Horan, who's visibly concerned but nods nonetheless. At his signal, Penelope rolls her eyes and puts away her knife. "All right, then," she says. "Let's get to work."

ELEVEN

HELOS

I thought I would be grateful to return to the hospital. My routine there, though draining, is what I know. The work I feel I was meant to do. Now fourteen people have died holding my hands, and I no longer know if *meant to do* matters.

They both tried to warn me. Finley insisted our old life is gone, and at the time, I heard it only as an ending. On the riverbank, Rora shouted that I should set aside my grief and recognize there's more at stake than our own problems.

And I'd actually called her selfish.

As I tend to patient after patient, with Bren and Tomas looking on, I'm beginning to suspect they were right after all. I've tried to recapture those golden years—Finley at my side, Rora safe, my apprenticeship paving the way to a practice of my own. And every time, life has set another obstacle in my path, barring the way back. The Vale, that prison. Roanin deserted. Each formed another step of the new track taking shape before my feet, but somehow it's Briarwend that has made the comforts in my old routine feel cruelly fleeting. Small, even, when so much else is on the line.

I don't want my life to change. But Jol has already made the call for me, distorted everyone's futures into versions they didn't see coming. The decisions made upon that throne will touch me wherever I am, whether I sit upon it or not. I can't go back as long as Jol keeps moving forward.

I have to start building.

The first idea comes to me two mornings after the battle, when I rouse from a nightmare in a sweat imagining Weslyn had not intervened, and that Eradain soldier had cut down Lilyn and me. I'd like to run it past Rora, but Rora isn't here. Finley is, but the thought of facing him after we left things the way we did has grown strangely confusing. I no longer know where we stand.

I want him. I've made that achingly clear, and the conversation I expected would end that hope for good instead revived it by suggesting he might want me, too. Which should be enough to make me delirious with joy—except the answer's still no.

Start building. If this, too, is going to change, I need to know how. No matter how much it hurts.

Finley answers my knock on his door that night rather warily. Still, he answers. I'd intended to start by picking up where we left off, but the questions die on my tongue when I see the exhaustion shadowing his features, the hunched stance and shifting weight. My eyes itch. Tonight is not the night for that serious talk.

Instead, I bridge the gap by sharing my nightmare-fueled idea in an undertone. A peace offering, until we can talk more. Fin's enthusiasm is so sudden, bright as the previous night's full moon, that it smooths the tension lingering between us. I can't help but feed off his energy. He's right. It *is* a good idea.

In the cold light of morning, the plan has decidedly lost its appeal.

"Maybe I should rethink this," I begin.

"You shouldn't," Finley says for the fifth time. "Stop fussing."

In his bedroom, Fin's going through the motions of preparing for the outside world, lacing his autumn boots and grabbing a long, charcoal coat and cream-colored scarf. He seems antsy today, itching to get on the move. Face flushed, hands restless. Even though my morning off from work overlaps with his usual trips down the hill, he still insisted on pushing that later and coming with me, because it turns out the old, distractible Fin isn't entirely gone after all. Admittedly, I'm grateful.

"Finish that first," I tell him, noting the mug of ginger tea abandoned atop the dresser.

He doesn't reply.

"Fin."

"I know, Helos. Please calm down."

"I am calm," I say, scratching my dark purple sleeves, then the back of my head.

After he wraps up in his scarf, Fin indulges me with another few sips.

"You don't have to come," I say, mindful of his obvious fatigue the night before. "If you're not feeling up to it."

Fin waves vaguely in my direction, dismissive. "If I wasn't feeling up to it, I would say so."

"Okay."

He must hear the uncertainty in my voice, because he glances at me critically before retrieving his sketchpad and walking stick from the bedside table. "Remember the days when we talked about something other than my health?"

I fold my arms. "Of course."

"Oh good," he replies sardonically. "I was starting to fear I'd imagined them."

I pace in the doorway, grimacing when the bell tower strikes the hour. Nine o'clock. In the corridor, someone barks a laugh while their rubber soles screech over the linoleum floor, and for whatever reason, the composite grates against my nerves. "Could they be any more—"

"Helos," Finley interrupts, padding over to my post just inside the door. "Are you feeling okay?"

"Me?" I ask, bewildered. "I'm fine! Of course."

"It's just, lately you've been a bit . . ."

"Smothering?" I supply. "Don't. You'll start to sound like Rora."

"I was going to say irritable. And—" He shifts his weight with a grimace. "You don't always seem like yourself," he finishes.

I study the blue sky peeking through the streaky window. "I'm sorry." It comes out quiet. "I'm fine. I'm me. I promise."

"Mm," he says, skeptical.

I follow him into the corridor.

"I know this can't be easy for you," he continues once we're past the dreaded staircases. Three whole flights; he's on an upper floor for safety, but that also means added pain every time he goes out. My heart bleeds for him with every ragged breath. "Rora being far away, everything in flux." He nods to the Royal Guards posted at the entrance to the Officers' Hall. "Me."

"It's not that," I blurt without thinking.

Finley keeps his eyes on the courtyard ahead. "Oh."

"I mean, it probably is. Or, I don't know. Maybe it isn't. I mean—" I tilt my head skyward, blinking away the sudden wetness. "I don't know what I mean," I murmur.

Half a step ahead, he swivels round. "You would tell me if there was something else going on, wouldn't you?"

"Of course I would."

"I mean it, Helos."

I shudder a little at the autumn chill. For a moment, standing only an arm's length away, Finley looks to me like the safest place in the world. His earnest eyes fixed on mine, hair billowing softly in the breeze.

Maybe that's why the words begin climbing to the surface.

"When I was—"

"All right there, Your Royal Highness?"

The group of four cadets that passed us that morning outside the hospital is back again. One grins when he spots me and nudges the handsome one with green eyes, who blushes and shoves his friend before glancing my way. Sheepish expression curving into a bright smile. This time, the flirtation acts like torchlight, repelling dark memories back into crevices and crawl spaces. When the silence stretches long, I tear my gaze away, back to Fin.

He's frowning.

"All right," he replies with less of his usual charm. "Any chance you've seen my brother this morning?"

"Yes, sir. Second Yard, not five minutes ago."

"Excellent. If you will excuse us, gentlemen."

Finley and I wind our way through the garrison, the pockets of space filled with careers and cadets. In light of recent events and growing need, the academy has cut its mandatory four years' training time in half, so they can push new admissions out faster. Now the youngest careers are sixteen, and fortune's sake, they barely look old enough to wear that uniform! These are the soldiers expected to fight in battles like Briarwend?

All of them bow to Finley as we pass. Some even nod respectfully when they catch my eye, assuming importance based on my proximity to the prince. I have always found it odd to watch Fin perform this shift into someone tighter-laced, reassuring in a less approachable way than he was with that group of four. While Weslyn's royal bearing and his natural one often seem cut from the same cloth, on Finley, it's like trying to fit two hands into a single glove: overly restrictive, not suited to the natural design.

Today I'm grateful for the attention, though, because I love watching his expression brighten with the purpose. Occasionally, I hover behind while he answers a question or listens to a tale of progress. By the time we reach the expansive practice yard, Finley's eyes are practically glowing.

Weslyn is standing alone near a covered walkway when we spot him, away from a unit of training cadets. No Astra this time—from what I can tell, most people on this base have responded to her newfound magic the same way they've responded to the messenger raven whose feathers sharpened into knife points, or the horse whose mane and tail sprouted flowers that wove among the strands. They pretend the evidence before their eyes doesn't exist.

Weslyn straps a belt over his dark pants and fitted navy shirt as if distracted, glancing more than once at the sky.

"Why does he do that so much?" I ask Finley. "It's like he's expecting the sky to fall."

Fin glances at his brother, grins, and doesn't reply. As always, he forms a decided contrast to Weslyn, who has spotted our approach and studies us with a frown.

Which reminds me.

"He knows about us," I say in an undertone. "You always said we were a secret." Back in the months before I grew tired of secrecy—and before my attempt to change it ended everything.

"We were," Finley replies, unabashed. "But unfortunately for us, Wes isn't stupid. And sometimes I'm just too lazy for lies."

"Who else have you told, then? Your sister? The whole court?"

"Helos," Finley chides with a click of his tongue. "My family may have known about my request to keep you away, but certain information is best kept between brothers." He closes with a wink.

What kind of information? I glance back at Weslyn, my mind scraping through some of the things Fin and I have done behind closed doors. To my horror, I can feel my face begin to flush.

"Good morning," says Finley cheerfully, stepping to his brother's side.

"Good morning," Weslyn echoes, like it's anything but.

"Helos has something to ask of you."

Weslyn begins rolling one of his sleeves to the elbow. "Does he."

"*He* is standing right here," I snap. "And never mind. This was a stupid idea."

"What is it, Helos?"

At a nod from Finley, I decide to come clean. "During the battle, when I was out on the field, that soldier would have killed me and the people I was with. I didn't know how to defend us." I chew the inside of my cheek. "I want to be able to fight back."

Weslyn looks up from his sleeve with narrowed eyes. "I believe Broden bears ample evidence of your ability to do so."

"Not against swords," I say, guilt bubbling up. "If I can learn how to use one, I'll be better prepared to retrieve wounded soldiers from the field."

"Fine," Weslyn says. "But I'm missing the part where I come in."

This time, Finley has to shove my shoulder for me to reply. "I thought you could teach me," I mutter.

His eyebrows lift. "Come again?"

"I thought—" I sigh, exasperated. "Will you teach me? Since you're not terrible at it."

Some mockery of a smile spreads across his face. "Interesting."

"What is?" I ask, regretting my question at once.

"You, coming to me for help." Weslyn shrugs. "It's interesting."

"On second thought, don't bother. I can find somebody else."

"You *have* been volatile of late," he continues, as if I haven't spoken. "Perhaps the discipline would do you good."

"What are you, my father?"

"I certainly hope not."

Finley snorts. I look at him, then at Weslyn's smug smile, and it dawns on me that he's actually making a joke. About my *sister*.

"Never mind," I say. "I don't know why I thought this could work."

"Come on," Finley whines. "It will be fun. A little bonding between friends, plus a free show for me."

Weslyn's expression darkens. "I seem to recall a time not too long ago when you asked him to stay away." He looks at me pointedly, as if I've dragged Finley here against his will.

Fin waves a hand. "Helos and I have reached an understanding. No need to protect me, Brother, though I value your concern."

"Mm," Weslyn grunts with obvious skepticism, starting on the other sleeve.

And what understanding is that? I want to ask. The answer is no—but is that truly what he wants?

"Let's grab you some training threads from the stock room," Weslyn says. "We'll keep to blunt blades for the moment. You're not ready for the real ones."

"We're starting now?" I ask, taken aback.

He crosses his arms. "Unless tomorrow would better suit your schedule? I suppose I could rearrange mine to fit yours."

"You self-important bast—"

"Now, boys," Finley interrupts. "Don't start bickering again. What would Rora say if she could hear you?"

The effect of these words is immediate. Eyes dropping to the ground, Weslyn clamps his jaw shut the way he always seems to whenever Rora's name is spoken aloud. I would relish the change in him more if it weren't for the hot flush of guilt trickling up the back of my neck.

I know what he does for my sister, having spent enough years with her to recognize the significance of earning her trust, of making her feel comfortable enough to shed her hard-wrought armor.

I know how I punished her audacity for wanting the person who does this to live. And now, Fin's and my voice of reason, our stabilizer, the strong one—she's out there alone. No doubt reassembling those protective plates, doing what she must to fulfill her part of the plan. And what was my part? Find Finley and—what? I shake my head. I can do more than that.

"Thank you," I tell Weslyn.

"Don't mention it," he mutters.

"By the river," Finley smirks. "I am going to enjoy this."

Weslyn leads me into the dark armory, which clatters with the sounds of fire blazing in forges and blacksmiths hammering out blades and pieces of armor. Off to one side, there's a smaller room dedicated to training gear. Weslyn tells the academy staff what he's looking for, and soon enough I've got a blunt sword belted around my waist and hardened leather pads encasing my torso, shins, and forearms.

"There he is," Finley calls with a grin as I return to the practice yard, tugging on a leather band and feeling ridiculous. He's seated himself in a far corner, sketchpad in his lap. Mercifully, the unit of training cadets has since departed.

"Leave it," Weslyn says, smacking my hand away from my wrist.

"Is this really necessary? I look like an idiot."

"It's for your own protection," he replies. "Don't want you getting hurt."

"Then why aren't you wearing all this? What if I hurt you?"

His mouth twitches, only a little. "You won't."

Before I can argue, he bids me stand a short distance from the yard's perimeter and moves opposite me, pulling a very much non-blunt sword from his side. "We'll run through the basics first. Grip, body positioning, balance, so forth."

"Weslyn is well-versed in such activities," says Finley helpfully.

With a grin, Weslyn points his sword at his brother. "Careful."

"My apologies. As you were."

The next hour passes in a blur of instructions. The blade is not overly heavy in my hand, which Weslyn says puts me at an advantage over many cadets. But the movements are strange to me. I'm not used to entrusting my safety to something not attached to my body. The closest feeling to this I can recall is warding others off with antlers in elk form, but that wouldn't do much good on a battlefield.

Weslyn proves to be a patient and nonjudgmental tutor. I can admit to myself that I'm grateful for it, particularly when a few passersby stop to watch and giggle. A short distance away, Finley has fallen silent for some time, trading teasing remarks for his pencils. I love watching him when he's like this—when sketching funnels his typically scattershot focus into a targeted beam. He keeps his head lowered, biting his lip in concentration, his hand moving rapidly across the parchment. What I'd give to be even a corner of that page.

"Fortune's sake!" I exclaim, doubling over where the flat of the blade struck my abdomen.

"Focus." Weslyn raises his sword for another blow.

After three additional unblocked hits, I suggest we take a break.

"Oh, come *on*," Finley says. "Even I could do better than that."

"Oh?" I meant it to sound irritated, but I find I'm smiling.

"Your aim is terrible."

"Yes, well, the sun was in my eyes."

"The *sun*?" Finley drops the pad and pushes to his feet, raising a hand to stem the flow of protests. "All right then, Helos. Give me your stick."

"It's a sword," I remind him, handing it over by the hilt.

He whacks the flat of the blade against my leg, hard. Why do they keep doing this? "Stick."

"You don't want to fight me, Brother," Weslyn warns, eyes bright. "That has rarely ended well for you."

"What!" Finley exclaims, raising the sword. "Your lack of confidence offends me. Brock always said I was a promising student."

"You skipped half his lessons."

"Yes, but whenever I showed, he said I held promise."

I'm discovering that illness—falling sick, getting better—is not a linear process. There are good days and bad days, and today is one of the good. It doesn't take long to establish that Weslyn is indeed much better, breaking through Finley's defenses multiple times, though never actually striking him a blow. Finley doesn't seem to care much, sometimes swinging his sword around with obvious showmanship. But even not taking it wholly seriously, he's far more skilled than I am.

"No peeking," he calls, when I reach for his sketchpad.

I've never spent much time with the two of them together. The experience is odd. Weslyn is like a different person, one who actually laughs and teases and even tosses out a dry joke now and again. He's more like Fin. It's actually fun watching the two of them spar, but the longer the metallic clangs ring out, the further my attention wanders. White walls start taking shape around me, windowless and lit by flickering sconces. There are figures as well, three or four, bending over to examine my wounds. Only, no, that must not be right, because the poking and prodding hurts, and they aren't heeding my requests to stop—

"Are you taking note, Helos?" Finley finally manages to get a hit on Weslyn, who swears mutinously.

I run my hands through my hair, recalling a smile. "You're a vision in swordplay."

"Good." He paces over with the practice blade, limping slightly. "Then let's hear no more talk of sunlight in your eyes."

By the time evening falls, I'm aching in muscles I never knew I had.

The brief joy I felt watching Weslyn and Finley spar faded all too quickly after I arrived at the hospital. In its place, I spent my afternoon shift in a prolonged state of tension, soaking in the main ward's collective panic. Three different patients died in the night, one of them Lyra. Though I did my best to take the edge off the remaining residents' nerves—delivering countless draughts of chamomile and lavender tea, sweetened with honey for the kids, and listening to their fears while they drank—there was only so much I could do. Helplessness is a unique brand of torture.

The sun dips below the horizon, and I drag myself to the mess hall, hoping for another moment's respite. An impossible ask, given how my patients' words continue to pulse between my ribs like a second heart. That, and the fact that I've been living on this base for eight days and still can't seem to stop my body from locking up, my chest tightening, in the presence of so many uniforms. The rationed beef stew sticks in my throat like dry bones as I try and fail to remember my life before, when an evening in a pub's lively crowd drowned out the noise in my head rather than inflaming it.

"Want some company?" asks a voice close to my ear, and I'm not proud of the way I jump in my seat.

Without waiting for a response, the four cadets who always seem to circle Finley slide onto the benches to either side of the table. A couple of soldiers I treated after Briarwend join, too, and judging by the tales with which they're already regaling the rest, I think my actions that day gained me some allies.

Forcing a smile, I order my brain to focus on their amiable faces and grateful words. I command my pulse to slow, because there's no reason their sudden closeness should make my lungs feel starved for air or my muscles tense as an animal sensing danger. The handsome boy with green eyes is at my side, giving his name, offering a pint of ale with a kind smile. I accept them both, knocking back the sour brew with vengeful speed, and ask for another.

Start building. If Rora's plan works, magic will once again flow east of the river. It will form a sort of test, an opportunity to revisit the past but do better this time. To choose acceptance rather than hate. My sister might be the one trying to awaken the land, but I can do more here to pave the way for its reception. *Should* be doing more. Like introducing people to a shifter's friendly face instead of hiding my abilities as Mahree requested, nudging public opinion toward a more tolerant atmosphere.

I can start by making friends, growing my list of allies. The shifter part can come later.

So I remain in the mess for a long time, returning my unexpected company's warmth. I talk, and I laugh, and every time they clap me on the shoulder or brush my arm, I take a drink. When memories of those other uniforms begin to prod the edges of my mind, searching for recognition, I drink. The images slosh away, back to their hiding holes. Victory. Which calls for a celebratory drink. I grab a third pint, then a fourth, until it doesn't matter that the leg touching mine beneath the table isn't Fin's. Until my patients' fears fade to a mercifully distant hum, and fourteen sets of hands no longer envelop my own in ghostly shrouds. Eventually, what starts as a mission becomes genuine fun.

When the mess's remaining occupants depart in favor of sleep, five of my newfound friends teeter away for home, while I let green eyes pin me against the granary wall for a few kisses. One hand wrapped around my waist, the other flat beside my head. The cement is cold against my back. There's no sun now to heat my skin. But the ale remains generous in its lingering embrace, and the body pressed against mine is warm, so I cling to those like the gifts they are, holding them close. Guilt tugs at my lonely heart for enjoying it, but after all, why shouldn't I? The answer is no.

By the time I stumble back to the Officers' Hall, the corridors are completely deserted. I slip into my room and kindle the lamp, wishing for the comforting presence of the books I kept stacked three volumes high along the walls of my one-room apartment in Roanin. Here, every painted wall is pitifully bare. I'm in the process of unlacing my boots when I notice the sheet of parchment someone must have slid beneath the door. I bend to pick it up.

The drawing of me in the training yard is eerily lifelike, sword dragging across the ground and face a portrait of sadness and longing. Scrawled along a bottom corner, an inscription reads, *For Helos, hopelessly unsuited to swordplay, who doesn't smile like he used to. Maybe one day he'll tell me why.*

Without bothering to undress, I lie back on the bed and shut my eyes, cradling the parchment to my chest. At some point, my quiet laughter turns into crying.

I wake to a pounding head and a mouth dry as sawdust, sensations which quickly coalesce into a singular, urgent need to be sick. The latter pulls me out of bed and into the nearest washroom, where I promptly empty the contents of my stomach into the toilet.

Cursed fortune. I can't remember the last time I drank enough for it to count the next morning. Two years, at least. Feeling angry with myself, I swallow the burning in my throat and pretend not to notice the sidelong glances from the person just outside.

When I plod back to my room, I find Finley standing by the door.

My stomach swirls.

"You're up early," I observe, rather pointlessly.

"Are you hungover?" he asks without pretense, eyebrows raised.

"No." The river take me. Out of all the mornings to come, he chooses this one.

"Don't get me wrong, I'm happy to see you're cutting loose," he says, following me inside when I open the door. "Only disappointed you didn't invite me."

I consider telling him I was busy kissing somebody else, just to see how he reacts. But that feels too petty. The sort of meanness that doesn't belong to me, and my ears burn in shame, my head still pounding. "You shouldn't be drinking in your condition," I say instead, swapping yesterday's shirt for a fresh one, long sleeved in a shade of muted gold.

Fin's mouth pinches tight. "My *condition*?"

"You know what I mean."

"How can I? You only bring it up every hour of every day."

I glare at him.

He glares back.

"I'm trying to help you," I remind him. "Which would be easier if you weren't so resistant."

"You're trying to heal me, not help me. There's a difference."

"Fin," I groan, not in the mood.

"On second thought," he continues, brow creasing, "I'm not sure I care for hungover Helos."

I laugh without humor. "Yeah, well, you don't seem to like me much better sober, so what difference should it make?"

Finley flinches.

I'm not sure how those bitter words escaped my lips. The days of uncertainty, maybe, or the weeks of heartbreak, or maybe it's just this *interminable* pounding in my head.

"That's not true," he says softly, sounding hurt.

I drag a comb through my hair, curling the strands behind my ear. "What do you want from me, Fin? To be your friend? To be more? No, forget me for a moment—what do you want for yourself? You didn't answer before and you're not answering now. You want me to watch you grow sicker and do nothing? Because I can't do that, Fin. I won't."

"I want—" Finley opens his mouth. Closes it again.

I let the silence hang, but he makes no move to fill it.

"Look," I press on. I didn't expect to be raising all this now, but here we are. "I'm not like you. This is hard for me. I can't pretend things are normal between us, as if nothing happened. I don't want to."

Still, he says nothing. Just chews his bottom lip, eyes glued to the floor. At the sight, my anger ebbs just as quickly as it flared.

"You can't run away from this conversation every time I try to have it," I tell him, more gently this time. "How can you expect me to be honest with you when you won't be honest with me?"

Finley twirls the top of his walking stick. "You're right," he murmurs, as I lace up my shoes. "I'm sorry. I— It's hard for me, too."

He doesn't seem prepared to say more, so I grab my travel pack and sling it onto my back.

"I'm going out, okay?" I place a hand on his shoulder, and he looks up at me with those crystal eyes, so warm and conflicted I feel I could drown in them. I long since have. "I'll see you later."

I don't ask if he wants to come. I leave him there, something I can't remember doing willingly before. Me going, him staying, and it's my choice. Feels necessary, yet wrong. As if the fraying edges of whatever's untethering inside me are twisting through the skin, starting in on the people around me. Spilling over, pushing, hurting.

My fists tighten around the straps of my pack. I need air.

At this hour, Bren and Tomas will be expecting me at work. Instead, I make my way out of the garrison and across the valley, desperate for distance. Herbs. I've been meaning to search the surrounding hills for lyrroot, which brought down body aches in the Vale. I start up one of the northern slopes, merely half the height of the two hills peaking to either side. The top of the pass would be a sizable climb, an hour's worth at least, and my ragged body objects sharply to the prospect. I overrule it. I *will* do this, because I choose to. I am the one in control.

Thighs aching, I throw myself up the scraggly slope, its patches of grass worn thin. There are no trees on this incline, but plenty of shrubs and low vegetation to source if you're willing to risk your neck. My head spins at the height, the massive Fendolyn's Keep reduced to a child's toy far below, and when a mountain gale sweeps my shirt around me like a storm, my pulse skips into double-time. Is this how Rora feels when she's flying? I search for the sense of freedom she's described and find only the pressing desire to remain on solid ground.

A better idea surfaces. When the air stills, I drop my pack, strip down, and pull from the magic in my core to release matter into the earth. Coolness drips down my limbs as my legs shrink, my face narrows and lengthens, and warming fur pushes through the skin. White along my chest, reddish brown covering most of the rest. By my fifth breath, my body has reshaped itself into a red fox.

The slope's newly sharpened sounds and scents hit like a bucket of water to the face, flooding my enlarged ears and quivering nose. A deluge that leaves little room for a wandering mind. Perfect. I press my nose against the springy earth, then lift it to the breeze, black paws padding across soil and rock, grass and weed, until I track down the minty scent of lyrroot in bloom. Pleased, I dig up the roots with my claws, kicking up dirt. The plant tastes foul in this form, and my ears lay close to my head as I carry them back to my pack.

I continue in this manner for the better part of the morning. Climbing, tracking, digging, until I've gathered enough to last me a good couple of months. Hunger nags at my hollow core, but the work is good, and sunlight gleams beneath rows of fluffy clouds, heating my back pleasantly. By the time I shift to human and return to the Keep, I can breathe a little easier.

I hit the mess hall, finding the kitchen in the awkward phase between breakfast and the midday meal. Food lines empty, tables deserted, the usual roar pared down to wooden benches scraping the floor and two cleaners' brooms sweeping the stone beneath. A wiry cook is clearing scraps away from the long table set perpendicular to the rest, where they lay out the food.

She grumbles at my approach but begins to thaw when I take the stack of plates from her hands and offer to clear up in exchange for the leftover crumbs. I bring one stack to the wide basin sink in back, then another, smiling at the kitchen workers' bemusement. The simple task relaxes me, makes me feel calmer. More like myself. After the fourth stack, the cook interrupts and places an affectionate palm across my cheek. Soft, the way I imagine a mother's touch is meant to feel. She hands me a plate of steaming eggs and a wedge of soft bread.

When I reach the hospital a full hour late, Bren catches my eye from across the ward, disapproving.

A blush heats my face. But I don't know how to explain to him that I couldn't come in until now. I just couldn't. Steeling myself, I prepare to attempt the truth when I recognize the figure at his side.

Finley. Returned to the hospital like he promised, milling among the healers and chatting with the patients in residence. The difference in atmosphere is palpable. Gone are the choked sounds of people trying to muffle their tears, the collective despair thick enough to seep beneath one's skin. Today, Finley has woven a net of calm over the ward. Children are laughing. Adults are smiling as healers make the rounds with renewed vigor in their stride. Even the room itself feels brighter despite the windows' narrow build.

Fin bringing the sun, the way he always has.

As if I've spoken aloud, his chin flicks up across the long hall, eyes searching, his mind and body attuned to mine. The smile falters when he sees me.

Our fight fresh in my mind, uncertainty fists my own heart. To stay or approach? I'm still deciding when a messenger catches me by the arm, swinging me round.

"You're Helos?" he asks. Lined, pointed face. Spindly figure shaped for running. Gold-dusted, warm beige skin.

I nod, adrenaline spiking. The white bands encircling both upper arms make him easier to spot at all hours—he works for the Danofers.

His expression is alarmingly grim when he says, "Her Majesty has requested your presence at once."

TWELVE

RORA

For two days, I don't see the sun.

Two days of living with three stories of solid rock overhead, feeling the muffled ache of a perpetual chill and breathing in the dank, stagnant air. It's nothing compared to how long many of these fugitives have been down here, especially the whisperers, who can't change their form and therefore rarely surface. Except it isn't nothing, because the closeness and the heavy walls and the feeling that I *can't get out* send the memories of that prison shed straight to the surface.

I have never been afraid of the dark. But in this darkness, I sense the bodies of the fallen strewn about like specters. Shadows made by flickering torchlight twist as the corpses did when I struggled through the sea of them, and those horrid skulls relentlessly remind me of death's finality, the blankness and the not knowing and the never more. So on my first day, I make Gemma walk me down each passageway and around every corner, then again when the lesson doesn't stick. It takes hours, or maybe it's only moments, and when I can't sleep I walk them again. I long for the security of lynx vision, lynx jaws, but since keeping my animal forms a secret has come in handy before, I construct my mental maps to the scant glow of candlelight. I have to know.

The rebels, for their part, seem to understand completely. Close to thirty are here at any given time, a mismatched group of people from different neighborhoods in Oraes, but it's Gemma and Merisol who decide to take me under their wing. Many of the shifters and humans, Merisol explains, walk the city in disguise trying to locate pressure points they can exploit, sneak fugitives into safety, and eliminate members of the local law enforcement, the City Watch. Underground, the whisperers take care of newcomers and help turn observations and information into tangible action. There are no forest walkers, but given Eradain's prairie landscape, I'm not surprised.

"Our numbers are small," Gemma adds, coming to Merisol's side and lacing her fingers through hers. Merisol leans in. "Most people want to get out, not stay and risk it, and honestly, who can blame them?" Her mouth twists to one side, forehead creasing. "The ones who join us are those who feel they have no choice but to try. Maybe it's foolish."

"It's not," I tell her firmly. "That's why I'm here, too."

The sad lines of her face slacken a little.

That first night, which I only know arrives because two people own pocket watches, Gemma and Merisol whisper stories of sorrow. How Penelope's husband, who used to work on the docks, supposedly died at sea, though his body was never recovered. That Penelope doesn't believe the official report, insisting he was murdered instead—just one of the magical civilians that vanished in the Prediction's wake, under Daymon's harsh rule. Merisol and her younger sisters were separated from their parents, a cobbler and a weaver, about two months ago, with no way of knowing whether they're still alive. One shifter was caught after adopting the form of someone their target knew to be dead, two more by shifting into an animal form when their emotions grew too powerful to subdue. An unlucky group was caught in the middle of smuggling a family to safety, and no one has seen them since.

Then the floor rumbles and the ceiling shakes, and every part of my brain flares into blinding terror. Feathers erupt from my skin as dust and grit sprinkle onto our heads, but Merisol holds my hand in the oppressive blackness—candles are precious here—and says it will end in a few moments. And it does.

An earthquake. Not a big one, but Gemma adds this happens often in Oraes.

My throat has shrunk so tight, I feel I can hardly breathe.

After that, they switch to more comforting tales—whatever cheer can be found in a place like this. Gemma is shocked when I tell her I've never been out on the sea and reminisces fondly of the wind in her face and the water droplets brushing her skin. Merisol speaks of her sisters, of days spent racing horses across the plains and eating sugared ice on the porch. In laughing whispers, they tell me of the first time they kissed, the happiness they manage to find in each other's arms, before asking me if I have someone waiting back home.

Doubts gnaws at the question. I want the answer to be yes so badly it hurts, but I have no way of knowing if time and distance will have reshaped what we were, whatever it was, into a closed event belonging firmly to the past. Anticipated grief squeezes my rib cage at the prospect. Since I'm not used to having this kind of conversation with near-strangers, I simply murmur that I don't know and let them do most of the talking. Not quite ready to reciprocate, but finding it's nice to listen nevertheless.

At last, day comes, and we begin to plan. Gemma claims a scratched-up table salvaged from a raided house and lays out maps she's drawn of the various city sectors and the strip of land surrounding Castle Oraes, which is built straight on the coast. When I compliment her drawing skills, she simply shrugs and tells me she used to work on a ship, as if that somehow explains it.

My stomach constricts when a group gathers around us early on with watchful eyes, but I breathe easier when it dwindles down to six. Penelope and Solet are back, along with Horan, the whisperer who heard the Telyan accent in my voice, and Kal, the redheaded shifter who leapt to the dead boy's defense. His older brother, I learned. I thought Merisol might join as well, but Gemma tells me quietly that Merisol won't participate in any rebel work involving violence. Instead, she divides her time between caring for her two younger sisters and searching the city for people in hiding and in need of protection.

As with the morning after we destroyed the prison, strategizing in a group rather than alone feels strange. Kal is a brash, jittery boy, short and spindly with freckled white arms and anger already grown so thick it flows through him like blood. If his rage burns red-hot like flames, Penelope's is the cool gray of a brooding storm. She's prickly, and clearly jaded, and I'd like to brush her away. But she still has a few human friends in the city and the castle kitchens where she used to work, and as a result has taken charge of maintaining that network of allies. So she stays.

Horan's presence, meanwhile, is a welcome addition. Apparently, he used to tend to the king's horses, and I can see the vestiges of that work in his thoughtful assessments and quiet firmness. Judging by the way glances slide to him before official decisions are made, he seems to be an authority figure down here along with Penelope. His measured manner reminds me enough of King Gerar that the likeness hits with a pang.

Solet holds the information that changes everything.

"You are familiar with the Royal Guard, correct?" they ask. "You know Carolette Dupon?"

I nod tightly.

"She's a traitor. She's here in Oraes, working for the king."

"You've seen her?" I demand, feeling the knot in my throat drop into my gut.

"A couple of times." Solet folds their arms across their dark red shirt, shrugging. "She's part of the task force dedicated to finding the same people we're trying to save."

"And did she recognize you?"

Solet smiles grimly. "I may not be able to change my face, but I know how to blend into a crowd."

"That's perfect, then," I say, old bitterness mingling with excitement, obvious even to my ears. "If you can hold her captive here, I can take her place. I've spent enough time around her to know how she speaks and behaves. I can pass as her."

"That would serve you better than trying to change your accent," Horan puts in, his hands flat on the table. "But we cannot bring her here unless we plan to kill her. Otherwise, she would carry our location straight back to the king." He peers at me over the top of his glasses. "Are you prepared to do that?"

I hesitate, and Penelope scoffs.

"This is war, girl, or close enough to it. Do you know how many people in hiding she has exposed? I say we kill her."

"Could she stay somewhere else?" I attempt, blatantly grasping at brittle threads. "Is there another safe house you control?"

No one dignifies that suggestion with a response.

I start to panic a bit under the weight of yet another life in my hands. Not an Eradain soldier, not strangers in the midst of battle, but someone with whom I used to work. Someone I know. Carolette sold us out to Jol. She's one of the reasons King Gerar is dead, and it sounds as if she's responsible for other deaths as well. But does that merit death in return? The debate remains the same every time, exacerbated by those fortune-forsaken skulls and their screaming silence. The constant balance of conscience and cool logic, a yearning for justice and the fear of becoming no better than they.

To permit to live or to kill.

They teach us how to do the job when we have no other choice, not to enjoy it, Wes told me once. *I don't think anyone should.*

And now he's heading for a war.

"We'll kill her if it comes to it," I say at last. "For now, we leave her alive. I need whatever information she can give me."

It's a lame out, but it's the best I can do, and even Kal is nodding. Everyone looks to Horan and Penelope. After searching my face, Horan nods slowly, raising no further objections. Penelope remains silent a long while before she throws up her hands. "Fine. Let's bring her in."

The day of the kidnapping begins as all days do here—in stifling darkness, the air crisp and stale against the back of my throat. But grogginess clears at once, chased away by the knowledge of what we're about to do. If all goes according to plan, I won't be sleeping in the catacombs again for a while. The thought fills me with both exhilaration and dread.

I stretch in an attempt to ease the tension in my neck and shoulders, which has grown near-unbearable after two days underground, then reach for the pile of borrowed clothes. My own won't work for the form I've decided to take.

True to their word, Penelope and Solet are already conversing in one of the narrow corridors, away from the main chamber where most people sleep. Mounted torchlight performs its usual sinister dance across the stacked skulls, and I step into its glow feeling as much a ghost as they.

Solet's jaw actually drops a bit when they see me impersonating King Gerar.

"Good," I say, blinking somewhat rapidly at the sound of my own modified voice. A voice that should still be among the living. "Let's hope Carolette feels the same."

Solet runs a hand along the back of their neck. "It's odd, that's all."

Which is an understatement next to how I feel.

After the group decided our best chance of success relies on separating Carolette from the guards with which she usually travels, I'd considered a number of faces before settling on one I suspected might shock her the most: the man she used to serve before she catalyzed his murder. The clothes Horan lent me are perfectly ordinary, wide-legged tan trousers and a beaten leather jacket slouched over a cream-colored shirt. The shoes are tight. Between the bland outfit and his assurances that Eradain leaflets rarely circulate images of southern monarchs, my disguise seems well poised to hold Carolette's attention without alarming locals.

Still, it feels slightly wrong to parade King Gerar around as if back from the dead. I haven't glanced in a mirror, but when I examine my hands, I see the palms he gently placed on the side of Finley's face whenever Fin made him smile. I straighten my spine and look out from Violet's height, Finley's crystal eyes, run a hand through Wes's thick curls and roll back his broad shoulders. I am all of them and none of them, the walking composite I always saw their father to be, and despite the unease, the idea of carrying them with me lends me strength.

"What time is it?" I ask.

Penelope pulls out her pocket watch and frowns.

"Nearly seven. I'll go wake Kal."

"No need," Kal says indignantly, coming up behind in his own borrowed form—cushier limbs, freckles gone, red hair muddied to chestnut brown. "That's you, I take it?" he adds with a critical glance my way.

Kal has made no secret of his irritation with me over the last couple of days, whittling down any communication into jabs or pointed silence. Like a child. Because he *is* a child, which was exactly my point when I argued against his involvement.

Penelope, however, insisted he was good for it. "You're both children," she'd snapped after several minutes of heated back-and-forth. Then, to me, "Whatever you've lived that makes you feel older than your age, he's lived it, too. So drop it."

"It's me," I reply with studied calm.

"Don't start," Penelope warns. "Today we place our lives in one another's hands. Are you ready?"

Her words are the reminder Kal needs, and he nods, suddenly serious.

And that's it. We've already run through the plan what feels like dozens of times, so the four of us walk the catacombs without another word. No goodbyes to the people we leave behind; we'll see them again when we're finished.

Up the old staircase and out of the shop, staggering our departures, and then it's fresh air and sunlight, *merciful* sunlight, warm on my face. In pairs, we make for the shipping district along the coast, Penelope with Kal and Solet with me. The outdoor market where Carolette has been spotted every week is a jumble of wooden stands strewn across sandy pavement, some covered, some open and set up like horse carts. Crowds run thick, and the smell of fish hangs heavy in the air.

After the catacombs, the noise level nearly overwhelms my senses—bartering customers, fishmongers' knives slamming down on boards, coins scraping together, and awnings snapping in the breeze. Infants wailing to get their way. I understand, readily, why

Horan was not concerned about locals recognizing a faraway monarch who's meant to be dead. It takes all my energy just to carve a path through the jostling bodies, distracted by the food and fabric for sale and the elbows digging into my sides. We're supposed to find Carolette in this?

When the sight line clears, I catch my first glimpse of Castle Oraes far back and to the right. The seat of Eradain's government coalesces in a heavy web of stone walls the color of sand, with rounded turrets shorter than Castle Roanin's gabled roofs and wings more compact than Willahelm Palace's elongated halls. Though I dread the kinds of decisions being made upon that throne, there's something elegant in the way the buttresses and towers curl up and in, rising at a slight slant like a breaching whale or a serpent steadying to strike.

The surrounding fence, however, sends a shiver down my spine. A tall, menacing mass of iron rods and curling filigree, topped with brutal spikes clearly designed to prevent people from climbing over. I can't help but wonder if my half brother ever felt trapped within that gate when his father was abusing him, or if my mother ever felt trapped behind the bars as I did underground, before her husband had her killed and mounted her head on one of the points. King Gerar's bloodless face swims before my eyes, and it's not until we're maybe thirty paces away that I spot a round mass speared atop the gate, blackened like carrion and half-picked away by birds. No one passing beneath it looks up. The head is not my mother's and it isn't King Gerar's, but still I feel the sudden and profound urge to retch.

I do retch.

"Keep it together," Solet murmurs through clenched teeth, their fingers tight around my wrist as people turn to stare or exclaim in disgust. In a loud voice, an onlooker berates me for thinking I could hold my liquor this early in the morning. Furious with Jol and his father, with these people, with myself, I run a sleeve over my mouth and swallow the acid burn scraping my throat. Attracting attention is the last thing we need. Not until Kal does his job.

Eventually, we find Carolette examining crates of jewelry

hewn from seashells, pieces one could never buy in Telyan. Rather than the purple-accented gray of Castle Roanin's Royal Guard, her City Watch uniform is a wall of navy fabric lined with gold. She's pulled her long, straight hair back into a tight tail, her broad limbs and bulky waist creating the impression, as ever, of sheer muscled power.

The sight fills me with rage.

It was her information that Jol used to justify skipping negotiations and starting a war. The same vicious tongue she leveled my way for years after King Gerar hired me as his spy in her stead, rendering her job useless and redirecting her to the Royal Guard. His death, Finley's certain pain, a sight Wes will never unsee, plus all the loss of life and grief still to come—and she's just standing there, fiddling with shells.

I remember her laughing with Ansley and sparring with Dom, treating King Gerar and Violet with perfect deference and threatening to make me pay if any harm had come to Weslyn on our journey through the Vale. Memory after memory cycles through, all the worse for how ordinary they look. I could have stopped her, but she played her part too well.

Carolette's head jerks up, and I twist away to rifle through some bundles of herbs. It isn't time, not yet. At my side, Solet is idly bouncing a red pouch in their palm, as if their mind is elsewhere. Carolette returns to the jewelry, and the pouch flies higher this time—and doesn't come back. Neither of us look at the awning on top of which it should have fallen. But Penelope must have seen, because a gray-and-white gull—one of her animal forms—swoops low overhead before vanishing from view.

My heart starts pounding hard in my chest, skin buzzing, waiting for the chaos to begin. One of the other uniformed women nudges Carolette and says something I can't make out, to which Carolette responds with a harsh bark of laughter. They move to the next stall. A small gap in the crowd has taken shape around them; some people glance at the group with a gleam akin to envy, while others maintain carefully neutral expressions. And yet, there are a few whose features pinch with obvious distaste: a pair of men who

speak in each other's ears, smoothing the angry lines from their
faces every time a City Watch member turns their way; a young
girl with clenched fists hidden in the shadows. I mark their presence with surprise, having thought the individuals responsible for
keeping Oraes's streets magic-free would be regarded as heroes.

Solet says close to my ear, "I see him," and I snap to attention,
filing the observation away for later. They peel away from my side
as I step closer to Carolette, staring and staring until her trained
senses detect the weight of being watched. Eventually, she spots
me—the only still person in a sea of moving bodies.

She stumbles back a couple of steps until she hits the table, her
eyes moon-wide.

It feels like victory.

"No running, Carolette," I say when I'm close enough to see the
sweat beaded along her tanned white skin, the fear warring with
rising fury in her brown eyes. "Not this time."

"Thief!"

The cry arcs through the air, stirring a collective shudder
among the crowd. Still staring at me, Carolette acts as if she hasn't
heard, but the rest of the uniforms are following the outraged ven-
dor's outstretched hand to Kal, who throws the stolen box at one
of them before pushing through the throng. He's got guts, I'll give
him that.

The City Watch takes up the chase, shoving and shouting at
nervous civilians to give way. One of the uniforms makes it only
a couple of steps before dropping to her knees, a stealthily planted
knife protruding from her side.

Now people are screaming, seeing the murder, trying to get
away. I keep my attention fixed on Carolette, piecing together the
rest from scattered glimpses—one of the remaining uniforms has
vanished after Kal, while another is jostled by the crowd, yelling
for everyone to stop. They don't. Holding my gaze, Carolette re-
treats slowly and crouches beside the body, checking for a pulse.
She finds none, I assume, because she pops up with rage contorting
her face. Then she stills abruptly.

Solet's knife is pressing into the small of her back, though no one around us seems to notice. "If you reach for your sword again, or call for help, you die."

Mouth pinched tight, Carolette stares at me again, only a couple of paces away. Surely she knows I'm a shifter, that I can't really be King Gerar, yet she seems transfixed, unhinged, by the sight of me nonetheless.

I feel a twinge of savage pleasure at forcing her to face her guilt, look it straight in the eyes. But it's not the same as justice, and all the remorse in the world won't bring him back. So I simply order her to take off her jacket.

When Carolette doesn't comply, Solet's shoulder jerks a little.

Carolette sheds the fabric roughly.

Left in a plain cream shirt, she's no longer recognizable as an official. I grab the jacket, and Solet and I guide her through the market and toward the grimy shop. At one point, Carolette inhales sharply as if to shout, but apparently Solet has the reflexes of a fox, because the next instant, Carolette hisses in pain. A small patch of red blossoms on her side.

"Don't get clever," Solet warns.

By the time we reach the shop, Horan and a woman I don't know are waiting just inside.

"Are the others back yet?" I ask.

He shakes his head. "Penelope'll be looking out for Kal. You stuck her?" he adds, noting the sticky red patch where Carolette clutches the fabric.

Solet fingers the knife. "She'll live."

"We need to bandage it," I say.

Everyone looks at me.

"That will have to wait until we're there," Horan says at last, frowning slightly. "We brought no supplies."

Down we go, back into the cold, close dark. I feel the descent resettling like a weight atop my chest. Farther ahead, Carolette swears when her head scrapes against the ceiling as mine had the first day; Horan and the other brought the lanterns, but nobody is making a particular effort to light her path. Nor has anyone bound her eyes with a cloth to prevent her from seeing our location, which is an uncomfortable reminder that none of them expect her to see the sun again.

Once they've shunted Carolette into a side chamber below, it takes some persuading on my part to gather wrappings for her side. Still, I get them. My sympathy has a limit, but I know that this, at least, is something Helos would do. Carolette won't let me bandage the wound, so I give her the wrappings as she sinks to the cold stone floor and ask the others to give us a few minutes alone. They allow it, and I watch Carolette patch herself up in charged silence. When she's finished, I crouch opposite her, clasping my hands before me.

Carolette's chin has dropped close to her chest, but she glares up at me with half-veiled eyes, clearly vexed. "Tell me who you are."

I tilt my head a little. "Why do you think this isn't me?"

"Because he is *dead*," she replies, her voice rising.

Anger spirals between my ribs. "At whose hand?"

"I didn't fire the bow." Her gaze, though still fierce, has dropped to the floor.

I laugh without humor. "Is that really what you tell yourself to lessen your guilt?"

"I have no guilt," she says.

"Really? None?"

"None."

I shrug, brow furrowed. "Then why won't you look at me?"

She clutches the sides of her head.

"You want to know what I think?" I persist.

"Stop talking."

"I think you're too weak to feel remorse."

"Stop playing games!" she snaps, then coughs and clutches at the movement in her side.

She's hardly in a position to be issuing orders. Suddenly, though, I want her to know.

I release my hold on the borrowed matter and let my bones shrink, my hips expand, my features return to my natural form.

When the quiet stretches long, Carolette glances up, balks at the sight, and utters one disbelieving, furious word: "*You.*"

Back in my natural form, the borrowed jacket hangs loose and the pants are too baggy. I push the shirtsleeves back so they bunch around my wrists. "Hello, Carolette."

"You survived the Vale, then?" she says, sounding decidedly unhappy about it.

I lift a shoulder and drop it. "Sorry."

"And the prince?"

"I'm surprised you care."

"I care about the Prediction," she clarifies, mouth thinning. "Do your friends here know about your part in that?"

My stomach clenches out of habit and old hurt. I hate, I *hate,* that she still has that power.

In truth, I've barely thought about the Prediction, its warning of *two shifters* and *death,* in the last couple of weeks. I've been too busy trying to make things happen, removed from the net of suspicion that ensnared me in Roanin. If we were back in our previous posts, the king's shifter spy and a member of the Royal Guard, I might have pointed out the lack of evidence supporting her conviction and worked to prove her wrong. Today, I am just too tired. Nothing I say will change her mind, and anyway, this is my interrogation, not hers. I refuse to let her dictate the conversation. That time has passed.

"Let me explain your position." I brace my hands against my thighs and push to my feet. "You have no authority. You don't call the shots. You're here to give us information, and in return, we might spare your life."

Carolette laughs. "Very nice," she says. "Can I give you a word of advice? People sound scarier when they're a bit older. Only cowards are afraid of children."

Now it's my turn to laugh. Families torn apart and magical blood persecuted. How could anyone growing up in this world still be a child? "Only fools underestimate them," I counter. "And you, Carolette, are both a coward and a fool."

I leave.

Penelope and Kal have returned to the catacombs at last, both luckily unhurt. When Penelope learns we succeeded, she volunteers at once for the uncomfortable task of making Carolette talk. A whisperer does, too. I'm reluctant to join, and Solet makes the decision for me when they pull me aside to add to a letter they're sending south to Violet via falcon.

Grateful for the distraction, I keep my message for Violet brief and to the point, telling her I'll be sending more information when and as I get it. For a long while, I consider including a separate message for Helos. Or for Weslyn, or Fin. My heart practically leaps at the thought. *Dear Wes—*

I swallow the burning in my chest, reality tamping down the fantasy. Paper is precious here, and a few short sentences would feel woefully inadequate given all I'd like to say. Besides, my gut shrinks away from the thought of Solet reading those messages. For now, the confirmation that I made it here will just have to be enough.

A couple of chambers away, Carolette has started to scream.

The agonized sounds echo like bells in the ghostly tomb, each one burying the knife of my guilt a little deeper. I have no desire to add yet another experience to my ever-growing reel of nightmares, but suddenly it feels wrong to hide out in here, too easy an out not to witness something I condoned when I agreed to this plan. No part of this should be easy. Besides, whispers the voice of reason I can never fully silence, I need to see how she behaves under pressure. So I return to the room in which I left her and force myself to keep my eyes open and my hands at my side, while Penelope and her partner chip away at Carolette's resistance with nails and wires and knives.

It doesn't take long.

"Do you have what you need?" the man asks, as I finish buttoning Carolette's jacket over my abdomen. The screams are still rattling through my brain. I wonder if they'll ever cease.

"As much as we're ever going to get," I reply, bile rising in the back of my throat.

"Then you should go. The longer they have to notice her absence, the more questions they'll have for her return."

Carolette must register the allusion to freedom, because she lifts her bloodied head. When she sees I've shifted to replicate her, she cries out in rage.

"How *dare* you pretend to be me, you filthy, duplicitous—"

"Believe me, I take no pleasure in it." I sniff in distaste, lifting the fabric from my arm and letting it drop.

"They will catch you," she continues, one of her eyes swollen shut. "As soon as they do, you're dead."

I don't bother replying.

By the time I reach the market, the body of Carolette's murdered companion has been cleared away. Blood, however, still stains the stone plaza. The number of City Watch members in the area has tripled, and what few market-goers have returned remain quiet. Some note my presence among them with raised brows and fearful expressions, while others retain that carefully deadened look. I ignore them all and march toward the iron fence enclosing the royal estate.

Four guards are stationed by the entrance, two in front and two just inside. I'm sure they must have heard what happened, but upon seeing my expression, no one asks any questions. The gate screeches open on metal hinges, and I don't stop to acknowledge any of the guards. I don't glance up at the head speared to the fence. Without slowing my pace, I walk through the gate and across the open grounds.

Here, there's no trace of the carefully tended lawn and centuries-old oaks that surround Castle Roanin. The earth separating Castle Oraes from the fence, maybe two hundred or so paces deep, has been tiled over with carefully hewn stone. Any vegetation has been cleared, rendering all who approach in full view of the towering glass windows stretched across the castle's façade. Behind the western wing, a thick band of greenish blue glitters in the afternoon sun. The Elrin Sea.

I skirt round the southern façade and circle all the way to the north, the side that faces the ocean. The tide oscillates merely three or four stones' throws away, climbing a pale beach studded with pointed rocks that sweep out to sea. Though I know these are protected waters, with Eradain's formidable fleet patrolling out of sight, this doesn't look like a very defensible position to me; placing the heart of their monarchy right on the water seems either a mark of arrogance, stupidity, or as is often the case, both. The air hums with the waves' lapping roar, and I can see a few individuals in white dresses and tan linen pants gathered by the water. Perhaps in another life, this grand estate would have been my brother's and mine, too.

Trying to ignore the feeling of stepping into the belly of a beast, I bypass a well-dressed man with two sleek hounds and a couple of servants beating linens, then cross the half-moon patio that leads to an entrance. The double doors are massive creations, at least twice Carolette's height, and they groan in protest when the valets tug them open.

I step over the threshold as if I have done it a hundred times before.

Though the atrium directly inside spans only two stories, the space has a bright, airy feel. Gauzy cream curtains are affixed to either side of the many windows, and the black-and-white checked tile floor has been polished to a shine. Opposite the entrance, two staircases rise in a semicircle that meets on a small landing, which opens to a corridor studded with columns.

Knowing better than to hesitate, I climb one of the staircases, my rubber soles clattering against the linoleum, and approach the line of valets stationed along the grand hall.

"Take me to the king," I command.

THIRTEEN

HELOS

I just stand there, bewildered, as the messenger goes on.

"You are to bring your healer's bag and come alone."

"Is the queen ill?" I ask, finding my voice. "What kind of symptoms do I need to treat?"

"It is not for her, and she didn't specify. Be quick, please."

Across the ward, Finley's gaze darts between me and the messenger. With some trepidation, I gather a few general supplies into a satchel, sling it over my shoulder, and follow the messenger outside.

Overhead, the cloud cover has thickened into broad strokes of gray. The day smells like rain. My spine quivers when the messenger leads me, not to the Officers' Hall, but directly to the Keep's outer wall. The formidable rampart stands several times my height, and I trail a hand along the chilled stone as we walk the narrow strip of land wedged between the wall and the buildings inside. "Where are we—"

"Just here."

He stops in front of a door I've never noticed, built right into the wall. Its hinges have been oiled into silence, and my sense of foreboding deepens when he pulls it open in a covert manner and quirks his head.

I glance behind. No witnesses.

Grasping the strap hanging over my shoulder rather tight, I

cross the threshold into a narrow corridor that snakes inside the rampart. The tunnel is dark, the air cold, any pockets of light cast by mounted torches keeping only the deepest shadows at bay.

The messenger eases the door shut behind me. "This way."

The sound of our shoes bouncing off the bare stone walls sets my head aching again. He stops at the top of a staircase leading sharply down. "After you," he says.

I study the darkening descent, finding little enthusiasm for the task. He's waiting, though, so I make my way down into the rampart's bowels. Muscles clenched, I try to ignore the way the stale air is thickening from merely unsavory to smothering. How my rib cage suddenly feels as if it's closing in, the two halves folding over one another.

I flinch at the hand on my shoulder.

"You all right, son?"

The messenger's hand. I barely realized I've stopped halfway down the staircase, my feet already turning on the step. Wanting to go back.

"Fine." I force them down, one after the other. Tell my brain to stop, just *stop,* because I'm in Telyan, not in a prison, not in that place. I run through the messenger's question again for distraction. Son—a casual word on his tongue, no doubt. But for me, it's long been laced with sorrow, and the former punch to the gut hits now with the hollow ache of an old injury. Duller, yet persistent. Lingering.

No one calls me son. Not anymore.

It turns out there's an entire complex buried beneath the Keep, remnants of a much older time. Hundreds of years, at least. A hidden network of torchlit passageways and wintry storage rooms and chambers with the doors sealed shut. We cross paths with a handful of people, few of whom spare me more than a cursory glance.

I barely notice. My shoulders hurt, and not from the messenger's palm. This is older pain, sparked by memory, baked into the muscles and bones. Pain from there. From them. With it, my mind starts drifting again, funneling like a draft toward the forbidden corners, windows I've kept successfully sealed for most of my life until the last three weeks. I don't know why this latest horror should be any different, why that night won't simply recede into the background like every other has before, but the needling insistence that I pay it any heed is beginning to drive me mad.

"I have him here, Your Majesty."

I snap to at the messenger's voice and lock eyes with Violet. She's standing farther down the corridor, donned in a crisp white collared shirt and sleek navy trousers, her hair pinned back on the sides. A handful of Royal Guards and advisors mill about in her wake, General Powell among them, along with the ever-present Captain Torres.

"Helos," she greets. "I have an assignment for you."

Down here? "Ma'am?" I say, the word somewhat choked.

She gestures to a door a few paces away. "Inside this room is a person we've taken captive. I would like you to tend to her injuries."

A patient—the whirring in my mind levels into smoother lines. "What kind of injuries are they?"

"Flora will bring whatever supplies you need," she says, not acknowledging my question. "First, I should tell you that this person is an Eradain scout." She pauses, watching me closely. "Will that be a problem for you?"

I see the faces among her entourage mold into portraits of distaste, as if they don't envy me the job. It's the same rhetoric as always, just unspoken. Their side. Our side. The healer in me hates the whole sordid business.

But those cages.

"No problem," I tell her, shoving that nightmarish place aside.

She nods, and I skirt past the group and through an open door, unease rising.

I stop.

The cheerless room is barren, with no windows to let in light or tapestries to temper the chill. The ceiling hangs low.

In the center, a woman sits tied to a wooden chair, a cloth bound tight over her eyes. Thick bands secure her ankles to the chair legs and her wrists behind the severe slatted back. Caked onto the lower half of her face, dried blood hints at a likely broken nose.

Tiny flames of panic begin fluttering in my chest.

The scene is too similar, memories of that night coalescing with the images before me. My body responds to the confusion, unsure whether I'm here or there, but knowing, now, what to expect in a place like this, what happens to prisoners like her. I feel lightheaded, shaken, my heart drumming a relentless rhythm. As the panic grows, so does the need for fresh air, for escape and freedom and *out*.

The guard who opened the door, a woman no older than twenty with raven-black hair, marks my hesitation. "You could have said no," she informs me. "People talk more when they're in pain."

It's the slap to the face I need.

"Bring me two buckets of water and spare cloth. Do it now, please."

She purses her lips but doesn't comment, just leaves me alone with the captive, shutting the door behind her.

The captive's head twists toward the door. But she doesn't speak, and neither do I. Not until the guard has returned with the supplies I requested and vacated the room once more.

Forcing my breath to slow, I place the buckets on the cold stone floor in front of her chair. She knows she isn't alone, but she won't be able to see anything through that cloth.

"I'm a healer," I say softly, crouching before her and pulling the satchel off my shoulder. "I'm here to help you." She sniffs as I begin laying out the supplies.

"Didn't you hear?" she replies. "I talk better under pain."

I look up from my work, not having expected a response. Definitely an Eradain accent—the words run together a bit, the vowels clipped short. I see the soldier I left bleeding in the mud at Briarwend, abandoned to die, and keep my tone light. "That's never been my approach. And I haven't come to make you talk, not if you don't want to."

The young woman laughs, a humorless sound. "You're a strange healer, if you choose to heal the enemy."

I soak a piece of white cloth in water and begin to clear away the blood caked around her mouth and chin. She flinches at the contact. "Where does it hurt most?"

"Don't waste your time," she hisses, jerking away from my touch. "I know what fate awaits prisoners."

"In your kingdom, maybe." I rinse the cloth in the bucket, the water clouding red, and return it to her face. "I don't think the queen will let you suffer."

I have no idea if that's true. Violet has never seemed cruel to me, just exacting. But these injuries—did they arise from a struggle not to be taken captive, or after?

The woman scoffs. "You are an innocent boy," she tells me. "Naïve. I'm the enemy, not a patient in a sickbed."

That word again. Enemy. It's the question from the Battle of Briarwend come back to haunt. The line in the sand separating us from them, and maybe I should see it that way. Lilyn certainly did. This woman does. But the truth is that it's not so easy for me, dividing enemies from friends. Not when the tools I trade in— injuries and ailments, traumas in the body and mind—don't see borders or ideologies. Ignoring the jab, I dunk the cloth in the clean water again. "Tell me where it hurts."

"First, remove the blindfold."

She says it like a challenge, like she's won the right to her silence because I won't possibly obey. I sit back on my heels, considering. When I study the room, searching for secrets, I see only rough walls and cobwebs gathering dust in the corner, the mounted torches with their barest offerings of warmth to keep the chill at bay. I'm sure her warden would disapprove, but the air down here feels old, and cramped, and there's only the one door I came in through. No hidden exits, or weapons she could use to free her ankles and wrists.

My shoulders hurt.

I rise and untie the fabric wrapped around her head. When I come back around and kneel before the chair, she stares in surprise.

"I'm going to fix your nose, okay?" I produce a small, blunt knife from the bag and hold it up for her to see. "I have to use this for alignment. I'll try to be fast."

"Don't come near me with that," she warns, eyeing the tool.

"I won't cut you," I assure her. There's real panic etching into her expression, though, so I lower the knife. "How about your neck, then? Where else does it hurt? I held up my end of the bargain."

The woman says nothing as I examine a long, deep scratch along her pale neck and sew a few stitches, then repeat the process for another laceration I find on her scalp, hidden beneath her golden hair. When I prod one of her shoulders, she winces.

"No serious damage, just bruised," I pronounce, finding the same is true of her ribs. She has another injury on her side, a cut that isn't healing well, which concerns me. It's older, though, not from today. Possibly the ribs are the same. "I'll make you a salve that will help with the pain."

Her brow furrows as she watches me crush the plants and blend them into a paste. "You're very strange," she says again.

"Maybe." I spread the salve over the tender spots, coming to a decision. "Though your kingdom thinks all shifters are strange, doesn't it? Or dangerous. So I'm not that different, really."

She stiffens beneath my hands, as if I've slapped her. She's still trapped, though, her wrists and ankles bound tight, so she can't move away. I finish the job.

"You are a shifter." Her voice comes out strained, disbelieving.

"Yes." I kneel by my supplies and clean my hands on spare cloth.

"But you're helping me."

I meet her narrowed gaze. "I'm a healer."

She says nothing, doesn't even protest or cry out as I lift the blunted knife once more and set the broken part of her nose back into place. When I ask if I've missed anything, she shakes her head.

I gather the supplies together and place them into the satchel, one by one.

"You look familiar," she murmurs.

My gaze flicks to hers, and I find her staring again.

I shrug. "I have one of those faces."

"No." She shakes her head once. "That's not it."

"If you have no other injuries, I'll be going," I say, getting to my feet.

"Wait."

I pause after swinging the satchel over my shoulder.

"What's your name?" she asks.

"Tomas," I tell her. "And yours?"

Her eyes glint. She doesn't reply.

I nod, grabbing the buckets. Still, I hesitate at the door, and after another beat, I turn. "Why do you ask?"

The woman looks down, away from me, her shoulders rolling forward. Her head dips, then rises again. "You have kind hands," she says softly.

Surprised, I nod again. "You could, too, if you chose to."

As I leave the room, a flicker of encouragement warms my core. An Eradain scout, a *soldier,* learned I'm a shifter and still called me kind. Perhaps a handful of people in that kingdom wouldn't want me dead after all, if I sat on the throne.

The raven-haired guard, who's been waiting in the hall, gestures meaningfully to a closed door nearby. Confused, I open it and find Violet waiting inside, along with the others.

"Shut the door behind you, Helos," she instructs.

I glance at the bloody water, then at her, and set the buckets down to close the door.

"You got her to talk," Violet says, lifting an eyebrow. At my bafflement, she runs a slender hand over a small hole in the wall.

"You were listening?" I ask, faintly indignant.

She nods. "Impressive."

The others are looking pleased as well, and their approval makes me feel somewhat rotten. Dirty. Like there cannot be simple kindness in times like these, only sympathy with intent. A series of calculated pieces and participants in a game I haven't yet signed up to play.

"I wasn't trying—"

"We don't have much time," Violet presses on, "so I'm going to get straight to the point. We have learned there's a band of infantry, two hundred foot soldiers and archers, moving south through the Smoky Rise. They are half a day's march from the valley." Distaste is written all over her features, similar to the look Weslyn wore on our furtive journey south of Roanin. The quiet, cold rage born of imagining these soldiers walking freely across her land.

Hearing they're already through the Rise, the same route Weslyn and I took, makes my skin crawl. We didn't miss them by much.

"The soldier we captured had been sent ahead to scout the way. It seems Eradain's army does not know the Keep is hidden inside the ring; likely, she scaled the pass for the vantage point alone."

I'm afraid to ask how she knows all of this, so I don't.

"This is yet another scattered attempt to gain ground, and like Briarwend, it will not stick. We have an opportunity here to thwart their advance. If their scout returns and directs them around the ring and up to where the road bottlenecks, our forces can encircle theirs and cut off any escape." She pauses, as if to see whether I'm following her.

I am, but there is one thing I don't understand, besides the fact that she's sharing all of this with me. "How are you going to convince her to betray her own people?"

"I'm not," Violet says. "I'm asking you to do this."

The silence in the room is broken only by the thunderous pounding of my heart.

"Do you understand?" she persists. "I'd like you to shift to impersonate this woman and lead her troops to the road, claiming safe passage. Our forces can ambush them there."

It takes a while for me to muster a response. When I do, all I manage is, "You want me to lead them to the slaughter?"

She doesn't flinch from my choice of words. "I want you to help us protect this valley, and everyone in it."

By steering others to their death. My throat squeezes shut at the idea, invisible ants dancing along my skin. *You have kind hands.* Hands meant for saving. For protecting, or making sure no one dies alone. Not for this.

"I understand this may be difficult for you," Violet says, and she does actually sound a touch sympathetic. "You are not a fighter, that much is clear to me, and normally I would not—"

"What am I, then?" The question comes out testily, and Captain Torres looks outraged at my tone.

"A runner, I believe."

My fingers begin tapping my leg.

"Normally, I would not ask something like this of you," Violet continues, nonplussed. "But Rora isn't here, and there are few on this base we know of who can disguise themselves as you can. We need you, Helos."

"Besides," General Powell adds. "You have spent time with the woman, even if only a little. You should have some insight into how she speaks and behaves."

At that, the rest of my speech comes flooding back, hot fury licking the hollowness in my core. "That's why you had me tend to her injuries?" I demand. "So that I could better impersonate her?"

"Wake up, boy. This is war." General Powell drums a hand along the table, his earlier approval giving way to impatience. "Unpleasant options must be weighed. Sacrifices made."

"Is this an order?" I ask Violet, the only question that matters now.

She considers briefly. "I could order you to do this as your queen, but I'm hoping you'll agree of your own volition."

"And why would I do that?" I press, ignoring Captain Torres once again.

"I believe there are some on this base you'd like to keep safe as much as I would," Violet answers. "We all walk a dangerous road, yourself included. So I ask you: are you prepared to step up when the situation demands it, or will you stand aside and hope that someone else comes in your place?"

This is the moment I know.

Not suspect, but understand with complete certainty. My life as a healer—or at least, as a healer alone—is over.

Gone are the afternoons lounging around Castle Roanin's estate—Finley doing his best to avoid responsibility, Rora enjoying a brief respite between jobs. Myself beside them, knowing I'd be content if the moment were to stretch on forever. Maybe that life ended when I learned the truth about our mother. Maybe it ended when my duties shifted from caring for the sick to failing to save the mortally wounded. Or maybe it was neither, only a single night of having my peace of mind shattered irreversibly, one unbearable night that changed all the following days into *afters*.

From now on, my world and that throne are intertwined. Rora doesn't want it. And if not me, who?

There is no one else.

"Fine," I relent. "I'll—"

"Violet, what in *fortune's name* is this?"

To my astonishment, Finley bursts through the door like a maelstrom, heedless of the trailing guard's protests.

Violet's entourage dips their heads in bewildered bows, while the guard stammers an apology, and through it all Violet just looks at her youngest brother, her expression withering.

"Not now, Finley—"

"Oh, don't play the mother, Violet, I beg of you." Finley's skin is flushed red with ire.

I have no idea how long he's been listening outside the door, or what I should do. Around the room, everyone but Violet appears to be feeling the same awkward uncertainty. Weight shifting, feet shuffling, attention flitting between the Danofers. Violet outranks him, yes, but he's still a prince.

"Everybody out," Violet snaps. "Finley, a word. Now."

Anybody else would quell beneath that tone, myself included, but Fin remains unmoved. I try to make my own escape, but he grabs my arm, trapping me inside while the rest flee.

I chew the inside of my cheek, for once not inclined to join him. "Fin—"

"You stay," he says, as the door clicks shut. Then, to Violet, "What are you thinking, sending Helos across enemy lines?"

Violet shakes her head. "I will not discuss this with you right this moment."

"Oh, you will. You absolutely will," Finley says, releasing my arm to advance on her. "Tell me what you could possibly be thinking."

"The same thing our father thought when he sent Wes to the Vale," she replies, crossing her arms. "The same thing you thought when you let them *all* go. It's the best chance we have."

"Oh—" Finley throws his arms in the air.

"You didn't put up such a fight then," she points out, which stings. I hardly need the reminder.

"This is different," he insists, unabashed. "You're asking him to pass as an Eradain soldier for hours in their company. We're talking about Helos, Vi. Not Rora."

"I know to whom I speak," she grits out.

"Helos!" Finley shouts, gesturing to me for emphasis, as if he cannot possibly believe she doesn't understand.

I'm starting to wonder, rather desperately, if the floor would open up so I could simply disappear. His point is plain. Rora is better at this type of thing, a fact I feel no shame in admitting. I've never been able to hide what I'm feeling the way she can. My face is too honest, too open. I know because she's chided me for it, seeming equal parts amused and exasperated, whereas more often than not, Finley has simply laughed.

He isn't laughing now.

"They will catch him," he continues, his voice low. "And they will kill him."

"You have little faith in your friend," Violet observes.

"Don't twist my words to suit your meaning. I know him far better than you."

"That is the problem," she says. "You are thinking with your heart, not with your head."

"Obviously!"

He speaks as if she is the foolish one for her approach, not he.

By the river, I love him.

"Do you believe you're up for this, Helos?" Violet asks at last, facing me head on. "If this isn't for you, tell me now, and you can go." Her gaze is piercing, her tone heavy with meaning, and I read in her question more than a reference to the task ahead. She also means the road as a whole. The risks in pursuit of reward, stepping into a role I never expected to fill. The path to take a throne, and to keep it.

"I can do it," I assure them both.

Finley looks horrified.

"Helos," he says. "It's too dangerous. Please don't do this."

Though I know it's not what he intends, his presence is having the opposite effect on me. It's the reminder I need of what's at stake, should Eradain's army discover our hiding spot and deliver that location back to their king. Fin, and all those like him.

"I'm asking you not to do this," he pleads, the words grown urgent, since he can likely read my decision upon my face.

"I'll be okay," I tell him. "I promise."

Finley's features are shattering into a thousand pieces, devastation written upon every one. After holding my gaze for an infinite span of time, he turns to his sister. "If he dies for this," he says, and I've rarely heard him sound so angry, "I will never forgive you. Do you understand?" He backs toward the exit. "I will go to my grave never forgiving you."

Hurt flashes across Violet's face, the first chink I've seen in her ever-present armor. "Fin—"

But he's already slamming the door behind him.

Only Violet and I remain, and the silence hangs heavy enough to choke on. Violet, a warrior queen if ever I've seen one, is wilting before my gaze, the tells small but visible all the same. Her head droops forward, her slender frame curling inward. For the first time, I see the strain of the burden placed upon her. A crown she was born to wear, but not this soon, and never easy.

"You understand, then. The kind of decisions that await you. And the cost." She fixes me with a look, the pain already receding in place of teaching, of purpose. "I will ensure that our troops lying in wait recognize this woman's face, so they know not to shoot. Get them to the road this evening, and General Powell will take care of the rest."

I nod, my fingers on the door.

"Helos." She scans my face, lifting her chin a little. "I'll see you when you return."

The scout's uniform has not been tailored to fit. The scratchy blue sleeves hit too low across the shoulders, while the cotton pants squeeze too tight around the thighs. Along the side, a hard patch in the shirt's inside lining must be dried blood from the poorly healing cut I found.

My fingers are ticking. Skin sweating. I've never much liked assuming other people's forms this side of the river. Somehow, it feels like giving in. Outside of the hills ringing the valley, I will myself to remain calm, trying to assemble the fragmented glimpses I received of this woman's personality into a cohesive picture. It's difficult to focus when Finley's terror and my own racing heart are blocking out most other thoughts.

I'm really doing this. These people will be dead at my hands. Unless they kill me first.

No, I can't go down that road. If Rora were here, she would tell me not to be ridiculous, even if the words were only a mask for her fear. Actually, if she were here, she would be doing this in my stead. But my sister is already crossing enemy lines abroad, so I can do it back at home, too. *Be brave like Rora.*

I inhale deeply, and the jittering subsides.

The first sign that I've found the scout's missing unit isn't the sight, but the thick smell carried on the wind. A sharp odor of unwashed bodies, doubtless the result of long travel. My hands ball into fists. Wrinkling my nose, I follow the trail into sun-dappled trees near the hills' base. Navy uniforms peek out among the foliage.

There are too many to count. Seated in small groups, chatting, pacing, napping, or playing some sort of game with stones—dozens and dozens of trained killers, all within a knife's throw of me.

Finley was right. I was mad to think I could do this.

"Tari's back," announces a voice from the mix. A few seated soldiers get to their feet and make way for the person striding through the crowd. A captain maybe, or a general, or however they rank their leaders here. I don't know how to read the uniforms. There is *so much* I don't know.

The woman is short-statured, sallow skin stretched thin across an unforgiving face. Skinny as a blade, as if the years have whittled away any cushioning or comfort, leaving only the bony remains of a weapon designed to strike. I stand at attention, remembering that much, at least, from living among soldiers.

"Report," she orders as a second person comes up just behind her, this one a bearded, bald man.

"I climbed the ridge and searched a short way beyond," I reply, the borrowed, higher voice strange to my ears. This much is true, since it's where our units found her. "The hill is one of many. There's a valley inside, and a great fort. It looks occupied."

The two appraise me without speaking, the nearby troops growing still. I work to keep my expression carefully neutral like I've watched Rora do so many times.

"This fort," says the woman. "Describe it to me."

Fortune save me. All I can do is imitate the accent as best I can and hope it lands. "It's made of huge stones, a collection of buildings surrounded by a high wall. I reckon you could fit hundreds of people inside. It's built on a hill."

I can read it on their faces and in the charged current stinging the air.

Something is wrong.

How can it *already* be wrong?

The bald man steps nearer and draws his sword. "Who are you?"

My eyebrows knit together. "What?"

He lurches forward, and white-hot pain scrapes across my leg. The fabric is torn, the tip of his blade red with blood. "Who are you?" he repeats.

The river take me, they know. *And I've scarcely said a word!* "Tari," I reply, because I must.

It's no use. My gut is screaming for me to run, but at a sharp word from the woman, soldiers have closed in around me, cutting off any chance of escape. I consider drawing Tari's sword, but my lessons with Weslyn have barely begun, and I've never, not once, been able to get through his defenses. Against a dozen, I would be dead before I nicked even one of them.

Surrounded by uniforms once again.

I cannot breathe.

"Grab her," the woman commands.

Heartbeats later, I'm caught tight between two soldiers. One arm twisted painfully behind my back, tugging at my reddened shoulders, the other gripped so firmly the skin is sure to bruise.

"I know you are an imposter," says the woman. Blood is seeping through the cut on my leg, the pain a line of fire. "I'll give you two choices. You can either die slowly or quickly. Your choice."

Time. I need time. *I cannot breathe.* "Are those the only two?" I gasp out, which earns me a fist to the gut.

The woman pauses as if to consider. "There is a third option our king reserves for people like you. Tell us what we want to know, and we'll provide safe passage across the river. A one-way trip, of course."

Panic spills over, suffocating heat, as I writhe in their grasp to no effect. My throat has grown so tight, it must surely have closed. I know it has.

I'm not going back. I can't. *I can't.*

Get them to the road.

"I'll talk!" I exclaim, changing tactics on a whim. "There's a way through the hills to the fort. A—a road. I'll tell you what you want to know. Just don't hurt me. Please!"

One of my captors loosens his grip, head tilting back. "That was easy."

"Too easy," says the other. "She's up to something."

My stomach plummets. I have to find a way to sell this, or I'm dead. There's a path before me plain as day, to make it seem less *easy,* but merciful fortune, I do not want to take it. I try to find another route, assess the situation from all angles like Rora would, but the panic has grown overwhelming, blinding, enough that my flailing mind can't hold onto the strands of reason.

"Where is the road?" the woman demands.

I can't think. I can only feel. So I take the path. "I— No, I can't. I won't."

Down comes a sword hilt, a boulder against my skull. My teeth rattle at the impact, black spots dancing across my vision. The fact that I expected this eye-watering pain does nothing to temper it.

"Careful," says the woman. "We need her conscious or we won't get answers."

"Careful gets you nowhere," the bald man retorts, raising his fist for another blow.

"Stop!" I cry, the act dropping away, becoming genuine. Foolish, really, because I've been here before and know this kind of plea to be useless, but the aching body is a stubborn thing, relentless in its attempts to get away.

He doesn't listen, of course he doesn't, and this time I black out before I can ask again.

When I come to, sprawled upon the ground, the woman leans above me, looking furious. The bald man has gone.

"Lead us there," she orders.

I would laugh, or cry, if my lungs had any air left in them.

The tiniest chance.

On the march around the base of the hills, back the way I came, all I know is pain. Pain in my head, in my leg, in my abdomen, pulsing and angry and terrifyingly familiar. Soon, the blood loss will become a problem, but if I pull in matter to stitch the wounds shut before that moment comes, I'm afraid they might notice and hurt me again. People talk more when they're in pain.

Rora will be here soon.

The thought emerges like moonlight breaking through the clouds, giving me strength. Rora will be here soon, and Finley is here already. They need me. Thoughts of them, and of General Powell's soldiers lying in wait, keep my feet moving. The promise of safety and home.

The road comes into view, the same one Weslyn and I walked so openly only a week before. I force myself not to look at the forested hills to either side, in case I give anything away. Once I feared the shifting shadows in those woods. Now I'm relying on them. *Please, let Telyan's army be there.*

When the infantry has moved nearly in sight of the valley, in the narrowest part of the road, salvation flies from the trees. First a volley of arrows raining like death overhead, then horses pounding down the slope and into the closely packed bodies. Both my captors fall with arrows in their necks, and I don't stop to look behind and see if we'll win. I set my gaze on the road and the valley before me, and I run.

Or at least, I try to run. What results is a series of lopsided sprints that end in collapse. Stumble forward, hit the ground. Push up and on, drawing toward the garrison like a beacon. Before I've gone far, I resume my natural form and desperately pull in matter from the air, stitching together the wounds I can mend, stemming the blood loss that is making my vision falter.

I'm moving faster now. Head still pounding like thunder, bile rising up my throat, but at least the cuts are temporarily healed. Behind, the fight's cacophony is arcing through the early evening shadows. Ringing steel, shouting, falling, horse hooves crashing over the earth. The instinct to stay and help and heal rises like the dying embers of a fire gasping for air, but far stronger now is the desperation to flee. Born from experience, it rages like a downpour inside, dousing the embers, urging me on.

"Helos?"

A voice from a dream, sunlight breaking through the storm. Only, it's not a dream, because somehow I've made it halfway up the hill, and Finley is there, collapsing beside me. Impossible.

"Helos!" My name is both relief and total panic. Finley reaches for me while another face swims into focus behind his, equally alarmed, warning him to be careful. Weslyn.

"Always keeping us apart," I grumble.

Then I faint.

FOURTEEN

RORA

Carolette admitted that Jol would expect her to report to him following the murder at the market. Still, I have to stand for several minutes outside the door before he permits me to enter.

Jol's private study is a close-quartered room, with paintings depicting old battles mounted between bookshelves along the dark, wood-paneled walls; their illustrated soldiers and rearing horses monitor the room with unsettling, empty eyes. Underfoot, a massive area rug, so thick and soft that my shoes create shallow imprints when I stand still for too long, is an intricately woven collage of blues, teals, grays, and glimmering golds—all the colors of the sea.

Most surprising to me is the polished wooden piano in the corner, near an elaborately inlaid hearth. I've only seen such an instrument once before, back in Castle Roanin in Queen Raenen's carefully preserved parlor. No one ever played it.

"There you are," says Jol, as if I haven't been waiting. "Shut the door behind you."

The last and only time I saw my half brother was at the prison compound, when I took Helos's place. Standing across from me now, he looks the same as he did before. The olive skin and tall stature that Helos and I share, though Jol's more muscular. Thick raven hair parted far to the side, a prominent nose that sits between vivid green eyes. By no means my twin, but enough of a likeness to Helos that one need only stand the two side by side to suspect they're related.

As before, the resemblance is uncanny, and I don't like it. The sight of him, this stark reminder of my mother's life prior to Father, Helos, and me, elicits a slew of uncomfortable emotions. Uncertainty for whether sharing family means I owe him a degree of sympathy. Resentment of the guilt his actions make me feel, as if that kinship makes him my responsibility to control, contain. A tiny, frustrating curiosity to understand how on earth he came to be this way, the blocks that built the man, and the pointless regret of what will forever be a what-if.

Then I remember Helos forced into a cage, his bleary expression bleeding into panic when he saw me take his place. King Gerar's hands on Wes's shoulders as he said, *Go safely, Son.* The bone shards pricking my bare feet and the grating's grizzled taste as I fought to escape the shed, and more recently, the aspen forest walker with barely enough strength left to flee.

The curiosity dissipates. I don't need to know him. I just need to stop him.

"Well?" Jol asks, folding his arms as he leans against a bookshelf. His pale blue collared shirt flutters a bit, caught in the breeze sweeping in through an open window.

"Forgive me, Your Majesty," I reply, dipping into a bow. "I searched for the culprit but could not find them."

Jol gazes idly at a painting. "One of those rebel rats, no doubt." When I don't respond, he glances over. "Don't look so shocked, Carolette. Even you are not infallible."

I straighten my features into a more neutral set. Do Horan and the rest know he's aware of their existence? "I can search again, sir," I hear myself offer.

"The Watch is out already. Come." He nods to a dark, wooden desk set near the window, its legs heavy and simply wrought. "I'd like your opinion, while you're here."

I join him by the desk, marveling that Carolette could be so valued—until I examine the parchment sprawled on top. Understanding dawns, and my insides constrict unpleasantly.

"Tell me," he says. "The southern towns. How are they constructed?"

I stare down at the map of Telyan, which is studded with small, colored pins in a few different places. Briarwend. The region below. What do they mean? "Sir?"

"This one here, for example," he says, placing a finger on Poldat, the fishing village on Telyan's southernmost coast. "Are the buildings made of wood? Stone?"

"Largely brick," I reply, having no idea where this is headed. "And some wood."

"Built on a river, yes?"

The answer is riven into the map for both of us to see. "Yes."

"This one?" Jol moves his hand northwest to Briarwend, where Seraline and her family live. Six weeks ago, I was worrying over her little sister making the sign to ward off bad fortune.

It almost feels like a different life.

"Stone," I say, nerves humming beneath my skin.

"And here?" he asks, pointing to an empty stretch of land to the southeast. No city or town appears on the map, only hills.

I look up at him.

I know the secret hidden in those hills, though I've never been. Fendolyn's Keep, the historic garrison where Weslyn was sure Finley and the rest of those evacuated from Roanin would have fled. No one outside of Telyan is meant to know its location. Even I don't, not precisely.

Jol's eyes remain fixed on mine, intent, like a wildcat's. I'm guessing this must be a test for Carolette's newfound loyalties, at least in part. After all, she's already turned once. I have no idea whether or not she's told him about the Keep, but then, if she had, why would he be asking this now?

"Forgive me, sir," I apologize again, playing for time. "I don't understand."

His face remains composed, expression cool, as the silence stretches long. "Perhaps I am mistaken, and that land is like the coast east of Grovewood, or the slopes north of Briarwend," he says at last. "Empty. Undeveloped."

I nod, relieved to be back on safer ground. "They're all empty, yes. Few people visit those regions, unless they want to do some hill walking or dip their feet into the water."

Jol taps the parchment with his palm, then nods. "Very well," he says, and I feel myself begin to breathe a little easier. Until he adds, "Have you followed up on Ember Street?"

Yet again, I have no idea what he's talking about, and a small bud of panic sprouts from my core. Maybe I was stupid to think I could impersonate Carolette so easily. I might only be grasping at the strings of what has been a lost cause from the start.

Get a grip.

"Not yet, sir." I speak right over the doubts before they grow deafening, because I did not come here to lose.

Jol holds my gaze a long moment. Without reacting, he walks slowly toward the window, his back to me. "Many have cautioned me against welcoming you into my court," he says, running his fingertips along the spotless glass until it smudges. "In this, I believe they underestimate your value, as Gerar did. Your information has been beneficial, your labors fruitful. I have never felt the need to doubt you." He faces me once more. "So now I will caution *you*. Do not give me a reason to."

"You can trust me," I reply with confidence. Carolette is many things, but easily intimidated isn't one of them.

Jol laughs quietly. "I deal in facts and observations, not sentiment. And the fact is, Carolette, you are hedging on Ember Street. Report to me by the end of the week."

There's a dismissal woven into the words, so I bow my head and make for the exit, fighting the urge to run. Though he didn't articulate the consequences for failure out loud, his meaning is clear enough. I'm eager to be gone, and almost at the door, when he speaks again.

"Remind me."

I swivel to find him still before the glass, his face partially cast into shadow with the sunlight bright behind. The effect is somewhat unnerving.

"The girl, Rora. You said she takes three forms. The lynx, the hawk." He counts them off on two fingers, then tilts his head. "What was the third?"

Apprehension roots me to the spot. At the sound of my name on his tongue, at the question so conveniently timed. Though his tone is casual as discussing a change in weather, his gaze remains singularly pointed.

"Mouse," I admit, reluctantly, since apparently Carolette has already robbed me of this leverage.

"Thank you," he says, somewhat quieter. "I must have forgotten."

I swallow. "Of course."

"Remember," he continues, and the edge reenters his tone. "Any sign of her or her brother, and you bring them straight to me, straightaway. No one else. And none of your interrogation tactics first. Understood?"

I nod.

"Go."

I sweep from the room and shut the door behind me, grateful for the barrier as I force back the feathers jutting up beneath my skin.

So Jol is expecting us to come, and openly. I'm not all that surprised, given the note he left and the certain measure of arrogance—or delusion—he seems to possess. I have no idea what he would do if he knew I'm already here. Kill me, according to Wes, and he's definitely more the expert on royal behavior and matters of succession.

Then why didn't he kill me in the Vale when he had the chance?

I see no reason to waste talent unnecessarily.

I could almost laugh. If he really believes I'd take his side even now, after *that,* he's in for a rude awakening.

Around the corner, and the hallway empties into a spiral staircase curving steeply up and down. I climb to the fourth level, my eyes straining in the watery light filtering in through slitted, vertical windows. I must be in one of the turrets.

Thanks to Penelope's ministrations, Carolette had provided rough directions for how to locate her sleeping quarters; unlike I had in Roanin, she's managed to secure a room inside the castle itself. Convenient for my purposes, if rather annoying. By the time I find the wooden door, I'm gratified to learn her hall is sparsely decorated and badly lit, at least. I make a mental note to start memorizing the castle's layout today and fish Carolette's small key out of my pocket.

The moment I'm inside with the latch refastened, I do a quick sweep to verify I'm alone. Her room is a simple affair, ten or twelve paces across, with a squat wardrobe and compact wooden desk against the far wall, a quilt draped over the brass bed, and a deep purple rug centered between eggshell-white walls. She's left the single glass window open, along with the shutters, so that the rhythmic hum of the waves drifts through. Fortunately, a small washroom is attached, so I won't have to share.

I unearth a bundle of matches in Carolette's bedside table and light the two oil lamps, drawing the wooden shutters closed. Probably no one could see inside at this height, but better to take no chances.

Safe from onlookers, I release my hold on the borrowed matter and regain my natural form, flexing my fingers with relief. Only a couple of hours have passed, not enough for me to begin feeling the strain of holding the shift, but I want to conserve my energy as much as possible. All the acting skills in the world would do me no good if I could no longer maintain Carolette's form.

My first order of business is finding out what in fortune's name I'm meant to be doing on Ember Street. I can't ruin this role, not until I have time to gather intel for Violet. One bit of reassurance at least—I'm growing convinced that Jol's questions regarding my animal forms were purely coincidence. If he suspected the Carolette before him were an imposter, I cannot imagine he would allow that person to simply walk away.

So, Ember Street. I shed the navy jacket and throw it on the bed, glad to be rid of the association. I half-expect the desk drawers to be empty, but luck may be on my side today after all, because Carolette's work is inside. She's filled an entire folder with potential residences and hideouts for magical people still living in Oraes, and beside each name, she's written either LU, FA, FD, or

VB. Other parchment contains tips she's received from citizens eager to keep their city safe by reporting suspected shifters in their midst. Penelope and Horan are both listed in the former, the letters FA having been crossed out and replaced with LU. My back tenses when Merisol appears as well, along with her sisters and two people with the same last name that might be her parents. The ones Merisol hasn't seen in weeks. Carolette has scrawled an LU beside all five.

By the time I locate an address with Ember Street among the pages, I've started grabbing handfuls of hair, frustrated. Four names are written there, and next to them, underlined, the word *sympathizers*. Which could mean any number of things. I'll have to—

Someone pounds a fist against the door.

I'm up and flying for the discarded jacket, pulling matter from the air and changing my form as I go. The wood rattles on its hinges before I've finished shifting, which is enough to send mouse whiskers shooting through my face. If I hadn't locked the door, the ruse would have been up already.

"What?" I shout, struggling to fasten the buttons with trembling fingers.

"What do you mean, what?" barks a man's voice. "Open the door!"

My hands falter. What if I figured wrong, and Jol guessed my secret after all?

"I'm not opening any door with you howling like that," I force out, trying to channel Carolette's confidence and short temper.

"Open it!" he says again, and his voice breaks on the words.

Well. I doubt Jol would send a crying man to apprehend me, and in any case, I'm starting to fear the attention his continued efforts might incur. I fling open the door and shove one quivering hand inside my pocket, clutching the knob with the other in a vice grip. "What is it?"

The man, whom I recognize as one of Carolette's party from the market, looks a mess. Uniform askew, amber liquor bottle in hand. Tears are streaking down his warm brown face, and the whites of his eyes are bloodshot.

"Dead," he says, more like a gasp.

It isn't hard to guess whom he's talking about. I say nothing.

"She's *dead*!" he repeats, as if I haven't heard him.

"What do you want me to do about it?" I ask roughly. "It's done."

His murky gaze blazes with ire. "She spoke up for you," he mutters, which is hardly an endorsement for Carolette's character considering the dead woman was part of the City Watch. "You should be out there, catching the bastard that did it. You don't even—"

"That was your job as much as mine," I retort. "And you lost him. Or her."

"These *people*," he says with a hiccup. An attendant rounds the corner, spots the drunken man, and flees after a fearful glance in our direction. "They've no sense of honor. These dirty, thieving—"

"Are you finished blaming everyone else for your problems? I have work to do." Anger is fusing sharply with disbelief. His king sends magical people to the slaughter, and he thinks *they're* the guilty ones for fighting back?

I start to shut the door in his face, but he blocks it with a hand.

"Listen." He staggers forward a step, then rights himself, drink splattering across the floor. I jump back with raised hands, barely missing the trajectory. "When are you going out next? I heard something about En—Ember Street. I'm coming with you."

Unease pricks my spine. "You're in no state to go anywhere."

"Let's kill 'em," he slurs, as if I haven't spoken.

"What?"

"It won't be hard."

"You can't do that!"

"What's it matter?" he demands, scraping a hand across his mouth. "It's not right, carting them off to live out their days in the Vale." He speaks as if reciting a decree. "Not when they come for our own. King's too lenient. I say, one of theirs for one of ours."

My grip has tightened on the doorknob. "Lenient?"

"'Course, trapped in the Vale, they're likely good as dead, anyway," he says, too caught up in his own narrative to notice me. "Maybe that's—"

"Get out of here." My breath is coming heavy now, too much to hide. I can feel the lynx claws threatening to break through.

"I'm going t—"

"Get out!" I slam the door in his face, this time not caring who might hear. My head is swimming. Dizziness dots my vision. King's too lenient, live out their days in the Vale—do they not know about the prison? Those lists, Ember Street—is that what the City Watch believes it's doing? Sending the people they don't want here into sanctuary?

I lock the door, stumble into the washroom, and pour water from a half-empty pitcher into a copper bowl. Splash the cool water on my face, splutter when some gets caught up my nose. Between Jol's easy confidence and the way Wes described the Eradain mentality, I've been under the impression that Jol had the full support of his human subjects. A unified front. So why keep the prison a secret?

I need to figure out who else is in the dark.

Pushing off from the sink, I grab the papers from the desk and make my way out of the castle. The sky has dimmed to dusk, and though I take a couple of wrong turns before arriving at the grimy shop, at least I've spent enough time as a king's spy to learn how to avoid being tailed.

Down in the catacombs, Kal sneers when he sees me. "Problem already?"

"Yes," I reply, brandishing the stack of files in his direction. "I need to talk to her."

On the floor of her lonely chamber, Carolette is sitting against the rough wall opposite Kal, who's apparently keeping watch. Her head's hanging low between slumped shoulders, her loose hair and stained clothing a grisly portrait.

Kal jumps up and kicks one of Carolette's bare soles. "Wake up. You're needed."

Carolette stirs and pulls her feet in to avoid further blows. Even knowing what she's responsible for, or at least a fraction of it, I'm rattled by the state of her face. Dried blood along her hairline and beneath her nose, eyelids swollen half-shut, a purpling bruise spread across her left cheek. I don't know if that's good or bad, to feel sympathy for someone who has wrought so much suffering upon others.

I imagine what Helos would say if he were here and let his words shape my own. "She needs water. Ice if you can get it. Or a salve."

"You're mad," Kal replies with a firm shake of the head. "She's our prisoner, not our guest."

"Wouldn't you hope for some shred of mercy if you were being held prisoner?"

Kal's face falls, and he takes a threatening step toward me, then another, fists bunched at his sides.

"My brother was a prisoner," he says in a low voice. "And they murdered him. Slowly."

At the reminder, I picture Helos back in the cage, what I would do if anyone ever treated him like they did Kal's brother, and find I have no response.

"Listen to me," Kal presses, sensing this. "Now is not the time to feel pity. She doesn't deserve it."

If Helos really were here, he might point out there's always a time to feel pity. More likely, he'd just walk away from Kal and fetch the supplies himself, uninterested in debating further when there's a patient in need of healing. But I'm not Helos, and to be honest, I think Kal may have a point. Anyway, I have a job to do.

I skirt around him and crouch before Carolette, who hasn't commented on our exchange. She meets my gaze when I say her name, but her eyes remain guarded.

"These letters," I begin, pointing to the pairs. *LU, FA, FD, VB.* "What do they stand for?"

"No salve for my cuts, then?" she rasps. "Pity. I had so much riding on you."

"Answer the question."

"For the life of me," she says, clearly reaching for the only weapon she has left, "I cannot figure out why Gerar thought you had value."

I shrug. "Maybe it's the fact that I'm here, asking the questions, and you're there, the prisoner meant to answer."

She huffs a laugh, mere wisps of sound. "Some mercy."

That stings. But I won't be deterred. "The letters," I repeat, holding one of the sheets close to her face.

Carolette worries her bottom lip, and Kal moves closer.

"Location unknown," she bites out. "Found alive. Found dead. Vale bound. You won't be—"

"About Ember Street," I barrel ahead, eager to end this reunion as quickly as I'm able. "You've written *sympathizers,* but nothing else. What have they done? What are you meant to do with them?"

"You won't be able to pull this off." Carolette's voice has dropped even lower, her upturned mouth mocking. "People will see I'm acting funny. They'll suspect. And that King Jol, he's clever, you can't—"

"What did they do?" I ask again, growing impatient.

She spears me with a look that's pure hatred. "They helped some scum escape the city and are suspected of trying to win others over to their cause. Other humans," she clarifies. "He—we mean to make an example of them."

"An example?" I echo, my stomach hollow.

Carolette smiles without humor. "The castle gate."

No. I recoil at her answer, my fingers crushing the papers' edges. I refuse to contribute in any way to that grotesque spectacle. "Just one more question. You're sending people to the Vale. What happens to them once they cross the river?"

A crease forms between her brows. "What?"

"When they cross the river. Where do they go?"

She starts to shake her head, then grimaces. "How should I know? Into the wild like all the rest."

So the drunken man wasn't the only one.

"Thank you for your help," I say, pushing to my feet. "Most informative. Try not to die before my next round of questioning."

Kal's eyebrows lift, but I'm already storming out of the room.

Back in the main chamber, a dozen or so people are spread among the tables or cushions on the floor. Though kept soft, their voices still rebound off the barren walls.

"What is it?" asks Merisol, rising when she spots my approach. Her younger sisters pause their game of small stones.

"Jol. He—oh, your parents! It's good news, I think," I add hurriedly, seeing the panic overtake her face. "Look."

Her sisters bound to their feet as I spread the papers across a table and find the one with their names. "FA—found alive. It's been crossed out and replaced with 'location unknown.' I bet they're in hiding, same as you."

Merisol grabs the parchment.

"Then why aren't they *here*?" asks the middle child, while the youngest simply watches Merisol. "They know the way."

"Maybe it isn't safe to leave where they are," Merisol says with a level of cheer I can tell is forced. Her hand is pressing the list so hard, the veins are jutting out beneath the skin. "They'll come when they can."

"Good news?" Gemma asks, coming to the table.

Though I know they deserve more time to sink into the relief, an inexplicable sense of urgency has been building in me for the better part of an hour, and I can't keep the next words in. "Listen. What do you know about the prison west of the river?"

Merisol's attention has shifted back to her sisters, but Gemma looks at me blankly. "What prison?"

And fortune's sake, in this moment, I can't decide which is worse—a place like that being widely known and condoned, or the idea that it could be hidden so easily from so many for so long.

It makes me wonder what else he might be hiding.

"The war against Telyan and Glenweil," I try again, struggling for calm as I search for the right questions to ask. "That's common knowledge, right?"

"Of course."

"And what reasons has Jol given for invading them?"

Gemma rubs her forehead. "It's been all over the leaflets. The southern realms have refused to ban magical people from their borders, which he argues works against Eradain's *noble* efforts to prevent another Rupturing." She conveys the last in a dry tone. "Supposedly, their resistance endangers our lives."

"There's also the Silent End," Solet puts in, joining our group. "That's their name for the Throes. Jol claims that rooting out magic is the best way to eradicate the illness, and as such, continent-wide compliance is essential."

Once again, I send a silent *thank you* to the Danofers, who have never pursued this line of thinking as a potential cure—even if they also haven't worked as hard as they could have to curtail this growing suspicion among the populace. "The Throes—the Silent End," I amend, glancing at Gemma. "Is it bad here?"

Her expression sobers. "It's bad. People don't talk about it much in the streets. The king encourages a more . . . stoic disposition." She pauses to place an arm around Merisol, who has sent her sisters back to their game. "'Magic is best kept out of sight,' you know? But it's here. They send the bodies of the dead out to sea."

Her words call another's to mind—panicked Gerig, uttering something about eliminating magic to protect themselves, how he hadn't signed up for . . . What? Soldiers, civilians, the City Watch—

He knew about the war, but not the prison or the campaign to take the Vale. None of them do.

Jol smoothed the chaos. That's what Wes told Helos and me back in Minister Mereth's palace, to explain why the Eradain people adored their young king after his father's more volatile reign.

Maybe it's time to change that.

"If I tell you Jol built a prison in the Vale, one for rounding up magical beings and murdering them—if we made that information public—how do you think the people here would react?"

Merisol and Gemma look horrified.

"How do you know this?" Solet asks, their expression grim.

I fold my arms over my chest. "Because I was there."

Steeling myself against the memories' bitter taste, I describe the prison's layout and operations—before we destroyed it. As I speak, others in the chamber drift over, dwindling conversations falling quiet in the face of my recounting. This group is larger than the six who planned the kidnapping, but for once my insides don't constrict quite so much under the attention of so many people. I want them all to know, down to the tiniest detail.

"This might be enough to make some of the humans uncomfortable," Horan says, when I've finished. He nudges his horn-rimmed glasses farther up his nose. "Exile is one thing, but mass murder, and not even in battle . . ."

Might. Some. Why not definitive, why not all?

"And they might not appreciate being lied to," adds an elderly shifter whose name I can't recall.

Penelope places her hands on her hips. "You know the humans won't care, Horan. Not all of them. They might even be grateful."

"Some is better than none," Horan insists, laying a palm flat upon the table. "Some is enough to create division among the people." His focus switches back to me. "This is big, Rora."

I think of the two men I saw whispering behind the City Watch members' backs, the young girl with her hands curled into fists. Maybe division has taken root here already, just behind closed doors, as Gemma said.

"How do we do it?" she asks. At her side, Merisol has rolled her shoulders back. "How do we get the information out like you said?"

A new sensation kindles in my chest. Something like warmth. I'm not used to working in a group, to admitting that I need help and relying on others to make the plan with me. No attacks, no shaming. Just teamwork. First Peridon and Andie, now Gemma, Solet, Merisol, and the rest.

Not only teamwork. Friends—or the beginnings of some.

"Leaflets have the farthest reach," says the elderly shifter.

Penelope throws up a hand. "The press is in Jol's pocket."

"The press also wants people to pick up its leaflets," Solet points out mildly.

"Would they take a story from Carolette?" I ask. "On behalf of Jol."

Horan shakes his head. "Word would get back to the king that you were the one to hand over the story. You would lose your position there."

"I'll lose it anyway," I reply, sliding Carolette's lists across the table. "I'm giving these to you all—use them as you will. Carolette is meant to be doing a raid on Ember Street, something about bringing a family of sympathizers to the castle to be murdered. I won't do it." I exchange a glance with Solet, thinking of Telyan. "Although it's true, I'd rather not lose my position this soon."

"I'll do it," Merisol says, her voice quiet but firm. "We can try an anonymous drop. If that doesn't work, we regroup, try a different approach. Now we just need to write the story."

"What if we print an illustration instead?" Gemma suggests. "Maybe an image would be more powerful than words."

My spine straightens.

Finley has argued the same to Helos and me several times in the past, when he drew political illustrations for Roanin's leaflets. Hearing his words echo in an ancient tomb miles away, spoken as a means of sedition against Eradain's king—I exhale softly. Finley would love this.

At the thought, homesickness crashes in, like a physical weight upon my chest. For my brother, whom I haven't seen in two weeks. For Finley, whom I haven't seen in six. This time of year has always been Fin's favorite, and spending days on Castle Roanin's estate made it easy to see why. Stifled by stale darkness underground, I conjure the fantasy in my mind: the babbling stream wends through gardens of marigolds in fresh bloom, clusters of blue hyssop stalks sweetening the autumn air. Fallen hickory leaves dust the old carriage house's roof with painted gold, while the forested mountains behind prepare for winter's clutch to cap them in snow.

With the heartache growing too loud, I wrap the memories around me like a blanket, drawing strength from their warmth. What I would give to be there now, fresh air in my lungs and Helos and Finley at my side.

"I'll have it ready by the morning," Gemma says, touching my arm. I blink rapidly, unsure how much I've missed. "Describe the prison to me again, clear as you can, and I'll draw it."

Though I'm as far away from home as ever, her offer makes me feel a little less alone.

I smile back.

That night, I return to the castle and follow other staffers and uniforms into the dining quarters underground. Few seem eager to talk to me, and I'm all too glad to eat in moody silence while keeping an ear out for any signs of dissension. I don't detect much—until the topic of war surfaces halfway through the meal. To my surprise, while most of the staffers speak of its necessity with passion, others respond with skepticism or muttered disapproval.

It's a start.

I wait for the safety of night before shedding my uniform, pulling from the air around me, and shifting to mouse. This is my first evening sleeping in the enemy's halls, and I don't intend to waste it.

Fine-spun runners help to muffle my footsteps as I scurry past footmen in red coattails patrolling the corridors and chambermaids dousing wide candles and oil lamps. My vision is painfully weak in this form, so to navigate, I have to rely on memory, sounds, smells, and my whiskers' ability to parse vibrations in the air. Fortunately, the darkened hallways seem quieter this time of night, almost peaceful. I reach Jol's private study undisturbed.

Piano music drifts through the fastened door.

Of course, it would be just my luck that the room is still occupied at this hour. I crawl through the crack and hurry to the opposite end, away from the piano and the hungry fire crackling in the hearth. The slow melody reverberates loudly in my tiny mouse ears, but my vision remains too blurred to make out who's playing. Jol, I suspect, but I'd like to be sure.

When the music swells, I use my mouse claws to climb a bookshelf's grainy wood, retreating into the pocket of darkness sunken between books. Knowing the risk but feeling bold all the same, I pull from my core and shift to goshawk, keeping still as a statue in the heavy shadows.

It is Jol, gaze lowered, head bent over the keys. Darkness cloaks this side of the room, but the space around him overflows with warm light—from mounted oil lamps, moon-white candles set atop the piano, the fire blazing in the hearth. Just as well I took shelter on this side; no one could sneak up on him there, however small.

Dressed in sleep attire, losing himself to music, he looks far more man than monster. Less intimidating than in our conversation earlier today. Frustration churns in my gut—that he would choose to be here of all places, on this night, at this hour. At the things he's done and will continue to do. That he would turn his mind toward such wrongdoing and choose to smooth the path to bigotry rather than opposing it.

Soon, though, satisfaction creeps in, because I finally feel I've found a way to hold him accountable for his actions. Not only by strengthening his opponents down south, but also those right here in Oraes. A task too big for me to handle on my own—but I'm not alone, not anymore.

And if they know already? Wes had asked the morning we said goodbye. *Know and condone it?*

We're about to find out.

The music stops abruptly, and my heart fires through my chest. But Jol's only reaching for a notebook on top of the piano, jotting something down before dropping the pen and running a hand over his face. He remains still for the span of several breaths before he lowers his hand, and the music begins again.

The scare was enough to jolt me to my senses, so I shed some borrowed matter and shrink back to mouse, my body chilled. I want to know what brought him here when he could be sleeping, whether I could use it to my advantage. For now, all I can do is wait until he finally brings the song to an end, douses the lights, and rests a hand briefly atop the doorknob before slipping from the room.

I remain frozen until his footsteps have retreated from earshot. Then I crawl to the floor, shift to human, and get to work.

FIFTEEN

HELOS

I wake to hazy morning light and a bed that isn't my own, the thin mattress less giving against my aching body. For a while, I lay staring up at the vaulted ceiling, where wooden beams arch beneath stone the color of storm clouds, and try to patch together the night before.

Memories surface in fragments. Flickers of consciousness while someone, maybe multiple someones, half carried me to the hospital. Bren tending to my wounds after I released the borrowed matter and telling me I'll heal without issue. Weslyn with blood streaked all over his clothing—mine?—staying long enough to learn the verdict before placing a hand on Finley's shoulder and vanishing abruptly. Finley—

My head screams in protest when I lift it from the pillow. Disappointment settles in my gut like stones. The seat he dragged beside my bed, where he sat watching me with wide, frightened eyes, is empty.

At some point during the restless night, Violet herself came to thank me and deliver the news. A decisive victory for Telyan. Two of the enemy taken captive, the rest killed before word of our location could spread. Our own losses kept small, thirty-seven to their two hundred. A triumph, she told me, but all I heard was a massacre.

Pointlessly, I glance at the chair again.

"Feeling better?" Bren shuffles into view and helps me sit up against the pillow. This morning, his face looks prematurely lined, his cool gray eyes and wide mouth kind but notably concerned.

"He left a couple of hours ago," he adds in a softer voice, nodding to the empty chair. "The queen's orders. He wasn't well."

"Why? What happened?" I swing my bare feet onto the floor, wincing as the movement pulls on the sword cut, but Bren stops me with a palm to the shoulder.

"Nothing too alarming. Just a fever, and his head was hurting bad."

Well, that makes two of us. Still, a fever—there's nothing "just" about it. Not when it comes to the Throes. "I should check on him," I say, as much to myself as to Bren.

"Let him sleep," he suggests, pushing me back down again when I start to rise. "Stay a moment. I want to talk to you."

My brow creases. "If you're referring to Fi—Prince Finley—"

"No." He holds up a hand. "I'm talking about you."

The words send a trickle of nerves along my spine. I work to keep my expression carefully blank.

"Last night, when I was assessing the damage, I noticed some—scarring. Couldn't have been from yesterday, but it does not look particularly old." Bren pauses, peering at me closely, and sighs. "Helos, I know I'm your boss, but I like to think I'm also a friend. If you need help, you must tell me."

"What do you mean, help?" I ask, the pitch of my voice rising traitorously.

"I will try to put this delicately." He pinches the bridge of his nose. "Is anybody—hurting you? I know there are some who are frightened of shifters. Or are you seeing someone, perhaps? Someone prone to violence?"

"Of course not," I reply, nerves spiraling into alarm. I tug at my shirtsleeves as if that will undo the damage already done. "Why would you think that?"

"The nature of the marks speaks to physical abuse. Quite severe," he states bluntly, abandoning the attempts at delicacy. "Helos, I know you didn't do this to yourself. I heard, as well, of the way you lashed out at that tall fellow, Broden. Quite unlike you, and I thought . . ."

"Thought what?" I demand, like a challenge.

"Well." His forehead creases. He looks uncomfortable, but

resolute. "An incident like that, or several, can stay with a person, as you know. That is to say, it can change them. And sometimes people who experience violence may themselves—"

"You've got it wrong," I interject, launching to my feet despite the way that makes my head spin. Panic is rearing its head in full force. "What you saw was a—a singular thing. It's in the past. I'm fine now." I scratch the back of my head, then run my hands through my hair. Itching to leave, to do something, *anything,* other than spend more time talking about this.

Bren reaches for my hand and covers it with both of his own. "Are you?"

"Yes," I insist, pulling free. "I—thank you for your concern, Bren. You're a good friend." This time when I inch toward the exit, he doesn't stop me. "I should go."

He nods, his hands folded loosely upon his lap. "I hope you know you can talk to me. If you ever want to."

"I know." I force a small smile, which fades as a new possibility drifts to the surface. "Who else was there, when you—" I pause to gather breath. "Did you tell anyone?"

Bren just looks at me, his countenance so sad I cannot stand it. "No one, Helos. I examined you alone."

Relief sweeps through me, like a sweet draft of cider on a cold winter's day. "Thanks, Bren. I'll see you later for my shift."

"You should rest—"

But I'm already gone, limping out of the hospital and toward the Officers' Hall. Fever and what might be a migraine . . . I climb straight to Finley's floor, turning over remedies in my head even as I feel the leg wound start to seep through the bandages. No matter. Helpfully, the corridor is empty, so no one asks questions as I knock on his door twice in quick succession.

When there's no response, I turn the handle myself.

I'm not sure what I expected to find, but it wasn't this. Finley curled up in bed, huddled beneath the covers, with Weslyn lying atop the blanket opposite him. One arm bent beneath his head, collared shirt wrinkled, Weslyn is looking at Fin with an unmasked expression that, for once, I'm able to interpret without trouble.

Misery.

His eyes find mine in the doorway, and the wall goes up. Emotion smoothed into a studiously neutral portrait. Moving slowly, Weslyn extricates his arm from under Finley's outstretched hand and rolls off the bed, following me out into the hallway. The door clicks shut behind him.

"He's just fallen asleep," Weslyn says in an undertone, leaning back against the wall with loosely folded arms.

My foot scrapes the linoleum floor. "Sorry. I didn't mean to interrupt."

Weslyn runs a hand along his forehead. With some concern, the healer in me notes how the skin has darkened beneath his eyes, as if he hasn't slept properly for days. "Shouldn't you be resting?" he asks.

My brow lifts. "Shouldn't you?"

He looks at me a long moment.

"Come back tomorrow," he says, shoulders slumping a little. "I know he'll want to see that you're okay."

Though the words hold a clear dismissal, I'm surprised to hear real sympathy in his tone. Maybe that's why I simply nod and walk away.

"Helos," he calls softly, when I've only gone a couple of steps. I twist to see him watching me carefully, gaze searching, as if working out a puzzle. "You are okay?"

The question and the memories it revives from last night—Weslyn hauling me across the Keep while Finley clung to my side, panicked—chip at the resentment I've harbored toward him for weeks.

"I'm fine," I reply, unexpectedly touched. "And thanks, by the way. For helping me get to Bren."

Weslyn nods. "It's a shame," he says, and when I open my mouth to argue, his curls up in the corner. "I rather liked that shirt."

For what might be the first time ever, we smile at the same joke.

"You'll live," I declare the next morning, once I verify that Naethan's wounded arm is healing well. Despite Bren's objections, I pulled myself to the hospital an hour before my shift even started, seeking distraction.

"Will you?" Naethan asks dryly. I've been limping as I maneuver around the crates on which I made him sit, to stop his pacing.

"Most likely." In truth, the sword cut stings and keeps leaking through the bandages. But my head feels better, my hands calmer, and Bren's questioning remains safely tucked away in a back corner of my mind. "This would go faster if you'd sit still."

Naethan does as I request, though he ducks his head a bit. "Don't like hospitals," he says, his voice quieting.

"Bad experience when you were younger?" I apply a thin layer of healer's balm over the raw flesh.

"Try many," he replies, and my hands pause in the middle of securing the fresh bandage. Naethan shrugs with his uninjured arm. "I've been good for a while. Listen, Helos," he goes on gently, before I can question the nature of his ailment. "Next time you try to be a hero, bring backup."

I nod, moved by his concern even though the circumstances made asking for help impossible. The precise details of my involvement in the valley ambush have been kept quiet, per Violet's concern that someone might harass me if they learned I'm a shifter. Regardless, word that I played a pivotal role seems to have spread throughout the garrison like wildfire.

I'm sure it didn't help to have Telyan's elder prince hefting my semiconscious, bloody body across the grounds for all to see.

Either way, I've already noticed new recognition in the eyes of people I've never met, nodding my way or patting my shoulder or smiling appreciatively. It makes me uncomfortable, to be praised for bringing about more than two hundred deaths. But I remember my resolution to make more allies who might in turn be more receptive to Rora's work, and I hold my tongue.

"Incoming." Naethan gets to his feet, inclining his head to the figure striding toward us.

Finley. He looks well this morning, thank fortune, sharp in a cobalt blue shirt that brings out his eyes.

"Naethan," Fin greets, before his attention switches to me. He falters a bit. "Helos. You're looking better."

Naethan makes his exit, glancing back with a rather prodding expression.

"I feel better," I reply, shaking my head once at Naethan.

Finley nods, his slender hand twisting his walking stick. "Good," he says. "That's good."

Neither of us speaks as I clean up from tending to Naethan's arm.

"How's your head?" I ask, just as Finley says in a rush, "I need to talk to you."

I blink at him. "What?"

Finley combs his fingers through his hair, roughing it up even further as his eyes search mine. "You see, I—"

"Your Royal Highness should be resting."

Out of nowhere, Tomas appears at our sides, his tone laden with disapproval. When Finley tightens his mouth and looks away, Tomas signals wordlessly that I should leave. At least there's little sign of concern for my well-being in his expression; Bren must not have shared his additional findings with his husband yet. I feel a twinge of gratitude.

"Sir," he presses.

"I told you, I'm perfectly well," Finley mutters, studying the ceiling. "Helos and I are simply having an—honest conversation."

Adrenaline kisses my skin.

How can you expect me to be honest with you, when you won't be honest with me?

"With respect, sir, that can wait," Tomas replies, and I'm torn between a desire to side with his healer's stance or shove him out the nearest door. "You suffered a migraine all of yesterday. And your fever has only just broken."

"As I said, I'm better now." Finley frowns.

"You won't be if you continue to inundate yourself with activity. All these outings, your riding—"

"I'm going to have symptoms regardless. What difference does it make?"

"Please, sir." Tomas takes a single step toward Finley. "There's a chance overstimulation leads to more than physical discomfort.

For all we know, the added stress could be lowering your body's defenses. Your health might decline more rapidly than it otherwise would."

A fist closes around my heart. Decision made.

"It's not a bad idea to take it easy, Fi—sir," I amend in Tomas's presence.

Finley looks betrayed. "Don't you want to hear what I've come to say?"

Yes. Merciful fortune, I do.

"Of course," I tell him, in a strained voice. "But if it makes your headaches, everything, worse . . ."

"So what?" Fin demands. "Isn't that my decision to make?"

His expression is pleading with me to take his side, but I can't, not when his health is at stake. "I'm sorry," I murmur. "I think you should do as Tomas suggests. We'll talk later today. I promise."

For a horrible stretch of time, Fin just stares at the knuckles whitening where he grips the walking stick. His body has stiffened with anger—even I can see it.

He leaves without another word, and the hurt in his eyes haunts me all the way through the end of my shift. *It's for the best,* I try to tell myself. Doesn't work.

Throughout my morning rounds, I dole out the first few doses of the lyrroot infusion I'm hoping may temper some general discomfort. Tomas looks on in interest, thin-rimmed glasses sliding down the bridge of his nose. I use willow bark to bring down fevers, eucalyptus to ease inflamed tissue in the joints, the peppermint I've found particularly effective at reducing tension in the head. I set a farmer's broken arm and soothe an elderly woman's rattling cough. When I'm done, I bring a salve to Willa, the cook I assisted with cleaning duty two days ago, remembering the hand she kept clutching to her lower back. She pats my face in that same motherly way, and I pretend not to notice the green-eyed cadet I kissed sitting a few tables away, trying to catch my eye; the need to be held and feel wanted is less pressing in the daylight, and right now, I'm mainly interested in swapping green eyes for blue.

My shift over, I try to check on the prisoners being held underground, as I'd like to tend to any who may be injured. Tari as well. Despite my mounting frustration, however, the guards bar me from entering. Resigned, I head to the practice yard.

"Are you sure you're up for this today?" Weslyn asks, the first I've seen of him since outside Finley's room. "You did spend the night before last in the hospital."

"I'm fine," I say curtly, brushing the point aside. "Do your worst."

I regret the words the moment training begins. He takes it much lighter than usual, probably for the best given my leg. But even with him barely breaking a sweat, the session is brutal. My body aches, and the part of my mind not distracted by thoughts of Finley feels as tired as Weslyn looks. There are a few triumphant moments in which I think I might actually be improving, but they're scattered, and Weslyn concedes defeat before the usual hour is up.

"Let's end it there," he says. "I have to take a meeting." He brushes the hair from his forehead and signals to the messenger who's hovering nearby, sent to collect him. "Go to the Officers' Hall. Violet asked to speak with you."

"Now?" I fret, having thought I was free at last to return to Fin.

"Go on."

Apprehension rolls through me during the short walk over to Violet's office. *Not another ambush,* I entreat silently, as one of the Royal Guards stationed outside the door announces my arrival.

"Helos, good. This will not take long." Violet is bent over a table covered in papers, dressed more casually than usual. A silk shirt the color of harvest wheat hugs her frame beneath a wide brown coat better suited to walking the hills. There's mud on her boots.

After the Guard has closed the door on us, she gestures toward a set of leather armchairs.

"How are you feeling?" she begins, grabbing a piece of parchment and taking the seat opposite mine.

"Fine," I say for what feels like the hundredth time. When her eyebrows lift, I add, "Your Majesty."

She grabs a cup of tea from the side table and sips it calmly. "I want to thank you again for your service to Telyan. I know it wasn't easy. To that end, I thought this might bring you some comfort as you're recovering. It arrived today."

I take the parchment from her outstretched hand, smoothing the many creases and curls. The paper is covered in tiny script, the upper corner dated to yesterday, and I don't see why it should interest me until Violet says, "Look at the bottom."

My gaze drops to the lines scrawled a short distance beneath the rest, and my heart skids into overtime.

Rora's handwriting.

I clutch the paper tighter.

"She's in Oraes," Violet explains, when I say nothing. "She has connected with a rebellion circuit, and one of my own." The quiet draws on, and she says, almost gently, "She's well, Helos."

Like Finley's before, my knuckles are pressing white beneath the skin where I clutch the parchment like a lifeline. Does Weslyn know? No, he was his usual self when I saw him, and anyway, surely he would have told me. My heartbeat flails unevenly, caught between relief and hurt. If she had the opportunity to send something south, why not write to me? It's been two weeks since we saw each other last.

"What have you asked her to do?" I respond, uneasy.

Violet simply waits.

"I know. You're the queen." I try to make it sound deferential. "But she's my sister."

"I have not asked for anything other than what she is already providing: information."

Which is barely an answer at all.

"Time runs short," Violet says, rising abruptly. "You may go."

Not needing to be told twice, I head for the door.

"Oh, and Helos." Her expression becomes difficult to parse. "I have noticed you spend a lot of time with my brother."

"Weslyn is teaching m—"

"Not that one."

My back tenses. I suppose the confrontation was inevitable, that I was foolish to hope she might see me and Fin spending time together and do nothing about it. "You want me to stay away," I guess, heart sinking.

A beat passes.

"On the contrary," she replies. "I merely want to be sure you plan to wish him well today."

I don't remember what day it is until the door has closed behind me.

Finley's birthday.

The sun has sunk behind the hills by the time I make my way to Finley's quarters, mug in hand. Tonight, no one is barring the entrance.

He doesn't answer my knock.

"Come on," I murmur, brushing the handle with my fingers. My forehead rests against the smooth wood. "Let me in, Fin. Please?"

The space beyond the door remains silent for some time. I don't leave. Finally, I hear him shuffle across the room and release the lock.

When I realize he isn't going to open the door himself, I turn the handle and close it quietly behind me.

The room is dark and depressing. An old gray curtain hides the window from view, and two flickering oil lamps cast eerie shadows along the colorless walls. Laid across the bed, where Finley stands with his back to me, are the colored maps that used to adorn his sitting parlor, a collection he spent years cultivating. I thought he'd left them in Roanin.

One by one, he's tearing them to shreds.

"What are you doing?" I ask, aghast. I know him. This is like ripping apart his entire being.

"They are mocking me." Finley speaks without turning around, and the anger in his voice stops me in my tracks. "I cannot stand it. Anyway," he says, the word almost lost amidst the harsh grate of severed paper. "No sense in holding onto places I'll never see."

Setting the mug atop the dresser, I reach around him and close a hand over his.

"Stop," I say quietly. The parchment pieces fall onto the quilt, and though my grip is gentle, he makes no move to continue his work. Beneath my palm, I can feel his skin trembling. "You have a fever, Fin."

"So?" he says.

The strained silence reaches into the far corners of the room.

"It's all gone wrong, Helos." Finley's words are barely audible, but still he won't look at me. A few rogue strands of hair have fallen across his forehead.

So close—it would take only a step, just a single step forward, and I could hold him, comfort him, like I once did. "What has?"

"My life," he replies. "Everything. Things were never supposed to be like this. Father gone, when he should have had another twenty years at least. I keep wanting to talk to him, and I can't." Finley's shoulders droop. "Our people are scared. Everyone's exhausted. Eradain's army will come, and Wes will probably die in battle. He hates it, you know, he should have gone to university. He should have had more time, too. He only joined so I didn't have to, and now there's not even a point to it, because I won't be here to use the time he gave me. I'm just a burden to—to everyone."

I stem the rush of bitter words by wrapping my arms around him, holding him safe, secure. "You're not a burden, Fin."

Heartbeats later, he leans back into me, folding his hands over mine. "I am," he says quietly.

I tighten my grip. "You could never be. Your family would say the same."

Fin releases a shuttered breath. "They do too much for me."

"I don't think they'd agree."

He doesn't respond right away, just rests his head against the rise and fall of my chest. "It's not fair," he whispers.

"No," I agree.

"I don't want to die."

I have to gather myself before responding. "I know."

After a while, he twists in my hold, curling in and closing a fist around my shirt, over my heart. I rest my chin atop his head.

"We're all wrong, too," he says. "You and me. And I don't just mean—that."

My chest aches. "What do you mean?"

"We used to tell each other everything." He shakes his head. "You're hurting, Helos. Something happened while you were gone, and you won't tell me what. But I don't blame you. It's my fault." His breath falters. "I pushed you away."

My attention drifts to the shredded parchment, stomach churning. I'm hurting. Am I hurting? The cavernous hole deep inside my rib cage tugs me closer, like a puppet. *What is it?*

It's everything. It's that worst of nights our journey west revived in full force, hearing a misaimed arrow whizz just past my face, clenching my jaw when Mother turned away. Watching Father bleed out before me, his skin peeling under the heat of the fire raging around us. Feeling my childhood friend's hand slip from mine while the soldier dragged him backward by his hair.

It's remembering most things about that friend—skipping stones together while the lake gleamed beneath the evening sun, playing the game we invented of pelting mystery objects at each other while our eyes remained closed, hearing the shyness in his voice when he handed little Rora a flower. Remembering all of that, but not his name. Making sure Rora doesn't remember him at all, because there's no need to make a bad thing worse.

It's white walls and smoking cigars, the night that seems to have jammed the door I've always kept shut, allowing everything else to spill forth. Encouraging it, in fact. That fortune-forsaken room with the blades and metal rods, the burns and the hands and the blood and the stop, *please* stop. But they don't stop, and I can't stop the loop, unstick this poison fused immovably between my ribs.

"Helos?" Fin says, tentative.

The words rise, unbidden, to the tip of my tongue. The ones Bren expected to hear. *I'm scared, Fin. I'm not the person you might have once grown to love. Something's wrong inside me. Something broken.*

But he and Bren, they don't understand any more than Rora did. I can't talk about this, can't even think about it, because as soon as I allow that door to open without resistance, the moment I stop fighting it, I'll never be able to shut it again.

In any event, how can I complain of pain from the past when his is real and happening now, right in front of me?

"We're not wrong," I say at last. "This is what I want, Fin. To be right here talking to you. It doesn't have to be anything more if you don't want it to. But I'll be here until you ask me to go."

Fin whispers, "I want it to."

When I stiffen, he pulls away to look me in the eye.

"I—that's what I wanted to say to you, before. I let you walk away twice, not knowing if you'd ever come back. I can't do that again. Not with you thinking I don't—" He hesitates. Takes a deep breath. "I'm afraid, Helos, I haven't been entirely honest." His teeth find his bottom lip. "With you."

Finley tilts his head toward mine, just a little, and my heart thrums when his gaze falls to my mouth in the sudden closeness. Only for an instant, but for the first time, in a long time, I saw it.

I lean a little closer, too, encouraged. "Go on."

Fin places a fingertip against my chest, tentative, before flattening his palm between my ribs. "You have to understand," he says, somewhat haltingly. "I'm used to being, to people saying I'm—too much. So the fact that you actually said you—" His gaze lifts from his hand to my face, sharpening with resolve. "You told me you loved me, and I didn't say it back. I let you think I don't love you." Finley shakes his head once, earnest gaze searching mine. "But I do."

The words are a song. They are warm as the sun, blasting away the cobwebs, flooding every part of me with light. *But I do. I do.* I can feel myself drowning again, lost in the sea of his eyes, the pull of his mouth, the—

"But it's not fair of me to ask that of you," he continues, like he doesn't want to. Like he must, even as I'm taking his face between my hands. "I meant what I said before, Helos. You deserve better than that. You deserve—"

I don't wait to hear who else this boy who loves me back thinks I deserve. I just kiss him.

At first, because I need to be sure this is what he wants, it's only the barest meeting of lips. Soft and slow. Waiting to see if he'll break away even as I am breaking apart. It's what I've waited so long to feel, the dizzying rightness of having Finley in my arms.

It turns out there was nothing to fear, because suddenly Finley pulls me into him like I've given the permission *he's* been seeking. I am delirious with this turn of events, struggling to breathe as he kisses me as if to make up for months of keeping us apart—hunger in his desperate hold, tongue tasting, lips parting beneath my own. Clinging to my neck and my shirt and my back as if he might be drowning in me, too.

I never want this moment to end.

Finally, though, he pulls away and searches my face, unsure. Waiting to see if he was—what did he say? *Too much.*

I grin like an idiot.

At that, the hint of apprehension lining his face brightens into a brilliant smile. Looking rather pleased with himself, he folds his arms across his chest, lifting his shoulders a bit—

And that's when I remember what his confession and his kisses kept at bay.

"You're still shaking," I say, startled into awareness. I return to the dresser and grab the tea that's probably gone cold. "Here, I brought this for you."

When I turn back, the lightness is fading from his face.

"Don't," he whispers.

"No, it'll help you, Fin. I promise." Smiling reassurance, I cross to where he's perched on the edge of his bed and place the mug in his hands.

Finley searches my face before dropping his eyes to the mug. "What is it?" he asks, his voice strained.

"Willow bark," I tell him, taking a seat at his side. "I brewed it for the pain, but it will help with the fever, too."

His chest rises and falls, breath still coming quicker from the kissing. "I don't want to drink it right now."

"You need to. It's good for you, Fin. Trust me."

Finley doesn't speak for a long while, staring into the mug, before he sets it on the floor untouched. "I want to ask you for something, Helos. Something you might not like. But I need."

"Anything," I say at once, and he glances at me sidelong, brows lifting. "Or, I mean, whatever this is."

A smile teases his features, but it fades when he starts to speak. "Every conversation we have these days starts and ends with this—this illness. I can't take it anymore. I get enough of that from the other healers."

"They're only trying to help," I remind him, laying a palm on his leg. Fortune's sake, it feels *so good* to be able to do that again. "There are medicines that can make you feel better."

"I know that, Helos. I take them all the time. That's not my point." He closes his mouth, considering.

"I know it must be exhausting," I offer, feeling a need to fill the silence. "You're very brave, Fin."

It seems this is not what Finley wanted to hear.

Pushing my hand aside, he folds over himself, grinding his fingers into his temples. "I wish people would stop saying that."

"But it's the truth," I say, confused. "I don't think I could do what you do."

"You could. You could because you wouldn't have a choice." Finley straightens suddenly, looking me in the eye. "Listen to me, Helos. I'm not going through the days trying to inspire people. I'm *not* brave for trying to do my best in a terrible situation. Anyone would do that." He runs a hand along the side of his face, then leans toward me. "The truth is I'm angry, so angry I could spend half my days screaming. I *hate* being sick. I don't want to die, and knowing it's coming doesn't mean I'm suddenly, I don't know, wise, or accepting, or whatever else people have tossed my way. The truth is I'm getting on with things the best I can because I have no other choice. If I did, I would take it. I would run to it." He tugs at his hair. "Living with an illness isn't bravery, Helos. It's just living without options."

I just sit there, uncertain how to respond.

"So stop trying to fix me." He leans away again, his eyes red around the rims. "Stop telling me to be strong. Don't warn me going down the hill or to the hospital or riding my fortune forsaken *horse* could make me feel worse, because I know that, I'm not blind to my own condition, but I'm going to do it anyway. Do you understand? I will do it anyway. I have to."

Finley stares at me for a long time, so quiet and still that I'm convinced he can hear my heart skidding through my chest. It's insultingly strong in the face of his own. I want to rip it free and swap it for his.

"I'm sorry," I say softly. "I didn't know. I just want what's best for you."

He bites his lip a moment and takes my hand. "Then tell me something will be hard when it will be. Let me walk when I want to, and let me cry when it hurts to. Catch me when I fall because I'm going to fall anyway, do you understand?" Tears are pooling at the base of his eyes. "Hold me even though it will hurt."

A flicker of understanding reaches me at last, one long overdue. I can't trade him my heart for his, but I can at least hold his against my own. I scoot behind him on the bed, pulling him into me, resting my chin on his shoulder. "I've got you, Fin," I promise, cradling his arms inside my own. His breath falters a little. "I'm not letting go."

And I don't. We stay like that a long time, my heart against his, the mug of willow tea growing cold. I don't care. He cries after a while—heart-wrenching, tortured sobs—and I hold him until all the tears are spent. Catharsis reached, at least for a time, and now there's only the oil lamps burning low, the cloak of night and the deception of peace its silence brings. Always, this silence is when the memories knock loudest. But with Finley in my arms, I find it easier to send them away, his presence warm enough to keep the growing shadows at bay.

"Happy birthday, Fin," I whisper into his hair, but his breathing has already evened into sleep. His birthday come and gone, what should be a guaranteed event cruelly turned achievement. Seventeen—how old does that make me now? Eighteen, nineteen? My birthday, and Rora's, have long slipped from sight, the dates lost like so many aspects of that life. A life of peace and normalcy before the fire consumed it.

Eventually, my own eyelids begin to droop. So when the garrison bells ring out, I nearly leap from my skin at the harsh clamor. A signal that, at this hour, could only precede trouble.

Fin startles awake, his swollen eyes finding mine, and he stumbles from the bed when a fist begins pounding on the door.

"Your Royal Highness!" calls a voice from the other side.

Finley straightens his shirt and glances to where I've already slipped into the dresser's shadow. A habit born from another life, when being one in a pair of shifters meant my presence in his sleeping quarters signaled danger rather than pleasure. Not a royal's harmless lover, but a risk. A threat.

Fin frowns.

"Sir!" The voice has grown insistent.

"No more hiding," Finley says, his voice low enough I almost miss it amidst the clanging of the bells.

The sentence tugs a smile from my lips, despite the circumstances. I cross to Fin as someone outside barks an order to stand aside and barrels into the room, rubbing drowsiness from his eyes even as they brighten into panic.

Weslyn, dressed in a loose sleep shirt and trousers. A trail of frost precedes him, and Astra blips into sight on Fin's other side.

"You're okay," he says to his brother, more a statement than a question.

"What's going on?" Fin demands, as Weslyn's attention fixes on me.

Finley grabs my hand.

Something passes between them, a wordless exchange I can't interpret. Whatever Weslyn sees in his brother's face, though, relaxes him, like a guard dog released from duty. He runs a weary hand behind his neck.

"I'm trying to find out," he tells us both without pretense. "But it sounds like Eradain has gained the coast. Our coast. Forty miles to the north."

SIXTEEN

RORA

As planned, Merisol slipped Gemma's drawing of prisoners and cages beneath the printing press's door. The next issue of their local leaflet is set to publish in three days.

We wait to see whether the drawing makes it in.

In the meantime, I slip back into the role I once performed for King Gerar, now with the intention of helping his three children. Ironically, I do so wearing the guise of his former Royal Guard.

It's uncomfortable to walk the castle as Carolette. To chafe against the gold-trimmed uniform's woolen clutch and meet the eyes of people younger than I am, older, wealthier or poorer, somber or brimming with cheer. Nearly all of them give way, the scattered individuals parting like crows at the sight of a cat. In Castle Roanin, people viewed me as a harbinger of death, and I knew it to be folly, refused to believe the Prediction's dire warning fell to my shoulders. In Oraes, people look at me as a harbinger of death, and they are right.

She already turned once. That's the message stamped into their watchful gazes, plain as day. *She betrayed the king she served. Who's to say she won't do it again?*

I know I'm running on borrowed time. Busy as he is, Jol will eventually learn of Carolette's absences and missed City Watch shifts, not to mention the lack of follow-up on Ember Street. Still, if avoiding suspicion relies on bringing people in for punishment, exile, or death, I'm not willing to make the trade. All I can do is take advantage of the days I have left.

And so, squaring my shoulders, I cast aside the pointed looks and hunt for information that Violet might find useful. First, I study the castle's vast interior, attempting to memorize the layout as best I can. I linger on dark stone staircases and press my ear to the doors in tapestry-lined corridors, searching for intel or individuals who may possibly break, if only I figure out how to apply the right sort of pressure. At meals, I camp out at the long tables and roaring hearths spiraling out from the kitchens underground, ready for the staffers to let something slip over their pints of ale and stories about the wealthy folk above.

Every evening, after Jol finishes at the piano, I dig through the contents of his private study. My first major find is a set of inked designs for evil-looking wooden contraptions on wheels—siege weapons clearly intended for battering stone. My stomach turns, imagining the horns ramming holes into defenseless old buildings like Briarwend's homes and halls, the wide slings flinging rocks large enough to crush soldiers and civilians alike, in addition to puncturing ceilings and walls. If these weapons were to reach Telyan, or fortune forbid, Fendolyn's Keep—

By the light of a single candle, I unearth blank parchment and copy down the designs, along with a commanding officer's report. In a pre-dawn visit to the catacombs, I pass them to Solet for their next falcon south.

As I search, I grow bolder with assuming animal forms around the castle, sneaking into barred rooms and working to commit as many of the conversations to memory as I can. Once, I'm spotted in mouse form crouched among the furniture and barely avoid the crushing sole of a boot. I spend the rest of that afternoon utterly terrified, certain that Jol, who was in the room, would have recognized the sighting for what it was. *The girl, Rora. You said she takes three forms. The lynx, the hawk. What was the third?* But no messenger tries to break down Carolette's door or summons me to Jol's side.

Two days pass. One to go.

Outside of the royal estate, I drop the Carolette guise with relief and walk the streets in borrowed bodies. There's a naval send-off one morning, transport ships with soldiers stacked along the decks like rows of teeth. I suffer the overwhelming crowd waving cuts of cloth stitched with Eradain's sun in order to count the ships leaving the docks: an alarming half dozen. In the afternoon, I use Carolette's salary to acquire supplies for the resistance. Food and warm clothing, fresh water, matches and candles, flasks of oil for the lamps, parchment and ink. Figuring it would be too conspicuous to bring all of these to a supposedly dilapidated shop, I pass them off through subtle handoffs and organized drop locations.

Publication day arrives at last. I throw on a casual black top and broad trousers from Carolette's wardrobe and slip into the city before the sun has risen. In an abandoned alley's shadowed safety, I consider which form to take and nearly fall back on an old disguise—the Royal Guard's Ansley—before remembering her past with Wes and opting for Evaline instead. Short and stout, broad mouth dominating a heart-shaped face, with thick brows and frizzy, shoulder-length hair. I like Ansley, but the thought of walking around in another body Wes once held has grown too weird.

Merisol has borrowed a stranger's form like I have. Even so, I recognize her by the excitement on her face.

"They ran it," she says, passing me a leaflet under the clay red awning where we agreed to meet.

And there it is, beneath the fold but printed on the front page nonetheless. Three crosshatched cages rendered in ink, each imprisoning a forest walker, a whisperer, and a shifter in turn. Behind, ghostly corporeal outlines drift out of a chimney, and the fine print along the bottom reads, *The king's justice for those exiled to the Vale.*

My back tenses at the dragged up memories. Gemma is good.

"It's awful to look at," Merisol says quietly.

Worse to live, I almost add, but she means well. In any case, my time there was nothing compared to that of people like Andie. "Let's hope other readers feel the same."

Merisol unfolds the six-page parchment, and we both bend over it as if to read. In reality, we're taking turns watching the leaflet stand a short distance away. A small queue forms of tapping feet and coins in hand, pocket watches withdrawn. People in caps and sea-stained trousers on their way to the docks, and parents clutching harried children's hands.

The man exchanging coins for leaflets smacks a stack of the papers over his assistant's head. "You're here to sell leaflets, not read them," he chides.

The younger man had been staring at the front page.

Among the recipients, reactions vary. Some fold the leaflets into satchels or under arms without even looking. One glances down, sees the drawing, and throws the crumpled leaflet into the street. Lynx claws threaten to poke through. On that same street, however, an older man is motionless, dissecting the front page. Indifferent to the approaching horse cart, he simply puffs on a pipe and shakes his head a bit. The queue starts to thin.

"Come on," Merisol murmurs, because we both know the danger of lingering too long in one spot.

Throughout the next hour, she leads me to a wealthier neighborhood called the Pearl District, then a louder stretch simply dubbed the Gull. Sometimes I struggle to gauge people's reactions when I spot a leaflet in hand, perhaps for the same reason I haven't seen a single person with the Throes, though Gemma assured me it's here. *Magic is best kept out of sight*—disgruntlement, too, it seems.

"Do you think it's working? Do people seem upset?" I whisper. I'm beginning to feel discouraged, but Merisol nods without hesitation.

"Yes," she replies, better able to read her people than I. "Not everyone. But enough for me to notice. And behind closed doors, they'll talk."

I clutch the hem of my shirt. "At least it's a start. A week ago, I didn't know if anyone would care."

"Things weren't always as strained as they are now," Merisol says sadly. "Used to be, the humans here only cared about magic not determining who has the right to rule."

A conflict stretching back to the realms' foundations, when some believed Fendolyn's daughter, Telyan, shouldn't inherit the crown purely because she had magical blood while her brother, Eradain, did not.

"This broader hatred, people believing the world would be better off, safer, without magic—that's King Daymon's doing, and his son's. And the Prediction's, of course." She breathes in deep, her borrowed face growing flushed, and I wonder which animal form her words have triggered, how hard she has to work to resist the shift. I've never seen her struggle with it visibly until now.

In some ways, it's nice to know I'm not the only one for whom it doesn't always come easy.

"I heard there were lists," I say.

"Lists, disappearances—King Daymon wanted to keep tabs on anyone magical. Only shifters the first year the Predictions aligned, but when they started to repeat . . ." She shakes her head. "A lot of us didn't take it seriously at first. Some humans may have resented magic, but they never went farther than that, so we didn't think things could get as bad as they did. The signs were there, and we still—" Again, she pauses. Inhales slowly. Releases. "So many lives destroyed," she goes on, even quieter. "You could barely step outside for fear you'd be next. *Your* family separated. Your home burned. King Jol with his exile, King Daymon with his lists—the Holworths are *so sure* the death the Prediction warns of means another Rupturing. The earthquakes only fuel that fear."

Dismay pinches my gut. I thought things were bad in Telyan—and they are—but listening to Merisol speak, long sorrow tinged with scorn, I realize I have no idea what it's been like to walk the paths she has.

Abruptly, she straightens her shoulders. "I imagine some people remember what Eradain was like before their reigns and this cursed Prediction. And some—well." She wrings her hands. "They can't all be monsters, right?"

I touch her arm, mindful of the night she held my hand when terror threatened to overwhelm me. Her assessment sounds rather generous spoken aloud, but the words aren't baseless optimism, nor wishful thinking. They're simply the truth, one we've both seen today for ourselves, and which she's best qualified to recognize.

I just wasn't expecting to find it here.

Wes once told me that Violet believed something was going on in Eradain the emissaries weren't relaying. After today, I intend to tell her she was right. Public opinion here isn't as united as Jol and his representatives led the Danofers to believe. Amazing, how convincing claims issued without evidence can be.

My insides perform their usual twisting dance when we descend into the catacombs and regain our natural forms. The sight that awaits Merisol, however, is enough to make me forget the three stories of solid rock overhead. At least, temporarily.

Both sisters are clinging to two middle-aged people with tears in their red-rimmed eyes. Her parents have returned. Somewhat thin, with worry lines etched into their bronze faces, but alive.

Merisol runs for them.

"It's great, isn't it?" Solet asks, coming to my side and nodding toward the reunited family.

I realize I'm staring.

"Definitely," I reply, turning away. "Did Carolette's lists help?"

"Not with that," Kal puts in with less bite than usual, joining our group. "But with others. The family from Ember Street you're supposed to hunt down—they're here now."

"So you're bringing everyone in?"

"Not all at once. We're not stupid," he retorts, folding his arms. "Have you found out anything else?"

"A few things." I scratch the back of my head. "Carolette is not particularly trusted—it's hard to get people to talk directly to her."

"Should have chosen a better disguise."

"This was the best option. I don't know anyone else well enough to imitate them."

"Speaking of information." Solet gestures for me to follow them to their makeshift office space—a water-stained table with stacked leaflets propping up the shorter leg—and lifts a rolled piece of parchment tied with twine. "I'm sending another batch to the queen. Anything you'd like to add?"

I hesitate, flicking at a splintered piece of wood. "Not to her," I say after a beat. "But there is something else I'd like to send."

I don't know when exactly I decided the time had come to write to them. Weslyn. Helos. Fin. Maybe it was on the walk over, watching the last of the morning light kindle an unfamiliar city filled with unfamiliar people. Maybe it was watching Merisol and her sisters get the reunion with their parents that Helos and I will never have. Or maybe it's the fact that I've spent most of my nights ghosting around the castle rather than sleeping, and right now, I'm just too tired to worry much about limited supply.

I tear a piece of parchment into three, sit with my back against the cold wall, and prop the pages on a borrowed book. Carolette's jacket hangs too large now that I've returned to my natural form, but at least the fabric is warm. Setting the small ink pot on the ground beside me, I hover my pen over the first sheet, debating.

Helos is the one who will be fretting the most, I think. So I start with him, insisting there's no need to worry, that I'm fine, I have things under control. It's a bit of a stretch. I also describe the glimpses of dissension I've been catching, because I think the fact that any sympathy could be found in Eradain's capital will surprise him as much as it has me. Mostly, I stress that I hope he's taking care of himself, not only others, and that I hope to come home soon. I haven't seen him now in, what, two and a half weeks? Almost three? This is the longest we've ever been apart, and right now, it feels like an eternity.

I move to Finley next, keeping my tone light as I did with Helos. Reassuring. I tell him about Oraes, the scent of salt in the air and the distant hum of ocean waves, almost like wind, folding onto the pebbly shore. I tell him how I rode a caribran, since I know he'll find that funny, and about the harbor I'm sure he'd love to explore. Though I express my condolences for the loss of his father, I don't mention the Fallow Throes—I imagine he would not appreciate the reminder.

Finally, there's Wes, and this is where my hand hesitates the most as longing strengthens its grip. I want him here beside me, not as well-worn images in my mind, but as the fantasy made real.

Instead of wondering what he's doing and thinking and feeling far more often throughout the day than seems reasonable, I want to see that cycle for myself. No, I want to be *part* of it.

Today, though, I have only the pen in my hand and the severed paper, and I need to make them count. Do I reassure him like I did my brother? Focus on the lighter aspects like I did with Fin? I shut my eyes and picture Weslyn's face by the fire that night in the Vale, when Helos was taken and we spoke our secrets into the darkness.

He wants the truth. As much as I'm willing to share, but only when I'm ready to share it.

The last time I saw him, he was grieving, and so that's where I start. I acknowledge how hard this must be for him, will continue to be, to face his people and go about his days as if nothing is wrong. I also encourage him, gently, not to shut down this time, to remember that he can get through it, that others are there to help.

By the river, I wish *I* could be there to help. I hesitate, then write that, too, before I lose my nerve.

I tell him some of the things I've done and am aiming to do. More an outline than the full sketch, because the page is already halfway full. I say I made the right choice in returning to the Vale and coming here, because I think I did, despite the rocky rate of progress. But I also share an echo of what I told Helos—that I hope I can come home soon. *Remember what I told you,* I write, pressed for space at the bottom of the page. *Look to the skies.*

With that, I'm off. I secure the letters with thread and ask Solet to send them when they can. This time, I don't pay Carolette a visit. I simply shake away the stiffness from too many nights awake and get back to work.

The war abroad may be out of sight, but here in Oraes, discord is spreading.

The signs are subtle. A fight breaks out inside a pub, and an argument drifts through an open window. Queues at leaflet stands grow longer, as if people are searching for, or dreading, another revelation about their king. More armed ships set out from the bay, but fewer civilians gather to see them off.

I can't predict what kind of effect this will have in the long run. I'm not naïve enough to imagine a city might change its heart overnight. Even so, I feel hope rising, and the more I'm able to chip away at Jol's armor, the brighter my mood becomes.

Until they print the next leaflet four days after the last, and I see the big, bold headline printed across the top.

Glenweil has fallen.

It's grown to be an unseasonably warm day, or maybe that's just the sudden rush of heat flooding my insides. I tug at the itchy collar hugging my neck as I read the article right there on the street corner. Eradain soldiers have taken command of the capital, Niav. Minister Mereth's location remains unknown. Rules are being set in place to govern the occupied cities and towns—curfews and local City Watches installed, with more changes expected in the coming days.

My stomach turns over.

I came to Oraes to get information for Violet that might help her drive off Eradain's forces. I came here to share the truth of Jol's vision with his people, maybe even to sow seeds of rebellion inside the castle. But things are moving quickly now, more quickly than I anticipated. While I've been planting seeds, expecting time to grow them into something substantial, the line has crept steadily toward Telyan. Entire realms are falling to Jol's influence, the jaws of Eradain's army pinching tighter, and here I am, scrounging the midnight halls for scraps.

Heart in my throat, I scan the rest of the leaflet for any suggestion that Telyan shares Glenweil's fate.

There's nothing.

I hope to fortune that's a good sign.

By the time I return to the castle grounds, I'm antsy enough to step right out of my skin. I thunder across the tiled courtyard and into the atrium, determined to double down on my efforts. To make my being here worthwhile.

An attendant rushes to meet me.

"What?" I snap, unable to blame my mood entirely on keeping in character.

The attendant shifts her weight, looking put out. "His Majesty has requested your presence."

Of course. He waits until the afternoon I have spent mostly outdoors, out of reach. "And how long have you been standing here waiting for me?"

"More than an hour, now."

Perfect. "Take me to him."

The attendant leads me up the staircase and through the narrow corridors, studiously avoiding my gaze. I struggle not to storm ahead, feeling restless. Useless. Itching to pick a fight, and as *myself*, not as Carolette.

She leaves me outside a set of whitewashed double doors. No guards bar the entrance, which seems strange and, given my current mood, recklessly trusting. But right now, it's mainly convenient, and I twist one of the knobs with scarcely a second thought.

The bright, airy space within is lit by a wall of glass windows overlooking the ocean. Painted seascapes dot the remaining three, the space between them coral pink, while an impressively intricate floral relief winds along the plaster-cast ceiling.

Across the room, Jol leans over a table, hands splayed on the wood. Unfortunately, he's not alone. I count five others—one keeping notes a short way to the side, three finely dressed in military attire, proud as preening geese and just as loud, and then—

My skin buzzes.

Carefully parted hair. Wide mouth. Sun-darkened white skin stretched tight across high cheekbones.

The prison commander.

Today, he's nearly purple in the face. "How dare you suggest—"

"I merely asked a question," says a tall, slender woman in uniform. Though her tone remains calm, she sizes him up through strikingly long lashes, a rosy flush tinting her warm brown skin.

"No, I took no *pleasure* in it," he grits out. "I was *protecting our interests*. Following orders, something you don't seem to have the stomach for."

The woman's eyes blaze. "Careful, Commander. Do not forget which of us has been shifting the line south, while you've been off in the woods—"

"You're out of line, Hariette," barks a man in similar garb. He's all greasy edges—shiny olive skin, slick black hair, a tongue that sits far too loose in his mouth. "You think you're so noble, as if you're not out there running people through with your sword every day."

"I took an oath to serve and I have, *Malhorn*," Hariette replies. "That's the nature of war. What you speak of is—"

"Carolette," Jol says, his voice low. "I do not believe I gave you leave to enter."

Instantly, the others fall silent.

"Forgive me, Your Majesty," I say, clasping my hands behind my back. *Wake up, Rora.* "I must have misheard."

To my satisfaction, Jol looks slightly less composed than usual. Veins jutting out along his neck, wisps of hair waving free from the usual part. The mouth so often curled in an arrogant smile is pinched rather tight. "Your report on Ember Street?"

The river take him. "I'll have it to you soon, sir."

Jol studies me a while, drumming a hand along the wood. I worry he might dismiss Carolette from his service here and now.

"General Malhorn," he says abruptly. "Take some uniforms to the Pearl District. Bring the Kierens in. I want a full report by the end of the day."

"Sir." The greasy man bows his head and glares at me imperiously.

"Leave us, all of you."

I'm not sure what reaction I expected this sudden dismissal to elicit, but it isn't the tranquil manner in which they all look at him. Not with fear or irritation, but with calm acceptance. Respect. Even now.

Well, except for the woman called Hariette, whose face remains a mask.

When the door closes behind them, Jol withdraws a decanter of warm brown liquor from a small wooden cabinet. His back to me, he pours a small amount into two crystal glasses set on top, then surprises me by holding one out.

"Please," he says, sipping from the other. "We have much to discuss."

Once I take the glass, Jol moves to the armchairs nearby and indicates that I should take the one opposite his. I perch restlessly on the edge, uncomfortably reminded of our conversations seated across from one another in the prison compound. Trying not to focus on how good it feels, despite everything, to sit.

"Is it no longer to your taste?" he asks, a crease forming between his eyebrows.

My hand tightens around the liquor I haven't touched. I'd rather not add to the murkiness in my mind, but he's looking suspicious, so I sip from the glass and work to keep a straight face as the liquor burns a hot trail down my throat. Nearby, a wooden model ship rests atop a chest of drawers, nearly the twin of the model Finley gave a position of honor atop his parlor hearth. I focus on the ship, on thoughts of Fin, until the urge to cough passes.

"The information you provided about Telyan's coastline," Jol begins. "It proved most useful."

I blink at him, wondering if in my present state, I've misheard. "Useful, sir?"

He nods, taking another sip. "Our ships were able to make landfall."

I hesitate probably half a beat too long. "Oh?" I say, attempting to sound relieved.

Jol twists the glass between his fingers. "The beach east of Grovewood was as empty as you promised. The assault was a success," he continues, and my heart picks up speed, tapping my rib cage, fluttering in alarm. "We needed a foothold. One that sticks." He watches me serenely. "Now we have one."

No. I can't be understanding correctly. The information I gave—I thought it was harmless. I deflected his attention from Fendolyn's Keep. It was supposed to be harmless.

Instead, Eradain has gained a foothold. Because of me.

Jol is smiling.

Gentle Helos, who probably couldn't wield a weapon to save his life, whose instinct is never to protect himself.

Finley, whose thirst for adventure never extended to war, whose well-being will surely only worsen under the stress and anxiety of an ongoing invasion.

Wes.

My Wes, whose job it will be, it *is,* to fight in the thick of it. I know him well enough to know that he'll make for the frontline himself rather than leaving others to do it for him.

They're all down there.

"Are you having a change of heart?" Jol asks, sounding genuinely curious.

"No," I reply firmly, my hand tightening on the glass. "Simply taking it in. And wondering, if I may, what comes next."

He folds an arm across his lap, casual. "With this new advantage, it is only a matter of time until we work our way inland. I believe I know where Violet is hiding."

He says it like a fox hunting down a rabbit, smoking out the warren and forcing his prey into his jaws. Which is absurd, because Violet is not one to hide. It isn't in her. If anything, she's the wolf to his fox.

"What will happen to the people?" I ask, striving to keep my tone light, unconcerned. "When Telyan falls."

That I framed Telyan's defeat as a certainty rather than a question seems to amuse him. "Our work with the magical communities continues, and will be no different with Telyans," he replies. "The humans will go under my watch. I have no quarrel with people who are willing to cooperate, nor any desire to waste talent unnecessarily, once our continent is secure."

Secure. Meaning, once he has obliterated magic—including his siblings—from its shores, and with it, any chance at another Rupturing. The idea is appalling. And that last part about wasting talent—it's an echo of what he told me in the prison, a sham of benevolence expressed with cool detachment. All I can manage is a nod. "And the Danofers?"

I'm treading dangerously now, even I can see that. But I could

not hold the question back. Perhaps it's better to go forward in ignorance, but I have no wish to walk blindly. I have to know.

Jol pushes off from his chair and sets his glass atop the cabinet.
For a while, he simply stands with his hands behind his back, his
face in repose. "I cannot allow them to live," he says at last. "They
won't be won over, not with their father dead."

Dead at his hands, he might add, but he doesn't.

"I will start with the queen, since she poses the greatest threat.
A worthy opponent, I admit, so I will give her a death befitting her
status. One quick cut. Painless—nearly." He glances at me, as if to
gauge my reaction. I attempt to give him none. "The elder brother
comes next. The rude one." At the thought of Wes, Jol's mouth
curls down at the corners, eyes turning stormy before he faces the
ocean once more. "Him—I think I will enjoy making him bleed."
He pauses. "Slowly."

In my free hand, my nails are blades against my palm. Threads
of numbness are teasing my core, whispering of teeth and claws,
fight and kill. And I will. I will cut him down in cold blood before
I allow him to see any of this through.

"The youngest is innocent," Jol admits. "He can't be blamed for
his elders' decisions. Still, I cannot risk him rallying support against
me down the line. All of them are threats to Eradain while they live.
The Danofers will die," he says, with an air of finality. "All of them."

The promise is nearly enough to send me over the edge. I long
to run from the room. Race all the way back down to Telyan, to
warn them what's coming. But I'm trapped here in this fortune
forsaken parlor, and Jol is grinning rather triumphantly—

Grinning?

I follow his gaze to my hands, where in spite of my best efforts,
the fingers have stretched into claws.

"Hello, Rora," he says.

SEVENTEEN

HELOS

Glenweil has fallen.

The mighty republic that Minister Mereth so deftly rules, all that separates Eradain from Telyan—overpowered. Its surrendering army scattered, its people divided between staying and fleeing.

To make matters worse, we've lost the northeast coast. Somehow they knew just the stretch that would be unguarded, and they deployed their ships, and now there are too many soldiers afield to encircle or destroy. Worse, the invaders have effectively blocked the land that connects Glenweil to Telyan, which means the surviving troops Violet sent to Glenweil's aid will struggle to link up with the rest of the army back in Telyan. A few hundred-bands ready and willing to fight for their queendom—stuck abroad.

A formidable number of soldiers still hold the line. Rumors whisper, too, of ships deployed to try to bring those stranded units home. But this is no scattershot attempt on guarded ground. Everyone expects the front will push inland. It's only a matter of weeks until combat reaches the Keep.

I had already thought time was moving quickly, that I didn't have enough. To decide about my birthright, to wait for Rora's work to succeed or fail, to be with Fin. Now it feels I have none. The valley grows jittery as a hive of bees as people panic and the army attempts to keep the order. Finley has an episode of delirium that renders him disoriented, then unconscious, a terrible half hour

I may never stop living behind closed lids. Five more patients die, leaving only imprints on now-empty beds and a circle of distraught family and friends. And all the while, the hours fly relentlessly by, determined to rub salt in my cavernous heart.

The day after the garrison bells ring out, Violet issues an order that sends joint spikes of comfort and anxiety rippling through the valley. Civilians and soldiers are to swap places. Civilians in the garrison to gain the protection of the height and the wall, soldiers relocated to tents below to safeguard the base. I make myself useful by carrying personal belongings or small children up the hill, trip after trip until my newly healed leg starts to hurt again. The work helps, but distraction can only go so far.

The crowds are growing tense, tempers flaring. This valley is not large enough to house all the new evacuees from the south, but many have come anyway, seeking refuge in the comfortingly large shadow of Fendolyn's Keep. Their presence means the already-rationed food will stretch thinner. On my fourth walk through the sun-baked encampment, I spot Ansley waving her hands in a heated argument with two sour-faced older people who might be her parents arrived from Poldat. Seven children mill around them, three with hair as red as Ansley's, all younger than she and looking as though they could use a few extra meals. They watch the fight unfold with unnerving stillness.

Through all the changes, the one bright spot is Finley.

Finley, this marvel of a boy who loves me back. My Fin, a designation I feared I'd lost forever, whose words and hands and heat make the descending darkness a little easier to bear. He rallies after his episode of delirium, and I catch glimpses of him working alongside Weslyn and Naethan on horseback, helping the hours-long move run more smoothly. While the latter two dismount repeatedly to help shift heavy objects or have a quiet exchange with civilians, Fin scours their surroundings for the next individual in need. He's become a trusted ally thanks to his daily visits; though blades of grass strain toward him, the sway and the silence still at play, few people even glance down.

Once, *I* become the person in need when I struggle to break up a group of young people taking their stress out on a boy with silver-rimmed irises and patches of silver and gold spiraling out from his hairline. Like a whisperer, but not quite. Not yet. Finley shoves his roan gelding, Cascade, through the circle and berates them in a voice he rarely uses in my presence. Stern and expectant both, so that he sounds more like Weslyn. Like a prince. Though he looks only two or three years older than the bullies, his tone makes them all stand up straight.

His interference on this boy's behalf must do something to me, too, because whatever he sees in my face makes him smile rather smugly before riding away.

Leave it to Finley to be the one who sets people's fears about magic at ease. Helping Rora from afar, his loyalty reliable as ever.

The move lasts well into the night. To every side, the valley stretches out like shadow monsters under an unbroken expanse of stars. All the while, the procession continues up and down the hill, lit by torches, oil lamplight, and the pearly glow of the moon.

By the time the majority of civilians have been situated in the barracks, the night sky has brightened to a mingled palette of cerulean and navy, a soft glow tracing the eastern hills. My weary body aches as if I've been trampled, and Captain Torres of all people is the one who finds me half-asleep on my feet and orders me to bed. I don't protest. I drag myself to the Officers' Hall and collapse on the mattress, asleep in the span of ten breaths.

In the morning, I learn of one more fear to add to the tally: after moving beneath the hill with the rest of the soldiers, Weslyn has left for the front.

His departure hits Finley hard.

"He'll be okay," I assure Fin, tamping down my own anxiety as I watch him wring his slender hands. "He's pretty good with a sword. Beats me every time."

"A child could overpower you," Finley points out, but he grins a bit through the nerves, leaning against the turreted wall.

We're up on the Keep's rampart, the dark stone track wide

enough for three or four people to stand shoulder-to-shoulder. This more private area is typically reserved for military personnel alone, but none of the soldiers on duty would say no to the sunshine prince.

Finley seems lighter at this elevation, relaxed for the first time since Weslyn departed a few hours before. The breeze in his hair and the sun on his face, each tent sprawled along the lakes beneath us reduced to the size of an egg. I stand back a pace from the waisthigh battlement, the height and buffeting wind enough to make my head spin, but Finley leans into it. Over it. When someone warns him to step back, he only bends farther.

"Look at it, Helos," he says, his gaze fixed on the hills ringing the horizon. They gleam yellow-gold under a clear morning sky, birds looping and diving around the peaks.

"Very nice," I say flatly, acutely aware of the steep drop just beyond the wall.

Fin glances back, rolls his eyes at my careful distance, and guides me to his side.

"You can hold onto me if you're scared," he teases, nudging my shoulder as he braces his forearms along the wall once more. His loosely clasped hands are hanging off the edge.

Slowly, I lower myself beside him until I mirror his position. Finley's not looking at me, but he smiles when another gust of wind whips our clothes and I seize his arm in a death grip. Not for the first time, I wish desperately that I could see the world through his eyes. To view the untamed as an invitation and the jagged peaks as possibilities, rather than echoes of a dangerous past. To look fear in the face and shrug it aside, even for a handful of heartbeats, because there are better ways to spend one's time.

"What would you do," I ask, "if you could do anything you wanted to, right now?"

Finley doesn't laugh at the question. He remains quiet for a time, staring at the hills as if he'll never stop.

"Maybe I'd climb every mountain in the Purple range, like that book you gave me," he says, a bit of humor in his tone. "Mount Caldain first, I think. Or maybe Feneran. Henriel." He rattles off the mountains' centuries-old names one by one. The faint smile fades. "I would take a ship," he says, softer. "And I would steer it toward the horizon. And just . . ." He shakes his head a little. "Go."

The words are those of the old Finley, speaking through the new. This yearning for adventure I don't think he'll ever be able to set aside, no matter how hard he tries. And he shouldn't have to. I glance at my hold on his arm, thinking how strange it is that he could ever think himself too much, simply because he's always wanted more.

"With you, of course," he adds kindly, patting my hand. It seems a fairly generous offer, considering how challenged I feel by a wall. "What would you do?"

"In this moment?" I pause, considering. "I'd like to check on the prisoners being held underground. The guards have turned me away each time I've tried."

Finley's eyebrows lift, his expression making clear that he thinks my abrupt pivot is a joke.

It's not.

"You care too much," he says. A sharp reminder that Finley may be the most laid back of the Danofer siblings, but he is still a prince of Telyan, the identity sewn into the tapestry of his being whether he chose it or not. And those prisoners threatened his people. Threatened me.

I brush my hair off my face, a futile effort given the wind. "I'm a healer. It's my job to care."

And it is mostly that, the innate compulsion to take something broken and make it new, to mend the cracks in the world he moves so confidently through. But it's also a whisper of intuition snaking through my thoughts—the notion that these people might one day be my responsibility. It's a night spent underground that ensured I'd never want another person subjected to the same, no matter their origin.

The way Fin rolls his eyes, disapproval mingled with fondness, tells me he sees the conflict on my face, even if he does not understand how it came to be. I suppose he sees this is important to me, though, because he relents as we make our halting way down the stone stairs that lead to the grounds. "I'll have a word with my sister."

Entirely too soon, the rampart's respite fades. We've scarcely walked ten paces from the wall when the brief levity leaves Fin's face, his eyelids drooping a bit. I, too, feel the weight settling over my shoulders like a shroud, back among other people and the grim developments they bring. Heedless of potential onlookers, I cradle his face in my hands and wait until he meets my eyes. "He'll be okay," I repeat.

Fin nods like he doesn't believe me. My heart twists, because really, didn't I feel the same when he tried to reassure me about Rora?

"I'll get you an answer on the prisoners," is all he says. "Find me tonight?"

I can't bear to leave him in this state, so I tug him into the narrow space between the granary and the rampart and kiss the hope back onto his face. When some semblance of peace rekindles his gaze, I leave for the hospital.

Tomas intercepts me at the door.

"I'd like your opinion on something," he says in an undertone.

A warning note sounds in my head; he rarely comes to his apprentice for healing advice. My misgivings increase when he leads me away from the hospital rather than inside, stopping at the same crates where I first asked Fin why he had said no. Today, a young man is pacing before them, squeezing his hands with the nervous energy of a cornered hen.

"Allon, this is Helos," Tomas says, sinking onto one of the crates. In an attempt to mask my confusion, I simply nod to the man with a smile. "I've asked him here to give his opinion."

"I'm not going in there," Allon says at once, training his eyes on the hospital entrance. There are markings along his face and neck, jagged across his light brown skin.

Tomas remains unfazed. "That's fine, Allon. We'll stay here. Please tell Helos what you told me."

Allon studies me a long while before murmuring an account of the gray-brown marks that appeared on his skin about a month back, dots he dismissed as a sign of some allergy. Except instead of resolving, they've stretched into thin lines and darkened to the point he can't ignore them anymore.

"May I?" I ask when he falls silent. He gives a tentative nod, and I lift one of his hands, turning it this way and that. The lines fall in a semi-regular pattern, everywhere they're visible. "Does it hurt at all?"

Allon shakes his head, then says, "Only—"

"Yes?"

"I feel—my chest hurts, sometimes. Well, it's not rightly pain, I suppose. But it feels funny."

I nod calmly, aware of Allon anxiously monitoring my facial expressions. Hiding the fact that my own chest has begun to prickle. "Like a pulling sensation?" I look up in time to see his eyes widen.

"Yeah." He sounds surprised. "I'd say so."

I push up his sleeve, feeling him flinch a little beneath my grasp, and find the same pattern extends up his arm.

Here is the point where I have to tread carefully. I meet Tomas's eyes, trying to read his thoughts on his face. All he does is nod, his expression the studied composure of long practice, but it's enough for me to guess he has come to the same conclusion. An impossible one—or would have been a few months ago.

He gestures for me to continue, back in teacher mode.

"I've seen this before," I tell Allon, releasing his arm and perching on a crate like Tomas. Not quite a lie, but not the full truth, either—that I've only seen it in a further state of progression, and never in humans. "The markings won't hurt you."

"What are they?" Allon demands, attention spiraling between us.

I rest my hands on my lap. "You've met forest walkers before, I assume."

Tomas watches Allon, who watches me.

"I don't understand," Allon replies.

"Those markings are not an allergy or a rash. They form a pattern. Bark."

"Bark," he repeats, tone flat.

"Some sort of oak, I'd say, based on the appearance."

Tomas cuts in. "These are the marks of a forest walker, Allon."

Allon stumbles back a couple of steps. "That's not possible. I'm human!"

Tomas rubs his chin. "The signs are clear."

"No," he says, furious. "Give me a salve, a draft of some sort. Get rid of it."

"I cannot."

"Then bring me a healer who can!"

It pains me to hear the desperation in his voice, the terror that the notion of living with magic has sparked in him. Perhaps, when magic first surfaced in humans centuries ago, they might have regarded it as a gift. Now it's only a curse. A disease. A facet to prod and to push away, to attempt to beat out of a person—and to punish when one cannot.

"Does the idea repulse you so much?" I murmur.

Allon looks at me sharply. Tomas frowns. It's not a question that belongs on a healer's tongue, not for me to judge how a patient reacts to their own diagnosis. I know this and endeavor to tamp the personal feelings down. But my façade is already shattering, agitation seeping through the cracks.

"I'm sorry," I say, getting to my feet before Tomas can ask me to go. "Tomas will finish here."

I leave. Hardly the behavior of a professional, but I can feel the scream building inside me like a wild creature, claws scrabbling for purchase, a hole through which to escape. I'm out of their reach and storming along the path, sending gravel skittering in my wake. Needing air, needing to move, needing—

A hand lands on my shoulder, and I don't think. I whirl, my fist already flying.

Naethan catches my wrist before the blow can land. "Whoa," he says, his forehead wrinkling. "Take it easy, it's only me."

Only him.

The river take me, I am *unraveling,* the ball of yarn sinking lower with every passing day. He releases my arm, and I run a hand over my face. "Sorry."

Naethan is dressed in a cream-colored sweater and dark trousers, the first time I've seen him out of uniform. I peer over his shoulder at the small group he's left behind: Ansley in casual wear as well, sliding glances my way alongside his father, Feryn, and a woman on his arm I guess is Naethan's mother. Of course. They must have moved into the Keep with the other civilians.

The hole in my chest stirs unpleasantly at the sight of his family, happy and whole. A mother and father left to call him son.

"Who were you expecting?" Naethan asks.

No one, is the terrible truth I can't share. The fact that in that moment, it didn't matter who was there, or why anyone might have followed. All that mattered to my racing heart was the hand touching my shoulder and the need to get it *off.* "Did you want something?" I ask, skirting the question.

Rudeness cuts through the words, biting, but Naethan only says, "What's wrong?"

By the river, I wish everyone would stop asking me that.

"Nothing's wrong," I tell him, though my traitorous voice breaks on the words.

Naethan searches my face, the pointedness in his expression reminding me that he's meant to succeed Captain Torres one day. "Why don't you come with us," he says at last. "Ansley wants to—"

"Helos."

We both twist to Bren, who's hastening toward me with a satchel slung over his shoulder. Something in the way he says my name makes my nerves stand on end.

"Is something wrong?" I ask.

"We've been asked to set up near the front to tend to the wounded," he replies in a rush. "As many healers as we can spare here. I'd like you to come with us."

My stomach plunges.

Leaving. For the front. Briarwend all over again.

Me.

"For how long?" I manage.

"Likely no more than two or three days. We'll try to rotate staff."

Two or three days! My heart races as my thoughts go to Fin, who's expecting me this evening. I imagine the devastation when he learns that I've gone miles away, first Weslyn and now me.

"Okay," I say, struggling to remain calm. Naethan has placed a hand on my shoulder, but I barely feel his touch. "Okay, I just need to talk to Fi—to someone first. I can be quick."

"Sorry, Helos," Bren says, and he looks it. "That will have to wait. Help us get everything ready, then pack a bag. We're leaving within the hour."

By the time our horse-drawn cart grinds to a halt, my exposed skin smells forcefully of herbs.

Exchanging a look with Emilia, one of healers closest my age, I hop down onto the packed earth. It feels bone dry, hard as a rock underfoot. We've left the hills far behind. Here, there are only a few large, hastily erected tents strewn across the yellowing grass, and a couple of isolated farms whose sleepy plow horses watch the proceedings with mild stares and flicking ears. Bren says something about the line being a mile or so farther north, but it's difficult to hear, and our view is blocked by the mass of people crowding the horizon and the makeshift village.

I know next to nothing about how wars are fought and lost and won. But even my untrained eyes can distinguish newer arrivals from soldiers who have been on the line. Not just because of the stains and the grime marking the latter, the injuries ranging from surface level to urgent. There's also something in the way they carry themselves. A certain lessening of fear, because for them, trouble is not ahead, but temporarily behind.

"Come on," Emilia says, nudging my side.

Endeavoring to focus only on what's here in front of me, not what's ahead, I help unload the cart with methodical precision. Metal instruments here, premixed pastes and medicines there. Needles and thread, mortars and pestles, scissors and saws, bandages and wraps. The purple healer's band secured around my arm. *Stop,* I will the slight tremor in my fingers and the nausea stroking my throat. The fourteen sets of hands are back, a gentle pressure encircling my own.

"We'll set up there," Bren announces to our group of seven after speaking with a woman in uniform. I follow his outstretched hand to a long wooden barn with an overhanging roof and shadows set under the eaves. "Emilia and Rian will take the field as discussed, the rest will remain behind. The wounded will be carted to the barn when possible."

When possible. When they don't bleed out where they lay.

"I can join them," I hear myself offer, leg bouncing. "Emilia and Rian." Weslyn's lessons filter through my mind. *It'll be okay. This is what I've trained for.*

"Absolutely not," Bren says, and holds up a hand when I open my mouth. "Start bringing supplies to the barn, Helos. *Now,*" he adds, in a tone he's never used with me before. Smarting, I turn on my heel and grab a box.

"About time," says a gruff voice to my left.

Two armored soldiers are lifting a third off of a cart, one who's making awful noises as his oddly bent foot drags along the ground. The soldier who spoke holds a cigar between their teeth as they press a blood-soaked scarf to the base of their injured friend's neck. "Javelin caught him," they tell me, eyeing my armband. The hand holding the scarf is shaking—not so calm as their words suggest. "Son of a bitch didn't fasten his breastplate properly. Patch him up?"

I drop the box and grab for a bandage and salve, needle and thread, as they set the injured man on the ground.

I was foolish to think the front would be Briarwend over again.

It will be far, far worse.

EIGHTEEN

RORA

For a long while, I simply meet Jol's satisfied stare, the blood turning to ice in my veins. My claws have retracted, mockingly late.

He knows.

At least, he knows I'm an imposter. Briefly, I consider adopting another borrowed body, pretending to be somebody else with a wildcat form; there's a chance that could work. Then again, being anyone other than myself might only increase the odds he would attempt to kill me here and now. And frankly, in this moment, I'm tired of pretending.

"Come, Rora, let's not play games," Jol says, as if anticipating my internal debate. He returns to the seat across from mine and rests his arms along the upholstered sides, watching me expectantly.

I take a second sip of amber liquor, this time to steel my nerves. After placing the glass on the rug, I release my hold on the borrowed matter.

The last time Jol saw my natural form, the resemblance to our mother, he went white as the moon. Today, he doesn't even flinch.

"I'm impressed," he says, resting his chin on one of his hands. "You played the part fairly well. A word of advice: try to keep a better handle on your emotions next time."

"Don't condescend to me," I snap. "At least I still have the capacity to feel. Unlike some."

Jol barely reacts. "I take it you received my invitation, then."

"You mean the one you had nailed next to King Gerar's head?" There is iron in my voice.

He appears nonplussed. "The very same."

"You're barbaric."

"I'm a realist," he counters, still maddeningly calm. "Threats must be eliminated. Surely you can understand that."

Bile rises in my throat. "You will never convince me that was right."

"Perhaps not," he concedes. "Yet here you are."

I fold my arms tight across my chest.

"Something wrong?" he asks lightly.

"I did not come to reconcile with you." Figuring the time to start planning my exit has arrived, I scour the wall of glass and feel my insides pinch. No windows.

"Ah. Perhaps you thought to kill me instead? Assassinated in my sleep, and poor Carolette, left to take the blame. Speaking of whom—" The echo of amusement drops from his face. "You will have to tell me where you're keeping her. I won't take kindly to having my members of staff murdered."

"Interesting choice of staff, considering the last king she worked for ended up dead."

Jol folds one of his legs across the other, appraising me. "You are loyal to the Danofers. Why? Do they have something on you?"

I release a huff of air, exasperated. "Not everyone has to resort to blackmail to gain loyalty."

"Money, then?" he muses. "Or wait, don't tell me." He smiles derisively. "Love."

"I'm loyal to them because they're good people," I answer honestly, shifting my weight in the chair. My abdomen has begun to ache with the stress. "They don't murder innocent subjects because there's magic in their blood. They're not arrogant enough to presume their way is always the right one."

Irritation flashes across Jol's features. He looks as though he's regretting starting with the niceties. "Has Helos come as well?"

If I thought it strange before to hear my name from Jol's lips, I like the sound of Helos's even less. "No," I reply, and for once, I'm fiercely glad of that fact. The farther from this man Helos remains, the safer he'll be. Even if Eradain's army is on the way. "He wants nothing to do with you."

If that stings, Jol gives no sign of it.

"So why did you ask us here?" I grip the sides of my seat, trying to distract from my stomach. "'Much I'd have you tell me, and much that you should know.' That's what you wrote to us. Well, as you say, I'm here now. What do you want me to know?"

Jol's attention drifts to the wall for several heartbeats. I scan the rest of the room for windows and find none. It will have to be the door.

"Do you think of her often?" he asks. "Mariella?"

An unexpected response.

I notice he doesn't refer to her as *our mother.* I notice how his bearing has hardened, a little colder now. Perhaps if he were someone I trusted, and not a criminal besides, I might confess that I used to think of her often. Too often, her presence an unmovable anchor weighing me down season after season. As it is, I feel no desire to start confessing my deepest sources of shame to him.

"I don't," he continues, and I can't tell whether or not he's lying. "I have learned not to, and I am better off for that. It does no good to dwell on the past." He leans forward in his seat, narrowing the distance between us. "When we last spoke, you said she left you, too. Abandonment leaves a mark—I know better than most—but I believe I can help you work through the loss. Or, perhaps, we can help each other. We must look to the future, Rora. Maybe even together."

The sincerity in his voice gives me pause. Help each other—it's an echo of the offer I made to him back in the prison compound. *You don't have to choose this path. Let me help you.*

Have I read him wrong? Is it possible that a part of him, however small, is as desperate for proper family as I've been most of my life?

I remember the cool indifference with which he threw me into the shed.

"That's it?" I ask roughly, the memory knocking me to my senses. "Is that the entire message?"

He assesses me with an indeterminate expression. "Is that not enough?"

I shake my head, ignoring the sharp pain that ignites. "You once told me that sentimentality had no place in your court. Yet here you are, talking of togetherness. I'm not stupid."

"I assure you, my intention is genuine," he says, looking almost hurt.

That's when I know he's lying. *You still believe there is value in sentimentality*—those were his exact words to me, spoken in the manner of one expressing disappointment. He's not saying all this because he believes in it.

He's saying it because he thinks *I* do.

"You're trying to manipulate me," I grit out.

The smile is back.

"Where are you going?" he asks, looking perfectly at ease as I shove to my feet.

"Outside," I say firmly, crossing the room with quick strides. "Back to Telyan. I don't know. Anywhere but here."

"Pity," he says, as my fingers graze the doorknob. "To have come all this way for nothing."

I hesitate at the door. When I glance behind, his expression has grown smug. As if he's certain he's figured out exactly how to get to me.

It sets my teeth on edge.

"Tell me," I reply, taking a couple of steps toward him. I blink away the black dots that flit across my vision, the ache that's spreading from my stomach to my limbs; by the river, I need to sleep. "What would happen to you if I walked through this door and showed everyone in the castle I'm a shifter? Surely they'd see Mariella in my features. They'd know I'm your kin. What then, when they learn their king has shifter blood?"

How *much* shifter blood is a different question entirely. Not for the first time, I wish I knew for certain whether our mother passed on enough magic for him to shift. Maybe not, if no emotions have triggered this already.

The smile slips from Jol's face. "The question is what would happen to you. Go ahead. Shift in my court. I guarantee you'll be dead before you leave whichever room you're in."

"And you?" I press, not so easily intimidated as that.

He sits back, studying me. "Do you care so little for your life that you would give it up simply on the chance I'd lose mine?"

The river take him, down to the depths. He's right. I want to live.

"Regardless," I say, folding my sore arms. "If I walk these halls in my natural form, people will guess we're related. You asked me to come; you must have thought of this already."

"My dear sister," he replies, the words mocking in their delivery. "If it came to it, it would be simple enough to kill you as proof of my commitment to the cause."

I narrow my eyes. "So, what, you asked me to come so you could try to get rid of me?"

"Threats must be eliminated," he repeats with a shrug. "Though, who knows. Perhaps we might yet come to an agreement."

I open my mouth to respond and sway on the spot.

"You're looking rather pale," Jol says, clicking his tongue in concern. "Why don't you sit back down."

The ache in my head. It's grown with searing insistence, too pronounced now to ignore, along with the fiery cramping in my torso, my arms, my legs. Instinct thrums a warning, throat tightening in alarm. Cursed fortune, it *hurts*.

"Painful, is it not?"

My gaze cuts to him, then to a small glass phial he's twirling between fingers.

My stomach drops.

"I believe I can help," he says, eyebrows lifting innocently. "For a price."

Panic beats its wings in full force. This can't be happening. I didn't come here to die, to let him win, I won't—the river take me, my *head*. How did things escalate so quickly? "Let me guess,"

I manage, swallowing thickly. Mouse and goshawk instincts are warring for prominence, but shifting won't stop the spread of poison. "The liquor?"

"Now, Rora," Jol chides, leaning back in his chair. "I don't think you have time to be asking the wrong questions."

"How long?"

"Still not the right one."

"Then what's your *price*?" I demand, saliva filling my mouth. Suddenly I'm eager to wring his neck, if only my hands didn't feel too weak to squeeze even a feather pillow.

Jol pushes to his feet, and his expression turns serious. "Let me see. Information, I think. On Telyan's army, Violet's weaknesses . . . You should just start talking. When you've shared enough, I'll let you know."

"And if I force it from you, instead?" I reach for the magic in my core, beckoning the lynx—but what's usually intuitive as breathing, easy as blowing dandelion seeds on the breeze, feels like trying to wrest a trapped limb free from underneath a boulder.

"In your condition? I recommend against trying." He withdraws a wicked-looking dagger from his boot. "I learned from the best."

My breath is growing shallower. I can't betray my friends. I cannot shift. I refuse to die, not today.

Not like this.

"You won't get far," he warns.

But my hands are already grasping at the door, pulling it open, the effort nearly enough to make me vomit.

No one's in the hall. I force my feet to move, scraping against the woven runner. Jol isn't following, which means he expects—he—

I clutch my head. *Focus.*

Which means he expects me to return to him. Only he has the antidote. But I can't hand him another piece of information that may result in Finley's death, Wes's death, *Helos's death*—

I stumble down the spiraling staircase, wading through the murky light. Tears are stinging my eyes. Helos would know the cure. If he were here—but I told him not to come, my brother is far away—and I just have this mad, insistent feeling that if I could only get outside—

"Are you all right?"

Someone is reaching for my shoulders, calling for help, but I shake them off. I'm not going to die trapped inside stone walls.

My shoes clatter against tile. The courtyard. Maybe one of the rebels will have the cure. Or an apothecary shop, I remember one not far from here. I can make it. *I will.*

I'm halfway to the outer gate when the ground rumbles beneath my feet.

That, at last, is nearly enough to make me give into despair. To sink to my knees and let the earthquake rattle my aching bones into oblivion. My legs, however, have walked too many miles to know the meaning of surrender, so I'm still on my feet when cracks splinter across the courtyard like fissures across a frozen lake, and I fall through.

I brace for the shuddering impact of packed earth against flesh.

Instead, my body meets a blanket of grass.

The blades are soft as lambswool. Gathering my remaining strength to sit up, I blink to clear my vision, wondering if this poison creates hallucinations on top of everything else. Because I feel, quite madly, as if I'm in the forest.

Patches of bright clover and moss creep over stones. Violet, bell-shaped polemonium flowers and stalks of magenta fireweed. Air that smells, not of fish markets or catacombs or amber liquor, but of fresh green. And winding their way through this shallow crack in the earth, like a dry streambed, are saplings. Elm and aspen and oak.

I think, *Peridon and Andie,* and feel hope.

I think, *Get up, Rora. Stand.*

I think, simply, *Helos.*

And then I think nothing at all.

NINETEEN

HELOS

After a certain point, the blood won't come off my hands. It's caked beneath my nails and in the crevices between fingers—red-brown, crusted smears that once flowed inside a person before that person's insides were turned out. I scrub and scrub, gritting my teeth, to no avail.

Bren finds me bent over the water basin. "All right, Helos?"

I recognize that look in his gray eyes, the concern that hasn't quite lifted since he asked about my scars. Grunting noncommittally, I try not to let my gaze linger on his purple healer's shirt, the front of which is as soiled as mine.

His forehead wrinkles at my vague response. He doesn't tell me to take the morning off after working well into the night, though, because he's done the same as I, and neither of us can spare the time.

Four days ago, we set up our makeshift hospital in the emptied-out barn. The owner was gone, likely evacuated farther south, and we spent a backbreaking couple of hours clearing the farming tools and hay bales to accommodate the rows of improvised beds. I've come to hate the dim, drafty space. A foul stench taints the air, with swallows flitting nervously among the wooden beams crisscrossed beneath the gabled roof. Under the eaves, the heaviest equipment looms as silent witnesses to our frequent failure, iron and immovable.

I've tried to keep count of the number of people I've lost.

I can't.

"You did your best," Bren continues, nodding toward a soldier with a severed torso. She's dead, in the process of being carried out to make space for another person, another chance.

I shake my head, still scratching at my hands. Empty words. My best was only enough for her to die with someone else's name on her lips. "How is the—"

"Bren!" calls a voice from across the barn.

Our brief exchange at an end, Bren gestures for me to follow and hurries over to the young man being half-lifted, half-dragged into the barn. By the river, this moaning boy with the crooked arm is a soldier? He looks like a child!

"Get his armor off," Bren instructs, as the boy's fellow soldiers lower him onto a stained cot. I help them undo the buckles fastening his breastplate into place, the ties around his metal shinguards; by now, I know the way.

The breastplate knocks the boy's broken arm when it slides off, and he screams.

I have not known proper silence in days. Even when I manage to catch an hour of restless sleep in the loft upstairs, the sounds are always there. People shout. They groan. They weep. Their suffering arrows straight through my core, tugging the fox instincts forward at a relentless rate. A draining, nearly ceaseless campaign to beat back the whiskers and scratchy fur prickling beneath my skin, gnawing away at the final vestiges of my strength.

On my second morning here, I actually slipped from the barn and shifted to fox, longing for the chance to try to clear my pounding head. The scent of grass and soil, the scrabbling of tiny paws across the earth—those remnants of my life in the wild, from which I've recoiled for so long, suddenly felt like a breath of the cleanest air. Far more peaceful than the consequences of human behavior I'd experienced in that barn. Even better, my heart leapt when I caught a whiff of magic's sharp scent, earth and ash, concentrated in a rabbit nearby. I didn't know if it was an ordinary animal gaining magic like Astra, or if I was not the only shifter in need of brief respite. But the encounter turned my thoughts to Rora, and instead of apprehension, I felt hope.

Then I returned to the barn to find three more people dead, and I didn't go out again.

"Prepare a splint, Helos," says Bren, after examining the arm. Trampled by a horse, I'd guess, judging by the bruising patterns on his skin. Mislaid hooves have caused at least a quarter of the injuries we're seeing.

"What's your name?" I ask the boy, gathering supplies while Bren continues his search for wounds. The boy doesn't answer, tears streaming freely down his face.

"It's Niall," says one of the soldiers who carried him in. No, she's an officer—there's the dark green band encircling her left arm. She hasn't budged, alarm painted across a warm beige face streaked with dirt and grime. "Can you save him?"

"Niall, I'm Helos. I'm going to set your arm, okay?" Not waiting for acknowledgement, I instruct the officer to hold him steady and grab strips of stiffened leather. I wish I could give Niall poppy for the pain, or whisky like I did in Briarwend, but our supplies are dwindling ever further, the steady stream of incoming patients unrelenting. He'll just have to be brave.

I shift the bone back into place, managing not to be sick myself when Niall vomits. Bren lifts the boy's head so he doesn't choke before staunching the blood flowing from a laceration on his abdomen.

The officer blinks rapidly.

"He'll be fine," I tell her, and he will be—in body, at least. I don't say that he might be one of the lucky ones, considering some of the others I've seen. Niall has a right to his pain.

"He's my responsibility," she says quietly.

"He'll be fine," I repeat. When Niall has been squared away, I glance again at the dark green band around her arm. This could be the opportunity for which I've been waiting. "Are you returning to the front?"

The officer nods, and my mood rises, just a little.

"Hang on a moment," I beg. "Please."

Without checking to see if she'll obey, I rinse my hands as best I can and race up the creaking ladder that leads to the loft. My pounding head swims from lack of sleep, a sick feeling lodged in my stomach and aching limbs, but I push through the dizziness. Cara is lying on the far end, trying to get some rest, but it's impossible to silence my footsteps as I navigate around packs and bedrolls to the dusty strip where I've left my own. Grabbing my pack, I dig out the rolled letter, make sure the tie sealing the paper is secure, and return to the officer's side.

"Is Weslyn there, where you're going?" I ask, slightly breathless. I haven't seen Weslyn since he left for this miserable place the same day as I, but surely a royal can't be that difficult to find. "Prince Weslyn, I mean. Have you seen him?"

The officer hesitates, and fear drives an icy dagger between my ribs.

"He's there," she replies after a time. My shoulders droop. "But we're in different bands."

I care nothing for military bands or who reports to whom. I care only for the letter, now stained, that's been burning a hole in my pack ever since I managed to return to the Keep yesterday morning. The visit had lasted only a few precious hours, an entirely insufficient time to reunite with Finley; he was working and didn't even learn of my arrival until shortly before I had to leave again. But it lasted long enough for him to hand me two letters.

"Can you get this to him?" I ask, shoving the rolled parchment into the officer's hands. "To Weslyn. Please, it's important. Prince Finley sent it."

Which is technically true—but the letter is from Rora. Arrived alongside the one I've since creased beyond repair, having read it over and over, twenty times at least. *Don't worry,* she wrote to me, which is typical Rora, and it makes me want to both laugh and scream. *I worry,* I would have written back, if I'd had an address. *I will always worry.*

The officer handles Weslyn's letter delicately, as if the paper is a priceless jewel or a fire log ready to combust. "It won't be easy," she warns.

"Please," I say again. "He'll want to read this. He needs to." I have no idea what's inside, not caring to pry, but I know I speak the truth. Weslyn may be an insufferable ass sometimes, but he also might be my friend, and my sister is mad about him, however much she tries to downplay it. The fact that she wrote him is proof enough.

The officer studies me a few moments longer, then nods. "I'll make sure he gets it."

Relieved, I thank her twice and return to my work.

Trapped in that barn for hours on end, time loses its meaning.

No clock tower tolls the hour. People bleed out before we've scarcely begun, and moments spent bent over a single person seem to last a lifetime. No one wants to risk a torch's open flames in an old wooden barn, and the weak light filtering in through scattered windows functions much the same as the few oil lamps we possess. Day blends into night.

And night—that should be the best time. The fighting stops when soldiers can no longer see, and so a merciful respite happens sometime between midnight and dawn; new arrivals no longer trickle in, and the patients still with us have stabilized. But after dark is when the memories knock loudest, and Finley isn't here to burn the shadows away.

All I want is to hold his hand. A five-pointed star that's strong enough to tether me to the light. Since I can't, I lay on my bedroll in the creaking loft and scour my pack for the one beacon I have left: a single creased, smudged letter. Rora's offering from afar.

The loft is too dark to make out the words, but I hold the letter close anyway. By now, I practically know it by heart. It's my fifth night in this barn, and I can't stop turning over the measure of division in Oraes she described. She framed the observation as a surprise, even a weapon to exploit, but what I hear is an opportunity.

It makes me think of that Eradain prisoner who learned I was a shifter and still said I had kind hands.

That day, I'd walked from the room daring to hope a few people in Eradain hadn't given in to Jol's vision. From the picture Rora has painted, it sounds as if there might be more than a few. I feel my hesitant desire for power morphing into certainty, the bodies on the floor below giving that conviction an urgent edge. The hands of the fallen are no longer weighing mine down, but pulling them forward, Rora's hopeful words and my morbid work weaving into a sort of tapestry. The strands point north, toward justice. They coalesce into a crown.

I fall asleep to thoughts of a faraway throne. When the sun rises and Emilia nudges me awake, it's back to unwashed soldiers and churned-up tissue and metallic warmth bleeding from bodies.

By the time I'm in a cart heading back to Fendolyn's Keep two days later, drifting in and out of sleep, I feel as though I've been trampled by a bear. The line has crept steadily south, despite the Telyan army's best efforts. We've had to abandon the barn, and Bren and I, along with a few others, are going home to rest and work the civilian hospital while fresh healers take our place.

All of us are slowly morphing into specters. Squeezed in among the sweet-smelling crates, I can see it.

Bren shakes me gently awake when the cart reaches the narrow pass that leads into the valley. Here, I once led more than two hundred soldiers to their deaths. I lift my aching head, my throat pinching at the sight.

Tents stretch along the lakefronts and slender weeds, an unnatural canvas of cream, gray, and green stretched into orderly rows beneath the setting sun. I've always slept soundest in a crowd. To close my eyes safe between four walls, to hear the grate of rubber soles against felled wood and wheels against cobblestone—city life comforts me with the knowledge that I am part of a collective, the breath that keeps the granite body running and sleeping and awakening every dawn. But I'm discovering it's one thing to be surrounded by people relaxed into routine, and quite another to be surrounded by frightened faces and the baffling composure of those trained to die in the service of something more.

The cart driver pulls the horses to a stop. We're hardly through the pass, and I sit up, shocked by the barrier before us.

A giant gash scores the earth, the ditch maybe four or five paces wide. Workers with shovels are spread along the bottom, churning up the dirt. In some places, only the tops of their heads are visible. The ditch stretches halfway across the narrow entrance to the valley, and someone has stuck long shafts of tipped wood into the bottom like a row of vicious teeth.

"What's this for?" I ask.

Bren shakes his head, as confused as I.

Nothing with wheels could cross that ditch, so the driver directs the horses to go around. Apparently the surprises aren't finished, because I can just make out a group congregating at the base of the plateau. Something is up.

When the cart finally passes through the rows of tents, I hop down on reluctant feet despite Bren's protest and push toward the swelling crowd. I can't judge how many there are. Dozens I'd guess, milling about the trampled grass at the plateau's base, with more descending from the Keep. Several soldiers have wandered over as well, but they're sticking to the edges, visibly uncertain as to their role. Maybe they're merely as curious and unsettled as I am.

A voice rings out from the crowd's center.

Fisting the straps of my pack, I wend through the mass. People part for me with uneasy expressions, noting the filthy, stained clothing I haven't yet been able to change. I'm sure the smell matches the sight. When I reach a small gap in the middle, four civilians armed with hunting bows are addressing the crowd. Two hoofed brown animals, both dead, are tethered to rods on the ground. Another animal's lifeless form sprawls unceremoniously at their feet.

My heart stutters in my chest. A wolf and two caribran.

Caribran east of the river.

Rora! Surely this must be her doing, at least in part. *She's in Oraes,* comes a niggling voice in my head, but that doesn't matter.

Even if she's had help—and she probably has—she was the one who set the string of events in motion, I know it. Ripples in a lake.

Stupid, *stupid* me for doubting her.

Hope is rising, strong and fast. Though it's probably crazy, surely too soon for magic to stop feeling threatened, I'm itching to race up the hill and into the hospital to see if anyone has been freed of the Throes.

And then reality sharpens into focus.

Gaze roaming the crowd, I see my own surprise reflected on strangers' faces. But theirs is layered with thinly veiled terror, as if the dead animals might stretch out their necks and swallow the gawkers whole.

"—entire herd, grazing the meadows!" one of the hunters is saying.

"We're going back," another adds. "Before we lose sight of them."

"But when?" a woman calls from the crowd.

"Before sunset. Don't worry, we'll drive them out."

"Caribran are one thing," the woman points out. "How can you drive out wolves you can't even see?"

One of the hunters nudges the poor wolf's snout with his shoe. "This one made herself known eventually. Follow the herd and you'll find the wolves."

Hold on.

Wolves you can't even see.

This is a changeling wolf?

The back-and-forth continues, but my mind is buzzing loud as a swarm of insects, blotting out their words. Magical animals have been sighted in Telyan. *Telyan,* where most have been driven out or hunted to extinction. There hasn't been a reported sighting of a magical animal in these parts in close on fifty years.

Magic came back, and they killed it.

They want to keep killing it.

I look at the changeling wolf, dead on the ground. Father loved these wolves, used to make them the heroes of his stories. He always hailed their presence as a sign that the world was at balance.

I lift my eyes to the pinched expressions around me, flyaway hairs framing scared, hostile faces. I hear their raised voices as fire flickering through the air, and I see history repeating itself, this rare, miraculous sliver of a chance slipping through our fingers like smoke.

I feel anger.

True, righteous anger, surging past the hope. The cavernous space inside me no longer black, but blazing red—burning the hands that hold me down, flying up the stairs and out into the open air. My sister is risking her life to save these people. And this is the thanks she receives?

"You are all out of your minds!" I shout, so loud the effort hurts my throat.

The crowd falls quiet. Many seem confused by this singular voice of dissent, searching for the source, and I'm only too happy to give it to them. Rora has never liked speaking in front of large groups, but I feel no fear at the prospect. Besides, I may as well get used to confrontation, if I'm aiming to take on Eradain's collective consciousness. This, at least, is something I can do to help her, despite the distance between us.

I step forward, into the center and the hunters' baffled stares.

The mild recognition to which I've grown accustomed kindles throughout the crowd. *Ah, him.* The mysterious healer who brought about an enemy unit's ambush, who used to spar with the elder prince and still remains a frequent fixture at the younger prince's side. My presence is unusual enough to be registered and remembered, even if facts are scarce, a topic of idle gossip for a stir-crazy base eager for distraction.

"What's your problem?" says one of the hunters.

"My problem?" I want to laugh. Or cry. And why not? These days, they're interchangeable enough. "My problem is that today you witnessed a miracle. The animals you destroyed and drove from their homes came back. And your first instinct was to kill them again."

"Magic threatens us all. It's dangerous." The woman who speaks is middle-aged, white skinned and hollow cheeked, staring me down with that characteristic strong Telyan brow. She's like a tempest personified, all weathered edges, her graying hair breaking loose from its plait. "Look at the Vale. Look at the Throes. The same force flows through these animals' veins."

"That wolf," I respond, nodding to the ground. "Was she bothering you?"

She stares as if she does not understand the question.

"You say magic is dangerous. Did she attack you? Did those caribran? Or were they too busy regrowing the grass they eat?"

"You're young," she says, and the dismissal grates my bones. "You don't remember what it's like to live on land where magic is awake."

I do laugh now, bitterly.

"We're better off without them here to stir up trouble—"

"Better off?" I take two steps toward her before I can stop myself. "Look around you! Crops are failing because the soil is poor. The land is dying. People are dying. How exactly are we better off?" She starts to speak again, but I interrupt. "And why should that even matter? Why do you people always make decisions based on what's best for you, *only* you? Why should human comfort always come first?"

"You're one to complain," she retorts, folding her arms.

"Actually, no. I'm not." I don't stop to consider the potential ramifications, because I just don't care. Not anymore. Especially not when Rora and I have spent years bearing the burden of suspicion, humans fearing the Prediction's warning applied to us. Now we're left struggling to clean up their mess, because *they're* the true heralds of death. It has always been them. I pull from air and earth and direct the matter into my skin, my lungs, my bones, shifting them all until I become this woman's twin.

The hunter steps back. Voices erupt among the crowd, and I wait until the count of ten before shifting back to my natural form.

"But you're—"

I don't know who among the onlookers started to speak, but they don't bother finishing their thought. Perhaps they're realizing the stupidity of claiming I couldn't be both the person they thought they knew and a shifter. My mind races beneath the rampart to that Eradain prisoner's shock. They all think they're so different, these people from opposing realms, but they're more alike than they realize.

"What do you want to do?" I ask no one in particular. "Drive me out? Go ahead. You can find somebody else to tend to your wounded and save your asses from invasion. I warn you, though. The Danofers might not take too kindly."

I dare to search the crowd, making eye contact with anyone willing to meet my gaze. Some look angry and confused, others pretend they don't see me at all. But some familiar faces are watching me fondly, the way they always have. Emilia, who must have jumped from the cart, same as I. The cook Willa, whose sore back I treated after I cleaned and she made me breakfast. A soldier I patched up in Briarwend. There are many I don't recognize, but who seem to recognize me.

"This is wrong," I tell them, exhaustion returning in one foul swoop. "The world doesn't exist to make your life easier. You just get to live in it. If every other species has had to make sacrifices, you can too."

Fisting the straps of my pack, I push my way through the crowd and make my way up the hill, silence hanging in my wake.

That night and the next, muted dread eats at the corners of my mind. Living openly as a shifter in Telyan would have felt risky enough a few months ago, what with the Prediction and the Fallow Throes serving as twin flames to stoke fear, mistrust, and unmerited resentment among humans. Now I've gone and done it when stress is at an all-time high.

Impulsive, I guess. But everyone has their limits, and turns out that skeleton of a mob was mine.

The hunting party still went out again that afternoon. At least the group had shrunk in size.

Word of my outburst seems to have spread like wildfire overnight, sparking tiny gestures most places I go. A covert glance here, a question there, heads turned toward neighboring tongues to swap impressions of the shifter in their midst. It sets my teeth on edge. I returned to the Keep to find respite, and instead I am surrounded by unrelenting eyes, a thrush forced into a cage and expected to sing for their entertainment.

Thank fortune, most people are treating me the same as before, whether because I clearly retain the royal family's favor, or because they simply don't care. I'm hoping for the latter, because for every three smiles, there's a pair of fists curling in dark corners, a pointed brow and murmured threat. The evening after my confession, four people stop me on my walk back from the hospital, hemming me in along the dimly lit path. In the end, they don't touch me, only laugh at the fear on my face before melting into the shadows. But their amusement is enough to make me run the rest of the way to the Officers' Hall, shaking. How did Rora put up with this all those years in Castle Roanin?

Nights have always been hard, but lately, they're growing nearly unbearable. Sleep is slow to come, my senses tuned to the hall on the other side of the door, waiting to hear the handle turn. When I relax enough to drift off at last, I wake to clothes drenched in sweat, the blankets a battered mess. The constant stares, the way they watch and prod me with words and silent warnings—it all takes me back to that horrible room, where threats were made vividly real with tools and faces and hands and flames. And always, now, I hear those soldiers, maimed or trampled or dying, crying out in that foul-smelling barn. On my hands, I feel the urine-soaked trousers of the unconscious and the blood of the mortally wounded. I scrub and scrub, my hands red and raw, but it won't come off, it won't come off.

In these torturous hours when the fear clamps down, I long to knock on Finley's door and ask if I could pass the remaining hours in his room. I'm sure he would welcome me. Past midnight on my second night back, I actually leave my room and make it as far as the hall with his door.

But as with every time I've tried, I just can't bring myself to lay this burden at his feet. Finley needs me to be strong. His stamina has dropped sharply in a short span of time, such that some days he doesn't have the energy to leave his room. Worse, his senses heightened four days ago, and I wasn't even *there*. Stuck in a barn while he was suddenly inundated with the scratch of pens on parchment several rooms away and the smell of the black smoke curling out of the armory chimneys. The onslaught is more than any human is built to take in, and with it comes a vicious headache that rarely seems to ease.

I know it won't be long until his voice changes to a stranger's. The beginning of the end. The duration of every patient's course is different, but I've tended enough of them by now to read the signs. It could take days or only hours, but soon his voice will change, and not long after he'll lose the power of speech. Just like Lyra had when he interfered on her behalf. Lyra, who's buried in the valley.

So I pause around the corner, biting my lip, before I turn on my heel and walk back to my room. I need to collect myself before he sees me in this state. I swap my sweaty sleep shirt and trousers for fresh ones, slide into bed, and pull the covers up to my chin. Longing to fall asleep. Afraid to fall asleep.

There's a knock on my door.

"Helos?"

The voice is muffled, but it's his. Shocked, I throw off the covers and yank open the door.

Fin is standing there, rumpled hair askew, wearing a matching set of sleep clothes the pale blue of a robin's egg. The sight is comfort beyond measure. We've barely spent time together since my return. He looks up at me with a slightly lowered chin, skinny shoulders hunched in the chilled, empty hallway.

"Can I come in?" he asks.

I step back quickly so he can pass and shut the door behind him. Fin stops only three or four paces in, his gaze flitting around the disordered state of my depressing room. I feel like crying. I feel like throwing myself at his feet and clinging to his legs like a child scared of the dark, so relieved am I to have him here. Instead, I lean against the doorframe and smooth the hair from my face, breathing deeply. "Couldn't sleep?"

He frowns at the distance I've set between us. "I came to ask you the same question," he says, scratching the back of his head. "I heard you down the hall."

My heart pinches. Of course.

I pace to the bed and sink onto the mattress. My back against the headboard, I press the heels of my palms into my forehead, hard.

Fin perches beside me, setting his walking stick against the wall. "What's wrong?" he asks, a bit softer.

"Nothing," I tell him. "Sorry I've been—away, more than I should. It's not your fault, I promise. I'm sorry," I say again.

"I don't mean us," he replies, lacing his fingers through mine. "I mean you."

My gaze falls to his hand in mine. That's supposed to be enough to keep the shadows at bay. It should be enough. So why is the noise in my head still there?

You can hold onto me if you're scared, he teased me once. He isn't smiling tonight.

"I've been having nightmares," I admit, finding it difficult to meet his gaze.

Finley nods. "About what?"

"People hurting each other. And—me."

Again, they feel like the words of a child, not a man nearly grown. Embarrassment heats my cheeks. But Finley doesn't laugh. He just scoots closer and lifts his free palm to the side of my face.

"How could anyone want to hurt you?" he asks.

The sincerity in his voice is breaking my heart. I want to tell him, *they already have,* but I'm afraid to see the change wash over his face, the sorrow color his crystal eyes. My composure is already hanging by a thread as it is.

"Helos," he says gently. His hand is still on my face, the only touch I still crave.

I cover his hand with mine, drop my head, and whisper, "I'm so tired, Fin."

"Then sleep." He smiles faintly. "I'll look after you."

I sink back into the pillows and shut my eyes, not letting go of him. My anchor. My lifeline. After a while, he squeezes in beside me and curls onto his side, our clasped hands a mountain between us.

"I'll look after you," he promises again, soft as breathing.

I want to respond, but I'm already fading, days of exhaustion tugging me into much-needed sleep. For once, my dreams bring me peace. When I wake the next morning later than usual, the sun already high in the sky, he's gone, the space beside me leached of his warmth.

I lay there studying my empty hands, wondering when he slipped away, or if he was ever even there at all.

TWENTY

RORA

I open my eyes to a dimly lit space. Water stains seeped into a mahogany floor. Musty air trapped between barren walls. The stuttering sounds of creaking wood. And—

"You know," says a low voice. "I had hoped you would come to Oraes. Just not with a knife already in my back."

I lift my head, wincing at the stiffness in my neck.

Jol is hunched in an unforgiving chair across from mine, arms braced upon his widespread legs. He's watching me.

I lurch forward, swearing when I realize my wrists are bound behind my own chair. The jerky movement exacts a toll—my body feels battered, as if I've been flattened beneath a caribran stampede. Still, the air down here feels mercifully cool, my skin no longer clammy, and the unbearable pain has dulled to a permeating ache. I test the bonds again. A mouse to slip free, then the lynx to—

I spot the knife hilt protruding from Jol's crinkled boot.

Perhaps it's best to wait until I've regained a bit more strength.

"This, from the man who poisoned me?" I rasp, my vision clouding temporarily while I assess the bleak, unfinished wooden walls for exit points. Unless I find another when I shift, there's only the closed door behind him.

"I did not give you a lethal dose," Jol replies, seemingly indifferent my ire. "Merely what I deemed necessary to make you talk."

I can't resist. "And how did that work out for you?"

His mouth presses into a thin line. "We've apprehended a boy in the streets," he continues, ignoring the question entirely. "He was helping another to dump a body into the river. Carolette's."

The shock stills my efforts. She's dead?

"He had quite a lot to say, when prompted." Jol's gaze remains fixed on me, arrow sharp. "Something about those so-called rebels operating in the city center. And you."

"I don't know what you're talking about," I reply, my rib cage tightening.

Jol remains silent for another beat or two, finger ticking, before he straightens abruptly. "Bring him in," he calls, smoothing a cuff on his dark red collared shirt.

The door bangs open, and two guards half usher, half drag a young person into the room. The skinny captive's clothing is torn, his face badly bruised with an eye nearly swollen shut, but he's recognizable to me nonetheless.

Kal.

"This is her?" Jol addresses him directly. "The girl responsible for the drawing?"

My heart twists as Kal looks at me, the breath rattling in his chest. I can feel us trying to read answers in each other's shuttered faces—who has revealed which truths, and to whom.

A bulky guard squeezes the back of Kal's neck, and his lingering defiance spikes into fear.

"That's her," he mumbles.

"Thank you, Kal. You've been most helpful." After Jol's focus cuts back to me, he adds, "Dispose of him."

The ground sways beneath my feet.

"It's my fault!" I say hastily, as the guards begin to thrust Kal out the door. I can't stay silent, not if my confession might earn him some degree of mercy. Whatever arguments Kal and I have had in the past, he doesn't deserve to die. "It was my idea. I drew it. Blame me, not him."

Jol raises a hand to halt the guards, eyebrows lifting.

"Let him go," I plead, resisting the urge to scream in frustration. Though my fingers stretched into claws, they only remained a handful of heartbeats before retracting. I'm still too weak to hold a shift, and I hate it, I *hate it*. "He's innocent."

"And Carolette?" Jol retorts. Behind him, the blood has drained from Kal's face. "I suppose you are responsible for her death, as well?"

I can hear in his mocking tone that he expects me to lie. "It was my idea to bring her in."

Head tilting back a bit, Jol appraises me thoughtfully, his countenance far too light for one weighing a young boy's life in his hands. "Back to his cell, then," he amends. "For now."

I release my breath and glance at Kal, who struggles against the guards' bodily clutch.

"I'm sorry," he tells me loudly, shunted across the threshold. "I told them about the mines—"

I'm studying the door long after it closes behind them, parsing the confession for the message buried within.

The mines—a false trail, I think. Maybe he didn't reveal the catacombs.

A small hope.

"You admit it, then," Jol says when we're alone. Without the audience, his voice has quieted. "You put the drawing in the leaflets. You attempted to turn my people against me."

Impatience surges forth, my temper flaring hot. When I try the claws again, I find they last a little longer this time. Progress. "I set your prison on fire, too, with the help of some friends," I reply, because suddenly I want him to know. To my immense satisfaction, he blanches. "Tell me, if your people are so supportive of your vision for the future, why did you feel the need to lie to them?"

In a heartbeat, Jol has shaken the shock from his features. Hostility rolls in, his temper the lightning to my thunder, as if his composure hangs on the edge of a knife. Finally, we're aligned. "I once offered you and your brother the choice of renouncing your ties to Telyan and siding with me." His fingers drum across his lap. "I see now I was mistaken."

"You poisoned me *before* you knew about the leaflets or the prison—"

"Perhaps if you had come as yourself rather than sneaking around my home in disguise, we might have begun things in a more civil manner!"

I blink at Jol, having never heard him shout. Confusion mingles with stark disbelief as, for the second time in my life, I catch a glimpse of the emotion that undercut our final exchange in the prison. That hint of loneliness, as if his invitation contained some small measure of sincerity alongside the intention of neutralizing the threat. *You know nothing of me or my life.*

Did some part of him actually think—?

"Side with you," I echo softly, shaking my head. "Who would willingly choose that?"

There again, buried in his features—the barest flicker of hurt.

Then he smooths the hair back from his forehead, and it's gone.

"The events in the courtyard have made it clear, there's no time to waste." His tone has grown businesslike, devoid of feeling.

The courtyard—fortune's sake, in my distraction since waking, I'd nearly forgotten. Land magic in *Oraes*. If Peridon and Andie were here, I would hug them.

But Jol is still speaking. "Because of you, my people need a reminder of what victory looks like. I intend to give them one. You might even help me with that, if you're lucky."

Apprehension needles my spine. "What, are you going to poison me again?" I ask dryly, though fear makes the question stick in my throat.

The ghost of a smile twists his severe face. "I think not," he says, as if he's given the matter serious consideration. "Your life may yet prove useful."

I'm coming to understand that Jol is always playing the long game. Thinking several steps ahead, assessing every word and course of action for strengths and weaknesses. Mapping out his future one projected step at a time, like pieces on a game board. I wonder if he learned this in childhood, whether years spent under the same roof as his father made this circumspection and bid for self-preservation necessary tools for survival.

"The time has come for us both to pay a visit to the kingdom you're so fond of," he goes on, and the smile hardens. "I believe I have some promises to deliver on."

At the reference to Telyan, a jumble of emotions war for prominence within. Relief at the thought of going home at last, quickly overpowered by the fear for what he plans to do. Finley. Violet. Wes. *I think I will enjoy making him bleed. Slowly.* "If you touch him—"

"*Him*?" Jol interrupts, shaking his head as if wounded. "So it is love. Oh, Rora, you disappoint me."

The air sweeps from my lungs. "It isn't—"

"And to think, I once believed your—arrangement," his gaze swipes down my figure after the pause, mocking, "with that family could be of no use. Tell me, after I make your presence known, what do you think *he* would give me in exchange for sparing your life?" The vestige of amusement fades from his face. "Because I intend to find out."

"He won't negotiate with you," I spit, though what I'm thinking is, *I will not be reduced to a bargaining chip. I'll be gone before you can use me for your gain.*

"Maybe not." Jol shrugs and pushes to his feet. "But I suggest you try for a little more optimism, because if he doesn't, I will cut your throat myself."

I grasp for the one advantage I have left. "You speak as if you plan on getting me all the way to Telyan as a captive. A lot can go wrong between now and then."

Horan and the rest will know Kal was taken. They'll come for him, and I can make my escape with them, too.

"You couldn't tell?" Jol asks, sounding genuinely surprised. "You're already on the ship. We left port several hours ago—I estimate we'll dock in Telyan in five, six days? After all, we control the northeast coast." He inclines his head. "Thank you again for your assistance in that."

All I can do is stare.

"Oh, and I recommend against any valiant attempts at escape," he adds, gripping the door handle. "We might turn your friend Kal loose once we reach the shore, or we might feed him to the sea instead. Up to you."

At last, I am heading home. Back to Telyan and the boys whose names I repeat like a mantra guiding my steps. *Helos. Weslyn. Fin.* The knowledge should be comforting, but the journey is far from the joy I once envisioned.

I understand perfectly well that Jol is dangling Kal's life to keep me in line, just as he plans to hold mine over Wes. I shift to mouse anyway as soon as I've recovered the strength. Free of my bonds, I squeeze through the minuscule gap beneath the door and past the two people stationed outside. Relying on my ears, nose, and vibrations in the air, I attempt to paint a picture of my surroundings. Below deck seems a bewildering maze of dim, dusty common rooms, narrow corridors, crowded passenger lodgings, and closed doors I make no effort to venture beyond.

By the time I make it above deck, it becomes painfully clear why Jol would choose to travel south with me by sea rather than trekking through occupied Glenweil.

I had hoped it might be easy enough to escape on wings once I'd done my best to free Kal as well. I was wrong. The ocean disorients me—blue in every direction, every angle the same. I have the sun, but I have no sense of where we are in proximity to land or how far I'd have to fly to reach land at all. For all I know, my strength would give out before I made it to shore. With a sinking feeling, I realize I'm nearly as trapped above deck as I am between four walls.

So I return to my room, shift back to human, and wait. Sit with my back against the wall and try not to think about the goodbyes in Oraes I didn't get to say. Unlike he had in the prison, Jol doesn't visit again.

Rather quickly, I realize I was built for earth and sky, but not the sea. The rocking motion makes me sick to my stomach, and I have only the one chamber pot in which to relieve myself. The windowless prison cell sports little more than an old, quilted bed pallet and a set of creaking drawers. If I stretch out my arms, fingers splayed, I can almost touch both sides of the room. The confinement alone is nearly enough to drive me mad, but worse is the idea of surrendering my safety to water's tumultuous grasp. It reminds me too much of that hateful river, the day Wes and I almost drowned. In the ocean's lurching embrace, I hear the river roar in my ears as its current dragged me down, stifled by murky darkness while I fought for air and freedom.

Day becomes indistinguishable from night.

I long to undermine Jol's control, and every time someone delivers hard bread and a glass of water, I consider shifting and telling the truth about our mother then and there. But every time, my will to survive comes out the stronger. I want to help create change, but I'm not so noble as to be willing to give up my life for the chance of securing a better future for others. Not if I have another choice. Maybe it's selfish, but I want to be a part of that future.

Anyway, I don't want the people of Eradain to turn on Jol because of his magical blood. I want them to turn on him because they disapprove of his actions.

Intending to reach Telyan alive, I bite my tongue and receive these rare visits in silence.

Save for one.

I have no idea what time General Hariette comes or why. All I know is suddenly she's there, the one whose argument I interrupted as Carolette, just before my half brother poisoned me. Stately in her red-trimmed navy military jacket, she shuts the door behind her as I jolt off the bed pallet and onto my feet.

She doesn't speak at first, simply studies me through her long lashes. My fingernails dig into my palms. If she marks the scent of vomit in the chamber pot, she gives no sign.

"You put the picture in the leaflets," she says, her tone neutral.

I don't know how she found out, but I see no point in denying this point of pride, nor in putting Gemma at risk by alluding to others' involvement. I nod stiffly.

"How did you come by the information?"

Her direct gaze is piercing, but I've spent too long in Violet's company to shy away. "I was there."

General Hariette's eyes drop to my hands, which are still balled into fists at my sides. "Your face looks familiar," she says, quieter.

Though I've decided not to shift in another's presence while trapped aboard this ship, something in this woman's manner sets her apart from the other high-ranking Eradain officials I've encountered. She doesn't seem softer, exactly, but—less hasty. Thoughtful, even, like she's determined to make her own decisions regardless of external pressures. It reminds me of Wes, and perhaps that's why I lift my chin a little and tell her, "I'm sure it does."

My pulse picks up as I brace myself for her reaction. But she simply looks at me with that same, unwavering focus before she nods and exits the room without a word.

And then, at last, land. The lookout sounds a horn when Telyan's coast appears on the horizon, the blare so loud that even I can hear it from my prison cell. My heart soars to be so close, and I force myself to stand and work the stiffness from my aching joints. I don't know how long we've been at sea, where my captors have held the upper hand. But Telyan is *my* domain, the realm I've roamed for the last four years, and I refuse to spend another night on the wrong side of the war.

By the time the ship teeters enough for me to suspect they've dropped anchor, I'm ready. I don't resist when four soldiers fetch me from my room, though I feel rather pleased that Jol believes I require so large a guard. For the first time, I see the ship as I couldn't in mouse form—three towering masts jut out from a deck at least the length of Castle Roanin's central atrium, while underfoot, the rich mahogany slats have been waxed to a shine, the salt residue scrubbed clean for the king's arrival. And just beyond—

Telyan, arcing green over gold after days of inexhaustible blue.

Early evening shadows lay scattered across the beach, but since the days have been growing shorter, I suspect it's only mid-afternoon. I breathe the palette in deep, drinking in the sight of the sandy shore and the forested mountains far beyond and to the north. Nearly two months ago, Helos, Wes, and I were trekking along the range's base with the Royal Guard, just there, finding refuge from watchful eyes in the sloping backcountry.

Home.

Helos, Wes—can you sense me coming?

At the procession's head, Jol smiles when he disembarks the royal flagship, running a hand along the railing. Alarmingly, I see no sign of Kal, and my body tenses further at the blocks of soldiers crawling up the beach, disembarking from the rest of the fleet. Jol's final push. A few guards escort me onto shore, and I resist the urge to sink my knees into the sand and kiss the earth.

Rather than making camp on the coast, Jol and his generals—Hariette and Malhorn among them—lead us on, unwilling to waste the dwindling daylight. Horses were brought over for their use, Jol's stallion suggesting a nervous disposition, so they ride in splendor while the rest of us march. Though the soldiers Jol assigned to my guard keep eyeing me edgily, clearly waiting for an escape, I know better than to attempt it with an army at my back. I'm waiting for the night, when velvet darkness shields me from sight and renders arrows ineffective.

At last, our sea-tossed legs are given a rest. The sun dips down and the tents go up, disordered clumps concentrated where the springy land lays flat enough. Thick rope chafes my wrists where a soldier tied it tight, but I feign indifference as the group leads me across the camp and between rows of hastily erected tents until we reach a trio three times the size of all the rest. I'm distracted by the sky, judging it nearly dark enough for arrows to miss their mark, when a soldier opens the flap to the largest tent and gestures for me to step through.

I stop just inside.

Jol stands before a mirror with rounded corners, the first time I've seen him up close since I woke on the ship. He runs a towel across his face, his bare torso gleaming with sweat and heaving as if he's just finished exercising.

"Leave us," he says.

One of the soldiers fingers his crossbow in a menacing manner before departing with the rest.

The first thing that strikes me is the amount of color brightening the tent. Deep red rugs, a couple of mahogany folding chairs, an illustrated map strewn across a wooden table. There are burnt umber pillows threaded with gold, a gleaming silver pitcher and a creamy white basin, and it occurs to me that it was somebody's job—likely multiple somebodies—to carry all of this here for him.

The second thing that strikes me is the state of Jol's upper half. His skin is a horrid spectacle, a collection of scars that cover parts of his back, his shoulders, his sides. Some are jagged and rough, as if someone sewed him up without a care for precision. Others are more neatly done, either the work of professionalism or pity.

"Rora," he greets when he sees me there, staring. I shouldn't, but it's hard to look away. "I trust your journey was comfortable." He speaks like he knows it wasn't.

Though Jol fiddles with the silver chain around his neck, he doesn't act embarrassed or ashamed of the marks. His confidence feels oddly like a challenge, a dare for me to comment, or to ask. I can't seem to work up the nerve.

Instead, my thoughts drift to my mother.

Our mother, who must have known what Daymon was and left her son there anyway to face him alone. I remember the times I caught Jol at the piano, his side of the room ablaze with light, and anger churns deep in my gut, hot and twisting. At the person who did this to him and the person who let him suffer it, the ones who didn't care enough to stitch him up properly. Has he ever felt a pair of gentle hands in his life?

I cannot forgive the man he's become. But for a moment, I pity the child.

"You're quieter than usual," he observes, pulling on a casual long-sleeved shirt. "Perhaps the ocean didn't agree with you after all. Nature is a cruel thing."

I don't voice the response taking shape on my tongue, that nature can be cruel and generous both. "Where's Kal?"

"Oh, I expect at the bottom of the sea," Jol replies. "You really believed I'd permit him to live, given his crimes?"

My eyes close.

Another person to add to the tally.

Sorrow heavy in my chest, I linger only a few heartbeats more before forcing my eyelids open again. Grief can't save Kal now, or me. I need to focus.

"Why am I here?" I force out.

Jol lifts a sheet of parchment and perches on the table's edge, one foot off the floor. "I've been writing to a certain friend of yours. Weslyn, isn't it?" He draws the syllables out in an exaggerated fashion, as though he doesn't care for the taste. I'd like to rip that precious name straight from his poisonous mouth. "Makes sense, now, why he'd risk following you into the Vale. Though you have poor taste, Rora, I have to say. Man as hard as that?" He shakes his head mournfully, and I find his lack of self-awareness staggering. "I'm wondering if there's anything else I ought to add. A lock of hair, perhaps. Proof that I have you here. Thoughts?"

"You have nothing," I say sharply, my wrists twisting against the ropes. I'm tempted to take my chances and shift to mouse, but given the soldiers waiting outside, common sense holds me back. Barely. *Wait for full cover of night.*

Jol pulls out a small knife.

"If you come near me with that, you'll regret it," I warn. Lynx instincts whisper against my skin.

Looking vaguely amused, Jol rises from the table. "Come now, Rora. It's only hair."

"You expect me to believe you after you threatened to cut my throat?"

"As I said." He closes the distance between us with slow strides while I take a step back, then another. "Your life may yet prove of use."

The lynx is clawing forth insistently, demanding I use its defenses. In a final bid to avoid the risk of shifting while the night remains light enough to see, I tell him, "Just like your father."

Jol stops.

He blinks at me, knife hand faltering. "What did you say?"

"I said you look just like your father, looming over me with a knife. Did I get that right?" I lift my chin, my tone full of scorn. "I bet he'd be proud to see you."

Jol can't be more than a couple of paces away, but he doesn't move. Doesn't speak. For a long moment, I see the anger rising in him, a clear inclination to lash out. His eyes glass over with something softer, too. Almost like hurt. Then he smooths the emotion from his features and folds his arms across his chest.

"I'm sure he would have loved to hear that," he says, watching me a heartbeat longer before pacing over to the silver pitcher. "Do you know what he used to call me?" His gaze stays fixed on the table in front of him, his voice turned casual once more. After another glance my way, he huffs a breathy laugh and raises the pitcher. "Useless." He pours water into a glass. "Lazy. Soft."

I think of Helos's gentle healer hands. Of Finley's kindness, Wes's heart. I think, *There is nothing wrong with softness.*

"Tell me, Rora." Jol regains his earlier seat. I can't help but notice the knife is flat against the table, out of his hands. "How would you like to be remembered?"

The question catches me off guard. He appears to genuinely want an answer, though, and I find my reflection in the rounded mirror, considering.

Tonight, there are no borrowed hands doing the work. No one's face but my own staring back. Bent brow, tired circles ringing angry eyes. Scattered lines and invisible weights that make me feel older than merely seventeen. Or eighteen, or nineteen. Whatever.

Once, when I looked at myself, I saw only a girl with changeable features. None of them enough to shape her into a person someone would stay for, could love. That girl is still there; wounds that burrow in the body for years don't just disappear entirely in a couple of months. Maybe ever.

But now she's more shadow than self. Beside her is someone on solid ground, more certain of her strength and the strength of her convictions. A girl who steps into the darkness rather than going around, because it's the best chance she has of bringing light, and because, for the most part, she is not afraid. She's learning to hold the good with the bad, and she is growing.

My gaze cuts to the man across from me, and I realize with abrupt clarity: he is stuck.

"I suppose I haven't really thought about it," I reply, trying to gauge where this is going.

"I have." Jol's manner has sobered. "I promised myself I would be a better king than he ever was. A better man." He looks at me, nods again. "And I am."

By the river, I want to shake him! I want to cry. I want to grab him by the shoulders and tell him how wrong he's gotten it, that for all his shrewd planning and calculating, he has badly missed the mark. *Turn back,* I almost tell him. *Even now, you can stop this course.*

Then again, perhaps he can't. Maybe he lost that path forever when he orchestrated that prison and those cages. That ghastly shed.

"You're not," I say instead. "It's as I said. You're misguided and cruel, just like he was."

Jol's hands clutch the table's edge, so taut the veins jut out beneath his skin. "I am nothing like him."

"Then prove it." Hearing the change in his tone, remembering the brief shift in his eyes, I decide to make one final appeal. Not as a southern spy to a northern king, but as a sister to her brother. "Jol, call off the attack. Reverse your legislation. No one else needs to die for this cause. It's wrong. You know it is."

Jol holds my searching gaze for what feels like half an eternity. To my amazement, I think I may have actually gotten through to him, until he runs a weary hand across his face, shaking his head as though he pities me. "If you believed the people you love were in danger, would you fight to protect them?"

"They *are* in danger," I remind him, exasperated. "Because of you."

"Would you?"

I don't respond.

"Whatever you choose to believe, Rora, I love my kingdom." Jol straightens, bracing his palms against his thighs. "And I will do what I must to protect it."

I know, then, that appeals are useless. They're wound too deep, the stories he tells himself to sleep at night. Jol will continue to do what he believes is right.

And so will I.

"Enough of this," he says, regaining the knife, and I agree.

I don't expect words to deflect his attention a second time, so cool air sweeps my numbing limbs as I shed matter into the air and shift to mouse.

The tent blurs at once, but I don't wait. Heart in my throat, I run toward the canvas wall, back prickling as Jol shouts and footsteps thunder inside. A heavy boot slams just behind, hard enough for the impact to rattle my tiny mouse bones, but I'm already shoving through a gap between sections nailed to the ground.

Fresh air fills my lungs, the sky outside beautifully dark. My core warms against the evening's chill as I pull from the earth and direct the matter into my limbs, mouse lengthening to goshawk. Though I can hear the thrum of crossbows firing away, I'm already a ghost to their human eyes. I keep my gaze fixed on the stars and the velvet night between them, letting my wings carry me up and away.

Toward home.

TWENTY-ONE

HELOS

The morning I'm meant to return to the front should be an utter misery.

Instead, the sunrise brings a miracle.

At dawn, the garrison awakened to find the valley had changed overnight. A vast field of wildflowers sprang up without warning, blanketing the grass in scarlet perennials and yellow coreopsis. Along the forested ridges to either side of the road, the trees *moved*. Down the inner slopes and a short way into the valley, so that the red-and-gold tree line now sits a few dozen paces beyond the hills and the ditch I've since learned has been dug to impede siege weaponry—another helpful tip from Rora. Untidy rows of wide-crowned oaks, towering hickories, and sprawling elms where before, there was only meadow.

The Telyans fought panic, this latest shock almost enough to send the already tense community over the edge. I shared their surprise and, if I'm honest, a little of their fear as well. Pain points from my childhood have become increasingly difficult to cast aside, along with the more recent memories of our summer journey through the Vale.

Alongside the fear, though, there is burgeoning relief, and hope. Ripples in a lake spreading farther each day. And later that morning as I work a final shift, another miracle greets me in the hospital.

At first, I think my sleep-deprived mind might be playing

tricks. The young woman sitting on the bed before me is a radi-
ant glow of white-toothed smiles and healthy curves, striking eyes
and raven curls framing deep brown skin. I examine her again,
repeating my questions, and at some point, we both start laughing while she answers. Because my mind is not misleading me; the
scene is real. Yesterday, this woman, Cait, could barely sit up, too
overwhelmed by her heightened senses, the pain in her head, and
a furious fever that wouldn't come down. Today, she has a minor
headache and a poor appetite, but otherwise she is the picture of
health. Her senses have returned to normal, and when we placed a
potted plant in her hands, nothing happened.

The Fallow Throes, gone. The magic has left her body.

Merciful fortune, it's glorious! If Rora were here, I would
swing her around until our heads spun. As it is, I can't stop laughing, something I'd nearly forgotten how to do. For the first time
in days, I am thoroughly unprofessional but giddy nonetheless, because the plan is *working*. The land is waking up, and the magic's
letting go. At least, it has once. But once is more than none.

I want to run to Fin.

More healers are coming over, other patients peering our way
with a mixture of curiosity and criticism, wary of this marked
departure from the hospital's usual sobriety. Cait meets the healers' baffled inquiries with studied patience, and I can feel the tired
spirits around her rising, too, a golden aura fanning out from this
inexplicable breakthrough. Word spreads like a long-awaited infusion of hope after months of stifling despair.

Since this morning seems determined to be good, Finley soon
appears at the door, leaning on his walking stick. Astra hugs his side,
recently a near constant fixture in Weslyn's absence. The beginnings
of a tentative grin tug at the corner of Fin's mouth as his gaze sweeps
over the animated group and locks onto me. *What's this all about?*

I beam at him. I want to race into the valley and its moving,
wonderful forest, throw my arms around the sturdy trunks and
thank them, *thank* them for being here. To ask what more I can do
to help, though I already know the answer. Their greatest enemy
will be the humans' fear. I can work on that.

At the other end of the long corridor, Finley's mouth moves, forming words I'm too far away to hear.

His face falls, going ashen.

"Fin?" I say, concerned, but he's already hurrying out of sight. The hour tolls—eleven o'clock, nearly when I'm meant to meet Bren for our ride—but forget that. I wasn't here when Finley's senses heightened and he needed me. I'm not leaving him again.

I'm on my feet and crossing the ward, the surge of positivity dripping away.

"Finley!" I call, when I'm out the door and underneath the graying sky. A cold breeze slaps my face, ruffling my collar, and I cross my arms against the biting chill. I catch a head of blond hair disappearing into the Officers' Hall and take off after him, climbing the stairs two at a time to Finley's room.

Ansley is pacing outside his door.

My skin prickles. "What's going on?"

"Helos." Ansley shakes her head, bemused. "I don't know, I was on my way out when he came flying through. He wouldn't speak to me. Maybe I should call the captain—"

"Finley!" I exclaim, knocking loudly. Ansley rubs her arms but doesn't interfere, so I guess she knows about us.

No response comes from behind the door, but there is another noise that sounds an awful lot like crying.

I knock again, softer. "It's Helos. Can I come in?"

The crying sounds quiet for a time.

Ansley glances down the hall. "I should—"

"Not yet," I say in an undertone. "I think I can—"

Without warning, Finley throws open the door, fists my shirt, and yanks me inside.

The room itself seems fairly composed. Nothing different save an empty teacup on the wardrobe, a jar of willow bark he can use for the headaches, and cotton wads to stuff in his overtaxed ears.

Finley, however, looks as though he's falling apart. He locks the door behind us and paces to the window and back, window and back, like this sudden adrenaline burst has lent him strength.

By the bed, Astra whines and paces a bit herself, clearly sensing his distress. His gaze lands everywhere but on me.

"What is it?" I ask, alarmed by the tears streaking his cheeks, the green shirt untucked roughly in the front, the way his shallow breaths are stuttering in his throat.

Without answering, he sends a mug skittering against the wall with the toe of his shoe and digs the heels of his palms into his reddened eyes. I realize more empty teacups are rimming the floor, broken into shards.

"Talk to me," I plead.

Fin shakes his head rapidly, his back hitting the wall.

I cross the room in a few short strides. I've never seen him panic like this, and I don't know what to do other than wrap my arms around him and hold his hammering heart against mine. Beneath my grip, Fin is all coiled tension, a deer trapped in a predator's line of sight. For a moment, though, he leans into me and buries his face in my chest. He's shaking. He still won't speak, but he's crying audibly again, and the sound—

My heart plummets straight into the earth. I finally understand.

"It's okay," I murmur, resting my chin on top of his head.

Finley lets me hold him a few heaving breaths longer. Then he shakes his head against my chest and twists free, unable to keep still. "It is not okay!" he cries, and the river take me, his voice. His *voice*. The pitch isn't right, too rough and different and *not his*.

A stranger's voice. The beginning of the end.

Unless—

"Listen," I tell him urgently. "There's hope things won't progress further. Today at the hospital—"

"Listen to me!" he shouts, fisting his hair.

I hold his gaze an endless moment, feeling helpless. "I'm listening, Fin."

The magic let go of Cait. If we're lucky, it will loosen its hold on others. But how quickly, if at all? The joy I felt mere minutes ago was cruelly fleeting.

Finley is running out of time. I know this now as surely as

breathing, and so does he. A month, maybe, given the rate of his course. If even that. Four weeks to spend time with those he loves, to look upon his mountains, to feel the sting of winter sharpening the breeze. To taste and listen and create and learn and move and *be,* before all of it blinks away into nothing. Never again.

Which is completely, *breathtakingly* unacceptable. He should have years and years.

Finley's pacing again, wringing his trembling hands. He rubs a palm across his chest and the base of his throat, breathing faster now. Too fast.

"Fin," I say, "you need to calm down."

"Don't tell me what I need!" he chokes out. Pressing his palms hard against his ears, he sinks to the floor beside the bed and bares his teeth in a tortured grimace. Fortune save me, I've seen that look in plenty of people with the Throes, but not in Fin, not until today. It's too much, the constant influx of sights and sounds and smells I can't sense at all, but he can't shut off for even one moment's respite.

"Then you tell me." I have to force normalcy into my voice as I crouch before him, watching him struggle to catch his breath. "What do you need? Tell me and I'll do it. Anything."

He hugs his knees to his chest and drops his face, shoulders shaking. Astra lays down beside him. After a long while, he murmurs a string of words into his knees.

"What was that?" I say, leaning closer.

He speaks again, the words breathy and broken from crying, and this time I make out "need" and "Wes."

My heart sinks. Not because the name on his lips isn't mine, but because his brother has been gone for days, stuck in that forsaken place of barren earth and sleepless nights, carnage and death. He is miles and miles away. "You want Weslyn?" I ask, and he nods. And what can I do? "I'll go look for him, okay? Stay here. I'll be right back."

I leave him there, hyperventilating on the floor. It nearly tears me apart, but I do it anyway, because I promised.

"Ansley," I say quickly, when I'm out in the hall. "When is Weslyn due back? Is he coming back?"

Some emotion tugs at her eyes. She must hear the urgency in my voice, can surely hear Finley falling apart behind the door, but she only shakes her head, looking scared. "I don't know."

Which isn't enough. I take off down the hall, skidding when she calls, "I'll stay with him! Find the captain. She might know!"

I hurry down the corridors, searching every open door for Captain Torres. When I finally find her, she's in some sort of meeting, gathered around a table with Violet and a bunch of other people I don't know. Using more intel from Rora's letters, no doubt. The ditch was already her doing. What next? Unfortunately, that's all I see before the guard posted outside shoves me back forcefully and closes the door.

Black hair, sallow cheeks, sour mouth.

Dom. The one who set Broden on me.

"Going somewhere?" he asks, features twisted in distaste.

"I need to speak with Captain Torres," I tell him. "It's urgent."

"Urgent," he repeats, deadpan.

"Yes, urgent, you bastard. Let me in!"

"Do you seriously believe—"

"It's about Weslyn," I add, desperate. "Do you know where he is? Is he coming back to the Keep anytime soon?"

Dom's eyes narrow. "You should address His Royal Highness as—"

"Yes, fine. His Royal Highness, Prince Weslyn Danofer, heir to the throne of Telyan, second biggest pain in my ass, next to you. *Where is he?*"

Dom studies my face, and maybe some of my panic starts to chisel at his ice-pick heart, because he says, "You're in luck, I suppose. Her Majesty called him back hours ago. She's expecting him today."

I am flying. Down the corridor, out the front door, and across the gravel paths. Civilians and soldiers both stare as I race past, a few calling out to ask if something bad is happening. Which it is, but not the military ambush or outbreak of magic they're doubtless envisioning. The chilly air cuts through my black cotton shirt, and I realize belatedly I should have brought a coat, because I will stand at the fortune-forsaken gate for hours if I have to.

As I run, threads of numbness spiral out from my core. At first, I think the elk instincts are tugging at my consciousness, offering a faster way to move and bring him home to Fin. But no, this is different. The buzzing, twisting sensation I felt the day I pummeled Broden is back, spurred on by images of Finley breaking down on the floor. Something else teases the lines of my body.

Something new.

In the far corners of my mind, the fleeting awareness of flapping wings—

But no, fortune must be on my side today despite it all, because Weslyn is there! Walking through the gate alongside other soldiers, devoid of armor but still dirty and visibly tired, beard untrimmed, curls disheveled. The buzzing in my core snuffs out like a doused candle.

Some of the soldiers are laughingly recounting a story, one walking backward at the head of the group as she speaks. Another says something I'm too far away to hear and claps Weslyn on the back, which tugs a grin from his usually stern face.

By the river, I've never been so happy to see him.

"Weslyn!" I shout. My lungs are heaving after my run, and I bend a little, hands on thighs.

Weslyn's head swivels. When his searching eyes find mine, the rare smile drops away almost immediately. He says something to the others and closes the distance between us with rapid steps.

"What is it?" he asks, like he's afraid to hear the answer.

"Finley," I huff. "He wanted— He's fine," I add quickly, seeing the color drain from Weslyn's face. "I mean, he's not fine, his voice changed because of the Throes and he's panicking. I can't calm him down, and he was asking for you—"

"Show me," Weslyn says.

Now we're both hurrying across the garrison. Twin flames of panic, though Weslyn's seems more a willow branch swaying in the breeze next to my crashing, thunderous ocean waves. The budding alarm with which onlookers marked my first run across the grounds intensifies with the sudden appearance of Weslyn keeping pace. For once, he doesn't stop to reassure them, only follows me in edged silence into the Officers' Hall and up to Finley's room.

Ansley's eyes widen with relief. "Thank fortune," she says. "Wes, something's not right. I've never heard him like this—"

Weslyn places a hand on her shoulder and murmurs thanks before knocking softly. "Fin? I'm coming in." He turns the handle, and I follow anxiously, not knowing what sight might await us.

Mercifully, Finley is right where I left him, knees to chest with his back against the bed. At his side, Astra lifts her head and wags her tail fiercely at Weslyn's appearance. Fin's breathing has quieted a touch, but when he spots his brother, he starts crying again.

"Hey, now." Weslyn's soft voice is admirably calm, I have to hand it to him. "What's happening here?"

Fin shakes his head.

Weslyn sinks down beside him, wrapping an arm around his shoulders. After a beat, he says, "Thanks, Helos. I can take it from here." A clear dismissal, though not an unkind one.

Fin glances my way. A sliver of guilt gleams in his miserable eyes, as if he's worried he might have offended me. I smile a bit, trying to convey that he has nothing to fear. "Just call if you need me," I tell him, before I shut the door on them both.

I stay away from the Officers' Hall for the rest of the day. The horse-drawn cart bringing healers to the front, the one on which I was meant to be, left long ago. I can't bring myself to care. Aimless, agitated by my flaring headache, I try the hospital instead.

It's no good. I fumble a basic wrap to counter ankle swelling and can't even remember the proportions for a simple fever brew. When Tomas notices the last, he tells me to take the rest of the day off, that I need to sleep or I'll be of no use to anyone. He doesn't chide me for having missed my trip with Bren, though, and gratitude pulses in.

I try to sleep as he says, I do. But I'm reluctant to step back into that hall, and when I leave the Keep entirely to curl up on the miracle forest's floor, all I get is a suffocating weight on my chest and rampaging thoughts that refuse to settle into slumber.

I shed my clothes roughly and pull from earth and air. As I shift, my frame lengthens and widens and sprouts a coarse brown coat and short tail, two legs turning to four. Antlers curve out from my skull, six tines on each, thankfully devoid of itchy velvet. The elk—an old comfort, one I very much need.

Because my mind has not gone blank. Far from it. Instead, the noise has grown nearly deafening.

I had thought that night in prison was the boulder wedged between the door and the wall in my mind, preventing me from shoving everything else away as I had done before. All the bad memories from my childhood, the callous fire, Father's death, and my mother's abrupt flight. The years of straining to keep Rora alive, to keep us both afloat, trials and errors with finding food and building shelter and healing injuries and maladies.

I pound a hoof into the soft ground, snorting loudly. But I crave a harsher release, so I lower my head and scrape my heavy antlers against a tree trunk. The points score long tracks into the bark.

I was sure that was why everything seems to hit harder now, and stays. The fear and anger and misery in those around me seeping beneath my skin and grabbing hold of my bones, clinging like burs. The distrust of shifters like me, and the way my bloodstained hands can only do so much. The fact that I was once somebody's son, and now I am no one's. I am still somebody's brother, but she is far away.

Now, I think I was wrong. That night was the boulder, but this is the avalanche—the boy I love falling apart because he is slipping from this world, and I unable to do a thing to stop it.

The bark is flaking. Twisting my head free when one of the antler's points gets caught, I sink onto the ground. Defeated.

The fear in his eyes. I can't stop seeing it, the way his bony frame trembled and his chest heaved, struggling like a fish out of water. I want to go back and tell him he sounds as perfect to me as he ever did. I want to assure him he has no need to feel guilty, because in that moment, I couldn't care less whether he wanted Weslyn or me.

The only thing that mattered was for him to feel better. I would move the world to make him better. My heart against his.

When the soft blue of twilight shadows the woods, I realize I had, miraculously, fallen into a dreamless sleep. I pick myself up, the rear leg joints bending inversely to human knees, and siphon the borrowed matter into the air with a shade of regret. The elk slips away as my body shrinks back to human.

I wend through the wildflowers until I'm back at the army tents. A few soldiers watch me curiously as I pass, and one or two invite me to share a pint. I only dip my chin in acknowledgment or ignore them entirely. I miss the feeling of unbridled conversation, without fronts or tension or restraint.

I miss my sister.

More than anything, I want to talk to her about this. Finley, my work, the war—all of it. I want the simple reassurance of knowing she's nearby if I need her. I want to ask how she has carried this weight with her for years and come out the stronger, whereas I feel as though I'm breaking apart.

I shove my hands inside my pockets, then fold them across my chest, then drop them again. My headache is back with a searing insistence, the forbidden memories creeping farther from their crawl spaces, but I shake the awareness aside in favor of the crisp night air stinging my face and the sound of my shoes scraping the gravel path.

The path—I'd hardly realized I climbed back into the Keep, but there is one of the night guards by westgate, nodding to me. I set my course for the mess hall, my stomach keenly aware of its yawning emptiness. Though midnight is still a few hours away, the garrison is quiet, the pathways dark and deserted. Most people re-treat to their sleeping quarters early these days. Perhaps in a hurry for the night to be over, because hope always feels more credible after dawn.

The training yard where Weslyn taught me to use a sword ma-terializes on my left. The concrete lot stretches out in a vacant, shadowed expanse, and I almost pass it by when I notice a lamp flickering in the armory windows. The door stands ajar.

After a brief deliberation, I pivot. Most likely nothing but a blacksmith working after hours, but no noise issues from the open entrance, and the sight's just out of place enough to pique a tendril of concern. Neck tensing, I peer around the doorframe and spot a lone figure bent over one of the workstations.

It's Weslyn. Shoulders hunched, elbows on the table, fingers curled into fists behind his lowered head so that his arms shield his face from view. An oil lamp flickers mournfully nearby, but the rest of the long room is lonely and dark. It feels wrong.

"Hey," I say.

Weslyn straightens abruptly like a child caught misbehaving. Almost at once, his features flatten into the hard, inscrutable expression he uses when he's acting the prince or the soldier or whatever—amazing, how quickly he does that. But in the heartbeat before they do, I can see they are a ruin of grief.

"Helos," he says, relaxing a little when he realizes it's me, though his gaze remains threaded with wariness. I guess I can't blame him for that. "Sorry." He runs a hand over his eyes.

I don't know why he's apologizing. "You didn't do anything."

"I just needed to—" He pauses. "Get away, for a moment."

At that, my feet are backing toward the door. "I'll go."

"It's all right, Helos." He circles the workstation and leans back against the wood, scraping a hand across his face again. "Did you need something?"

It's a genuine question, not an accusation, and I realize the last thing I want is to give him something else to do. I shake my head. "I came to get away, too. Everything is just . . . a lot."

After a beat, he nods.

"You look terrible," I add. Because he does. He's cleaned up since I last saw him, but still he looks utterly exhausted, his gray collar askew, royal posture abandoned. His red-rimmed gaze is slightly distant, slightly haunted. I haven't seen much of him lately, but I'm certain he's grown thinner, and the sight unnerves me. "Have you been eating?"

Weslyn's mouth curls with a hint of amusement. "What are you, my father?"

I start to smile, too, in spite of myself. "Don't dodge the question."

"I'm fine."

Which is obviously a lie. "Right. Come with me."

His brow furrows. "What do you—"

"Will you please just trust me? Please."

Clearly skeptical, Weslyn follows nevertheless until he sees where I'm bringing him. Then he digs in his heels.

"I'm not sick," he says.

"You're not well, either," I tell him bluntly. "And there are things in here that can help."

Even in the darkness, I can see him fold his arms. Too stubborn for his own good.

"Please trust me," I say again. "I won't jab you with anything, I promise."

Weslyn sweeps his fingers through his hair, but at last, he relents. I lead him through the hospital—or at least, I would, if only he wouldn't insist on stopping and speaking with every person who reaches out—and finally wrangle him away from the rest and into the supply room in back.

Weslyn leans against the doorframe, unimpressed with the dingy space. "You've brought me to a closet?"

I throw up my hands. "Has anyone ever told you you're an idiot?"

A subtle smile works at his jaw. "Perhaps."

"Good. Sit," I say, gesturing to one of the wooden crates.

He frowns but does as I've instructed.

"I brought you here to avoid another scene like that," I continue, pausing my work to gesture vaguely toward the rooms with all the patients.

Weslyn runs a palm along the back of his neck and mutters something about duty.

I refrain from commenting, focusing instead on the glass bowl I've nicked from a shelf. I toss in a peppermint sprig and a pinch of sage. Grab a ginger root, then change my mind. After a while, I remark, "I've noticed you spend a lot of time helping other people."

"Have you," he says, voice flat.

I nod, grabbing a jar of lavender petals to add to the brew. "You learn to notice things in my line of work."

Weslyn folds his hands, then cranes his neck to examine the herb mixture I'm preparing. "What are you doing?"

"Helping you."

Weslyn looks down at his hands. Not the answer he expected, perhaps, but it amounts to the same thing. We spend the next few minutes in silence, I preparing his tea and scouring the shelves, while he stares at seemingly nothing. Up close, I can see new shadows ringing his eyes, worry lines etched into his face that I don't remember seeing before. How old is he, twenty? Today, he looks older.

"Do you want to talk about it?" I ask after a time.

"What?"

"The thing that's upsetting you." I pause, considering. "Or things."

Weslyn laughs once, an entirely humorless sound. "That would take half the night at least."

"I don't mind."

His features soften at that, but he doesn't answer my question.

When the tea is ready, I hold out the steaming mug.

"What is that?" he asks, sniffing warily.

"Poison," I tell him.

He rolls his eyes but takes the mug.

"This too," I say, shoving a small plate of oatcakes drizzled in honey onto the crate beside him.

He looks at me.

"Healer's orders." I shrug. "Sorry, kitchen's limited here."

Slightly surly, Weslyn downs one of the oatcakes and blows on his tea. "Do *you* want to talk about it?" he asks.

I lift my eyebrows.

"The thing that's been bothering you."

I finish preparing my own cup of tea and take a seat on another crate nearby. "I think you know already."

We fall quiet again, both of us lost to our own thoughts. Hunger is gnawing at my insides, but I ignore its nettling, determined to see this job through. Weslyn sips at his tea and eats another biscuit. Though I'm trying not to mark his progress, since that would likely add to his discomfort, I can't help but notice he slows when he's only halfway through.

His eyes have taken on that hollow look again. I think of him sinking onto the floor beside Fin after what was likely a hard day of riding. I look at him and think, *He has to go out again tomorrow, and the next day, and the next.*

"Rora will kill you if you die in battle, you know." Sipping my tea, I watch his face for any sign of change at the name. There's barely a flicker. "So you have to stay alive, okay?"

Weslyn nods a little, the mug steaming in his hands. "Okay."

He's still not looking at me. His voice and his expression are hedging too close to ones I've seen on certain soldiers these last few days, the ones resigning themselves to an early grave. Or losing hope. I don't like it.

"I would also like you to stick around. Now that we're friends and all."

That works—he looks up.

"Listen." I smooth the hair from my face. "I haven't been fair to you. You're a lot nicer than I gave you credit for." I pause. "Well, maybe not a lot."

He smiles, surprised.

"I'm glad Rora gave you the stardust," I press on. Determined, again, to see this through. "You're good to have around. And you're a good brother, you know."

Weslyn takes another biscuit from the plate. "You are, too."

The tension eases further with this newfound common ground. Mutual respect, because we've both been there, the older brother, and we get it.

"Since we're confessing things, as friends," he says, eyebrows lifting. "There's something you should know."

I take a long drink, leaning back on my free hand. "Oh?"

He nods, growing somber. "You're terrible with a sword."

I snort. "Yes, well, weapons never really suited me."

"Me neither."

I chew the inside of my lip.

Nonplussed, he grabs the final oatcake. "Finley really loves you, you know. More than anyone."

I nearly choke on my tea. Weslyn appears vaguely amused as I sit there, hacking out my lungs. "You think so?" I reply, rather weakly.

He shrugs noncommittally. "Just thought you ought to know."

I can't think of what else to say. I am a prize idiot, my mind swept clean temporarily, all the noise drowned out by my suddenly surging heart. *More than anyone.* The words are like a rush of golden haze, like starlight spiraling down from the treetops.

Weslyn still looks entertained, and I realize he's reading all of this on my face.

"Anything else I should know?" I say roughly, recovering myself.

He's silent a long while. Downing the last of my tea, I stand and pace over to the tiny washbasin against the wall. *More than anyone.* Stop. Wash the mug.

"I really wish your sister were here."

I swivel round, caught by the emotion in his voice, but he won't meet my gaze. He's folded over himself, hunched over his mug. Something tells me he got her letter.

"I do, too," I say, and by the river, I mean it. After a beat, I add, "Finish drinking that."

"Bossy," he mutters, but he raises it to his lips.

When he's done, I take the plate and mug and dunk them in the water. I feel better, somehow, knowing he's got those things in him. There's only so much I can do for a grieving heart, but at least it's a start.

"Helos."

This time when I turn, he's looking at me. He smiles a little. "Thanks."

I nod. "I'm not Rora, but you can always talk to me if you— you know. Need someone to listen." I finish scrubbing the dishes. "Anyway, I'll see you in the morning."

"The morning?" he echoes.

I hold up the mug. "For your next dose."

I have only one more stop to make before grabbing supper. I walk the short distance to the Officers' Hall, nodding to the person on duty outside the doors. Tonight, I have business with the third Danofer sibling.

I realized something just now, talking to Weslyn. Whether with a person, a hospital ward, or an entire realm, my instinct is and always will be to heal, not to hurt. In this, my hands can only do so much. But I also have my voice, and I'm starting to think the way to affect change might not be one or the other, but both.

I've already started building. The time has come to act.

Despite the early evening hour, Violet admits me into her office as soon as her door guard announces my presence. She's seated alone, bent over a stack of papers, reading by close candlelight.

"Helos," she says, beckoning me over. Her attention lingers on the parchment before her. "I assume this is important."

"It is." I move to the other side of her desk, hands clutched behind my back. "You asked if I was ready to pursue the throne."

She lowers the paper and meets my gaze directly. "I did."

"My answer is yes," I say, and I'm surprised by how right it feels. How good.

Clearly pleased, Violet sits back in her chair. "I'm glad to—"

"But I don't know how I could manage it," I carry on, even as her eyes narrow at the interruption. "In a letter, Rora said the Eradain people are divided, that many don't support Jol's agendas. Which might help, but even so, how could a shifter ever be accepted in a place like that?"

Violet appraises me for some time, lifting her chin. I resist the urge to fidget beneath her steady gaze. "Rora has shared this information with me as well," she says. "I'm glad to hear you're thinking this way, Helos. Circumspection is important in a leader. You will make a good king." My heart hammers to hear her speak of such a tenuous future with confidence, until she adds, "But I agree with you. Taking power will be difficult."

My spirits deflate just as quickly as they rose.

"I believe you know as well as I that there's no guarantee of success in a venture such as this. Nevertheless," she raises a hand, "I would not encourage you if I felt the situation were hopeless. Remember that Eradain does not elect its officials as Glenweil does. That monarchy stretches back to the kingdom's foundation. The crown is an institution, and the people there have been conditioned to respect it, however much they begrudge the individual currently at the helm. In short, blood inheritance has always governed who sits their throne. And you, Helos, have direct kinship to Jol, and by extension, a title granted to you by birthright. I assure you, these are tools that you can use."

My thoughts drift to Finley at Lyra's side, the difference he managed to make in an instant with only his manner and his title. Still—

"Eradain was also founded on the principle that magical blood shouldn't dictate who holds the throne," I point out. "Both practices are equally old, so who's to say which the people will value more when faced with the choice? The throne's survival, or who sits upon it?"

"You, I think," Violet says.

I close my mouth.

"You have a way with people, Helos. You are the kind of person others naturally open up to. You have a good heart, and you listen." Her eyebrows arch. "Perhaps you can persuade them toward the former."

I run a hand through my hair, face flushing. "Why are you trying to help me with this?"

She rests her elbows on the chair's cushioned arms. "Because I believe you would be a better ruler than Jol."

"And?"

She smiles wryly. "And it would benefit me to have an ally on the throne." At my reaction, she says, quite calmly, "Both can be true at once. So you tell me, Helos. Do you believe you can persuade them?"

I think of Rora, already off doing the work. I think of the victims of that prison, of the Holworths' legislation, this war, all depending on a change for the better. *You have kind hands.*

The strands harden into resolve. "How do we remove Jol from the picture?" I say in answer.

Violet's mouth curves into a sharp smile. "Take a seat."

TWENTY-TWO

RORA

The flight south is like medicine to my weary bones.

Though I've never been to Fendolyn's Keep, I have a rough idea of where to go. I've seen the maps. Sure enough, after an hour's flight beneath the waning moon's pearly glow, a smattering of faint lights twinkle far below once I've passed over a ring of hills. My heart lifts at the tents taking shape in the valley, as well as a giant stone structure gleaming from the top of a plateau. Oil lamps and candles in the windows, like a trail of stardust guiding me home.

I don't know where to find the people I need, so I circle lower, trying to make sense of the layout before me. The garrison is more brightly lit, and walled besides, so I'm guessing the royals are staying within. Would Helos be there, too? Likely he'd try, if Finley's inside. Since I need clothes before I go searching, I drop to the encampment, figuring I can nick a set from the darker tents.

After several ungraceful minutes of hopping along the ground and trying to keep out of sight, I locate an unoccupied tent and root through the stranger's small truck, grabbing a simple blue top, underthings, black trousers, and a belt. I leave the shoes; they're far too big, and the long years of living outdoors have left the soles of my feet plenty calloused, anyway.

Once dressed, I make my way through the rows of tents toward the Keep. A few soldiers huddled around fires appraise me curiously as I pass, but fortunately they leave me be. Until—

"Rora?"

I turn on my heel, a short distance from the base of the plateau. Naethan is hurrying toward me.

Thank fortune. A familiar face.

"Where did you come from?" he asks, looking me over with a baffled expression. The clothes are clearly not mine; I had to roll the shirtsleeves several times to prevent them from swallowing my hands.

"It's a long story," I reply. "Have you seen my brother? How is he?"

"He's fine," Naethan says, and relief rushes in as he gestures to a large tent behind him. Another member of the Royal Guard is posted outside, glaring, but Naethan appears unfazed. "He's in there, in fact. The queen called a meeting."

I blink at him, temporarily lost for words. Since when would Helos be invited to an official council meeting? "Can you show me?"

He scratches the back of his head. "We're not meant to admit anyone. Queen's orders."

"Please, Naethan," I press. "I have information she needs, right now. I've just come from Eradain's ranks."

After he considers this a while, Naethan exhales softly. "Come on, then. But if I lose my job, it'll be on your head."

"Wes would never let that happen," I reply without thinking. Naethan's mouth twists in amusement, and heat rises to my cheeks.

"How is—" I pause, not wishing to give myself further away. Then I just decide not to care. "Have you seen him recently? Weslyn? Is he okay?"

Naethan doesn't reply at first, and worry spikes through my gut. "He's okay," he says at last. He glances at me, a wry expression on his face. "About to be more than okay, I'd guess."

Before I have time to ruminate on that further, we arrive at the tent.

"What are you doing?" the other Royal Guard demands, but Naethan ignores her and opens the tent flap for me to step through.

The space is dimly lit, with oil lamps flickering over the canvas walls and a threadbare rug covering the earth. For a handful of heartbeats, nobody notices the newcomer in their midst. I catch sight of Violet, in the middle of posing a question, then Captain Torres and a couple of generals I don't recognize. A scribe is seated at the round table in their center, scratching away. And standing a short distance to the side—

My heart threatens to climb right out of my throat.

It's Wes. Hair curling loosely over his forehead, white sleeves rolled just below the elbow like always. He leans over the table, weight braced along his forearms, studying a map sketched in ink and entirely unaware of my presence.

Violet pauses mid-sentence. "Rora?"

Weslyn's head snaps up, the map forgotten. After an endless moment of searching, his wandering eyes find mine.

He straightens in shock.

Then my view is blocked, because closing the distance between us with rapid footsteps is—

"Helos!" I throw my arms around my brother, squeezing tight and resisting the inexplicable urge to laugh. He's okay! He's here! He pulls away and holds me at shoulder's length.

"Are you okay? Are you hurt?" he asks, and it's nice to know that some things, at least, never change.

"I'm fine," I assure him. Turning to Violet, I bow my head. "Forgive me for interrupting, Your Majesty. I didn't think it could wait."

"Speak freely," she says, looking mildly astonished.

I tell them about the droves of foot soldiers heading for the valley. That Jol himself has made landfall and is planning to lead them into what he views as the decisive battle. Winner takes all. As I speak, Helos bounces on his heels nearby, his face a landscape of utter relief. Weslyn simply stares, frozen, as if at any moment, he'll blink and I'll be gone.

Fortune's sake, he is standing there, *right* there, and I cannot go to him. Is this how Helos felt with Finley, all those afternoons at Castle Roanin? I don't know how he could stand it; it hasn't even been five minutes. Amidst the crowd of onlookers and the relentless timeline pressing down on our necks, all I really want in this moment is to hold and be held. To run across the room and bury my face in his chest, feel his arms around me and just be still for a moment, two, and breathe him in, in, in.

But I can't.

And absurdly, he *smiles,* just for me, because he knows.

"We expect the line to reach the valley in two days at most," Violet says, her tone all business. "How many new arrivals do you estimate?"

"Several hundred," I reply, alarmed by the concern that blossoms in the generals' faces.

"And Jol himself intends to lead them." Violet tilts her head, thoughtful.

"He will try to kill you, ma'am," I say, my gaze flicking back to Wes.

Violet waves a hand. "He will not succeed."

"Ma'am, you know my advice in this," says one of the generals.

"I do, so there's no need to recount it again."

I have no idea what that means, only note the general's countenance is a mixture of concern and grudging respect. "He will also come for you, and Finley," I tell Wes. "If not himself, then he'll send others. He wants the Danofers gone."

In the corner of my eye, Violet's looking slightly more concerned now. I should have used the more formal address in this company, I know, but in this moment I'm struggling to focus much beyond Weslyn holding my gaze. The two of us working together like we did across the river. A long while later, he nods. "We can make sure Finley is safe."

And you, I want to shout, but I know it'd be fruitless. This is why he made the choice he did, years ago. For this moment right here. Finley can stay far from the field, but Weslyn has to serve, added threat of assassins or no.

It is why I made the choice I did days ago, sipping poisoned liquor while Jol mused on murdering Wes with pleasure. I will not allow it.

"I don't like it," Captain Torres says abruptly. "Fighting the enemy on our front door. The terrain is limiting, too enclosed. It will be difficult to evacuate, should we need to." She looks at Violet meaningfully.

"I will not flee," Violet replies.

"If the situation grows dire, you must," Captain Torres persists, undaunted. "The line must continue. It's my job to see it done."

"You speak as if the battle is already lost," Weslyn observes in a low voice. "It's not. Prepare to evacuate Finley, if it comes to it. But there is hope. Eradain's forces are strong, but most are conscripted soldiers fighting a campaign set by their king. Ours are fighting for their home. That will make them stronger."

The generals appear heartened by this reminder; Telyan has never had to conscript. Courtesy of the military tax King Gerar levied three years ago, the army provides a good life—food and a stable career, rigorous training, plus high enough wages that those enlisted can send a portion to families back home. I feel sure if it weren't for King Gerar's foresight, his children would be less equipped to challenge Eradain's assault.

I send a silent thanks.

"With respect, sir, where will I lead His Royal Highness?" says Captain Torres, whose face has remained grim. "Over the hills, which seem liable to shift at any moment?"

I glance at Helos, confused, but he's preoccupied with staring at Captain Torres, drumming a hand along his thigh.

"There is also the matter of succession," she continues delicately, with the air of choosing her words with care. "We must consider the prince's health. If the worst should happen, we have to be prepared."

Helos's face turns stricken, and my insides tighten in fury, despite the brutal logic lining her words.

She is asking if Finley is the right royal to save, since he cannot carry on the Danofer line if he's dead.

"There is hope for Finley, and the Throes," Helos says through gritted teeth. "The magic you fear may in fact be doing us a favor. When the forest moved, a patient with the Throes was cured. Surely you heard. The magic left her body, as it did with two others today."

"The forest moved?" I ask quickly, adrenaline prickling along my skin.

Helos nods, smiling a bit. "Yesterday. A herd of caribran have also been sighted a short way to the north."

"Then it's working!"

Everyone looks at me. Wes's eyebrows tick up.

"What, exactly, is working?" Violet says.

I clutch my hands behind my back. The fact that the land might actually be waking up, that the magic *let go* of three people with the Throes, is encouraging enough to make my head spin. And a herd of caribran! The changes must be Andie and Peridon's doing, theirs and the rest of the whisperers who agreed to drive animals east.

Still, this group half-filled with strangers, some of whom are appraising my outburst with disapproving expressions, does not seem the best company in which to admit that reviving the land was my idea.

"I believe the Fallow Throes surfaced in time with Eradain's efforts to rid the continent of magic," I say at last. "The magic is fracturing, searching for a way to survive. That's what's causing it to latch onto humans. Maybe if we can help restore its natural state, it will stop seeking shelter elsewhere."

"Weslyn has explained this theory to me already."

My gaze cuts to him.

He nods.

"Rora raises a good point," Helos puts in, stepping up to the table. "We should be focusing on removing threats to magic, not fearing signs of its return. Prohibit people from hunting magical creatures. Change your public messaging, frame the awakening magic as a good thing."

"We were discussing the future of the royal line, and the war," Captain Torres says, a bit testily. "Not the Throes or common hunting restrictions."

"The subjects are linked," Wes argues, coming to our defense. Again, I have to fight the overwhelming desire to go to him. "If we win the war, allowing magic to flourish in Telyan could be the antidote to the Throes we've been waiting for. Doing so could save

Finley." He fixes onto Violet. "Our army is strong, but the people sheltering in the Keep are frightened. We can take steps to mediate that fear. Enact the hunting ban. It will send the message that you're thinking of Telyan's future beyond this war."

Violet presses her palms to the table and remains silent for a short time. "Your theory is possible, but tenuous at best," she says. "Still, I agree about the ban, for the sake of morale if nothing else. Have a draft on my desk by morning," she tells the scribe, who nods and begins a separate page. "There is more to discuss, but it merits a more private audience. Rora, I'm glad to see you back. You've done well."

My spine straightens.

"We will speak more tomorrow. In the meantime, you need food and a place to sleep. Helos will show you to the Officers' Hall; I'm sure space can be made."

I spot a few raised eyebrows around the group.

"She can stay with me," Helos offers, seeing this.

"Space can be made," Violet repeats. "Tell one of the Guard. Go on, now."

I dip into a bow as Wes catches my eye, looking alarmed by this sudden turn of events. As if he's not yet ready to let me out of his sight, when we've only just reunited after weeks apart. I'm inclined to agree, but Helos is already taking my elbow and ushering me out into the night.

"You made quite the impression," he says in a humorous undertone, clapping Naethan on the back as we pass. I really have missed a lot. "By the river, I'm glad to see you. What do you need? Are you hungry? I can—"

"Rora."

Helos and I twist in time to see Weslyn jogging from the tent. My breath hitches as he slows to a stop a couple of paces before us, glancing between Helos and me uncertainly.

"I've just remembered," Helos says after a beat. "I owe Naethan an explanation for something. Won't be long."

He leaves.

In the silence that follows, Wes and I just stand there, our gazes locked.

Adrenaline heats my core, to have him merely an arm's length away after the long weeks apart. Close enough to reach out and touch. Wes has grown thinner, but aside from this source of concern, he's the same as he was the day we parted. The curling hair and thick brows, the beard shaved to shadow, the faint scents of cedar and sage. Those deep-set honeyed eyes resting so intently on mine. It's overwhelming, almost, to take in the breadth of his stance and the fall of his shirt across his chest, to tie that thought to my impatient hands and realize how badly I want to run them over every inch of him.

I force my arms to stay at my sides. Whatever I may want, uncertainty still nags, his sudden nearness also reviving the earlier doubts I set aside in favor of hope. My heart sinks as wishes dampen to remembered wariness and the tension threaded between us back in Roanin, after the choice I made on the riverbank.

"Won't they be missing you?" I ask at last, nervous now, as I gesture to the tent.

That's not at all the first thing I'd like to say to him alone. Not even in the top ten. But my traitorous mind has drawn a sharp, sudden blank. How to pick up where we left off, to judge where we stand, when so much has happened in between. And if his feelings have changed?

His eyes don't leave my face. "They can wait."

So maybe they haven't.

Naethan and Helos have indeed entered a quiet, spirited conversation. With a glance their way, Wes shifts us a few steps farther into the shadows. His pale shirt glows faintly, a beacon in the moonlight.

We're more alone here. Squeezed in between canvas tents, Wes glances down and rolls my comically large sleeves between two fingers, looking amused.

Like an idiot, my heart pounds loud enough to wake the dead.

"You came back," he says softly.

The words sound like an invitation, enough that I manage a small step toward him despite the doubts. "I told you I would."

Weslyn seems to mark my hesitancy. Maybe he, too, is thinking over where we left things last, or maybe he's learned to read me better than I realize, because he meets my gaze directly and says, "I meant what I told you, Rora. I never blamed you for doing what you thought was right. I just—needed time to process, that's all."

To hear him say my name. Not in a memory, but here tonight, aloud.

"So you still—" I break off, casting about for what I'm trying to ask. "I didn't—"

Ruin things, I nearly say. A fear I'm not sure will ever fully go away.

Exhaling softly, a quiet sound of disbelief, Wes searches my face before slowly, carefully raising a hand to the side of my head. His fingers brush aside the rogue strands of hair.

The motion is the mirror of what he did the morning we said goodbye, his touch as achingly gentle, and hope overpowers the fear. Beautiful, restful hope. My pulse drums a quickening beat as he bends his head toward mine—only a little, as if in answer and question both. Certain of my own response, I lean closer myself.

"Sir, there you are. Her Maje— Oh. My apologies."

Wes drops his hand. We both turn to the messenger standing nearby, whose eyes have shifted tactfully to the ground.

I take a reluctant step back, recognizing how this must look. Belatedly trying to make this into a more casual scene.

Wes notices my retreat and frowns.

"Yes?" he says, pivoting from quiet Wes to firm Prince Weslyn in the span of a single word. Only now do I really hear the difference in the voice I grew used to hearing across the river. The way he speaks with me.

"Her Majesty is asking for you," the messenger replies. "Forgive me, sir. She was quite insistent."

Frustration flashes across Weslyn's face, there and gone in an instant. He nods once. "I'll be there in a moment."

"Sir." The messenger bows his head.

When we're alone again, Wes looks back at me with a torn expression. He shakes his head a little, helpless.

"It's all right," I tell him, smiling through my disappointment to try to ease his guilt. His obvious dismay is making me feel rather bold, so I reach out to smooth a wrinkle from his collar. "Duty calls."

Wes covers my hand in his, trying to reclaim the distance I put between us. "When can I see you again?"

Skin humming beneath his touch, I raise my eyebrows and remind him, teasing, "I'm not the one with meetings to attend."

Weslyn glances toward the tent, rubbing the back of his neck. "Tonight?" he suggests hopefully.

I laugh lightly. "It's already night."

"True," he says. "But there are many hours yet."

Anticipation whispers in my ear, the what-ifs taking on a rose-colored tint given what is in his eyes. Still—

"Won't you be tired?" I ask.

A smile tugs at his mouth. Amused again, he shakes his head.

Helos is walking toward us now, so I force myself to step away, out from the cherished warmth of his hand. "All right," I say, and Wes's smile broadens. "Tonight."

TWENTY-THREE

HELOS

I can hardly believe it. Rora, here. Safe and in one piece.

After I peel her away from Weslyn's side, I usher her up to the garrison, choosing to ignore the way she glances back more than once. I am just so relieved, babbling like an idiot. She must be hungry, so I take her to the mess hall, and it's not until she pauses outside the door that I realize she isn't wearing any shoes.

"What happened to your things?" I exclaim.

Rora seems a bit sad. "I couldn't carry them with me. I had to fly."

"We'll replace them all," I assure her, kicking off my boots. "Use these for now. I have another pair."

"What about you?" she says, but I'm already stepping inside so she can't protest further. At least I have socks.

The shoes are roomy on her, but better than none. I take her through the food line, filling two plates as far as the rations will stretch while she looks on, half exasperated, half amused. Nobody pays us much heed, which is good, because I need her to talk.

"Tell me everything," I say, making for a table near the corner and swinging my leg over the bench.

Rora grabs her plate and sits opposite me. "First, you tell me. Finley. Is he—?"

I hesitate, not knowing how to reply. She deserves the truth—all of it, I think—but one piece at a time. "He's alive." She nods, like I've confirmed something she already knew. "But his voice changed. Yesterday."

Her hand hovers over her fork a few moments before she picks it up. "You said the magic has started letting go. That some people have been cured of the Throes."

"Some."

Her gaze finds mine. "Some is more than none."

Leaning over my plate, I blink away the burning in my eyes. "We can go see him after we eat. Now tell me about you."

Rora takes a careful bite and shakes her head. "I don't even know where to start."

"The Vale," I suggest. "The pri—" The stupid word catches in my throat, and her forehead creases. "That prison compound," I try again, beating my voice into submission. "In your letter, you didn't say. Is it gone?"

The thought of Rora returning there at all, let alone by herself, is enough to make me want to tear the hair from my head. She's nodding, though.

"It's gone," she says.

Upon hearing the news, raw emotion threatens to overwhelm me once more. I scoop boiled potatoes into my mouth, waiting for the rest.

"I had help. Someone named Peridon—you haven't met him. His cousin was in a cell near yours." She chews her stew thoughtfully, avoiding my gaze. "And one of the soldiers working there. He helped us break in."

Nerves buzz deep in my gut like angry bees. "You didn't."

"It was the right move," she insists. "We needed his insight."

"Rora, that was dangerous!"

She glares, critical now, and I get it. Everything she's done has been dangerous. I knew what she was setting out to do when I let her go alone weeks ago. But this is hard for me.

"So you broke in," I say, shoveling another forkful with forced calm. Trying not to imagine what our father would say if he knew I wasn't there to help her. "Then what?"

I listen with what I believe to be admirable composure as Rora walks me through that day and night, then the days to follow. The journey to Oraes. The catacombs. Respect mingles with belated concern, alarmed by the could-haves and might-have-beens. While she speaks, she's doing that thing she does with her food—devouring every piece, but in tiny bites, as if she has to make each mouthful last. The remnant of our past makes my stomach twist, but I don't think she even realizes she does it.

When she comes to Jol, she hesitates and looks at me strangely.

"What?" I ask, glancing down at my shirt for stains.

She's quiet a while longer before she shrugs. "You look like him. But you're so different." She shakes her head. "It's odd."

"Hm," I grunt, not keen on the idea of resembling him in any way. Funny how Rora has spoken with this newfound brother of ours several times, and I haven't even met him once.

At least, not yet.

"I'm going to do it, Rora." I keep my voice low, wary of eavesdroppers. "Violet and I have been talking. The longer he remains in power, the more people will continue to suffer and die." I bend closer. "I'm going to take his throne."

Rora raises her eyebrows. "That's dangerous, Helos."

Her tone is prodding, and I wave a hand to show I've taken the point. But a long time passes, and she doesn't offer more.

"You think I'm wrong to try?" I ask, a bit hurt.

She worries her bottom lip. "It's just—" Another pause. "Have you thought this through? I mean, really thought it through, Helos."

"Rora, give me some credit."

"I am," she says. "But you can be somewhat . . . rash."

I lower my fork.

"You can," she persists.

"You think I'd be bad at it?"

"Don't twist my words," she retorts. "That's not what I'm saying, though even you have to admit that you have no idea how to rule an entire realm. But beyond that, you do realize that, *if* you succeed, you're talking about making a commitment for the rest of your life to a kingdom you've never even seen?"

I drop my gaze, stung by her doubts, even if they're grounded in truth. "I may not have seen the realm, but I've seen the people flowing from it. Dying for it. And the cost of fighting back." I don't add how it changes you, to not only see but *feel* their bodies and their blood between your hands. No longer distant figures or numbers in a report, but individuals, each with a different gleam in their eye and words on their tongue and their own beating heart. I don't say it because I think she knows already, from how she spoke of the prison shed. I lift my eyes once more. "I've seen what will happen if he remains in power. That's enough for me." I pause, considering. "Maybe for others, too. You said yourself the people there are divided."

"They are," she says, almost reluctantly. "But I'm sure the reality is far more complex than what little I saw. I wasn't there for long."

"Of course it is. But that's all the more reason to feel encouraged," I argue. "Think about Roanin. The Prediction," I add, rolling my eyes. "The angrier humans became, the more frequently you witnessed tension in the streets. When things were calmer, incidents were rarer, more spread out. If you already picked up on that anger in Oraes in so short a time?" I shake my head.

"I suppose."

I study her downcast features, growing frustrated. "What aren't you saying?"

She doesn't respond.

"Look," I say, so low she has to lean closer to hear. "I just— I have to start building somewhere. Especially if Finley—" I bite my tongue, forcing the rest out. "I don't think I could stay here, if we run out of time. If he dies. It would hurt too much."

I've never voiced that thought aloud, not even to myself. Maybe I didn't realize the truth of it until this moment. And yet, now that the words are out, I feel—oddly lighter, somehow. Only a fraction. But still. *Merciful fortune, please. Let him live.*

"I would be here," she says at last, looking at her plate.

Understanding dawns.

I'm at a loss for how to respond. The feeling is new to me. Ordinarily, words pass between my sister and me as easily as breathing.

This, however, is a fork in the road I don't think either of us saw coming. The separation of these last few weeks has always been a temporary measure, born from necessity. I've never considered our paths may continue to diverge by choice.

We're both nearing the end of our plates, but the food is sticking in my throat.

"Would you come with me?" I ask. "If it came to it."

She pushes her hair behind her ear, and a tiny knife pricks between my ribs. She doesn't have to say the answer aloud. I already know.

"You would stay for him," I say, not unkindly. I should have realized Rora's feelings for Weslyn went beyond a passing fling. How could they not? Back when we started in Roanin, months passed before Rora lowered her guard around even Finley. It means something big, to earn her trust.

"It's not just that," she says, then straightens under my look. "I mean it, Helos. I like it here. I like my job. I'm good at it, and I can make a difference."

She still looks miserable as she says it.

"You are good at it," I agree. "Come on. No decisions tonight. Nothing is certain, anyway." I wait until she sees me smiling before pushing back from the table. "Let's go. I want to see the look on Finley's face when you walk in."

At the mention of seeing Fin, she brightens a little. Depositing our plates in the appropriate bins, we make our way out into the night and toward the Officers' Hall.

I stop us in the courtyard.

"Rora." I run a hand nervously through my hair. I resolved to do this, and I will. "There's something else I have to tell you. About Finley."

She waits, apprehension coloring her face.

"He and I—" I hesitate, having trouble finding the words. "Fortune's sake, this shouldn't be so hard. "Look, I haven't been honest with you."

She folds her arms, but a smile teases her features. "Go on," she says.

"You remember the message he told you to give me. About the answer being no."

"I remember."

"Well." I drag a foot along the ground. "It's because I sort of told him I loved him. And I asked him to be with me. Publicly. If he felt the same."

I say it all in a rush, and Rora looks at me long enough I feel embarrassment heat my face. "You're in love with Finley," she says, her tone giving nothing away.

I nod, shoving my hair aside. "That's right."

And then she smiles, wide and true. "Well. That's obvious."

"You knew?" I say, my voice cracking a bit.

"I'm not blind, Helos. I already told you. I've seen the way he looks at you."

I glance toward the Officers' Hall, a flurry of emotions warring for prominence within. Excitement. Sadness. Longing. Dread.

"I wish you would have told me sooner," she continues. "I was waiting for you to tell me. Why didn't you?"

I shake my head, abashed. "I don't know. I grew so used to keeping things a secret, and then I didn't wa—"

"How long?"

I blink at her. "What?"

"How long were you keeping things a secret? Exactly how long have you been seeing each other?"

I toy with my hair again. "A year?"

"A *year*?"

"Well. Two."

"Helos!" Rora is laughing now. Proper laughter, the kind that's all too rare from her, and I feel a sheepish smile spread across my face. "I can't believe you," she says. "I wouldn't have judged. Well," she amends, still grinning. "Maybe a little. You couldn't have fallen for someone with fewer strings attached? You had to choose a royal?"

I fold my arms. "You're one to talk."

For the barest sliver of time, she looks defensive, her habitual response. But then we're both laughing again, loud enough that a group of people nearby pauses to stare at us. The slight chink I felt in the chains encasing my heart widens a bit more—first over supper, and now this. As if she's taking some of the burden away just by listening. Or I have, simply by speaking the thoughts aloud.

"My poor, lovesick brother," Rora says, shoving me toward the Hall. "Let's go."

Ansley is standing outside Finley's room again, the third time in two days. I can't help but wonder if Weslyn asked her to do this. When she sees Rora at my side, her mouth drops open.

"You're here!" she says.

Rora smiles back, tentative. "I'm here."

"Does Wes know you're back?"

At the question, Rora tenses so subtly that probably only I catch it. I understand; Fin and I may have kept our relationship a secret, but clearly, Weslyn has confided in his friends. Or in this one, at least. "He—yes," Rora says. "I saw him."

Ansley nods, looking pleased. "Good. Were you coming to see Finley? He's inside."

Whatever Rora was worried about seems to have passed, because her smile has broadened. Before she can respond, though, the door swings open and Finley himself steps through, his lavender shirt unbuttoned an extra notch at the top. His hair falls in a state of gentle chaos as he stands in the hallway, staring at Rora.

She grins. "Lowering your standards, I see."

"Rora!" Finley reaches out and grabs her hand, tugging her inside. Forgotten, I nod to Ansley before following them in.

"Tell me everything," Fin is saying, an echo of my earlier request. He forces Rora to sit on the end of his rumpled bed, and if she's noticed his slower movements and hollowed cheeks, his altered voice and the remnants of treatments sprinkled throughout the room, her expression reveals nothing. A talent I've never managed to master.

"It will keep," she replies. "I want to hear about you."

"Nonsense. There's nothing to hear. My life is dull."

Rora's eyebrows shoot up. "I was under the impression that this valley is about to be under siege."

"Oh. That." Finley scrapes the hair off of his forehead, feigning indifference, though we all know there's nothing casual about this particular subject. "Helos, there's no need to hover by the door. We don't bite."

His teasing is the permission I needed, and I sink onto the quilt, feeling happier than I have in weeks. There is much I've longed to reclaim from my life prior to the onset of the Throes, but this here might be what I've missed the most. Rora, Fin, and me, seated in a circle and talking for hours about everything and nothing. Well, Finley and I would talk, at least; Rora has always listened more than cutting in.

Tonight, however, she takes the lead. Throughout the next hour, she recounts the stories she began telling me in the mess. Finley is rapt, hanging on every word, and the sight bolsters me.

"Fortune's sake, Rora," he says, when my sister has cycled through the highlights. He runs a hand along his face. "I don't know whether to compliment you or shout at you for risking your life like that."

She gives him a look. "You're just jealous I made it north before you did."

"Rora, please. I have done *some* traveling in my time. I am a prince, you know."

She laughs, which makes Finley smile. Back in Roanin, I think it became a game between us, though one we never acknowledged. A slight thread of unspoken competition to see who could tease a smile or peal of laughter from my serious sister. In the end, we were pretty evenly matched.

At her prodding, Finley launches into his own rendition of the last several weeks. He dances around the heavier topics I know are in his thoughts—his father's death, his fear for Wes, his own diminishing health—but Rora doesn't seem to mind.

"Helos has been quite the hero around here," Fin adds, startling me.

I scratch the back of my head, uncomfortable. "Hardly anyone's hero."

"No, it's true," Fin insists, and Rora smiles at me. "You should see the way people look at him. I finally have some competition."

"I could never compete with you." I meant it as a joke, but the words come out more earnest than I intend, and Fin's expression sobers a bit.

"Although," he says. "I wish I had known about your mother sooner." He glances between us before settling on my sister. "That's big, Rora."

Her smile fades. "It doesn't change who we are."

"Maybe not," Fin concedes. "But it changes what you could do." His gaze turns on me, and I nod emphatically, because by this point, I'm on his side. Indifference is a luxury we can no longer afford.

Rora isn't speaking, and after another beat, Fin relents. "Well, give it some thought," he says, leaning back on his hands.

We stay like that for another hour at least, talking and lounging and lapsing into comfortable silences. Part of me wishes I could freeze this one night, a memory to revisit and relive years from today. The three of us together, where we belong. But we're all growing tired, each of us stretched too thin these last few days, and eventually, Rora calls it a night.

"I forgot," I say, sitting up abruptly and looking to Fin. "I was supposed to ask about a room. Your sister said Rora can stay in the building."

"Leave that to me." Fin ambles into the corridor and calls to someone out of sight. He returns a couple of minutes later, beckoning to Rora. "Halin will take you. Find me again tomorrow?"

My sister rises from the bed, promising to stop by in the morning. Before she goes, Finley halts her by the door and whispers something in her ear with a smile. Whatever it is makes her glance at him with a slightly disarmed look, but he only winks and adds in a louder voice, "See you tomorrow."

Then she's gone.

For several heartbeats, Finley lingers in the doorframe, glancing between me and the hall. I remain seated on his bed, waiting for him to decide. Now that we're alone, I'm trying hard not to dwell on what Weslyn said to me, but mostly, I am failing. *Finley really loves you, you know. More than anyone.* I knew he loved me, yes, but somehow hearing the words from someone else feels different. *More than anyone.* It feels good. No more hiding.

At last, he asks, "Fancy a change of scenery?"

My heart rises. So it isn't time to say goodbye, not yet. Happy to stay in his shadow as long as I can before the nightmares claim me, I nod and hand him his walking stick.

I'm prepared to follow Finley back out into the night, maybe for an evening climb up to the rampart. To my surprise, he only leads me one floor down and stops outside my room.

"This okay?" he says.

I don't respond right away. I can feel myself staring, trying to read his intention in his eyes. Aside from the night he bade me sleep while he kept watch, an invisible weight has hung between us ever since I returned from the front. As if each is trying to shield the other from our burdens' spiraling reach. I can feel the cruel memories I've collected gathering steam, on the verge of overflowing, the endless hours between sunset and dawn growing nearly impossible to endure. Worst of all, even Finley's light no longer seems enough to prevent the terror from creeping in, and I hate, I *hate,* that the creatures in my mind have set in on the two of us, too. Daring to interfere with this perfect happiness I struggled so long to regain.

Tonight, though—

Maybe it's only Weslyn's words banging around in my head, or maybe it's the way Fin is returning my stare directly, but this feels new.

No, not new.

It feels old, the motions belonging to a former time, the way things were before our prior lives vanished for good. Unbidden, the possibilities bob to the surface, a collection of scenes from the past that heat my neck and tighten my chest, that might actually repeat in the present if only I could focus my *fortune-forsaken mind* on what's important.

Finley blinks, deflating ever so slightly in the silence. "Then again, it's late, and you might want to—"

"Here is good," I say, one hand already on the doorknob, the other fumbling for my key. "Here is—I just needed to find—Sorry. Come in."

Fortune's sake, *get a grip*.

Finley's mouth twists in amusement as I unlock the door and gesture for him to step inside. As I follow, I'm dismayed by the wholly unwelcome feeling that settles in the pit of my stomach, the clenching uneasiness that seems to claim me nowadays every time I enter this room.

Not now, I beg the monster in my mind.

I feel it smile smugly and dig in its claws.

Finley paces over to the chair by the curtained window, where he massages his ankle idly. I sink onto the bed, rubbing the back of my head, then stand again and grab a half-filled glass of water from the dresser. Pace a little. Then return to the bed.

"Rora seems well," Finley says, sounding relieved. "I really can't believe she did all those things." He pauses, wincing when he switches ankles. "Well, I suppose I can."

I nod, raising the glass to my lips. "What did you say to her, back in your room?"

Finley adopts an entirely innocent expression as he leans back against the chair, appraising me. "I told her to tell Wes 'hi' for me."

The water catches in my throat, and Fin's eyebrows rise as I erupt into a fit of coughing. "Tell—what?"

"Don't look so shocked, Helos," he chides. "Surely you know that's where she's going."

I clear my throat, rubbing my chest a bit. "You sound pretty happy about it," I observe, unable to keep a note of accusation from my tone.

"Why wouldn't I be?" Fin replies. "He's my brother."

"But he's so—"

"What?" Finley demands, suddenly defensive. "Wes is what?"

I fall silent, finding I have no response. It's not that I haven't grown to like his brother. I've already admitted that I have. And fortune knows Rora deserves to be happy. It's just—"I don't want her to get hurt," I say at last, because that much, at least, will always be true. "She's been hurt enough."

Fin shakes his head, though calmer now. "You wouldn't say that if you'd heard the way he speaks about her." He's fiddling with his sleeve, but when he sees my face, he drops his hand and smiles. "Helos, you needn't worry about Wes. He may not let many people in, but when he does, he gives them everything." He fixes me with a meaningful look. "Not unlike certain people I know."

"Weslyn and I are not so alike," I protest.

He huffs a laugh. "You'd be surprised."

I wait for him to say more, but he remains quiet, staring at a corner of the curtain drawn across the window. And truly, I'm ready to move on from the details of my sister's love life.

"I envy you, actually," Fin says after a while, pinching at the curtain. "I wish I were more like him."

I roll my eyes. "What are you talking about?"

Fin pushes to his feet and paces to the dresser, leaning against the wood. "Wes knows how to hold onto a good thing when he has it." He studies his hands.

"What, and you think you can't?"

In answer, Finley looks at me, sadness in his gaze. He opens his mouth to say more, then shakes his head. "Helos—"

I rise from the bed and close the distance between us, sensing something is coming. Something that's been building inside him.

Finley searches my face when I stop barely an arm's length away. "Tell me what's wrong," he says. "Please."

I step back without thinking, brow furrowing. "What?"

"I can see you hurting," he pushes ahead. "A part of you isn't here with me, hasn't been for a while, and you won't tell me why, even now."

My throat tightens as my shoulders twinge with remembered pain. White walls are swimming before my eyes. Not now, not now, not now.

"Do you still not trust me?" Finley asks, scarcely louder than a whisper.

His self-recrimination is the call to action I need. I will not let Finley think my recent distance is somehow his fault, not after the doubts he's already had to bridge to reach this point. "Of course I trust you," I assure him, taking his face in my hands.

He rests a palm over my right, eyes glassy. "But you won't—"

"Just—just kiss me, okay? That's what I need."

I press my lips to his. One final, desperate attempt to blot out the tide.

Finley kisses me back, but only just. His hesitation is obvious, and suddenly I'm terrified that I'm too late, that I've already lost this one good thing. That the hand pushing me into the blackness has won.

But soon he stirs and answers my plea for closeness with his own, and the fear slips away.

Finley's kiss is sunlight made flesh, the sudden break in the rain I've always run out to meet. This time my hands move before my legs can, grabbing his hips and pulling him against me, drawing him close before he doubts again. It's instinctive, old habit, the way every part of me opens to his touch—my stance, my mouth, the strings restraining my heart. No, this isn't sunlight. It's the lightning strike.

Finley leans into me, a hallowed weight. His movements are slower than they once were, his embrace a bit weaker, his lips a little less forceful. None of it matters. My reckless heart races as quickly as it ever did. Reveling in the feel of his forearms pressed against my chest, I hardly realize he's nudging me backward until my heels hit the bed.

I am only too happy to comply. *This* is what I was hoping might happen tonight. Not a journey into the dark, but keeping afloat on the clouds. I slide over the blankets, bringing him with me, mindful of moving slow enough for him to follow. It's a break from his usual pattern—nothing about Finley has ever been slow.

Even now, there's a hungry glint to his wandering eyes, and yet also—hesitance, a hint of self-consciousness coming back to haunt him. Shaking his head, he looks down at himself, then back at me as if to say, *Really? This is what you want?* Which feels faintly absurd, considering my entire body is on fire for all of "this." With a smile,

I pull him near like I've always done, until he's leaning over me, breathing hard.

I want to say something, to tell him how much I missed him, how I want him. But I'm terrified that speaking aloud will break the spell, so I simply close my eyes and command myself to feel. To stop thinking for a minute but remain in this moment, *this* moment, where everything is beautiful and familiar and good. *The answer is no,* he told me once, but now we're speaking an older truth. My fingers are tracing the curve of his spine, his teeth are tracing the plunge of my neck. His hands are on my abdomen, exploring, teasing, then tugging my shirt up and off and following its ascent with a line of kisses. My stomach. My ribs. My collarbone. My breath hitches.

Beneath my hands, his body stills.

"Helos, what is this?"

I open my eyes to find Finley leaning over me, looking scared and pale as a ghost.

Scared?

He places a delicate palm on my shoulder, and cursed fortune, I forgot.

"It's nothing," I assure him, reaching to pull him close again.

Fin shakes his head and sits back. "What happened?" he asks.

"Finley—"

"Don't lie to me, Helos. Please. Not tonight." The buttons on his shirt are half-undone—my interrupted work—and his hair falls in a state of ragged chaos. But his crystal gaze remains singularly pointed.

Knowing there's no point in arguing when he's like this, I sit upright, scratching the back of my head. "I'm not sure where to start," I murmur, wishing we could just go back to the kissing bit.

Fin's eyes aren't leaving my face. "How about by explaining where you got those scars?"

I stare at him.

He stares back.

The monster smiles again, settling in for the show.

"Helos," he says, softer now. "Talk to me. Please."

A simple request. In fact, the same one I've made of him before. So why does it suddenly feel so difficult to speak? I open my mouth to try, but no sound comes out. No *breath* comes out. Instead, the base of my throat squeezes tighter.

"Helos?" he says.

I clutch the sides of my head, desperate to stem the tide before it overflows. The jeering words, the white walls, the cigar smoke thick enough to choke on. It's all pouring forth too quickly, the details sharpening with every added moment I allow my mind to dwell on that night. Finley's hands are on my knees, and I see the person I've become. A person who buries and pushes and hides the truth from even those he loves. I don't want that to be me.

But fortune save me, this *sadness*. I feel the weight of it like a stone on my chest, cutting off any attempts at sound. The ghostly hand is back, pressing me down, pushing me into the echoing black. The images grow overwhelming, foul creatures crawling from the crevices in my mind, and with their approach, the room around me starts to shift. I blink to fix my vision and find that my eyes are wet.

"Do you want me to—"

"I asked them to stop," I tell him, breathy, like an apology. An odd noise is ringing in my ears. The lights around me are too bright, my ribs too taut, my lungs too empty. Everything in excess, nothing fitted to its proper place. "I told them to stop, but they wouldn't listen."

"Who, Helos?" Finley's hands lift from my knees to the backs of my own. Lacing his fingers through mine, he peels my hands from my head and grips them tight.

I stare at our clasped hands, once a mountain between us. I will myself to view them, instead, as a bridge. "The prison that Rora destroyed," I say, knowing it will hurt him to hear but saying it anyway. Testing the words. "I was there, for a night. Before she got me out. The soldiers, they—"

By the river, I am trying to speak, and it's *hard*. To find the needed breath and shape it into the right sounds. To allow my mind to lean into the details rather than forcing them around. I blink Fin's face into focus and realize he, too, looks ready to cry. "I don't know," I tell him, and for some reason it feels like pleading. "They didn't like that I'm a shifter. They wanted to hurt me. The— They laughed." The air stutters in my throat. "And then they didn't. Fin, I can't—"

They, they, they. This monster has too many heads.

Finley has shifted closer so that he can wrap his arms around me. Almost like his birthday all those nights ago, except I'm the one trembling now, needing to be held. His grip remains steady and uncharacteristically still.

"I'm here, Helos," he says quietly. "Hold onto me."

So I tell him. The blades they used to cut me, the smoking cigars they pressed into my flesh until it burned. The mocking hands that scorched vengeful trails across my skin. The metal rods they slammed against my shoulders, popping them out of their sockets, then back in. The vile insults they hurled, with threats of more to come in the days ahead. *We have to make you pretty for your audience with the king.* I'll never know if they tortured every new prisoner to pass through those doors, or if I was one of an unlucky few. From what I've gathered, they didn't touch Rora after Jol stepped in, and that, at least, offers relief beyond words.

Finley doesn't comment on each of my confessions. He lets me speak, and he cries, and he tells me none of it was my fault. "I've got you," he says, keeping himself together while I break apart. "I'm not letting go. You're safe now. I love you."

He keeps saying that, even after my breathing has quieted and my words are spent. *I love you. I love you.* I can feel the anger swelling inside him, a near-tangible thing, ready to burst. Not for me, but for the ones who did this to me. His arms around my waist somehow both soft as water and rigid as a sword's sharp steel. But I don't want to think about those monsters any longer, and maybe he understands this, because he keeps his focus and his promises on me, not on murmured threats or talk of vengeance.

Gradually, though my body feels wasted from the confessions, it also grows strangely lighter. The blackness inside my chest brightened incrementally, just a touch, now that its burden has spread onto the lap of another.

Fin continues to whisper his promise, and the words weave together into a rope, one from which I manage to pull myself out of the cavernous hole and onto my feet. Not yet fully in the sun, but at least somewhere in between, and fortune's sake, it feels good to learn that future isn't lost to me after all. That I can speak the words aloud and still remain on solid ground, with safety by my side. I've opened the door, and Finley's still here. We both are.

I meet his unflinching gaze and understand at last. *No more hiding*—not only us from the outside world, a shifter and a prince together whatever the fortune-forsaken Prediction might warn, but from the shadows in my mind, the memories lurking behind the door. No more hiding. Only forward.

I reach for him.

I had thought I knew everything there was to know about being with Finley already, but this feels new. Better, even. The burdens weighing us down, not gone, but shared between us. No part of him or me holding back. Instead, we hold each other.

At some point, the clasping and quiet words turn into quiet kissing, which turns into fervid clutching, which turns into me pressing him softly against the bed. The safest place in the world, here beneath my hands, rising to meet me. And when he breaks away to confirm, do you want to—? I tell him, I do. I absolutely *do*. But do you?

He does.

Because they tried to rob us of this joy, but they couldn't. Because today, he and I are both alive, and maybe by the end of this war, neither of us will be. Because I love this boy more than the earth itself, and if I can't move the earth to save him, I can at least move with him. Holding my heart against his. So I do, until the mountain between us is nothing more than memory.

TWENTY-FOUR

RORA

The room I've been given is far more comfortable than my prison aboard Jol's ship. A wide bed, a small desk, simple curtains draped across the window—the idea of sleep is tempting, but I linger just long enough to take it all in before pulling open the door and stepping out into the velvet dark. While my heart is full from reuniting with Helos and Finley at last, there is one more visit I promised to make tonight.

I descend the hill and wind through the lines of sleepy tents, endeavoring to be little more than a ghost passing among them. Wes told me where to find him, but even so it's an effort to navigate this pseudo-city in the moonlight. As I count the rows, doubt rears its head for a final attempt, whispering that I should return to my room and let him sleep while he still can, that I shouldn't run the risk of someone seeing me here. Or perhaps I haven't waited long enough. Maybe he's still in meetings, bound to uphold his position's duties before personal ties, and I'm wasting my time.

Stupid. My feet are already moving toward his tent.

I slow when I reach the entrance. His is a rounded, sizable thing, larger than a lot of the ones I've passed and yet smaller than some. Perhaps befitting the delicate balance between standard officer and blooded royal. There's no door on which to knock, but Wes solves the dilemma for me by pulling the tent flap aside practically the moment I reach it.

I open my mouth to speak and shut it again. "Hi," I say at last, somewhat lamely.

Weslyn smiles. "Hi," he says, and gestures for me to come inside.

I step under his outstretched arm and hear the flap swing shut behind me. I am excited and uncertain both, nerves buzzing, finding this all feels much more real now that I'm actually here with him, properly alone.

Clutching my hands before me, I walk the length of the room, maybe nine or ten paces across. The furnishings suit a person of his station, I suppose—a small, square table, a cot draped in cabled gray, a washing basin and wooden chest, even an extra cushioned chair set near the table. A corded purple rug spans the entire width, and squat oil lamps give off enough warm light to keep the deeper shadows at bay.

I take the measure of it all before turning back to Wes, who has waited through my appraisal without speaking, barefoot in sleeping trousers and a loose gray shirt. A small fire heats my chest at the sight of those clothes hugging his sturdy frame—the public presentation dropped away, revealing this version of him that exists only behind closed doors. The boy beneath the title I'm lucky enough to see.

"There's so much to catch up on," I tell him, since this seems a good place to start. The quiet is making me smile; he has never felt the need to fill silence with idle chatter. "So much I want to hear, and to tell you." I lift my shoulders a little. "But I can't seem to remember any of it right now."

He takes a couple of steps toward me, then stops, a careful distance still between us. In his movements, I see echoes of the way he so often speaks—calm, but cautious. A door left open, waiting to see if I'll step through. "I feel the same."

When my gaze flits to the furnishings, I force it back to Wes, resisting the ridiculous temptation to start counting once more. Part of me struggles to believe that our conflict born on the riverbank wasn't an ending, that this is really happening. I here, Weslyn there, the wanting plain on his perfect face.

This future I thought I'd lost that day, with the impossible boy who learned the very worst of me and wished to stay—it's playing out before my eyes. The choice I believed to be right and he wrong—I made it anyway. And he's still here.

Wanting *me*.

"It's been a while," I say, my breath coming somewhat quicker than seems reasonable. Willing him to move closer.

He does. Another few tentative steps, searching my face from only an arm's length away. I feel like a willow branch stripped of leaves, laid bare beneath the intensity of that gaze.

"It has," Wes agrees.

I release a huff of air, crossing my arms. "Are you just going to repeat everything I say?"

Rather gently, Wes peels my arms apart and laces his fingers through mine. "That depends," he replies, "on what you're going to say."

Something is rising in me. Heady and strong, like thunder rolling through the night sky, building toward a storm. "I missed you," I admit.

And there it is, the quiet smile I have grown to love.

"I missed you," Wes says, tugging me closer when I start to object, right into his chest. "I missed the sound of your voice, and the way your hair looks in the morning." He winds a hand through the wavy strands, cradling the back of my neck. "I missed watching you do all the little things, like building a fire or lacing your shoes. Studying the horizon. I looked for you every morning, you know. To the skies, just like you said." He tilts his forehead down until it's grazing mine. "I missed you, Rora. I missed saying your name."

My lungs are burning. Surely they'll soon catch fire. Wes must certainly be tired, no matter what he claimed before; I can see new shadows coloring the planes of his face. Even so, to drink in every detail, each heartfelt word, and feel his body brushing mine—it's all of the memories I've clung to, but suddenly they're here again before me, tactile and tempting and so very much alive. Daydreams are one thing; the reality of him is something else entirely.

I clutch the front of his shirt in my newly freed hand, our faces so close I can feel his breath on my skin. "You looked for me?" I whisper.

"Every day," he replies, just as softly.

I lean closer still, no longer looking at his eyes, but at his mouth. A mere inch away, maybe two. That subtle grin. "That's a lot of days."

Wes nods, the movement barely perceptible. "I'm good at waiting."

He speaks with a hint of humor, but it's the truth, and one of the parts I like best. Wes has always been patient. Never pushing. Across the river, speaking secret words into the dark. Here in this tent. Still waiting.

"Wes?"

"Yes?"

I smile, eyelids drifting shut. "Say it again."

"Which part?" he asks, without judgment.

"My name."

I open my eyes after a time to see Wes watching me. "Rora," he murmurs, and in a way, it sounds like breathing.

It's a name. Only a name. But it's my name, and no one has ever uttered it quite like this.

I pull his head toward mine.

It is that day by the riverbank. Skin against skin, his mouth moving on mine. The same feeling of rightness, to have this quiet, warmhearted boy beneath my hands. To revel in the heat seeping through my limbs like liquid as I wind my arms around his neck and mold my body to his. Erasing the space between us until there's nothing left.

But tonight is also something new. Instead of pulling away to catch my breath, I want to *inhale* him, my body taking on a mind of its own. When Wes kisses me deeply, with confidence, I tangle my fingers through his hair and give my all in return. The old me would have felt safer acting on these feelings in a borrowed form. Now I don't want to be anyone other than myself as I let him tug me, gently, down on the chair and onto his lap.

It is a collection of moments that feel instant and endless at once.

Learning new lines on his body with every kiss, feeling the muscles shaped for fighting realigning to a softer, better purpose. The press of his chest easing me back, broad hands skimming the skin beneath my shirt when I pull him with me. Back tensing amidst the delicate pressure of my own hands, which are tentatively exploring new territory after charting a course across his heart like I wanted. Eventually, my wandering fingers find the base of his shirt and grip the fabric tight before slipping under and up. Judging by the sound Wes makes against my mouth, I don't think he minds.

Outside of this tent, forces are gathering in the darkness, pressing closer with their weapons and clamor and hate. But here in his arms, it's only quiet edges and careful, reverent touches. Him and me, rivaling the warmth of a fire's glow, as night's protective hand cloaks us from view.

I jump when something cold presses my ankle and find Wes's dog nosing her way between us with a wagging tail.

"Astra," Wes grumbles without looking, drawing the syllables out through gritted teeth.

His tone makes me smile. I scratch Astra behind the ear, figuring that will appease her. Instead, she shoves closer.

"Go away," says Wes, trailing kisses down my neck. "Bad dog."

"You'll hurt her feelings," I protest faintly, even as I close my eyes, trying to linger in this moment a little longer. "She only wants attention."

"I'm busy right now," he says, his lips somewhere around my shoulder where he's brushed the borrowed shirt aside. "She will understand."

Astra barks, and I can't help but laugh.

With a groan of defeat, Wes drops his forehead to my shoulder, then sits back and looks at Astra. "I've spoiled you," he informs her somberly.

Astra is all innocence, hearing only the reluctant affection in his tone. Wes gives in, stroking her head with a resigned smile.

In the sudden stillness, sobriety returns, and I pull away.

"It's late." My voice sounds unsteady even to my ears. "I should go."

Wes lightly sweeps the hair off my forehead. "Stay," he whispers.

And I want to. Fortune help me, it's all I'd like to do right now after the long, hard weeks apart—to stay, to talk, to touch. To sink into the moment because tonight, there's nowhere else I need to be, no job to complete. It's a night for doing, not what I need to do, but what I want.

With this pause, though, I've grown acutely aware of the late hour, the evening shadows pressing close outside. The bed nearby, and how very alone we are in this tent.

And I don't want that. Not yet.

"If I stay, I'm not—" I begin haltingly. I don't know what he might expect, and my gaze cuts to the bed. "I don't want to—do more than this."

Wes is shaking his head before I even finish. "Just sleep beside me. Nothing more." He brushes the hair from my face again, earnest eyes locked onto mine. "Please. If you walk out that door, I don't think I could bear it."

There's an undercurrent to the gentle appeal, a sliver of fear slipped through a crack in his usually calm veneer. The people he's loved and lost imprinted on his heart—gone too soon, unfairly, cruelly.

And yet. I know if I chose to leave, he would not try to stop me. He'd open the tent flap for me on my way out.

I smile and trace his collarbone with my fingertips. "I'm not going anywhere," I say, bending my forehead to his. "I'm staying right here."

It's a funny thing, to think that we spent years roaming Castle Roanin's halls, determinedly avoiding one another's paths. How blind we both were. Now we doze in each other's arms, intent on not being anywhere else.

The words come later, when need has sobered into reluctant awareness of the circumstances beyond our door. The roads we've walked between our parting weeks ago and tonight. As we talk, I come to understand that divisions which once felt large as mountains lose their edges with time and distance, shrinking as new challenges rise up to take their place.

Wes doesn't shy away from the confessions I speak into the dark, the people I killed or allowed to be hurt in the service of trying to right a wrong. Nor does he murmur empty reassurances about it all being okay, because it's not. The memories are cruel, their burden heavy to carry, and noble intention is not enough to cancel that out.

He listens with interest when I recount the catacombs and the people I befriended. He presses his lips to the top of my head when I speak of missing Helos, and the hardship of spending weeks apart for the first time in my life.

When I speak of my conversations with Jol, and the poison, he is silent.

"What are you thinking?" I ask.

Wes places an arm behind his head, staring up at the ceiling. "It's—difficult to think of you there alone. How close he came to—"

He breaks off, as if he doesn't wish to give the what-ifs more power by speaking them aloud. We're discussing the same man who killed his father. I stare at my hand on his chest, rising and falling in time with his breath, and decide not to mention the fact that Jol planned to use this protectiveness against him. "I'm all right," I say simply.

"You were hurt," he replies.

"I'm not anymore."

He's quiet again. "I should have been there. For you."

The words nestle deep in my core, soft as flower petals entwined around my ribs. That I somehow managed to find someone who cares in this way, who wants to offer shelter rather than a closed door—it's still new for me, and the concern is nearly as seductive as hearing him speak my name. I squeeze a little closer. "You're here now."

He tightens his hold a bit but doesn't respond.

"Before I escaped," I continue, attempting to steer him away from this unwarranted guilt. "There was a moment I thought I

might actually get through to him. Jol." My tone grows bitter.
"But he wouldn't listen."

"Rora." Wes brushes his fingers along my arm. "It is not your
responsibility to change him."

Now it's my turn to say nothing.

"You share a difficult past, but the paths you chose to take are
vastly different. Yours being rather better," he adds with a touch of
humor. "But it was a choice, and so was his. You can't blame yourself
if he won't now choose the same." He turns his head toward mine
and smiles a little. "You cannot fix the whole world."

"I can try," I murmur, only half joking.

We lay without speaking for a while.

When Wes's turn comes, I can feel the change come over him
like a physical thing. His silence grows weighted, as if he's choosing
his next words with care.

I wait.

"My father is dead," he says after a time, quiet.

I know the kind of courage it takes to speak truths as crushing
as those aloud. I take one of his hands, holding it fast. "Yes."

He breathes in deep, an obvious effort not to fall apart. That he's
been here before—the untimely, grossly unjust loss and its brutal
nature—wouldn't make this second time any better.

But he doesn't say more on the subject, so maybe for tonight,
it's enough to share the words with someone who's been here, too.

Instead, I learn that Wes has grown overwhelmed by the vol-
ume of demands on his time and too many sleepless nights. Always,
it seems, there is another person beckoning, needing his opinion
on one course of action or approval on another. Food rations'
allotment and distribution, expanding sanitation efforts to keep
up with the influx of civilians, meetings among military officials
strategizing Telyan's defense—all are matters in which he's had
a hand.

There is bitterness when he speaks of killing in battle, and fresh
pain when he skirts the edges of what it's like to have to watch
fellow soldiers die. The strained dynamic of how to balance being
a leader with serving in the army same as the rest. His body has

tensed beside mine, and I can hear the hatred he's harboring for himself and this particular role he's never wanted.

"I wrote to the giants," he admits after a time, startling me. "Two weeks ago. I asked if they would bring stardust to Telyan, so we could bury it underground."

"You *what*?" I demand, propping an arm beneath my head so I can see his face better.

He meets my gaze calmly. "Do you disagree?"

No. If anything, I feel the opposite. But I'm remembering the day Hutta told us that stardust's presence alone in Telyan would not be enough to awaken the land, that it would have to be buried in order to have any restorative effect—and her subsequent criticism of Wes's obvious relief. *You see? You want the magic only when it benefits you.*

At the time, I would have struggled to believe I might come around to the idea of replicating the Vale east of the river, even only in part. But I'd have flat-out refused any possibility that *Weslyn* would not only change his mind on the matter, but also actively work to make that scenario happen.

I feel a rather strong desire to kiss him again.

So I do, enthusiastically.

Wes laughs against my mouth, surprised, and in that moment, I decide that rare sound might be the best sound in the world. "Apparently not," he manages.

"What would you trade them in response?" I ask, settling back at his side. "And what did they say?"

"I haven't heard back. But if Eradain wins this war, they will destroy the Vale in its entirety. I think the fact that Telyan is opposing them should be offer enough."

"Does Violet know you asked for this?"

Wes sobers. "No," he murmurs. "But it seems the right thing to do."

We're quiet again, each turning over the other's words. Sleep has begun to tug on my tired limbs, and it would be easy to just give in, to not bring up the one subject he's avoided in all the time we've been talking.

In the end, I voice it.

"And Finley?" I prompt gently.

Wes, so often the picture of stillness, sits up.

The cot squeaks as he shifts around me, swinging his legs onto the floor. I rise slowly, watching him stare at something I can't see. Lying by the entrance, Astra lifts her head.

"Wes," I say softly.

"I can't—" he starts to say, then drops his head into his hands. Rising with a stretch, Astra paces over and lays her head across his feet.

I move to sit beside him, my leg pressed against his.

"I can't bear it, Rora," he whispers at last.

My heart breaks for him. For me, and for Helos. Most of all, for Fin, my closest friend, whom I can't imagine a world without. The whole situation is astonishingly unfair. But that's not what Wes needs to hear. "You can," I say, surprising myself.

Weslyn doesn't lift his head. He doesn't say a word. After a moment, though, he takes my hand and grips it tight, like a lifeline. And how many times has he kept me tethered to sanity, and the feeling of safety, since our journey through the Vale? I rest my head against his shoulder as he cries for his brother, the person he has tried so hard to protect, and for this one cruel thing he cannot save him from.

In the morning, I wake to murky light seeping into the tent, and the gentle sounds of the world around us stirring to life. I turn over. Wes's arm still curls around me, his breathing even with the sleep he desperately needs. He looks younger like this. Not the overburdened man from the meeting last night discussing battle strategy and lines of succession, but a boy who loves his dog and is trying his best. Part of me wishes I could lie here forever, waking up to someone else's warmth beside mine.

Extricating myself carefully so as not to wake him, I slip from the bed and straighten my clothes. Astra watches me from her post by the door without raising her head. In the early morning light, with Weslyn asleep, I notice what I didn't the night before—a piece of parchment splayed on the chest of drawers. I lift it closer, emotion strengthening its hold on my chest. The paper is worn along the edges and marked with new creases, as though it's been folded and refolded a dozen times. The letter I wrote from the catacomb floor.

I drop the paper and run my hands over my face. The river take me, I need tomorrow to be just another day. Not the coming of a storm, but a day like any other. The sun rises and falls, and all the important things remain.

But it won't be, and the reminders are all around. After patting Astra goodbye, I weave through the encampment and meet the somber eyes of soldiers merely hoping to see past tomorrow's sunrise. Some of them are little older than I am. Up in the garrison, a ghostly sort of quiet hangs in the air. Not sleepy, but expectant. Waiting for an army to break through the sun-kissed hills' protective net. The atmosphere makes my skin prickle.

Everything looks different in the daylight, and it takes me a while to find the Officers' Hall where I was meant to spend the night. Naethan and Ansley are huddled under the eaves of a practice yard nearby, their heads bent low in conversation. Neither of them notice me, but their clasped hands chip at some of the tension that's been building inside. I suppose there were a few good developments mixed in with the bad, these last few weeks.

Luckily, the Officers' Hall is quiet when I make my way up the stairs. Sleep still drags at my eyelids, and I have no desire to weather awkward reunions with members of the Royal Guard who used to make my life difficult in Roanin. As I've long since lost my pack and everything inside, I'm uncertain what I can do in the way of changing. But when I return to my room, I find that someone has placed on the bed two sets of clothes in my size—a deep green, long-sleeved dress, as well as a cream-colored sweater and purple pants so dark they're almost black. The forest and the night sky.

I run a palm over the dress. The fabric is beautiful, feather-soft and thickly woven. I'm not sure who was responsible for this gift, but I can tell the garment is more expensive than I'm usually able to afford, and the idea of wearing it makes me nervous. With some regret, I opt for the sweater and pants and step into the washroom.

After weeks of moving from job to job, it feels strange to suddenly slow down, adrift. But bent as I am on seeing Helos, Wes, and Fin through another dawn, I've realized I have no formal role in the battle to come. I stop by Finley's room as he requested, craving his familiar friendship amidst this sea of change, but the guard outside his door informs me he is out. I knock on Helos's door a floor down, but there's no answer there, either. I frown. Maybe they're usually gone by this hour.

By the time Helos finds me in the mess hall, I'm almost done with my modest bowl of loose porridge, made with water instead of cream.

"I went to your room half an hour ago," I inform him as he squeezes his long legs under the table across from me. "Where were you?"

"Out," he replies vaguely, though there's a suspiciously happy look about him. It fades a bit when he tastes the meal. "Listen, when we're done, Finley's meeting us—"

"Here," Fin cuts in, slowly lowering himself onto the bench beside Helos. "I finished earlier than expected."

He's dressed more neatly than usual, his green collared shirt properly tucked, though his hair remains as wind-tossed as ever. From the corner of my eye, I can feel people watching our table now that Fin has arrived, but I've been waiting so long to see him again that the added attention doesn't bother me as much as it once did.

"Nice night?" he asks me.

Helos takes sudden interest in spooning porridge into his mouth.

"Finished what early?" I reply, choosing to ignore the question.

Finley grins. "Oh, you know. This and that. Royal duties to perform."

Helos coughs, and my eyebrows arch.

"Listen, Rora. Any plans this morning?"

Rubbing the back of my neck, I shake my head. "No, but I wondered if there's something I could do to help. Seeing as tomorrow—"

"No, you've done enough," he interrupts, smile leveling into seriousness. "Tomorrow isn't here yet."

"But—"

"For one morning, at least, you can leave things to others. Come on." He pushes from the table and holds a hand out for me. "I have an idea."

TWENTY-FIVE

HELOS

For a few precious hours, life feels like old times.

Finley has brought Rora and me to the forest that blankets a small corner of the valley floor, though he's tethered Cascade a fair distance downwind. I can tell the ride tired him out; after he removes the cotton from his ears, he lies back in the grass, inhaling deeply. As Rora and I have been trading yawns since breakfast, we're only too content to lie beside him.

I don't know how long we remain beneath the broad oaks and quivering elms, nestled among the brown-gray roots pushing up through the ground like tributaries from a stream. Wildflowers wave among the ankle-high grass—white wood asters with moonlike petals encircling gold button centers, and pointed purple larkspur in the season's final throes before the blossoms fade. Though the sway and the silence makes its presence known, Rora, Finley, and I stick so close that the straining branches don't look like they're reaching for Finley alone. Instead, under a pearl-gray sky, they form a jagged circle around us three.

These aren't old times, of course. Castle Roanin is far away, and none of us can forget what tomorrow's clashing armies might bring. But hidden from the valley's watchful eyes, we can at least breathe a little easier.

Funny, that. I never thought I'd find respite in the woods.

"All right, then, Rora," Finley says when he's recovered his strength. Shaking the hair from his forehead, he opens his leather satchel and pulls out his sketchpad. "Indulge me."

Which is her cue to shift.

Rora scrapes the dirt from her palms, straightening her sweater against the mild chill.

"The magic can only help keep things moving, right?" Finley adds, meaning the land, I think. Rora doesn't seem to require as much persuasion to shift as she once did, though, and she duplicates a stranger's form readily enough.

Fin bends over the sketchpad, his attention narrowing into that singular intensity that mesmerizes me. Gaze razor-sharp, forehead creased, mouth serious and straight—one of the few times I see his brother in him, now that I think of it. While he commits Rora's new form to charcoal and paper with eerie accuracy, I sketch a mental model of *him* in my mind.

Yes, it has all the features that make my heart race—the ready smile and capable hands, the slender neck my head fits so neatly beside. Rose-dusted skin as warm as a summer night, and lithe legs made for blazing new trails. But this morning, another facet woven into the design might be the one I love best of all: the heart that walked alongside mine into the darkness and didn't let go.

"You're next," Finley says, glancing my way with that signature knowing gleam in his eyes.

Clearing my throat, I reply as I always do. "Rora's the better subject."

"Only in the daylight," he mutters with a wink, which is enough to make my sister blush.

I widen my eyes at Fin, trying to signal there's a time and a place. Finley shakes his head at me, his face a studied portrait in bewilderment.

"Losing your touch?" Rora prods, though she's smiling now, as Finley's charcoal has stopped moving for a good few heartbeats. Probably for the best—my sister always was willing to rein Fin in while I was blinded by the sun.

"Rude as ever," he replies, but he gets back to work.

I push my hair out of my face, tilting my head to the sky.

Until last night, I feared that if I stopped fighting the door in my mind, I'd never be able to close it again. I believed it was meant to remain shut. Had to, in order for me get through the day.

This morning, seated beneath these trees that once loomed like enemies and today feel closer to friends, I'm coming to understand I was wrong.

Rora is using her magic with perfect ease in front of someone other than me, though I remember her former reluctance as clearly as she. As he sketches, Finley ignores the unnatural silence enveloping these woods—not forgetting the significance, not pardoning it, but setting aside the fear for a while in favor of something better to do.

Maybe the door is not meant to remain shut, after all. In this moment, with light and dark mingling across an unbarred threshold, I finally feel I can get through the day holding both.

We linger a while longer once the portrait is complete. Not speaking, simply soaking up each other's company. Neither Rora nor I are eager to return to the Keep's confinement, and I'm guessing Finley senses this dip in mood, because he soon rescues us.

"I'll race you back," he says, using my outstretched arm to get to his feet. "My horse, your elk. What will you give me when I win?"

"You forget I have wings," Rora puts in.

Finley grins, clearly surprised. "Fine. I warn you, though, Cascade does not like to lose."

"By Cascade, you mean you?"

"Typical royal arrogance," I observe, shrugging at Rora. "It's in their nature. Too showy for their own good."

Finley folds his arms. "I'm not the one about to take off my clothes."

Rora laughs. Another point for Fin.

Unprompted, Finley turns his back when Rora reaches for her sweater, then twists still further to give me privacy as well. The gesture is so utterly human, I can't help but grin; nudity holds little weight to shifters, as this body is just another form. I shed my shirt before he makes it around, and it's my turn to feel rather smug when he swallows visibly.

Pulling from earth and air, I direct the borrowed matter from head to toe. My back folds over, the forest's musty scents twining through my nostrils as the fur along my neck darkens and antlers stretch from my skull. The pleasant rush of heat sweeping my body subsides as I settle into the elk, but luckily, my thick coat tempers the chill.

Rora has already perched on a low-hanging branch opposite Fin, fluttering her wings impatiently.

Looking behind, Finley pats my nose fondly before scooping up our clothes and stuffing them into his satchel. Cascade stands patiently, ears pointed toward Fin while he maneuvers into the saddle.

"Let's wake these people up, shall we?" he says, gathering the reins and clutching his walking stick like a crop. "Straight to the base, no stopping."

We run.

Out of the forest and into the valley, the wildflowers rippling in our wake. All around, the ring of hills stretch old and proud as mountains, while the windswept autumn leaves swirl overhead like stardust raining down. Finley is laughing, but I can barely hear over the wind roaring in my furry ears. Faster, faster, my lungs heaving for air.

I don't care. With Fin and Cascade galloping at blinding speed to my left, just behind, and Rora flying overhead, another part of my old life slips away for good. I no longer feel as if the wild is working against us, striving to beat us down. Instead, we're racing to meet it, adrenaline soaring nearly as high as Rora in the sky. As my hooves strike the earth, I imagine invisible tendrils strung between my antlers and the grassy ground below. I toss my head and stretch my legs to the breaking point, willing the magic buried deep underground to rise, urging the land to wake.

We don't stop until we reach the plateau. In the end, Rora wins. Of course she does.

We've scarcely arrived back in the Keep and shifted to human when Rora and I receive a summons to Violet's office.

Confused and slightly breathless from the run, the three of us head to the Officers' Hall. Violet tries to make Finley leave, but she relents when I insist I'll just tell him everything anyway when we're through here. Victorious, he and I take seats around a small table, while Rora remains close to the door, standing with her hands behind her back.

Not five minutes later, Fin and I have both grown heated with outrage.

"Absolutely not," I say, as he nods vigorously.

Seated behind her desk, Violet remains impassive. "Yours is not the answer I require."

"It doesn't matter. It's absurd," Finley cuts in, a verdict with which I wholeheartedly agree.

Most worryingly of all, Rora says nothing.

When Violet said she'd asked us here to discuss a delicate matter, I assumed it would be about the throne—which it is.

I wasn't surprised when she began by raising the conclusion she and I reached two nights ago, after Weslyn and I shared tea in the supply room: that Jol must be removed from the picture.

What I did not expect, what Violet and I never discussed, was the possibility of asking *Rora* to do it.

"I will remind you, again, that the decision is not yours to make." To my healer's gaze, the eldest Danofer appears more strained than usual today; though her erect posture and tailored cerulean blouse are crisp and refined as always, I detect a new heaviness to her manner, her eyelids drooping slightly.

"You're asking her to murder one of the most powerful people in Alemara *in the middle of a battle*," Finley practically shouts. "Rora's no assassin. She's not even a soldier!"

"Keep your voice down," Violet says through gritted teeth. "Rora, I will not ask you to attempt this at the onset of battle. I have others already who will bear that burden. But I need to know, should those efforts fail, if you would step in and take their place."

I'm just watching my sister, my leg bouncing, pulse racing as I silently plead for her to look me in the eyes. To assure me that she won't endanger herself in this way. Instead, Rora's gaze has angled toward the window, her brow bent in thought.

Fortune's sake, she's considering it.

I'm ready to end the whole affair when the door swings open, and Finley and I jump.

Weslyn walks in and runs a hand through his curls, his navy shirt crisp and collar aligned. All in all, a more put together version of himself than the one to which I tended two nights ago. "I heard raised voices—"

"Finally." Fin and Violet speak over each other, as if they've both just won.

Weslyn glances between them and slows his pace. "What?" he asks, appearing vaguely ambushed. Though he's not looking at Rora, I can't help but notice the way his fingers brush her back ever so slightly in passing.

"Our little brother believes me a villain," Violet says, leaning against a window with folded arms.

"What? Why?" Weslyn fixes Fin with a frown.

"She plans to order Rora to assassinate King Jol!" Finley counters.

"What?"

Fin smiles at Violet, smug.

"I am not *ordering* anything," she says with a sigh. "I'm simply exploring our options."

Weslyn doesn't reply, his face unreadable.

"Father would never have asked it of her." Finley raises his eyebrows, like he intends this to be a winning blow.

Violet shakes her head. "The circumstances have changed since the crown passed to me," she says, in a somewhat softer voice. "And I am not our father. I'm perfectly aware of the risks, as well as the family connection, but I believe it fair to ask. You underestimate her abilities, and that is not something we can afford to do with the people we employ. Not right now."

"It's not people we employ," Weslyn says quietly. "It's Rora."

A long look passes between them.

I cannot stand the way they're discussing her. As if she's not standing right there. Like this is a war council and she the army of one, a blade to wield or sheathe at their discretion. Rora may have claws, but she isn't a weapon. She's my sister.

Rora shifts her weight, folding her hair behind her ear, and I can tell she's growing agitated, too. "It's my decision," she says a bit impatiently, speaking for the first time since Violet posed the question.

Weslyn studies her closely before he shoves a hand into his pocket, turning to me. "You realize it will be difficult for Eradain's people to accept a shifter on the throne. Let's say, for the sake of argument, that Jol is killed and you convince his circle to crown you. Convince," he repeats, holding up a palm when he sees me open my mouth to object. "The public doesn't know you exist. It would be easy enough to make you disappear."

King Gerar's assassination hangs heavy in the air.

Rora blanches, and seeing this, Finley taps his fingers on the table. "Wes—"

"He needs to know," Weslyn persists. "If you secure the crown, what then? How will you maintain it?"

"We could send some of the Guard with him," Finley says. "As a loan."

"No." Weslyn's still looking at me. "The people there will know you've been living in Telyan. You don't want them to think you're Violet's puppet on top of everything else."

"Thank you, Weslyn," Violet says pointedly.

"Are you trying to frighten me into saying no?" Rora asks, causing Weslyn to pivot abruptly.

He appears almost hurt by the suggestion. "It's not for me to tell you what you can or can't do, Rora," he replies, his tone softening. "I'm simply saying make sure the risk is worth it."

A few heartbeats pass, and Rora nods. Forgiven.

"Rora said the people there are divided," I tell him, discomfort swirling in my core. "It may be difficult, but not as difficult as Jol's ambassadors have led you to believe in the past. Look, I've thought of this already. And I'm not entirely helpless," I can't resist adding.

"A group of rebels is operating in Oraes, not all of them magical," Rora points out, glancing at Violet as if nervous at the prospect of speaking so openly in her presence. Violet gestures for her to continue. "Some used to work in the castle. I feel sure they'd work for you if you asked them to. They're not bodyguards, exactly. But they'd be people in your circle you could trust."

Weslyn runs a hand along his beard. "It's a start," he admits.

I glance at Finley, who hasn't spoken much since the focus switched from my sister's safety to mine. His hand is flat against the table, gaze distant as though his mind is elsewhere, someplace grim. A smile flickers across his face when he catches me looking, but the gesture is clearly forced.

Rora isn't the only person I'd be leaving behind.

Panic flares.

"Weslyn, you raise fair points, but the fact is, we are out of time to deliberate further." Violet unfolds her arms and crosses back to her desk, dropping into the chair without ceremony. "Jol is here. Rora has said that he's planning to enter the battle himself, which puts him at risk. We have a singular opportunity, and I will not allow it to pass untried, not without making every attempt to see this job done." She pivots to my sister. "Rora, as I've said, this is a contingency plan. A last resort, but important to establish nevertheless. If you receive a call, are you prepared to answer it?"

All heads turn toward my sister.

Keeping her hands behind her back, Rora says, quite firmly, "Yes."

Pressure builds in fixed points beneath my skull. The elk responding to the fear, urging antlers and speed and escape. A way to take her far from this mad endeavor that could very well mean her death.

Stricken, Finley's staring at Weslyn, wordlessly pleading for him to interfere—but Weslyn does nothing. Only holds Rora's gaze a short while, then nods.

"Very well," Violet says, her expression grim but resolute. "Stay a moment, please. The rest of you can go."

TWENTY-SIX

RORA

Three months ago, the prospect of killing someone in cold blood would have made me feel ill. That hasn't changed, particularly when the person in question, however vile his actions have been, is family.

It should mean little, I suppose. The fact that my mother gave the life I've just agreed to take away. The ties of blood and memory feel small beside the bonds of here and now—friendship and loyalty, obligation and love. Equally strong is my acute awareness of those who came before—the victims in that shed, King Gerar, Kal and his brother, and all the rest I'll never see. Even so, I can't help but feel the tiniest seed of a question taking root in my mind.

What does it say about me, that Helos's healer hands save lives while mine continue to end them?

It doesn't matter. The truth is, I made my decision before I knew Helos would try to take the throne. Clarity came in Jol's parlor with a glass of poisoned liquor. *Him—I think I will enjoy making him bleed. Slowly.*

If the call comes, I will answer.

"Have a seat," Violet says, once Helos has closed the door behind him with a final, frightened look. She returns to her desk and gestures to the chair opposite. "There are a few further matters I'd like to discuss."

I do as she asks, clutching my hands in my lap.

"First, there is the matter of payment for your journey through the Vale. I have not forgotten. Four hundred gold pieces was the agreed-upon fee."

Off guard, I shake my head a little. Money seems almost insignificant these days. "We did not succeed, ma'am," I remind her, my voice low with shame.

"Payment was not contingent on success," she replies briskly, sipping a cup of tea. "You did a great service to Telyan in trying, as you have continued to do these last few weeks. I am happy to pay what I owe. Ursa will find you to coordinate payment. Though, I fear, it will have to wait until after tomorrow."

Her words lift me up a bit, despite the loss of the stardust. That still stings, no matter how generous her assessment.

"Next," Violet continues, "there is the matter of employment. As my father is no longer with us, the arrangement you made with him no longer officially stands. That said," she dips her chin in acknowledgement when I straighten in alarm, "I would like to offer you the same position. You would be working in a similar capacity, and with equivalent pay, but you would be working directly for me. I understand if you'd like to think this over before deciding."

"I'll do it," I reply at once, and she lifts an eyebrow. "I mean—thank you. I accept."

Violet smiles, looking pleased. "I'm glad to hear it."

Again, she speaks of Telyan's future as though it stretches beyond tomorrow night. I don't know if her conviction is genuine or a façade, but it strengthens me.

"Finally," she says, and her voice shifts a little. "There is the matter of my brother."

Unease pricks my shoulders, and I wring my hands before me. "Finley is—"

"Not that one."

My stomach sinks like a stone. So she knows, at least in part. Here it comes, the inevitable end to the happiness I've only just found.

"Ordinarily, my brother's personal life would be little business of mine. However, given the present circumstances—" She pauses.

"As I'm sure you can understand, his position has changed, and so must mine."

I quirk my head a touch, wishing to vanish into the earth. "Ma'am?"

Violet sits back in her chair, drumming a finger idly along the armrest. "We are living in uncertain times. While my father was king, the likelihood that Weslyn would ascend the throne remained reasonably slim. With my father's death, however, that likelihood increased. And with the onset of this war, it has increased still further." She looks at me matter-of-factly. "It's important you understand. At this point in time, Weslyn is next in line to the throne. If something were to happen to me—tomorrow, a week from now—he would become king."

The reminder is sobering, as I suspect she intends it to be. I knew the possibility, of course, but throughout our journey in the Vale, or falling asleep in his arms—it is all too easy to forget. "You're saying he's not for me," I guess quietly.

Violet actually smiles a little. Again. "I will be blunt," she says. "I like you, Rora. I admire the way you think. Were I not in a position that forced me to prioritize alliances over friendship, I like to think we might even be friends."

I lift my head, surprised. "I would like that."

Violet nods. "And if we were discussing this as friends, I would tell you that I believe you're very good for Wes." She sips her tea. "In fact, I'd suggest my most stubborn brother might have met his match."

I do my very best to maintain a neutral expression.

"As his sister, I want to support him," she says, and here, her tone grows more somber. "There are many unreliable people in this world, but Wes is one of the good ones, and I wish to see him happy." She sighs. "However, as his queen, I'm afraid the situation is more complicated than that. A relationship with Weslyn is not the more casual matter it may have once been. He has a duty to serve the kingdom and the crown. And people will be watching. They will always be watching," she stresses.

My gaze shifts to the window, where sunlight is beaming onto the tile floor. The implications hang like daggers from my heart.

Weslyn cannot be with a girl like me. A girl with no clear past, no advantageous connections except to a foreign monarch currently seeking to kill him. Even if he could, what would that life be like? Months—years—of being watched and waited on and discussed, my image and actions dissected in relation to his, the people's prince. Telyan's rock, the one whose eyes give strength in the darkest of times. That would be a kinder designation than being one of the Prediction's two shifters, perhaps, but even so. As Violet says, they would always be watching.

My throat constricts as Weslyn's words float to the surface of my mind, the ones he murmured to me that day on the riverbank. The promise to which I've clung these last few weeks, like a trail of starlight guiding me home.

I really am an idiot, he had said, laughing a little. *All this time searching, and it's always been you.*

Fortune is cruel. To hand me this person who sees me for me, who knows the worst of me and still wants to stay, only to take him away. How could I have let myself pretend? Feathers are pricking beneath my skin, seeking an escape, but there is none, because this is the reality. Before me, I see the fragments of the future I thought I knew slipping from me like leaves in the breeze.

It's a fantasy we've built between us. A fantasy, but nothing more. Untenable.

"Rora," Violet says, her voice uncharacteristically soft. "There is another side to this, one that might hearten you. Have you considered that your position has changed, too?"

I blink at her rapidly. *Get a grip.*

"If a day comes when Helos ascends the throne of Eradain, you will no longer simply be my employee. You will be the sister of a king." She considers this. "Publicly, this time."

The sister of a king. Not a king who has caused so much harm, but Helos. The healer, the hope. The image is tempting, but my mind sees only the one word. "If," I echo, my voice flat.

Violet studies me carefully. "There are no guarantees of success, but it's a chance nonetheless. These days, I think we should all take the hope we are given."

I nod slowly, remembering myself. "Thank you, ma'am."

She folds both hands neatly on the desk, brisk manner returning. "My intention has not been to hurt you. Nor am I asking you to—what was your brother's phrasing? 'Stay away.'" She pauses. "Not today, in any case."

My brow furrows. What does Helos have to do with this? "What are you asking me to do, then?" I say at last, striving to be polite.

Violet rises, indicating our meeting is at an end. "Consider what I've told you," she replies, as I push to my feet. "And be certain it's the path you want."

I pace back and forth in my room, unable to keep still. Though I'm trying to accept the hope, panic is edging in far stronger. Helos, going north or killed in the attempt. Finley, gone if the Throes won't release its hold. And now Weslyn, perhaps near, but forever out of reach. If I lose them all, who will I have left? When counting the objects around me doesn't work, I throw open the window and shift to goshawk.

Aside from the morning's race, weeks have passed since I've flown simply for the joy of it. The day has grown crisp and bright, scarcely a cloud left in the sky, and the breeze on my wings feels like coming home to myself. I climb higher and higher, until the sprawling tents are merely dust below. For the people there, the hills ringing the valley are a barrier, protection. For me, they're a door, and I race between the slopes and over green meadows and rolling hills.

I don't know how much time I spend in the air. An hour, maybe two. Enough to feel the knots in my stomach gradually unwind as I decide that today is not the day for mapping out the rest of my future. To acknowledge that, whatever might come from further thought, today I cannot imagine giving Wes up.

So I don't. I return to the Officers' Hall, re-dress, and make my way out into the garrison. Either fate is on my side, or it's intent on rubbing salt in the wound, because I find him strangely quickly.

He's in one of the practice yards, speaking with a group of people in uniform. I don't know their names, their stations, or anything about them, but I recognize the warmth in their eyes as easily as my own. The camaraderie, the respect. Because he may be mine, but he is also theirs.

Today, I don't feel like sharing. Today I am selfish. Greedy for these few precious hours before everything might change. I loiter just close enough to snag his attention without catching theirs, the balance perfected after years in his father's employ. Wes gives little sign that he spotted me, but after a moment, he tilts his head to a squat building nearby. I take the cue and cut around back, into the narrow stretch between the building and the garrison's outer wall.

Long moments pass before Wes meets me there, looking so earnest and hopeful and perfect I cannot stand it. He smiles in surprise, a question in his eyes, but before he can voice it, I take his face between my hands and kiss him, hard.

This kiss is different than the ones we shared last night. I cannot name it. Not an ending, but not familiar, either. I think, perhaps, it is a plea—to not let me mourn what I haven't yet lost, to stay alive through tomorrow. To come back to me. *Don't leave, don't leave.* Wes must sense the change, because after a few moments, he pulls away and looks at me.

"What happened?" he asks, concerned.

I shake my head. "Nothing," I murmur. "I just—I needed to see you, that's all."

Wes continues to study my face. "Tell me," he says quietly.

The simplest answer is ready on my tongue. *I don't want to lose you.* But I also don't want to lay this burden at his feet, not when he has so much else with which to contend. My fear won't give him strength. So I smile a bit and run a hand through his hair, shaking my head a second time. "Can you get away again, later? Just for a little while."

Though he clearly isn't fooled by the lie, he, too, has learned not to press. He nods. "Give me a couple of hours, then I'm yours."

I'm yours. The words carry me through the day, through my conversation with Finley when he takes us up to the rampart to share a meal and find comfort in each other's presence. Through the heart-stopping moment when we learn the ships sent to try to fetch the Telyan units trapped in Glenweil succeeded; the rescued soldiers march into the valley along with a number of Glenweil forces and Minister Mereth herself, smuggled aboard a ship in secret. Telyan's defense grows.

They carry me through an hour in the hospital, lending Helos what assistance I can. Which isn't much, mostly pulling supplies at his behest, but he seems glad of the company, regardless. Finley was right when he spoke of a change surrounding Helos. My brother has always moved about the world with greater confidence than I, but there's something different now in the way the world moves back. Subtle change flickers over the faces of those around him when he passes a building or walks into a room. Their eyes hold recognition and respect. Helos has built a reputation for himself while I've been away.

At last, Wes and I manage to steal time alone, wrapped in conversation or tangled up in each other's arms. An empty office, behind the stable, against the wall. Secreted into the Keep's shadowed corners, I long to stop the clock and stretch the hours into days and weeks and weightless time we don't have.

Wes doesn't speak of the battle to come, but I can feel its looming shadow in the way he kisses me, the times his hands linger ever so slightly on my waist before letting go. How his eyes trace my outline until I've passed out of sight. His own sort of pleas. As if he's storing up the memories while he can, not for after, but for now. In case now is all we get.

All too soon, evening falls. Though I've been given my own room, and to some trouble from what I gather, I can't bring myself to spend the night there alone. Not with the total upheaval and inexcusable loss that tomorrow threatens to bring.

I return to Weslyn's tent, and he doesn't question my being there, doesn't seek an explanation, because he doesn't need one. He pulls me close and we curl up in weighted silence, my head resting on his chest, fingers tracing patterns on his skin. Drinking in the sound of his still-beating heart. I'd like to build a sheath for that heart, an iron cage to keep it safe from arrows and blades and spears and hooves. I'd like to give him wings, so he can take to the sky when the ground becomes untenable. Protected. Free.

"Come back to me," I whisper, when I think he's finally fallen asleep. But he must have heard, because his arms tighten around me.

And so we remain, holding each other, until the morning comes.

TWENTY-SEVEN

HELOS

They close the gates at dawn.

Westgate. Southgate. North. Enormous wooden doors reinforced by metal plating, stretching up to the rampart and locked by three different crossbars. Soldiers armed with bows line the turreted towers to either side of the gates, prepared to cut down any who try to break inside. Though, really, if Eradain makes it as far as the Keep, things will be as good as lost, anyway.

The sky has grown mockingly bright, an unbroken sea of blue indifferent to the carnage about to unfold on its watch. Mounted high atop the towers, Telyan's standards wave limply in what little breeze there is. Today, I find the sight more depressing than inspiring, so I focus instead on the medical station some healers and I are setting up at the base of the plateau. Civilians may be locked inside the Keep, but healers are the exception. We're needed down here.

The group numbers fourteen in total, including Bren and Tomas. Fourteen people attempting to assume responsibility for an entire army. Thirteen healers—and Rora.

"Grab the other end," I tell her, nodding to the table I've cleared.

My sister helps me lift it without comment, still smoldering from our earlier argument.

Things got unusually heated between us. Enough that a passerby actually tried to step in, as if at any moment, we might start throwing punches. I wanted Rora inside the garrison, protected by those

archers and heavy walls. She flatly refused, wouldn't even entertain the notion. She did, however, have the audacity to suggest that
I should remain uphill. Me, a healer! "I have a job to do, Rora," I
reminded her, which only led her to respond, "So do I."

Which, of course, only increased my nerves exponentially.

"You're not supposed to go out unless they call. What other
job is there?" I demanded, alarmed when she said nothing. "That
is an army," I pressed on, pointing toward the long blocks of gray
uniforms dotting the valley. "And you are not a soldier. You're not
even armed."

Still, she didn't reply, and after another round of fruitless questioning, I reverted to progressively desperate attempts to make her
see reason. It was no good. The only argument that gave her pause
was when I suggested that Finley could use the extra guard where
he's being kept in the Officers' Hall. But even that was not enough
to sway her.

Now, as we continue setting up the station—a collection of
tables and blankets, crates of glass jars, and heaps of bandages and
antiseptic—she is quiet as the grave. Folding in on herself the way
she does, and today, it grates my teeth.

I'm starting to understand why she and Weslyn get along so well.

I am grateful, though, that at least she agreed to stay here, by
my side. I could use the extra set of hands, not to mention the reassurance her company provides. Besides, at least this way, I can keep
an eye on her.

Soon after the garrison bell chimes the ninth hour, deep horns
bellow out from the hills. Rora and I exchange a worried glance,
our disagreement forgotten in an instant, and Bren paces over to
place a hand on my shoulder. The signal that Eradain's forces have
been sighted.

"Listen to me," he says, angling to Rora. He knows she's my
sister, and that her presence here is nonnegotiable, but little else. "If
this becomes too much for you, I want you to go back up the hill.
Okay? We can manage well enough without you."

It's Bren, so the lie about our capabilities is meant to be reassuring, but Rora's eyes narrow like he's offended her. She may not

have a healer's stomach for blood and gore, but nor is she squea-mish. Neither of us have been afforded that luxury in life.

"It won't be too much," she tells him.

Bren appraises her doubtfully but doesn't object.

Beyond the encampment, the bulk of Telyan's army sits in wait. Infantry armed with swords, archers, and a sizable number of units on horseback—six hundred mounts at least. Thanks to Minister Mereth, a few hundred green-and-brown uniforms are mixed in with the green-accented gray, aid Telyan so urgently needs. While I can't see much beyond the rows of tents from way back here, I'm sure they're waiting for Eradain to reach the toothy ditch.

We know when they finally arrive, not only by the sound, but by the trembling underfoot.

Hundreds upon hundreds of steps send shivers through the earth, a low vibration I feel all the way down to my bones. Since I don't understand battle strategy or design any more than this level vantage point allows me to discern, I cannot pinpoint the exact moment when the armies engage. But the sharp clang of metal striking metal, of indecipherable shouting and whinnying horses, reach across the valley with painful clarity.

The wounded arrive slowly. They are only those well enough to drag themselves behind the lines; this morning, none can be spared to give the fallen a fighting chance. I rely on the nature of their in-juries to tell me how the battle goes; the number of trampled limbs trickling in suggests that Telyan's defense has begun on horseback, though plenty of puncture wounds crop up among the damaged bones. A perverse composition of the front and Briarwend both.

I feared the reminders might push me over the edge, but today, their suffering centers me, puts my adrenaline into productive use. I work hard, flitting from wound to wound with as much efficiency as I can muster. And all the while, I endeavor not to think about what exactly is happening a few hundred paces away. The young and old dying alone on rocking ground, their last sight perhaps a wildflower like those Rora, Finley, and I sat among, or the blades of sticky grass nearest their face. I don't know if we're winning or losing, but my job remains the same either way.

After a while, I realize Rora's disappeared.

My hands still over the patient to which I'm tending. I'm searching like mad, scouring the small crowd for her face, but save me, I can't see her. *I can't see her.* When the patient groans, it takes everything I have to snap back to work rather than dropping it all to find my sister. My body grows strained with the effort.

I don't know how much time passes before she reappears. Half an hour? Less? Gait stiff but without visible injury, she emerges from the encampment, and the movement snags my attention as if she and I were tethered by ropes. I finish stitching a hole I've rid of metal shards and rush to her side.

She pauses at the sight.

"What is wrong with you?" I exclaim, wiping my bloody hands on my shirt. "Where did you go?"

Rora's eyes are wide and scared. Almost haunted. "I lost sight of him," she says, her voice breaking on the words.

Clarity dawns. Weslyn can sit a horse well, if Briarwend is any indication; he must have been in the first or second push. Maybe even alongside the soldiers I've been treating.

My anger melts away, and I reach to pull her into a quick hug before remembering the state of my clothing. Instead, I place my hands on her shoulders and look her in the eye. "He's going to be okay," I say firmly, though truthfully, if he *is* among the units whose stragglers have been trickling in, I am scared for him. Enormously so. "He's a prince, not a common soldier. I'm sure there are people out there assigned to watch over him."

It's guesswork at best and empty promises at worst. I know it, and so does she. There are no guarantees either of us can make regarding Weslyn's safety today.

Rora looks close to crying.

"Listen to me," I continue. "He's good with a sword. We've both seen it. Trust him to do his job." The reassurance is merely an echo of what I said to Fin what feels like months ago, though it hasn't even been two weeks. As I was then, I'm reaching, grasping at straws. Mercifully, however, Rora seems to steady a bit. "I need your help here," I press. "These soldiers need your help. Please, Rora."

The last is no feigned excuse to keep her at my side. It's the truth, and she appears to take it as such.

Over the next couple of hours, we work together, Rora helping as she can—handing me the tools I request, putting pressure on flowing wounds, holding bodies down when they start to struggle. Two shifters together, just like their stupid Prediction warned, but for once, no one around utters a single remark. Fortune's sake, the reprieve makes a nice change.

The valley, meanwhile, is roaring, the tumultuous din enough to set anyone's head pounding. As time passes, the horse-related injuries begin to dwindle, surpassed by the gruesome work of arrows, spearheads, and swords. Perhaps the bulk of the action has switched to hand-to-hand combat on the ground.

When we start to run short on certain remedies, I realize someone is going to have to check the hospital for more. Rora volunteers, but she wouldn't be able to identify what we need, so I go instead. Up the hill, my shoes scrambling against the dirt road, all the way until I reach westgate.

"No admittance," calls one of uniforms from the bordering tower. "The gate has already been secured."

I bend over with my hands on hips, panting heavily. "I'm a healer," I call back, uncertain why I have to explain when the purple band hugs my upper arm like always. There's no reply, and I glance at my arm, only to find the band has grown too obscured with gore to be visible. "I'm a healer!" I repeat. "We need supplies. I have to get to the hospital."

"No admittance."

"*Open this door!*" I shout, pounding my fists against the wood.

My plea changes nothing, and I lean back against the barrier, hitting my head. This is the first time I'm glimpsing the battle from above, and the sight nearly makes me sick. Merciful fortune, how many people are in the valley? A thousand? Two? Five? I can hardly make sense of it, only see the colors strewn about like ants, swept across the ground thick as storm clouds. Eradain's forces are pushing through the narrow pass, across the ditch, and onto the field—slowly, it seems, but advancing nonetheless. The defense's mounted units have shifted to the outskirts, flanking the hundreds of units on foot.

That's all I see before the door groans open behind me, so unexpected I nearly fall on my rear.

"Be quick about it," says one of the women at the door.

I'm already gone, racing inside. The grounds are largely deserted; most people must be taking shelter. I can't blame them. When I reach the hospital, I don't stop to answer any of the patients who ask what's happening below. I just rifle through the supply room and fill a crate with phials of liquid, torn cloth, and jars of salves and balms and roots and herbs. As I work, I try not to think about the time only three nights ago when Weslyn and I sat on crates in this same room, finding peace over cups of tea, because my mind seems far too bent on reframing that particular memory as an ending.

Arms full, I'm crossing the main ward and out the hospital's front door when I catch movement in the corner of my eye.

Odd. I thought it was coming from outside the Officers' Hall, but now I don't see anybody there. Not even—I approach the building, peering closely.

There *are* two guards outside the open doors, as there ought to be. But they're both on the ground, the pavement beneath them staining red.

No.

I drop the crate of precious supplies and *run,* a horrible, plunging sickness knifing through my gut. I don't understand what's happening, only see the guards with their cut throats bleeding out onto the pavement, the doors behind them thrown wide. The doors to the Officers' Hall, where Finley was meant to remain safe.

Nausea coats my throat at the corridor inside. More bodies slumped in grotesque displays against the walls, the linoleum tile smeared scarlet.

This cannot be happening. How have the soldiers upon the rampart not noticed? Too fixated on the action taking place outside the walls, no doubt.

Finley.

I'm hurtling up the stairs two at a time, ignoring the screaming in my thighs, past the second floor and straight to the third. The swarm of bees is buzzing again in the pit of my stomach, numbness spiraling out from my core. The fox, the elk—which would help? Would either? Merciful fortune, don't let me be too late.

I'm onto his floor, and the next person I see bleeding on the ground isn't a stranger.

It's Dom.

"What's happening?" I ask, sharp pain rattling my knees as I throw myself down. A lump rises in my throat at the sight of him clutching at a hole beneath his ribs, his pallor having grayed to a sickly, dying hue. I've never liked him, but he certainly doesn't deserve to die like this, and I reach to examine his wound in case there's anything I can do.

Dom shakes me off and lifts his sword with a weakening grip.

"Take it," he says, the words sticking in his reddened mouth as he holds out his hilt. "Royal Highness, quick—"

I hate to leave him there like that, but I cannot bring myself to stay. Not while there's still a chance for Fin. Assuring Dom I'll be back, I take his blade and hurry the rest of the way to Finley's room. To my horror, sounds of a struggle are cutting through the open door.

For several heartbeats, all I can do is stand in the entrance, trying to make sense of the scene.

Far too many people have crammed inside, too few of them dressed in purple-accented gray. I spot Ansley first, her long hair beacon-bright. She's on her feet, her sword cutting a wide arc around her, but she goes down at a blow to her leg. Her attacker looms with dirty skin, rumpled clothes, a bruise blossoming up her arm . . .

It's the Eradain prisoner whose broken nose I set beneath the rampart, the scout I impersonated behind enemy lines.

Shock makes my hair stand on end. The other attackers, grimy and battered—how did they—

I find Fin, and all other thoughts are lost.

He is mercifully, *beautifully* alive and shouting obscenities, struggling to break free of the two prisoners—*former* prisoners—trapping him between them. "Bastards!" he cries, dragging his feet across the floor. I see his gaze lock onto a sword, see him fight to reach it, but their grip is too strong.

"Let him go!" I shout, charging forward with no other plan than to get to him. Finley's gaze shifts, but in an instant, an outstretched blade blocks my path. It's all I can do to intercept the horizontal blow with Dom's sword.

My opponent's weapon matches the one in my hand—she must have nicked it. No time to see more before she slams it against mine again, then again, strong enough I feel the blows ripple up my arm. Fear spikes a sour taste in my mouth as she forces me back against the wall, the unforgiving stone cold, and my blade clatters to the ground.

Instinctively, I throw my hands up as her sword reaches toward my throat.

The blow doesn't come.

I peel open my eyes to see recognition dawning in my would-be killer's face.

The Eradain scout.

"Tomas," Tari says, sounding confused.

"No witnesses," calls one of the prisoners holding Fin, just as Fin yells, "Helos, go!"

Still, she hesitates.

"You owe me," I remind her desperately. Ansley hasn't risen from the ground, nor have the other two in gray. "I'm calling it in. Your life for his." I nod to Fin. "Let him go. Please."

Tari shakes her head. "He's our way out."

"Helos, get *out* of here!" urges Fin, and one of his captors strikes him on the head.

The buzzing in my core grows louder, angrier. Nearly deafening. My bones are burning like the day I pummeled Broden, the spreading numbness sharp as fire licking my restless limbs. The call to shift, but not the fox and not the elk.

Something new.

The other prisoners are shouting again, and Tari's face hardens with resolve. To end me or spare me, I don't know, but I know that if I die, there will be no one left to rescue Fin. Fin, who is struggling with all his slender might, his frantic eyes begging me to save myself even as his captors take increasingly violent measures to contain him. The moment one puts his sword to Finley's throat, I'm gone.

Heat roars in, slamming against my core as my rib cage expands. My stomach, my neck, my head. All of me growing larger, huge, arms and legs widening like tree trunks, the ends stretching into claws nearly as long as my fingers. Rounded ears and chestnut fur and *teeth,* heavy and razor sharp. Ready.

For half a moment, my mind doesn't recognize this new form. My final of three that's taken shape without choice, years after Rora gained her third. I'm frozen, registering only the terror dawning on the prisoners' faces. Their haggard breaths grate loud as snapping flames to my ears, while their fear's musty scent twines through my nostrils with startling clarity, so barbed it's nearly blinding. Tari has backed against the wall, the color drained from her face. Distantly, I realize my clothes sit in tatters on the floor.

With that, the knowledge settles safely between my ribs and around my heart, warm and certain as breathing.

Brown bear.

Finley's mouth is hanging open.

Stolen sword raised, one of the prisoners rushes me with a cry. It is easy, so easy, to bat him aside. My paws are wide as supper plates, and the man feels fragile as glass beneath them. Little harder than brushing a fern from my side. Encouraged, I stand on my hind legs, tall enough now that my head nearly grazes the ceiling, and roar.

The window behind Fin and his captors rattles on its hinges, and one man actually drops his sword, urine staining his trousers. No one else moves toward me, so I decide to go to them.

It works. I don't even have to use my teeth. The prisoners scatter, racing for the newly freed exit. Only a battered Finley remains before me, standing wide-eyed.

The battle still rages in the valley below. I don't know where the prisoners have gone, or if Telyan is winning or losing the fight.

I need to check for survivors among Ansley, Dom, and the rest, and the healers will need the supplies I came to fetch. But I can't go anywhere. Not until I know Finley is safe.

I need to know he isn't afraid.

Rather slowly, Finley raises a hand to the fur between my ears. His palm is a delicate weight pressed to my forehead. Wanting to reassure him, I lift my head and release a gentle puff of air that sweeps his hair back like grass in the breeze.

Finley laughs a little, quiet, and the sound is music to my ears.

"On second thought," he says, a tiny smile blooming across his ashen face. "Perhaps you'd better stay."

TWENTY-EIGHT

RORA

The noise is like nothing I've heard before. Loud as a thunderstorm and just as earth-shuddering. Sheltered behind the encampment, at the base of the plateau, Helos and I are too far away to make out words or individual voices. But we can hear them dying.

All I can think about is Wes.

Wes, who held me in his arms the last two nights and whispered my name. Wes, who I know, I *know,* will be among the first lines of defense.

Helos appears better able to tune it out than I; ever since the first survivors began trickling in for treatment, some of them falling from their horses, he has acted almost like a different person. I've watched him work before, of course, but not in such a large capacity, with so many different patients to juggle. And not with wounds that look like these. Though his face is grim, he moves with a steady precision born of habit. I can see why his bosses value him so much. It makes me wonder what other horrors he's seen in the weeks I've been away.

I remain at his side for as long as I can stand it. But at a certain point, I have to know.

I lose myself in the encampment, choosing a tent at random to stash my clothes, and shift to goshawk. Then I'm off, soaring far above the Telyan lines, making straight for the mounted units in front. I'm enormously relieved to see the massive trench severing the valley, just inside the gap between hills where the road spills out from the bottleneck onto open land. The ditch looks deep, maybe three paces across, with pointed sticks stuck along the bottom. Enough of a challenge to slow the progression of foot soldiers, and more importantly, to prevent those wheeled siege weapons whose designs I sent south from entering the valley entirely.

But it's narrow enough for horses to jump.

Which is Telyan's opening strategy, judging by the sight: for swordspeople on horseback to leap the ditch and cut through the rows of Eradain soldiers trapped in the bottleneck, unable to proceed. The plan might be effective at overwhelming the invading units, but it's also dangerous—I can already spot a few horses who haven't managed the jump.

I duck lower, diving until I'm only a handful of paces above the battle. The ground has morphed into a bewildering tangle of bodies crammed close. Spears propelled, swords clashing, broad war horses barreling through those on foot. The proximity is enough to set my heart racing, but I will my nerves into submission. If he can do it, so can I.

Under normal circumstances, I could easily distinguish Telyan's green over gray from Eradain's red-trimmed navy. The soldiers below, however, are half-covered in chainmail or thin plated armor, and dust, blood, and gore are spreading fast. So I look to the ones on horseback, weaving through the upturned spears and helmeted heads as I would around trees in a forest.

When I spot Wes at last, I'm relieved beyond measure to find that he's still on horseback—a huge gray stallion with its dark mane in plaits. Naethan rides nearby on a dark bay, driving his sword into an opponent's neck. I resist the urge to fly close to them, wary of spooking the horses or distracting them with my sudden appearance. Instead, I offer what little aid I can, scoring my talons across an exposed shoulder or scalp when the Eradain colors shine clear. I may not be a soldier, but this, at least, is something I can do.

Unless the call comes.

As I fight, a fresh line of mounted units leap the ditch, some of whom are armed with bows—Glenweil's, I think. Closer to the encampment, blocks of foot soldiers are watching, awaiting their turn. Grateful, perhaps, to not have to lead the charge.

A wooden shaft flies my way, tipped with a curved blade the length of my entire winged body. Alarmed, I twist in the air to avoid the blow, but I'm too slow—the silver edge catches me on the side.

I lose my balance for a moment, then clamp my beak shut and beat my wings hard, lurching up and out of reach. The pain doesn't come, so miraculously, I think the blade must have only caught feathers. When the adrenaline subsides, I swing lower to offer my limited assistance once more.

I can't find him.

I do another sweep, panic flaring bright and hot as the sun. He was there. He was *just there!* But I can no longer discern Wes or Naethan among the jumble, and Eradain's harried soldiers seem to have grown tired of the flying pest haunting their heads, because more spears are arcing my way.

Admitting defeat feels like the worst kind of betrayal. Sharp and bitter as knives scraping my insides, or an iron fist clenched around my heart. I relent even so, retreating to the tent where I left my clothes and shifting back to human.

The healers station has grown much fuller than before. Despite what I've just witnessed, the scene playing out at the base of the plateau is gruesome enough to make my stomach churn. The makeshift tables and beds are all occupied, while other arrivals await their turn on the ground. A short ways to the side, some people have taken it upon themselves to begin laying out corpses. All those they couldn't save.

Helos rushes over, and I halt at the sight.

The front of his tunic has smeared brown and crimson. Not only his clothes, but his skin as well. His lithe figure is filthy, draped in other people's blood, and though I know it isn't his, the picture before me calls bile to the base of my throat.

"What is wrong with you?" he demands, half frantic. "Where did you go?"

I don't know how to explain, having no wish to argue again. I try to tell him anyway, but all I manage to confess is, "I lost sight of him."

Speaking that truth aloud breaks open the wound once more, and my throat constricts rapidly. I don't expect Helos to understand, but he must, because his features slacken with pity.

"He's going to be okay," he says, taking me by the shoulders. "He's a prince, not a common soldier. I'm sure there are people out there assigned to watch over him."

Helos sounds so sure of himself, but I know he is lying, and his face suggests he knows it, too. He may not have seen the chaos I did, but he must have a sense of what's happening out there. He's been tending to the wounded.

I feel tears welling in my eyes.

"Listen to me," he continues, grip tightening. "He's good with a sword. We've both seen it. Trust him to do his job."

The words call another memory to mind. A day in the Vale when I was preparing to scour the prison compound for any sign of Helos, and Wes started fretting. *This is what I do,* I told him. *And I'm good at it.*

I force a deep breath and try to internalize the words. Reminding myself that trust works both ways.

Helos nods, as if he can read my thoughts. "I need your help here," he says. "These soldiers need your help. Please, Rora."

I only have to see the state of his clothes to know he's right. Besides, I have to be useful somehow, and if this is the only way, so be it.

Following Helos back to the base, I spend the next couple of hours helping him however I can. Many of the words he mutters to himself are meaningless to me, but we're used to operating in tandem, and this morning is no different. I do my best to obey his instructions and match the composed manner with which he speaks to the soldiers.

The worst moments are when a patient is too far gone for him to save. In these cases, there's more than just sadness in the way Helos scrubs his hands and wrists and flags two runners down to remove the body. Frustration mounts, sometimes anger, usually directed at himself. I don't comment, but I can see the emotions bubbling closer to the surface the longer we work.

When one of the healers announces we're running short on certain supplies, I'm not surprised when Helos overrides my offer to help and runs up the hill to fetch them himself. He looks agitated and exhausted both, and it's scarcely even midday. I can only hope the brief respite will do him good.

In his absence, I quickly discover I'm fairly useless at this without him giving me specific instructions. I suppose I could volunteer to assist one of the others, but I'm afraid of making a mistake, and feeling rather shy of their company despite the circumstances. Instead, I switch to acting as a runner, taking on the horrible job of helping to lay out the corpses.

Very slowly, they're beginning to encircle the hill.

The healthier soldiers bring us reports of the ongoing battle. They aren't good. At some point after I left, Eradain pulled its infantry back from the pass and pushed archers forward in their place. The patients murmur, too, about a wicked kind of spear, one that Telyan's army has not encountered before—wooden shafts designed to break upon impact, so that they cannot be thrown back into enemy lines. The onslaught of arrows forced Telyan's mounted units to retreat, and in the interim, Eradain began crossing the ditch. Now foot soldiers are bearing the brunt of the main action, horses relegated to the outer flanks.

I take in the updates and close the eyes of the dead. Trying, trying, trying not to imagine Wes among them. Half an hour must have passed since Helos left, but he hasn't returned.

My gaze lifts to the garrison, where Telyan's standards are billowing hopefully in the breeze. Soldiers line the rampart, no doubt watching the action unfold below. What's keeping him? I'm tempted to run up and check, but would they open the gates just for me?

Stupid. I have wings.

Back to the tents I go, shedding my clothes and rising into the raucous air. Gaining height, I'm dismayed to see the Telyan lines have moved a little closer to the garrison than they were before. Eradain has started pushing them back.

Attempting to quell the sinking feeling in my stomach, I turn toward Fendolyn's Keep, intending to fetch my brother or offer assistance. But movement below snags my sharpened hawk eyes, shapes among the masses unexpected enough they halt me mid-flight.

Animals have scattered across the valley.

I sweep toward them, aiming for a closer look. No, I haven't imagined it—there are mountain lions and their magical counterpart, caegars. Lumbering brown bears and timber bears. Changeling wolves operating in a pack.

They're fighting.

What is happening? I fly over the clashing armies with renewed intention, searching for streaks of silver and gold behind the lines. And amazingly, I find them—whisperers cutting holes through Eradain's ranks with rapid-fire arrows, easier to spot from above with their metallic hair gleaming in the sunlight. After two long passes overhead, I find a find a jaguar snarling among the throng, and near his side, a figure I recognize.

Peridon!

He's fighting with the grace of a mountain cat, alternating between a silver blade and his wooden longbow. Hair tied back, leather armor covering his chest and forearms. Without thought, I'm diving toward him, adjusting my hold on the borrowed matter as I near the ground so that I shift to lynx upon landing.

By the river, it is *loud*. I can hardly hear myself think! Swords thudding against wooden shields, the twang of bowstrings releasing arrows, the squelch of spear tips rending flesh. There are voices shouting names, voices shouting pain. Boots striking the earth and climbing over fallen bodies. My tufted ears sift through them all, a cacophony of violence I've never experienced.

I spot navy sleeves peeking around plated armor, an Eradain soldier cutting a path toward Peridon. She's five, maybe six strides away from him. I fight toward her, the lack of space around me bordering on stifling. Spiraling arms, stumbling legs—there can't be more than a couple of paces to navigate in any direction. On the ground, I can feel what I couldn't from the air—a trembling deep in the earth, the impact of hundreds upon hundreds of footsteps.

I reach the soldier and leap from behind, digging my claws into the unprotected stretch of skin to either side of her neck. She goes down, fully unprepared for my attack, and I command myself not to hesitate before clamping my jaws beneath hers.

Peridon whirls around, sees the soldier on the ground with me on her back, and nods. "Rora," he greets, shouting to be heard above the din. "We figured you could use some help."

We. I glance behind him and notice what I didn't before—a long tumble of dark, curling hair. Andie's fighting, too, her jaguar close by, and I startle at the sight of her left arm. This is the first time I've seen the skin not covered by a sleeve. The gold rings stretch all the way from shoulder to wrist.

"Down!" she yells, the instant her eyes connect with mine. I crouch low, and she fires an arrow so close to my head I can feel the draft ruffle my fur. Another soldier drops just behind. High cheekbones, wide mouth bent in a final sneer—the prison commander.

The only word that comes to mind is, *Good.*

I have no time to ask how on earth they came to be here, or how many others they brought. I simply fight beside my friends, alternating between lynx and goshawk. On one of my trips into the air, I spot a dark mass moving in from the west and feel a jolt of excitement. Widow bats.

It feels right, to have forestborn joining the fight. To operate as a team rather than standing alone. Magic itself takes no sides, but those who wield it can—and should. If Telyan falls, there will be no other defense against Jol's rule of law. Far better to resist as a unified front while we can.

A sword catches Peridon in the leg, and excitement quickly morphs into fear.

Andie and I hurry toward him, and I shift to human just long enough to shout, "There's a healers station!" before returning to lynx and pressing against his side. Peridon leans on me, his body weakening, as Andie struggles to cut a path for us in the direction I'm headed. I know in my gut we have little chance of making it there before Peridon bleeds out, but I forgot about the gold bands ringing her arms. Animals appear from nowhere—three wolves, a brown bear, the jaguar, and two enormous golden eagles. The birds might be Peridon's doing, but I know he hasn't mastered the larger mammals; that Andie can hold them all in her mind while fighting herself seems a breathtaking feat.

Peridon climbs atop the bear, and our group manages to escape the fray with only one loss—a wolf whose high-pitched yelp carves a hole in my heart. I race ahead to find the tent with my clothes, then shift to human and hurry back to their side.

"Don't bring the animals," I tell Andie, relieved to be able to use my voice again. "They'll frighten the healers."

"Who cares?" Andie asks, and I hesitate before realizing she's right. There are bigger problems today.

Peridon's leg has been bleeding for an alarming length of time, and he's nodding in a dazed manner on the bear's back by the time we reach the station. The nearest humans—healers and patients both—spot the incoming bear and freeze.

"He needs help!" I shout, just as Peridon begins to fall. Andie strains to catch him.

At that, the healers snap into action once more. A young woman rushes toward us and helps Andie usher Peridon to one of the cots. Once he's safely in her hands, I hurry through the small crowd, searching for Helos.

I can't find him. Still.

"Have you seen my brother?" I demand, cornering Bren.

He only shakes his head. "He sent another down with the supplies."

Fear spirals through my core as I look again to the Keep atop the hill. Helos would not have stayed inside on account of nerves.

I'm partway up the plateau when the ground trembles beneath my feet, enough that I almost lose my footing. It's only the battle, I think, or an earthquake. Except it's neither, because striding into the valley, tall as trees, are giants.

Giants.

In Telyan?

Wes's letter.

The thoughts all come at once, jumbling into a single tangled mass. I can hardly believe what I'm witnessing. Seven have arrived, grabbing soldiers like matchsticks and hurling them to the side. The sight feels as out of place as that of the ground beneath their feet.

It's changing.

Roots are spiraling out from the stretch of forest spilling into the valley. The gnarled, twisting limbs rise several hands-widths into the air, cutting through the ranks regardless of uniform, streaking the valley like gold bands through ore. Whether the magic is a mark of the giants' influence or that of forest walkers, I can't say. Blades of grass grow taller, darkening to brown as they wind around soldiers' calves and trap them in place. I remember the iron-like strength of that grip from the day Helos, Wes, and I first met the giants in the west.

Once, the idea of seeing shades of the Vale replicated in Telyan was enough to send me over the edge. Now, the convergence just feels right, the environment edging back to the way it ought to be. Forestborn and humans standing together while the magic takes root in the land around them, disparate threads bound together to reclaim what was stolen.

Eradain's army doesn't share in my delight.

Many of the units nearest the sprawling ditch are backtracking toward the pass, visibly spooked and seeking an exit from the fight. They steer clear of the patch of forest that produced all those roots, though, as if no one dares to step beneath its shade as Helos, Finley, and I did yesterday. At the suggestion of retreat, a cry goes up from those in green and brown and gray. The call sounds like hope, dangerous and fleeting but growing a little stronger nonetheless. With magic's arrival, the tide of battle is shifting in Telyan's favor.

Victory. A win is beginning to feel possible.

A horn sounds from the north.

I pivot to the lakes, where half a dozen or so riders on horseback are shouting with raised arms, attempting to rally the retreating soldiers toward them. My heartbeat stutters in my chest. Only high-ranking officials from Eradain fight on horseback, and one of them lifts a mounted standard bearing a massive *H* embroidered atop Eradain's sun-encased crown.

The king's banner.

The call still hasn't come.

Uncertainty steals the breath from my lungs. I think of the soldiers fighting to stay alive back at the healers station. Gentle Helos covered in blood. I think of the ones that already lay fallen throughout the valley, trampled before or after death by fellow soldiers around them. I think of Wes, who was alive two or three hours ago, but now, I don't know, I don't know.

The call hasn't come.

I'm running.

Hair whipping across my face, wind burning my cheeks, my blood-splattered boots pounding the earth. Keeping behind the Telyan lines, I leap over the rising roots, over grass that bends toward me but does not darken, doesn't bind, only seems to whisper as I pass. *End this,* says the voice on the breeze, or maybe it's only in my head. Either way, I intend to. I don't need someone to tell me the time is now. I am deciding for myself.

If anyone thinks it strange to see a girl with no weapons or armor racing across the war-torn valley, I receive no sign. No one tries to stop me, surely preoccupied with pushing their opponents in the opposite direction. Animal instincts stir beneath my skin, offering flight or claws, but I ignore them. For this, I need my voice.

I wait until I'm close enough to make out Jol's figure atop the timid chestnut stallion with white socks before screaming his name.

Jol doesn't hear—the battle still rages too loud. Instead, his gaze remains fixed on one of Telyan's mounted units flanking the infantry's outskirts. I'm too far away to identify any of the riders, but I can see the horses, a patchwork of black and brown and gray.

Gray—

I can't make out the rider. It might be him, or it might not be, but the possibility alone is enough. I see Jol's rapt attention and put the pieces together even as my feet continue to fly. His army is unsettled. His soldiers need a boost in morale, a reminder of what victory looks like. And Jol intends to give them one.

I change course just as he kicks his horse forward and throw myself before it, arms spread wide. "Jol!" I yell again, the word a blade scraping my throat.

The horse skids to a stop in front of me, ears flat against its skull, and rears. I edge as close to his flying hooves as I dare, willing the breeze to carry me right to him. This horse has been trained to remain steady amidst the chaos of battle, but apparently not in the presence of a shifter. How could it be, raised in the north?

Fiery pain sears my side, so sudden and sharp a gasp escapes my lips.

The stallion rears again, and Jol slips from the saddle, slamming into the ground. My attention flits down. I thought a hoof struck me, but no—a patch of scarlet blossoms across my sweater. My fingers grow sticky as they graze the tear in my side. Whoever launched the arrow or dagger or whatever it was clearly missed their mark, but the river take me, it *hurts*.

"Hold!" Jol shouts to the uniforms pointing swords in my direction, a half-circle of blades straining toward me like the tree limbs encircling Finley in the forest.

As he pushes to his feet, I pull from the air around me and direct the matter to the blazing cut, stitching the fat and torn skin shut. The pain blinks out, though the stain remains, and I train my focus back on Jol.

"You need to stop this," I tell him, raising my voice to be heard. It's absurd, really, to try to have a conversation with a battle raging maybe twenty paces behind. "Enough blood has been spilled. Call it off."

Jol straightens, looks me in the eye, and says, "You are in my way."

"Look around you!" I shout, while his guard pushes closer. "You're losing. Your people are dying. Is this what you want your legacy to be?" His eyes dart away from mine, fixing on something over my shoulder, and I take a step toward him, desperate to keep his attention.

Jol pulls his sword and points it at me.

I make no effort to sheathe the claws that spring from my hands.

"Last warning," he says, taking his own step forward. His blade has come close enough that I could reach out and touch it. "Get out of my way."

"Or what?" I retort, the realization dawning with abrupt clarity. "You'll kill me? You've had that chance a dozen times already, and you've always held back. You are *still* holding back. Why is that?"

Jol's mouth is pinched, his eyes brimming with hatred.

"Weakness," he says, in a voice low enough I almost miss the reply.

Behind me, the battle is edging away. I can see a couple of his guards growing distracted, uneasy, torn between the threat from a weaponless girl and that of armed, angry soldiers pushing Eradain's forces closer to the valley's exit.

"No," I say, taking half a step forward until his sword nearly touches my chest. "Not weakness."

Jol remains motionless a few moments longer. His gaze flicks over my shoulder once more, and he starts to step around me, clearly bracing to launch into the fray.

With only half a thought, I twist around and score his hands with my claws.

He doesn't drop his sword, and maybe that's why the guards don't seem to notice. But blood wells in the deep lines I carved.

Jol stares at me, apparently heedless of the pain in his hand, his eyebrows raised in minor astonishment. His mouth settles into a smile. "Are you going to kill me, little sister?" he asks.

I don't respond. I only meet his mocking gaze, numbness spiraling out from my core. The lynx whispers in my ear, urging me to pick a better form for this fight.

In my silence, the smile drops from his face.

I wonder what our mother would say, if she could see us here now. Her firstborn and her forestborn, each preparing to destroy the other. Perhaps it's her haunting presence that stays our hands even now, this tenuous connection she threaded between us when she left us both to grow up on our own.

In the end, as it always does, logic wins. I have a job to do.

I throw myself forward and slash out with my claws, aiming for his throat. They catch only air—he twists away before they can connect. I'm bracing myself for another blow before his guard takes me down, but suddenly Jol is bent double, his clothes ripping, his body lengthening, growing—

Shifting.

I stumble back as his body settles into a different form.

Four enormous paws. Pronounced shoulder blades and golden brown fur with the chainmail half-hanging around his new body, the other half dragging where it tore. Long whiskers, a pink nose. A curved, twitching tail.

Mountain lion.

The stallion tears past me in fright, but none of the uniforms behind Jol have moved. All they do is stare. We're all stunned, I think, but none more so than Jol.

For an endless time, he simply stands there, motionless. Still as an aging statue carved from stone. As the moments drag on, I catch subtle changes taking shape. His tail brushes out. The fur rises along his spine. His pupils dilate as they stare at seemingly nothing.

A minute ago, I was ready to end his life, but the prospect feels altogether different with him so obviously afraid.

"Jol," I manage.

An ear flicks in my direction.

I don't know why I say it. "It's okay."

Trembling, Jol raises his head and looks at me.

"You can shift back, if you want to," I tell him. "Just let go." I place my hands over my stomach.

The spiked fur along his back begins to lie flat just as a black-fletched arrow thrums past me and sinks into his chest.

I cry out, twisting around to see who shot. I can't tell. The arrow is Eradain made, but on a battlefield riddled with arrows, anyone could have grabbed it.

Jol collapses on the ground, breath rasping in his throat. For an instant, a scene from another time pulses before my dry eyes—a caegar trapped in the woods, ensnared in an Eradain net while Helos, Weslyn, and I looked on, horrified. A question leveled my way. *Who the bloody ends are you?*

I look again to his guard, the uniforms backing away, their

features contorted in horror. Loyalty gone, it seems, with the truth of him brought to light. My half brother alone, again, as he has been for most of his life.

Except today, I'm here.

I drop to my knees and examine the wound, confirming what I already suspected. Whoever fired the arrow, their aim was true. Jol's stomach rises and falls unevenly now, so I do the only thing I can think to, which is to place a shaking hand on his shoulder. Probably he doesn't deserve it. But he isn't going to die alone.

Jol shudders a little at my touch. Within heartbeats, his body is shrinking, the fur receding, shifting back to human. He coughs, an awful sound scraping his lungs as blood bubbles up from his mouth.

I don't know what to say, so I simply sit there, one palm on his shoulder, the other holding his hand. Jol's eyes find mine. He looks as if he might try to speak, but when he opens his mouth, pain rips through my body.

Sharp. Searing. Burning. Like the fire in my side but worse, so overwhelming that I can't tell where it's coming from. An arrow? A sword-tip? A spear?

Panicked, I release Jol's hand and dip my head to search for the wound, needing to heal it temporarily. My neck twists, and I catch a glimpse of black protruding from my back. Father swims before my eyes, a fate I refuse to share. *Not today.*

Before I can do more than grasp at the air around me, my vision goes black.

TWENTY-NINE

RORA

There is pain. Pointed and brutal, searing as flames, all around my shoulder. Pulsing like waves throughout my skull.

There are hands I cannot see, and voices I can't make sense of, and foggy darkness that overwhelms my senses for indistinct stretches of time.

And then, there is softness beneath me. A lightweight blanket draped over my lower half, and a warm glow waiting on the other side of closed lids.

I open my eyes.

Wooden beams stretch across the ceiling, with dusty shafts of light drifting lazily just below. I tilt my head toward the foot of the bed and have to shut my eyes against the dizziness that slides in. When I open them again, I see a shock of golden hair bent over lanky legs, thin hands pressed to either side of his downturned head.

"Finley?" I rasp.

His chin shoots up, and then he's struggling to his feet and calling Helos's name. When Fin sinks onto the side of my bed, I note with alarm that his eyes are red.

"Rora," he says, grabbing one of my hands. "You gave us quite a scare."

There's no humor in his voice as he speaks, no gentle teasing when Helos suddenly appears in an obvious state of distress. My brother has changed into fresh clothes and a new healer's tunic, but the skin around his hands is still tinted red.

"Don't try to sit up," he says, sinking onto my other side and placing a palm on my shoulder when I start to rise. The other one is aching, but not with the searing fire of before. "You're in the hospital, but you're okay."

"I feel dizzy," I say, my voice coming out quieter than I intend.

Helos nods. "That's the medicine. And you took a pretty hard blow to the head."

I blink at him, trying to collect my thoughts. "Why didn't you return? After you went up the hill."

Helos bites his lip. "I meant to," he replies, sounding guilty. "But Fin needed—I had to—I'll explain later," he finishes.

Finley says nothing, only holds my hand. The silence sets my nerves on end.

"Jol—"

"Dead," Helos says.

It's difficult to identify the emotion that spirals through me at the word. I'm not surprised, and if I'm honest, there's even a good degree of relief—that it's over, and that I didn't have to do it myself. But the fear in his eyes remains branded onto my mind.

Helos starts to smile. "Rora. Eradain surrendered. We *won*."

For a short while, all I can do is stare at him and Fin. *We won.* It's over—or the worst of it is, at least.

Except it's not, because Finley still isn't speaking, and though their faces are two of the ones I most need to see, one is missing.

"Wes," I say.

I mean it as a statement, but it comes out like a question, and panic grazes my insides as I realize I'm terrified to hear the answer.

Fin blinks rapidly, and Helos places a hand on his shoulder before telling me, "They're still searching."

They're . . . still . . . "How long has the battle been over?" I ask.

Helos hesitates.

"How long?"

He sighs. "Half an hour, maybe."

No.

That's too long. Helos and Fin both stammer protests, but I'm rising anyway, pulling from the air and directing the matter to anywhere I can find that hurts. My shoulder, my head. The cut in my side. I might be undoing some of Helos's work when they reopen later, but I don't care. Fear is coursing through my veins and seizing my heart in an icy grip. I cannot sit here doing *nothing*.

"You need to rest—" Helos starts to say, but I'm already winding through the hospital, past a mass of red hair—Ansley? I don't stop long enough to be sure—and out into the Keep.

Before, the garrison was a ghost town, save for the soldiers lining the rampart. Now the grounds are crowded as Roanin on Prediction Day. Civilians and soldiers alike are hurrying about, some weeping, others beaming with relief and joy. Whisperers and forest walkers, maybe even shifters, are scattered among them, exchanging quiet words or mugs of steaming drinks. The gates have been thrown open, and people are toting the fallen inside like ants on a log, heading for the hospital or the nearby practice yard, which appears to have been converted into a makeshift wing.

I push through the crowd, ignoring them all, and rush downhill on newly steady legs. Near the base of the plateau, I can see the giants milling about, heads bent together in conversation. The giants who wouldn't be here if it weren't for Wes. My breaths are coming fast, my heartbeat pounding like drums of war, and it has nothing to do with the sudden exertion.

I am going to find him. I will, even if I have to comb the valley a hundred times over. People are already walking the fields, but they're not me. *I will. I will.*

The words bang against my skull like a mantra. Like a plea. *Come back to me.* No, I won't let myself believe that night was our last. I have been here before, the creeping return on desperate feet to find inexcusable loss awaiting me, but today, that pattern changes. I'm going to make it so.

After the hours of blinding clamor, the mournful quiet draped across the valley lingers with eerie intensity. It is loud in my ears, louder than the mantras in my head. All around me, bodies blanket the ground, an undulating spread of mud-streaked, mangled limbs and torsos gleaming scarlet and brown. Armored plating lies dented, chainmail links broken, spears snapped a handspan above their deadly tips. A horrid stench floats through the air, sharp and nearly thick enough to grasp.

My stomach churns with nausea as I navigate the maze, terror lending speed to my feet. Telyan gray, Glenweil green, and Eradain navy all jumble together like splatters of paint. *Where are you?* Here an older woman, her broad neck torn where it meets the shoulder. There a young man, his uniform colors too dirty to make out, his honeyed eyes sightless, the dark hair—"*No*," I gasp, forcing myself to stumble past. It's somebody else. It isn't him. Two arrows pointed in opposite directions have been etched into the young man's breastplate.

Fur is creeping beneath my shirt, giving form to the fear. I fight to steady my rapid breathing and glance farther out, where other survivors have embarked on their own searches. The silence born of shock is growing new legs in the battle's aftermath, shouts and sobs and names offered up like pleas. In the distance, someone dressed in Royal Guard gray turns over fallen soldiers with remarkable speed.

"Weslyn," I murmur, adding my voice to the rest of them. Saying the name aloud seems to lend it more weight, like a tether stretched taut across the earth. In my head, I grasp the end with shaking hands. "Where are you!" I call, more loudly this time. Then, flouting self-consciousness completely, "Wes! Where are you?"

In my peripheries, someone is watching me. Tall and mud-bound, regal even in despair. Violet's wide eyes catch mine, and their usual certainty is ringed with fear.

Part of me wonders if she'll chastise me, insisting on formal address even here. She only heads in the opposite direction, now calling the same, her movements increasingly urgent.

I go on like this for a time, shading my eyes with a dirty hand, apologizing to empty ears when my feet catch a hand or outstretched arm. Hope dangles from my rib cage on trembling fingers, on the verge of losing its grip and surrendering to the misery lodged deep in my stomach. I walk farther still. *Where are you,* I cry, over and over, along with any number of requests. *Say something. Hold out a hand. Answer me. Please answer.*

I can feel my mind switching directions, reluctantly angling toward a new, forbidden set of instructions—how to prepare for a life without Wes. When everything he is morphs into memory, and I won't get another hour together, not a single moment more. That I've faced this crossroads before on the riverbank does nothing to make it easier. The base of my throat feels so tight, I can barely breathe. I cannot breathe. *Please no,* I beg silently. *Not him. I'm not ready. Give me one more day.*

Someone is shouting my name from far away. But it's not his, the voice all wrong. And maybe that's all it will ever be from this day on—the voice I need to hear sounding only in my head. My calls give way to steady tears, even as my legs plow onward instinctively, not yet willing to concede defeat.

I don't know what it is that makes me twist around. Not a sound, not a sight. Just a feeling inside, one without shape or name.

I turn my head and there he is. There's my Wes.

Not dead. He's walking.

His gait is uneven, his bearing that of someone struggling to stay upright. Most of his armor has been shed, his shirt and trousers ratty and stained, skin tricolored with layers of grime, expression warring between purpose and pain and something haunted, broken. But there he is, walking toward me.

Whatever he's starting to say breaks off as I throw my arms around him, feeling the need to be gentle and utterly unable to manage it. His shirt is stinking and already slick where I bury my face in his chest, and I don't care, *I don't care,* because his heart is beating wildly as mine and his mouth is in my hair and his arms are steady as they hold me. Not a memory. He's *holding* me. Dimly, I notice the jagged pattern of his breathing and realize he's hurting, but he isn't pulling away, so neither do I.

We remain that way for a while, neither of us willing to break apart. I can feel the exhaustion dogging his body and the sorrow lodged in his controlled breath. After a time, I shift to look at the space around us. Wretched sounds still pierce the air, and the bodies lining the battlefield haven't changed. But new people are standing among them. From a short distance away, they hover with mingled expressions of relief and confusion, watching their prince embrace an unknown girl. I doubt any of them know that I'm a shifter, but perhaps this sort of public display is inappropriate for a royal. I don't know the rules. I lift my eyes to his, ready to step away, but his grip remains tight as he looks back at his people. He already knew. He doesn't care.

"Don't go," he whispers, and then I'm back in the night I returned home. A night, it seems, which may not be the last of its kind, after all. Farther afield, Violet is moving toward us, a small entourage of guards just behind. Relieved, I spot Naethan among them.

I close my eyes, my lips curving into a smile. "I told you," I reply, squeezing him tighter. "I'm not going anywhere."

HELOS

Rora ignores my warnings and hurries out of the hospital before I can stop her. Not that I tried too hard—I really can't blame her, and truthfully, I'm just blindingly grateful that she's *alive*. If that giant, Hutta, hadn't intervened and carried her to the hill, I expect the outcome might have been quite terribly different.

My eyes cut to Fin, who didn't try to stop her at all. I gather myself a moment, then murmur, "He might—"

"Don't," Finley says, dropping his head into his hands again.

So I don't. Resting a palm briefly on his shoulder, I rise and check on Ansley, who's a little out of it but luckily should heal well enough. That leg, however—she'll need time to build her strength back up. Rora must have temporarily healed her own wounds; she moved far too easily for someone who, not long before, was shot in the shoulder, sliced in the stomach, and banged in the head hard enough to lose consciousness.

Back in the main ward, I offer assistance to anyone who needs extra hands, guilt pricking my consciousness while I make the rounds. *Why didn't you return?* I intended to, but I just couldn't bring myself to let Fin out of my sight. Not after that scene in his room. Together, we had gotten the survivors to the hospital, which I decided abruptly was the next-safest place for him to be. Unfortunately, by the time I'd returned to Dom, he was dead.

I carry on working for some time—stitching wounds, preparing calming remedies, checking on patients with the Throes—until a minor commotion draws my eyes to the entrance.

Relief flares like river water released from a dam. Weslyn is at the door, leaning rather heavily on a bruised Naethan but indisputably, wonderfully alive. Rora paces nearby, tracking their progress. Scooting around stragglers lining the corridor, I hasten toward the group and reach the entrance at the same time as Mahree.

"Out of the way," I tell the crowd, wrapping an arm under Weslyn's other shoulder while Mahree leads the four of us to the more private ward in back. Weslyn stumbles once, his face an alarming, ashen pallor, and he keeps swallowing as though he might be sick. Fortune's sake, it's a miracle he made it up the hill.

The best moment is when Finley hears us coming and looks up. His eyes grow wider than the moon when they latch onto Weslyn.

"*You,*" he exclaims, tugging the cotton from his ears and pushing to his feet while Naethan and I lower a wincing Weslyn onto the edge of a cot. "How *dare* you make me think you were dead, you selfish, spiteful, *idiot* of a brother!"

The angry diatribe is rather ruined by the fact that he's crying.

"Sorry, Fin," Weslyn says, screwing up his face at the pain but grinning a little all the same. "Bad day."

Rora puts a hand on the back of Finley's chair, chewing on a smile. As soon as Weslyn has been safely seated, Naethan hurries a few cots away, where Ansley is watching us through half-closed eyes.

"Out," Mahree says, looking at Rora.

"No." Weslyn's voice is firm. "She stays."

Mahree rolls her eyes but doesn't object again, only beckons me over and points to Weslyn's head before prodding his shoulders and arms. "Sprained," she says, noting one of his wrists.

I crouch in front of Weslyn, holding my finger a short distance from his face. "Follow this."

"I'm fine," he says, which is a lie, because he's blinking as if the windows are letting in too much light.

"Actually, you're concussed," I inform him, hearing him wince when I search his head for cuts or bumps. "Lucky you're so thick-headed."

Mahree adopts a scandalized expression, but Finley laughs, and it's the most beautiful sound I've heard all day.

Weslyn doesn't protest again as we continue our search, just closes his eyes for increasingly long stretches. I force him to drink a cup of water, then another, while Mahree pronounces dehydration and significant blood loss. Like most I've treated today, he has some unfortunate scrapes and contusions, and we peel away his grimy shirt to reveal spectacular bruising along the ribs.

"Two broken," Mahree says, which makes Rora suck in a breath.

I grab something to ease the pain and glance at my sister, wondering why she suddenly looks guilty. "You're next," I remind her.

Weslyn's head shoots up. "What? What happened?" he demands before pressing his lips together as if, once again, he might be sick.

"I'm fine," Rora says with a shrug.

Finley squeezes his forehead between weary fingers. "The pair of you."

After Mahree finishes wrapping Weslyn's ribs—nothing to do there but wait—Fin shifts to the edge of his brother's bed, and Rora agrees to release the borrowed matter erasing her injuries. Placing a hand on her good shoulder, I steer her back to her original cot and watch her grimace as the pain returns.

"Sorry," I say, "the poppy will have worn off."

Though my stitches were sound, the shoulder wound starts bleeding again at the renewed trauma. I press linen to the area while Rora grits her teeth, and Weslyn tries to stand like an idiot.

"Don't you start," I warn him. "There's enough that needs doing without us all having to redo our earlier work."

"What happened?" Weslyn asks again, pressing a hand to his head.

Fin exchanges a long look with my sister. I can read in his eyes the same curiosity I've felt since Hutta rescued her—whether it's merely coincidence that Jol's death corresponded with Rora taking the field. But too many potential eavesdroppers remain nearby, and Fin doesn't voice the question any more than Rora offers an explanation. Time enough for answers later. "Rora decided to act the hero today."

"Act the—"

"Sir!"

We all look up at the messenger heading our way. She's panting a bit, her posture slumped in relief. "Sir, Her Majesty has requested your presence at once."

It takes all of us a moment to realize she's speaking, not to Finley or Weslyn, but to me.

Sir?

"Me," I say flatly, just to be sure.

"Yes, sir. Right away."

Rora stares at me.

"I— All right," I say, flustered. Disposing of the linen, I shrug at Rora and an equally baffled Finley and follow the messenger outside. She leads me out of the bustling garrison and down the hill without a word, even when I ask her what this is about. We stop outside the council tent, and I count ten soldiers at least, all standing at attention, before one at the entrance tugs on the flap to admit us.

"Helos," Violet says when I step inside.

The space is crowded, such that it's difficult for me to take in everyone at once. Violet is seated at the table, with Minister Mereth to her left and an array of papers spread before them. A number of people in uniform are standing around; in one corner, two bear the Telyan and Glenweil standards, while in the other—Eradain's.

Minister Mereth studies me with a curious expression. I wonder if she's remembering the day she expelled Rora and me from her realm as clearly as I can, even four years later.

"This is him?" asks the man seated opposite Violet, narrowing his eyes critically.

I glance at Violet, waiting for a cue.

"Helos is Mariella's son," she supplies. "You see the resemblance to Jol, surely."

The man's mouth twists at the mention of his late king, his oily olive skin and black hair greased to one side, putting me in mind of a lizard. I still can't decide if it's bad that I hear them speak of Jol's death and feel nothing at all, save for relief.

"You must be joking," he says.

Indignation swirls in the pit of my stomach, along with a hint of self-consciousness. I resist the urge to look down at my clothes, which are a mess, I know, hardly the appearance of royalty.

"Perhaps you're unfamiliar with the queen's style," I reply, pushing the hair back from my face. "She is rarely one to laugh."

The barest hint of a smile crosses Violet's lips. "General Malhorn here has come to deliver Eradain's surrender." She pauses, so that we all linger in that fact just a little longer. "When we raised the matter of Eradain's line of succession, I told him there was already an heir ready to ascend the throne."

"Where is the proof?" General Malhorn demands, slapping the table with his palm. Minister Mereth lifts her water glass mildly, still watching me. "A lot of people look alike. Coincidence, I say."

"The proof is in his face, as you can very well see," Violet says, somewhat impatiently. "But should you wish for more, it so happens we can provide that. Fetch Rora," she tells the messenger.

This, I decide, is the moment I need to say something clever. Persuade them of my right to be here, as Violet advised. Under General Malhorn's critical glare, however, with the morning's casualties haunting my mind and their blood baked into my skin, what comes out is, "I'm sorry for your loss."

His head tilts back. "What's that, boy?"

"You must have lost a lot of good people today," I push on, not bending to his condescension. "I'm sorry."

General Malhorn drums his fingers along the table, apparently unable to think of a proper rejoinder.

Faint amusement traces Minister Mereth's features. "Helos," she says. "Helos what? Tell me, do you claim Holworth as your family name, or have you taken Mariella's prior to marriage?"

Expectancy clouds the subsequent pause as I try to determine how to fill it. A reasonable question, but the sting of not knowing the answer never fully fades. "Neither, ma'am," I say.

General Malhorn shakes his head. "This is ridicu—"

"My father's," I decide, the impulsive words feeling right as soon as they leave my lips. "Helos Wolridge."

In truth, I can't remember Father's family name any more than I can the precise pitch of his voice. But I remember the heart of the stories he used to tell, with changeling wolves at their center. Animals with the ability to blend into new surroundings, a sign of good fortune to come. And after the atrocities at Caela Ridge, who has learned better to adapt than Rora and I?

Violet knows I'm lying, but I detect approval in her tone when she says, "Have a seat, Helos."

General Malhorn folds his arms, but no one outwardly objects when I take a chair midway between him and Violet. Instead, the three leaders move onto smaller points of the surrender, two scribes scribbling furiously to the side.

A murky feeling seeps out from my core.

If I take the throne as I intend, this is about to become my life. Meetings, negotiations, politicking, persuading. Working out the finer details of countless categories of life. I will have to say good-bye to my job as a healer. Or at least, redirect that energy toward a broader, indefinite purpose: healing a kingdom.

I knew this already, of course. Still, up in the hospital, working at people's bedsides—it feels like more than a sense of purpose. It feels like home. And I am choosing to leave it.

To my horror, my eyes begin to itch. I blink the suggestion of tears away, knowing that now is the last time I want to start crying. But the weight is settling over me with renewed intensity, exciting and frightening and heavy. Surprisingly heavy.

When Rora arrives, she's moving far too easily for someone with her injuries. Again.

Fortune's sake. That'll make treatment number three.

General Malhorn's eyes narrowed when he first saw me, but he sits back in his chair when Rora bows to Violet.

"This is Helos's sister, Rora," Violet says, in the manner of one who knows she's just been handed a victory.

A muscle works in General Malhorn's jaw. But he doesn't try to deny the resemblance between her and Mariella. I suppose this is one gift, at least, our mother left for us—the echoes of her visage etched into our features, beyond the point of contention.

Rora glances at me, uncertain, and I smile encouragingly, trying not to dwell on the conversation I've been too distracted to focus on until now. The fact that she wants to stay in Telyan, even if I go.

My stupid, itching eyes!

"They are blood-forsaken shifters," General Malhorn bites out.

And *there* it is, the brand of anger I last felt facing that skeleton of a mob. "Hundreds have died today," I say, finding my voice, "and that's what you care about most? Who led them into battle, General? A pair of shifters or you?"

"My orders were—"

"I'm not questioning your ability to do your job. I don't doubt you do it well. I'm asking why you believe shifters are responsible for deaths you can't see, when the consequences of your own actions are there before your eyes."

General Malhorn grows red in the face. "I tell you the people won't stand for it!"

"A conversation." I force myself to breathe in deep and let the air out slow. "That's what I'm asking for. I'm here to work with you, General Malhorn. Not against you."

"You will not have the support of the army."

"Actually," says another general posted beside Eradain's flag bearer. "He might."

The woman who spoke is tall and slim, no visible injuries aside from a scratch along her warm brown face. Her long-lashed, deep-set eyes are studying me, not with trust, exactly, but with interest.

In the corner of my eye, Rora straightens in recognition.

"Insubordination, Hariette," General Malhorn barks. "You swore an oath—"

"To lead fair fights between soldiers while minimizing civilian casualties," General Hariette interrupts, her steady gaze cut from steel. "Not to condone mass murder. There's a difference."

"That is treason."

"It is treason to deny a blood relation of King Jol what is rightfully his." Hope sparks as General Hariette addresses me directly. "There is blood on your clothing, Helos Wolridge. Why?"

I see no reason to lie about it. "I'm a healer."

General Malhorn exhales dismissively. Distantly, I realize neither Violet nor Minister Mereth have spoken in a while, but I resist the urge to check the former's face. It feels important not to look away from General Hariette's piercing gaze, and anyway, this is not Violet's mediation. It's mine.

After a long while, General Hariette nods. "I will speak with you," she accedes, and I can't help but smile, whether that's regal or not. "For now, I believe there are terms still to discuss."

For the next half hour, debate continues regarding the terms of surrender. When at last, Minister Mereth suggests we take a break, I'm only too happy to agree. I can follow the conversation well enough, but each new point is yet another reminder that in many ways, I am out of my depth.

I rise stiffly from the table and realize Rora has already slipped away without my having noticed. Eager to ask why and how she seemed to know General Hariette, I walk from the council tent and make for the hill.

She didn't go far. Standing a short way from the plateau's base, Rora is gazing up at three seated giants, a sapling in the shadow of ancient oaks. And sticking close to her side—

"Are you determined to make my life more difficult?" I ask Weslyn when I'm close enough.

He glances at the giants and rubs his head. "This is important."

"Helos," says Rora, who's suddenly beaming. I'm not used to the sight. "We decided to—"

"Wait a moment," says one of the giants—Corloch. I remember him from over the summer. "We agreed."

"We can tell Helos. You know him," Rora replies, familiar impatience now coloring her voice. She tugs me closer and murmurs, "The giants brought more stardust—Weslyn has been writing to them. They buried it while we were up on the hill."

I blink at her happy face, marveling at the change. Three months ago, the mere thought of bringing stardust into Telyan terrified her. "You buried it?" I repeat, somewhat stupidly.

"The time has come to reawaken the land," says Guthreh, another I recognize from the Vale. "It will take time, and a little assistance. As I told these two before," she gestures to Rora and Weslyn, "rain may cure a drought, but not overnight. Still, magical creatures are beginning to return east. Their presence will help."

"Have you told anyone else about this?"

"Not yet," Weslyn answers. "But it's the right move."

Guthreh appraises him thoughtfully. "Perhaps. Perhaps not. Your realms are at a turning point. Will you choose better this time, or will you revert to old patterns? Time will tell. Regardless, we have decided to give you the chance. You made a compelling case."

Rora turns her smile on Weslyn, whose typically stoic features soften at the sight. He looks at her like he looks at the sky, and I realize Finley may have been right. Maybe I don't need to worry quite so much after all.

And yet—

"Finley!" I exclaim, the ramifications catching up with me. "Why didn't you save some for—"

"That was not the trade."

"But then, how quickly will the magic stop feeling threatened?" I ask desperately. "Will it let go of those with the Throes?"

"A rain may cure a drought, but not overnight," Guthreh repeats. Dismay stabs deep in my core at the lost opportunity, until she adds in a kind voice, "However, this valley has seen quite a lot of magic today." That's an understatement—roots still twist out of cracks in the ground, the grass around them having returned from brown to green. "I believe you will find it has already begun releasing its hold. Particularly if you give the burrowing magic somewhere else to go."

I trade troubled looks with Rora and Weslyn, wracking my brains for a solution.

Somewhere else to go.

An idea hits. Foolish, maybe, one that probably won't work, but why not try? I open my mouth to explain, then shake my head and simply say, "I'll be back."

Rora calls after me, but I'm already gone, hurrying up the road to the top of the hill as quickly as my tired legs will allow.

Inside the garrison, I push through the crowd toward the hospital. My heart rises at the scene that awaits: a sprinkling of smiling faces, more patients with the Throes sitting up and looking happier than they have in weeks. I head for the back, but the healer there informs me that Finley has gone.

"Gone where?" I demand.

She shrugs.

I try the Officers' Hall, doing my best not to watch the team of cleaners scrubbing at the mess on the floor, the spot where I returned to find Dom's open eyes glassed over.

Finley's room is empty, too.

Frustrated, I pace to the window and back, feeling antsy enough to step out of my skin. Where would he go? His heightened senses, he's always gritting his teeth lately at all the noise. And right now especially, the garrison's throngs are making a racket. He'd want someplace quiet, but most of the buildings on this base have grown full to bursting. Except, perhaps—

I turn my feet toward the stable, a building I've never stepped inside before, given the way horses respond to my presence. A number of stalls are empty, their former residents no doubt still lying on the valley floor below. I search each one, and the stablehands take little notice, too preoccupied with removing tack and rehousing the horses that have been fortunate enough to return.

At long last, I spot him, a narrow pillar of fatigue dressed in black and robin's egg blue. Anticipation tightens its hold.

Finley's in one of the occupied stalls, running a brush over a dark mare's neck and murmuring words too low for me to make out. The horse throws her head back as I stick my own over the low stall door, and Finley whirls around, fixing me with a frown.

"You might have warned me," he says, face flushed. "I've just lost several minutes' worth of work calming her down."

"Sorry," I breathe, though I struggle to feel properly subdued. Not when he has this chance. I retreat to the empty stall across the aisle, too fired up to stand still. Maybe by now, I should know better than to get my hopes up, but I can't help it. My stupid, reckless, hopeful heart.

After he's soothed the horse's nerves, Finley shuts the door behind him, shaking his head. "I've never liked it," he mutters. "Sending horses to fight a war that isn't their own. Hardly seems fair."

The sober assessment quiets me temporarily. Then I'm bouncing again. I walk the perimeter, kicking a little at the straw on the ground.

"Well," Fin says slowly, watching me from the entrance. "Either something very good or very bad has happened."

"What makes you say that? It doesn't matter. Listen, the giants buried stardust in the ground—"

"Stardust—"

"Shh," I plead, crossing the stall and placing a gentle palm over his mouth. "It's supposed to be a secret for now. Or, I don't know, I just—" I take my hand away, forcing a deep breath. Finley stares at me like I'm unhinged. "The point is, with the added magic, I think it could be enough."

Finley shakes his head. "Enough for *what,* Helos?"

I search for the words to explain before realizing I might not have to. *Somewhere else to go.* Taking his free hand, I guide Finley into the stall, his walking stick carving a ravine through the bedding.

"Do you trust me, Fin?"

His mouth purses as if he's unimpressed with the question.

"I want you to try something for me," I persist. "Please."

Fin studies me a long moment, forehead creasing, before he gives me that look he's used before. Exasperation mingled with fondness. "What exactly do you want me to do?"

I place a hand on the back of his head, winding my fingers through the waves. "I want you to focus on the magic in your core," I say with a faint smile, bending closer. "And I want you to let it go."

Finley huffs a humorless laugh, the ghost of a grin dropping away when he sees I'm entirely serious.

"Oh, that's all, is it?" he says dryly. "Helos, this isn't a bedtime tale. I can't just will it away. And anyway, as if I haven't wished it gone a thousand times be—"

I don't let him finish. I just wrap an arm around his waist and kiss him.

Finley's resistance lasts only an instant before he kisses me back. Because we're not living a bedtime tale, and I might be talking nonsense, but this, at least, will always feel right between us. And while he kisses me, I try something I've never done before, would never even have *thought* to attempt until Guthreh's words—

Drawing on the magic in my core, I pull from the world around me as if to shift. Only this time, exceedingly slowly, gentle as breathing, I try to pull from *him*.

Heat flares in my core, just as it does when I'm borrowing matter from earth or air. Finley tenses a little, and I worry I might be hurting him, but he doesn't break away, so I don't either.

I know it's working. I know because I can feel the magic, as natural to my body as it is foreign to his, warming my limbs and my core and my bones like a taste of summer breeze. Like a break in the downpour. Like the sun.

The connection slips away like a spigot run dry, and Finley stumbles back, unsteady.

For an endless moment, we just look at each other, his chest heaving a bit.

"Helos," he says, tentative, as if he's not sure what just happened. *How* it happened.

I grin.

"Helos!" he exclaims, smile spreading, and now he's laughing as I wrap my arms under his and spin him around.

It is joy, spiraling through my veins and around my heart, so fiercely it burns. Warmth and light as strong as a thousand suns. Relief so powerful the sensation is blinding, mind-numbing. As if I've been holding my breath for years and can finally breathe easy again. I'd almost forgotten how.

The weeks of torment, at last, at an end. The Fallow Throes, gone. Finley, free.

Free.

Why didn't I think to try this before? *Idiot,* I think. I could have at least—no, the conditions weren't right, it wouldn't have—

"What?" I ask, scraping away my tears, when I realize Finley's still laughing.

He grabs my shoulders lightly, his hands an anchor for my jumbled thoughts and racing heart. "Your face," he says, the answer breathy. "I don't know how you expect to rule with a face like that. It's like reading a book. Every thought you have shows clear upon it."

I sniff a bit, casting about for a response. "Maybe they're only clear to you?"

He matches my smile. "Definitely not."

"Well." I pause, considering. "Maybe I should try harder to control it."

"No." Finley sobers with the word, earnest eyes searching mine. "Don't do that."

And drinking in the sight of him, a wild thought surfaces, one I didn't allow myself to consider until now. "Come with me."

He drops his hands. "What?"

"Come north with me!" I say. "I have no practice being royal. You can show me how it's done. And you've always wanted to see the world outside of Telyan. Why not start now?" I lace my fingers through his. "Come with me, Fin."

Finley looks rather bewildered by this sudden flurry of words, but I have never felt more certain in my life. This is what I know to be right: to do the work ahead of me, but with Finley at my side.

When the idea settles, he smiles a little, mischievous. "Are you proposing a strategic alliance between our great realms?" He rests his arms upon my shoulders, hands behind my neck. "My father did warn me such responsibility might fall to me."

I shrug, touching my forehead to his. "I just want you."

Finley's smile broadens. "Well then," he says, quieting. "You have me."

THIRTY

RORA

It's harder getting Wes back up the hill the second time. I think we're both anxious to see where Helos ran off to and how Finley is doing, but the return trip seems to have drained whatever was left of Wes's strength. By the time we pass through the gate, he's leaning into my support pretty heavily, one arm over his chest.

"You should have stayed in bed," I chide, attempting to mask my concern.

Weslyn laughs shortly. "Not a chance."

As we cross the grounds, onlookers note his halting progress with alarm—the steady soldier prince scarcely able to walk. I know it's a mark of his pain that he isn't feigning wellness for their benefit, so I steer him toward the hospital.

Wes shakes his head and says, "Not there."

I roll my eyes but don't argue, just try to think of another place he can rest. "I have a room in the Officers' Hall," I suggest.

He raises his eyebrows in a manner entirely unbefitting his current state.

"Don't get clever," I warn, which makes him grin. "You're asleep on your feet."

By the river, I can still hardly believe he's *here*. Injured and weakened, but warm and alive and clutching my arm, his human heart beating strong. My gaze keeps flitting back to him of its own accord, as though he might disappear at any moment. Seeing this, he slides an arm around my shoulder, quietly reassuring.

Ignoring the garrison's prying eyes, I help Wes into the largely abandoned Officers' Hall and up to my room. He hesitates once over the threshold, apparently having second thoughts.

"Fin—" he says.

"Can wait," I tell him. "Sit. You'll be of no use to anyone if you make yourself worse."

He winces as he lowers himself onto the bed and leans against the headboard, eyelids drifting shut. "You sound an awful lot like Helos sometimes," he mutters, though he's smiling.

With a shrug, I linger near the doorway, uncertain now.

Wes peels open his eyes in the silence and searches the room, brow smoothing when he finds me shifting my weight from one leg to the other. "Come here," he says softly.

I tuck my hair behind my ear, torn. "What if I hurt you?"

He lifts a shoulder. "I don't care."

"Don't be an idiot."

"We established long ago that I already am."

Weslyn's smile broadens at the sound of my sudden laughter, and the sight melts away the last of my reserve. Circling the mattress, I perch by his side, facing him, and take one of his hands in my own. A treasured weight.

With a delicate touch, I trace the grooves lining his palm before running a finger along his wrapped wrist. "Is the sprain very painful?"

Weslyn's eyes don't leave my face. "A little."

And despite the answer, happiness kindles in my chest, because even hearing his voice feels more special now, a gift I almost lost forever. Determined to appreciate that gift fully, I move to his heart, the navy shirt creasing beneath my fingertips. "What about your ribs?" I sketch a small pattern, light as a feather.

"A little," Wes concedes, sounding amused.

I continue exploring until I'm rewarded with the tiniest change in his breathing, amusement shifting to an altogether different reaction. Encouraged, I run a hand through his hair, to the back of his head. "And this?" I ask innocently.

"Nothing," he says, swallowing.

"Nothing at all?"

"Maybe a little." He pauses, expression thoughtful. "You'd better check again."

I work my mouth into a frown. "You're teasing me."

Wes grabs my wandering hand, honeyed eyes bright. "You're teasing *me*."

Well. "A little," I agree, smiling. I can't help it. This morning, I woke desperately pleading to fortune that it wouldn't be our last. And here we are, having reached the other side. It makes me giddy, almost reckless, to think about the time stretched before us. Suddenly, we have so much.

Wes raises an eyebrow. "Perhaps you should broaden your search."

Still grinning, I roll my eyes—on principle—before kissing him softly. Unlike our reunion on the battlefield, I'm careful not to press too close. But soon enough, he places a hand on the back of my head anyway, drawing me in.

Someone coughs behind me.

I pull away and twist around, heart skittering through my chest.

Finley stands in the doorframe, a bit wide-eyed. "I mean, I knew this was a thing," he says, "but I think now I needed to see it to fully believe it."

"Don't you have somewhere else to be?" Wes asks good-naturedly, running a hand over his face.

"What, and miss the show?" Decidedly entertained, Fin turns back to the hall. "It's okay. You can look now."

Helos pops his head around the corner, pink in the cheeks.

Which pretty much reflects how I feel. "How long were you there for?" I demand, somewhat weakly.

"Long enough," Fin says, pacing over and plopping down on the end of the bed without a concern. Though he uses a walking stick as usual, his movements seem strangely lighter, nonetheless. And the look on his face—he's happy. Really, truly happy.

Excitement thrums in my chest.

"It's lucky I found you, really," he says, glancing between us. "Because I came to tell you something's happened."

Helos opts for leaning against a wall, features brightening.

"Something good?" Wes asks, watching his brother carefully.

Finley grins. "It's gone."

Gone. There's no need to specify what.

Adrenaline pulsing, I glance at Helos for confirmation and feel I might burst from the emotion on his face.

"You're certain?" Weslyn says, disbelieving.

"I'm certain," Fin assures him. "Although Helos says there may be some lingering effects for a long time. My head still—"

He doesn't get any farther than that, because I've thrown my arms around him, blinking away tears. It worked. *It worked.* I can scarcely believe it's real—to have endured so many years of things going wrong, so many hopeless nights, only for them to finally start going right. A reality I once believed could never be mine, and yet here I am living it. Here he is.

Here we are.

Finley laughs over my shoulder as he hugs me back, holding tight. "She's touchier now," he says to Wes. "You've been a bad influence."

When Wes doesn't respond, I twist around to find his face is in his hands.

"Oh dear," Finley says. "I've broken him."

We stay this way for a while. Talking, laughing, *being,* nothing to rush off to, no other place we have to be. A new peace of mind I have trouble wrapping my head around. We're here, and the war is won. We're here, and Finley is healthy once more. Not I, but *we*— three boys I can't imagine a world without, and I no longer have to.

I'm not used to this feeling. The sense that weeks and years of trouble are largely behind me, as if everything might actually be okay. This joy, so powerful it burns my chest—how could I have gone so long without knowing it? It's bright as stardust, pure as the sharp scent of pines caught on a winter breeze. Warm as a campfire smoking on a summer night. I want to wrap this golden feeling around my chest and never let it go.

After a time, however, Helos snaps up, muttering something about a meeting. With a hasty apology, he bolts from the room.

The joy loosens its hold, just a little.

"I should go, too," Finley says, and my ribs tighten further. "There's a lot that needs doing."

I blink in surprise. Since when has Finley cared about that kind of thing?

"You watch yourself, Rora," he says, placing his hands on my shoulders and adopting a voice of mock gravity. "My brother is not as noble as he likes to pretend."

"You haven't a shred of nobility in you!" Wes protests.

Fin winks at me. "And thank fortune for that."

I stare at the door long after Finley has closed it behind him.

In their sudden absence, I find it harder to avoid the subject I've been flying circles around in my mind. The fact that the one constant throughout my life will soon be hundreds of miles away. I don't know what I'd expected to see, following the messenger into that tent, but it was not my brother sitting among leaders of realms while smiling at me.

The sight had taken me aback. Helos has always been more comfortable speaking his mind to strangers than I have, but this was more than that. I don't know if it was the quiet confidence in his bearing, or simply his eerie resemblance to Jol, but he looked like he belonged. An impressive achievement, and one I should be celebrating—

So why does his victory feel like a loss?

"Hey," Wes says, placing a hand on top of mine.

The gentle pressure doesn't erase the sorrow pricking my heart. But it comforts me nonetheless. Even injured, he's still here.

And so am I.

In the coming days, the people of Fendolyn's Keep begin to rebuild. By the second sunset, the bodies have all been buried or burned.

Too many died with fear in their hearts, dreaming of a day they never got to see. The giants and forest walkers send the towering roots back underground, and Telyans work together to fill in the ditch as well, shifting the valley closer to its former state. The stretch of upturned grass and trampled wildflowers across which Finley, Helos, and I raced, altered to a vast burial ground.

Alongside the somber mood, however, quiet joy begins spreading like wildfire. With the dissipated threat of invasion and Eradain's army ordered to vacate Telyan within the week, people speak of returning to their homes. South to Poldat, west to Briarwend, north to the capital. After these long weeks of upheaval and uncertainty, I find myself craving the familiar stability of a home and a life I already know. Roanin is calling, but burgeoning excitement mingles with anticipated loneliness. However much I wish he could follow, my brother will be gone.

Peridon and Andie leave the Keep the evening after battle, having spent the first night in the practice yard's makeshift healing grounds, each contending with their own injuries. As the sun begins to set and the western hills dim against a purpling sky, Andie and I linger on the yard's outskirts while Peridon exchanges a few parting words with a blushing girl who appears either human or shifter. Andie's fist is wrapped around her brown pack's strap as she watches her cousin with something akin to guilt in her bearing.

"He's always followed me into crazy situations," she murmurs after a while. Moss-green sleeves cover her arms once more, hiding her mastery from view, but I know the rings are there, now. "One of these days, he'll have to stop."

I nod noncommittally, thinking that would be his choice to make. She and I haven't spoken much since reuniting, a careful distance wedged between us, but a splinter of tension seems to have lifted from her shoulders since our last parting. I'm glad for it. "What will you do next?"

Andie releases a breath, her long curls fluttering in the gentle breeze. "Feren has always intended for me to lead the clan after her."

I lift my chin, surprised by the admission. I've seen a few members of her clan in the valley since the battle ended, Feren and Andie's father among them. Though Feren and I didn't speak when we locked eyes across a cobbled path, mugs in hand, she nodded my way with grudging respect in her eyes before turning aside.

"I don't know if that will happen now," Andie goes on. "Or if it ever would have. I've never cared much for politics."

My thoughts turn to Finley. "Is there something you'd rather do instead?" I ask, and her silver eyes flick to me at last. "Or be?"

For the first time since I met her, Andie's mouth curls into a genuine smile. She doesn't reply when her attention shifts to the hills, but I think I can guess at the answer she holds close to her chest.

Free.

"I envy you," she says instead. "The power of flight. I can only hear about it secondhand."

My eyebrows lift, and she gestures to her mind, that ever-present link to the animals around her.

I feel myself return her hard-won smile.

"Listen, Rora," Peridon says, coming to our side. He's still favoring his uninjured leg, and my heart pinches at the scrapes and bruises coloring his lithe figure, his formerly bloodied hair pulled into a low knot. Even so, his expression is bright. "Will you be staying here in Telyan?"

"Roanin."

"Good. I may be passing through in the coming weeks. I'll see you there."

Andie rolls her eyes. "You can't be serious, Peri."

Peridon shrugs her off, while I peer around him and resist the sudden urge to laugh. The blushing girl is still looking.

"We'll say goodbye, then," he says, folding my hand between both of his. "We did good work, huh?"

"We did," I reply, feeling my spirits lift at the idea of seeing him again. "Thank you for—well, you know. This, the land, it wouldn't have happened without you."

I twist toward Andie as I say it. Already a leader, I can tell, though what she chooses to do with that gift will be up to her.

She nods. They know.

I walk them to the gate and watch their figures shrink into the distance.

In all this time, I barely see Helos. He's been spending his days shut up with Eradain officials, working to persuade them to his cause. In the evenings, he returns to the Officers' Hall looking exhausted and slightly disgruntled, not in the mood to delve into details. So on the third night, I suppose it shouldn't surprise me that the person who knocks on my door isn't Helos, but Finley.

"They're going to crown him," he tells me in an undertone, sounding a bit surprised himself. "Tomorrow. They're keeping the ceremony fairly private, but you're invited, of course."

I just stare at Finley loitering in the doorway, attempting to steady the anxious drumming of my heart, to stem the confusion and disappointment at the fact that Helos himself isn't bringing me this news.

His new life beginning, and already, my part in it is slipping further away.

"That General Hariette has volunteered to be his Captain of the Guard," Finley goes on, amused. "She has a few trusted individuals she's recruited to ensure he reaches Eradain safely. Didn't take long—he must have impressed her."

"And she—they all know he's a shifter?" I ask, when I find my voice.

Finley nods, ruffling his hair. "Jol was an only child, and his father's siblings died before producing heirs. The Holworth line is broken; a half sibling of Jol's is as close as they're going to get." A crease forms between his brows. "They don't want to leave a power gap for long. Empty thrones breed chaos, which is the last thing that kingdom needs on top of a lost war."

I shake my head. I believe him, but there must be more to it than that. The stakes are too high—if the top officials were unimpressed with what Helos has to offer, it would be simple enough to make him disappear, as Weslyn said.

I've always thought of Helos's gift with people as a talent, but I'm starting to think it's also power.

"Are you okay?" Finley asks.

I fix him with a look. "Are you?"

Helos going north would mean more than one farewell. Finley fidgets a bit, but nonetheless, he looks remarkably composed for someone facing a future without his love.

Suspicion roils in my gut.

"I think he's going to be good at it, Rora," he says at last, summoning a small smile. "Our Helos, a king. Who would have thought?"

"Finley—"

"The ceremony will be early, shortly after sunrise," he presses on. "Come to the academy building on the western side. The white one. Second floor." He quirks his eyebrows playfully. "Wear something nice."

Before I can question him further, he heads down the hall, walking stick snapping against the polished floor.

I shut the door and spend the night in a state of restless unease. I should be happy for Helos. I *am* happy for him. Yet nerves and sorrow have been warring with the joy in my stomach all day, and tonight, they're coming out the stronger.

The following morning dawns just as clear and crisp as the day of the battle. I slip on flats and the beautiful long-sleeved dress, which flares ever so slightly at the waist, the neckline curving a short way beneath my collarbone. The design is fairly simple, perhaps not as formal as one might expect for the sister of a soon-to-be king, but the finely spun wool is deliciously soft against my skin, and the dark fabric is the reassuring color of pine. It feels right to me.

The Keep is still subdued when I walk to the building Finley mentioned. The room where the coronation is set to take place, on the other hand, is not. Perhaps it's quiet by coronation standards, but the long hall—framed paintings and maps decorating the white walls, flower arrangements hastily strewn among the rows of chairs squeaking against wooden floorboards—must hold twenty or thirty individuals at least.

I feel a slight shift in the crowd when I walk in. Heads turning, murmured conversations dwindling momentarily. The sudden awareness of my presence reminds me vaguely of the attention I garnered walking the halls of Castle Roanin, but the faces before me aren't pinched with suspicion or distaste. Instead, they're the smoothed features of innocent curiosity. Respect, even. Courtesy of my newfound status, I suppose.

Nerves dancing along my skin, I resist the urge to ball my hands into fists as I scan the slightly raised platform in the front. No sign of Helos. My footsteps slow.

I jump when I feel a slight touch to my waist.

"Does the princess require an escort?" says a voice close to my ear.

I turn on my heel, and the clenched fist constricting my chest loosens its grip.

Wes is dressed more formally than I've seen him in a while—tailored navy suit fitted over a light gray shirt and charcoal tie, silver ring slipped onto his middle finger and shoes polished to a shine. He's shaved his beard to shadow and smoothed the thick curls into relative submission. All together, it's a consciously regal portrait that might have distanced him from the boy who slept on my bed, were it not for the quiet smile just for me. That part is the same.

I open my mouth to tell him I'm not a princess, then shut it again as he leads me to a seat near the front. Because, of course, Helos's coronation means I am. And strange as that feels, much as it will take getting used to—the title and abruptly elevated status, the faces looking on with interest—in this moment, with Wes's arm bent beneath my hand, I'm also beginning to feel being a princess might come with certain advantages.

"There you are," says Finley, when we slip into the second row. He's cleaned up well, too, handsome in a suit a shade lighter than Weslyn's and a white collared shirt that, for once, isn't coming untucked.

Seeing him like this, it dawns on me.

I destroyed that prison and enabled magical creatures to return to the homes from which they were hunted, with the help of former strangers I now call friends. It was my idea to reawaken the land.

Weslyn's words persuaded the giants to cross the river for the first time since the Vale's establishment, more than seven hundred years ago, and bury stardust underground. A trade no other human has been willing to make.

And once the magic felt safe enough to let go, as I've since learned, Helos—the healer, my hopeless romantic of a brother—kissed the magic out of Fin.

The road didn't look the way we expected, when we set out for the Vale two months ago. But the three of us saved him after all.

"You look nice," I reply, smiling. A few seats away in the front, Violet is conversing steadily with someone I don't know, but I see her gaze dart toward us a couple of times. "Anyone would think you're enjoying yourself."

"I do what I can," he says, tugging at his collar as if it itches. "Nice dress."

Standing between us, Wes has said nothing, only stares at my dress in a way that makes my face feel flushed.

Finley smacks him on the head with a leaflet.

"Hey," Weslyn grumbles, hunching his shoulders against the blow. He tosses a glare over his shoulder, to which Fin responds by widening his eyes, before turning back to me. "You look—"

"Miss?"

We all twist toward the messenger standing at the head of our row.

"His Royal Highness is asking for you," she continues.

Rarely in my life have I ever been addressed as "miss," and I suppose I'm going to have to get used to it. His Royal Highness, though—Finley and Weslyn are both behind me, so she must be talking about my brother. Silently marveling at the strangeness of it all, I gesture for her to lead the way.

She takes us back out the door through which I entered, then down the echoing, empty corridor and to a room on the next floor up. Guards in red-trimmed navy have been stationed outside the door, and if the expressions on their faces aren't friendly, exactly, at least they're civil.

The messenger knocks and reaches for the handle, but Helos throws open the door himself a heartbeat later, face crumpling in relief. He beckons me inside and closes the door behind us.

The low-ceilinged space looks like an abandoned classroom—a blackboard situated on one end, small wooden desks spread about, and dusty morning light filtering in through high windows. Almost at once, Helos begins to pace between the rows of desks, running his hands through his likely once-tidy hair. Now the brown waves are sticking up in disarray, and his navy suit jacket—where did he get these clothes?—is unbuttoned where he's tossed it aside.

"Nice suit," I say, by way of a greeting.

"What am I doing, Rora?" he asks, pacing the length of the room.

I raise an eyebrow, sitting on one of the desks. "Panicking, by the look of it, which I don't think will help."

"No," he says, waving a hand and moving to a window. "I mean, what am I *doing*? Here in this room, in these clothes, preparing to take a fortune-forsaken *crown*." He shakes his head and sinks onto one of the desks opposite me. "I must be out of my mind."

I watch him scrape a hand over his face, trying to find the right words that will comfort him. Instead, all that comes out is, "Probably."

Helos's head jerks up.

Before long, we're both laughing. Bent double with it—two wilderness-raised orphans crinkling our ceremonial clothes. Because it *is* absurd. Me in this fancy dress, a princess seated in the second row. He in that regal suit, preparing to accept responsibility for an entire kingdom. It's absolutely, unequivocally *mad*.

Yet I can't stop smiling.

"The river take me, Rora," Helos says, when he's regained his breath. "I don't think I can do this."

"You can," I say firmly, nodding for emphasis when he eyes me dubiously. "If you couldn't, you wouldn't have made it this far."

He snorts, but it comes out halfway a sob. "I don't think that's how it works."

"I'm not saying things will be easy," I continue. "But you have allies now, or at least the beginnings of some. Powerful ones," I add, thinking of General Hariette. "You can use that."

Helos dips his head. "I'm not a politician," he murmurs. "I know nothing of lawmaking or treasuries or armies or courts. I'm just a healer."

I consider this a while. "I think a healer might be what that place needs."

And it is. Eradain is already a kingdom in change. Their monarch is dead. The land is waking up, as are some of the people. They're going to need someone who can guide them through the changes and teach them to respond differently this time. To adapt to the shifting landscape rather than beating it down, to find the beauty in the flourishing magic rather than focusing only on the danger. Not just cruel, as Jol once believed, but cruel and generous both. The light and the dark, woven into one.

Who better to heal a realm than my brother?

"You'll have advisors there to help you," I go on. "You're pretty smart, Helos. And you have the right intentions. Don't sell yourself short."

Helos twists his hands before him, staring down into his lap, before meeting my gaze and saying, "I asked Finley to come with me."

I try my very best not to shatter at those words, to keep my head up despite the torrent of conflicting emotions.

I am desperately happy for Helos, and for Fin, and relieved that my brother won't be going there alone. Given Finley's behavior when we spoke last night, I suppose I'm not entirely surprised, either. But I feel the loss. Helos and Finley, my two closest friends for so long.

Gone away.

"What did he say?" I ask, suspecting the answer already.

Helos smiles, as though a memory is playing before his eyes.

"He said yes. He's going to teach me how to act like a royal, though he's going to wait a month or two before coming. Help Telyan to rebuild." He chews his lip. "He hasn't told his family yet."

My mind flashes to Wes, to yet another goodbye forced upon him. And he doesn't even know.

Helos's smile fades, mirroring my own somber thoughts.

"I won't ask you to come, Rora," he says. "I know you like it here, and you shouldn't give all that up just for me." He nods to himself, coming to a decision. "I think you should stay in Telyan."

Sweet Helos, so often the portrait of a torn heart, however brave his words. The comfort I feel knowing Finley will be there with him dims at the thought of my brother spending his first couple of months in Eradain feeling overwhelmed and completely alone.

And just like that, I reach my own decision.

"Telyan feels like home," I agree, watching the light leave his face. As though he knew this was coming but dreaded hearing it anyway. "But I'm coming with you. For a little while, at least— until Finley arrives."

Helos's eyes grow wide as the moon. "What?"

"I'm coming with you," I repeat, feeling in my bones that it's the right decision. A goodbye is coming, one that will be more painful than any I've faced before. But I don't have to face it quite yet. North or south, we go together, always. "You don't have to do it alone."

For several moments, Helos appears as if he might cry. He crosses to the desk and hugs me, and as usual, no words are needed.

"Come on," I say, pushing off from the desk and straightening my hem. "You have a coronation to attend."

He laughs a bit, swiping at his eyes, and smooths his hair back into place. Together, we head for the door.

"Oh," he says, pausing abruptly as he buttons his suit jacket. "I forgot to tell you." He grins. "I got my third form."

My heart skids through my chest.

"What? When?" I demand, shaking my head in bewilderment. "How could you not tell me?"

"I am telling you!" he points out. "I just forgot."

"You *forgot*—"

"Anyway," he says, shifting his weight onto his other leg. "It's a bear. A brown bear."

I blink at him, trying to take it in. My brother, a *bear*. Maybe he really does have more fight in him than I'd realized. I want to hear the story, and some time later, I'll make him show me the shift. But for now, I simply laugh and say, "Well, then. Those Eradain officials had better not get on the wrong side of you."

The ceremony proves to be a quiet and somewhat brief affair. One of Eradain's representatives officiates, and Helos makes his vows before the seated crowd, back straight, chin raised. At one point, I peer around Wes to steal a glance at Finley, wondering if he's feeling the same swell of emotion I am. Mostly, he just looks proud as he beams up at Helos, no royal reserve in his bearing.

When it's over, everyone rises as Helos strides from the room, wearing a gold, ruby-encrusted crown with five points. My insides twist unpleasantly as I realize that crown must have traveled south with Jol. I haven't told anyone the story of his death yet, or the mountain lion that came before. There has been too much to do, and an overwhelming desire to look toward the future rather than dwelling on the past. But I was not the only one who saw him shift.

I can't help but wonder why it took so long, if our mother left enough magic in his blood for him to take an animal form after all. Maybe his body sensed intuitively that shifting under his father's roof would have only placed him in greater danger, bringing more hurt than help. It seems fighting me was a different situation entirely.

The story will spread. How it will affect the legacy over which he obsessed, I can't say, nor do I wish to spend any more time thinking about it. Not today, at least, with my brother newly crowned.

When Helos vanishes from the room, I wring my hands behind my back, uncertain of what comes next. Before I have time to worry too much, though, the messenger is back.

"If you'll just follow me," she says.

I gesture for Finley and Wes to follow, because I don't think Helos will mind, and the messenger leads us to another abandoned classroom much like the first.

Helos visibly relaxes when he sees us, tugging the crown from his head and roughing up his hair.

"Having regrets already?" I ask, biting back a smile.

"It's heavy!" he says, brandishing the crown for emphasis.

Finley crosses the room and swipes it from him. "The weight of royalty," he declares solemnly before placing it on his own head. The crown falls to the side a little, too wide for his narrow skull.

"Don't think it suits you, Fin," Wes observes, leaning against a wall.

"You flatter me."

"Not intentionally."

"Finley!" Violet barks, making me jump as she strides into the room unannounced. "Take that off at once. If someone from Eradain sees you—"

"Shove off, Vi," Finley whines, plopping down on one of the desks. "You worry too much. And Helos doesn't mind."

"I don't," Helos agrees, grinning as he grabs another desk.

"Anyway, he's basically your equal now, right?"

Violet rolls her eyes.

"*Diplomacy,*" Finley chides.

Violet folds her arms. "Why I thought this was a good idea . . ."

"Not everything is *your* idea," Finley says, waving a hand in my brother's general direction. "This is Helos's birthright, whether you wanted it or not."

"Exactly. Helos's birthright, not yours."

They both glance at Weslyn, who had been watching Finley with amusement. Now he raises his hands, abruptly wary. "Don't involve me."

"Weslyn agrees with me," Violet says, which is, frankly, a stretch. "Take it off."

Finley does, though he sighs dramatically before restoring the crown to Helos's head. Helos just watches Fin like he's waiting for the sun to rise, and the whole thing makes me laugh, because it strikes me as faintly absurd that Helos is planning to look to *Fin* for royal etiquette and advice.

All too quickly, though, the laughter sticks in my throat.

A goodbye is coming. I can feel its edges creeping closer, tightening their painful grasp on my chest. The weight of it sits like a river stone lodged in the pit of my stomach. A future in which anything might happen, unexpected or wonderful or difficult or tragic, and Finley won't be there. Helos won't be there, once I leave him in the north. This time, our paths are branching apart with no end in sight.

The prospect is terrifying, sorrowful enough that tears prick my eyes. And just like that, I'm seized with an overwhelming desire to rewind the clock. To have one more day together, back in Roanin. Only, not as we were back then, but as we are now. The people we've become.

By the river, give me one more day. One day with Helos, Finley, and I walking the Old Forest or roaming the castle grounds the way we used to, unconstrained on lazy afternoons. With Weslyn there, too, this time, a stranger back then but now an indispensable part of the picture. Cursed fortune, how could we have wasted so much time?

Time.

In the battle's wake, I had marveled at how much we suddenly had. Now I realize it was an illusion even then, because this day, all of us gathered here in one room—I can't predict when any of it will happen again.

And yet.

Yet—looking at their smiling faces, as familiar and comforting as ever, it occurs to me that maybe, just maybe, not everything has to change. As Finley and Violet continue to bicker, with Helos periodically interrupting or coming to Finley's defense, I feel a pair of arms wrap around my waist, steady and strong. Brightening through the tears, I place my hands over Weslyn's and realize that some changes might even be for the better.

A goodbye is coming. But here in this room, I see only my brother's face lit with unbridled joy, and my best friend chasing down the future once more. I see my queen as steadfast in her opinions and dependable in her leadership as ever. I see Wes, the fixed point north, the oak, patient and unwavering and unquestionably mine. And despite the sorrow, I'm still smiling.

I want one more day, and maybe somewhere down the line, I'll get it. But in this hour, I have Helos and Finley laughing louder than I've heard in weeks, while Weslyn holds me in his arms with a smile just for me. And for now, I decide, it's enough.

TEN
MONTHS
LATER

HELOS

It's strange, after so many years hemmed in by overbearing wilderness or cracking walls, to awaken each morning to the sea.

At dawn, with my head sinking into feather-soft pillows, I open my eyes to find early morning light peeking through the gaps between curtains. My room is a long, low-ceilinged collection of white-paneled walls, just one in a set of three comprising the private royal suite. It's far more space than any one person needs, but I'm told Jol's suite used to occupy five, and Rora warned me about the dangers of acting too much of a pushover. Moving quietly, I blink away the vestiges of sleep and slide from the massive four-poster bed.

The first few days, chambermaids snuck inside and tried to open the curtains for me. I put a stop to that before the first week was out, though, because this moment is mine. To pad barefoot across the plush, pale blue rug and sweep aside the curtains, slip through the glass balcony doors, and breathe in the crisp ocean air.

Today marks my tenth month in Eradain. When the clock tolls the eleventh hour, my court scribe, Gemma, will formally bestow upon me the red-and-gold loropin feather reserved for Eradain's monarch, the quill which writes the truth about the future—but only for the one gifted a feather, and only on each anniversary of the day it was given. At my request, as rehearsed, guards will open the iron gate rimming the estate, whose spiked rods I ordered tipped instead with metal curled into shells. My people will file across wooden bridges that arch over the grassy ravines winding throughout the tiled courtyard, each strip of wildflowers and

moss-covered stones and fledgling oaks within having been carefully tended by my groundskeeper, Horan. All will flood to the
beach, the endless ocean at their backs.

After shaking hands with Telyan's ambassador, Solet, and Glenweil's Padric, arrived to bear witness, I will walk onto the patio
and write a message that solidifies my role as the wielder of truth
and unites my kingdom with Alemara's other realms. When the
quill guides my hand, all I'll be able to do is hope it doesn't produce
the three words which have plagued my sister and me for years.

For now, I simply lean against the filigreed balcony railing,
staring out to sea. I have never liked waking to silence, and I used
to think it was the city grinding to a start that lifted my spirits. I
think, now, that I was wrong. It is this: the wordless roar beating
its uneven tempo upon the shore, the open horizon stretching
before me, and salty breeze ruffling my hair, while back inside, Fin
simply rolls over in bed, determinedly asleep.

Life in Castle Oraes has been a profusion of firsts. I wake to
three rooms and the ocean, and when I walk the tapestry-strewn
halls, my way has already been lit by attendants who move through
the castle like ghosts. There are rooms reserved for council meetings, and a long hall kept clean for biweekly audiences with the
public. Penelope's kitchen serves three meals a day on porcelain
plates spread upon a varnished wooden table. And three times a
day, an older man handpicked by my new captain of the Royal
Guard tastes the food in case of poison.

There are countless names and faces to learn, protocols to which
I adhere, boxes of documents to read and sign off on. Distant towns
and local neighborhoods to get to know, the latter of which I insist
on walking myself, though Captain Hariette sends half a dozen
Royal Guards with me every time. There are meetings that leave
me half hoarse from debating so much, and meetings that leave me
battling the urge to fall asleep.

In these ever-changing days, sometimes I can't help but wonder
if I made the right choice. Sitting in my fourth meeting of the day,
or lying awake in bed, it's easy to long for the simpler life I once

had. When my responsibilities were limited to my patients and my sister, Finley and my own sporadic whims.

But I can feel myself beginning to make a difference, and these are the moments that make it worth it. Change is a slow-moving beast, some days little more than a whisper of tolerance or a formerly closed door held slightly ajar. I see resentment in many of the faces around me, often disapproval or mistrust, but there is curiosity, too. A gradual willingness to listen, to engage, to work together in the interest of a brighter future.

I'm starting to think this might be how change happens—not all at once, but one day, one conversation, at a time. In my mind, this kingdom has always been a place of harsh rule and hardened planes, but I'm determined to soften the edges, bit by bit.

The sun has climbed above the horizon, so I push off from the railing and slip back inside. With the curtain drawn, the room is still dark, but lately I don't fear the nights the way I used to. The haunting memories I shared with Finley haven't faded away; shadows still linger in the crawl spaces of my mind, ready to creep forward whether I call them forth or not. They are, nonetheless, easier to bear. As if even the simple act of voicing them relieved some of their nagging pressure.

It makes me want to try it some more.

The door remains open.

"Fin," I whisper, bending over his side of the bed. I shake his shoulder a little, and he groans in protest, rolling his face into the pillow. "Fin, wake up," I continue, smiling. "I want to show you something."

"Can't it wait until morning?" he mumbles against the silk.

"It is morning."

After a beat, Finley flips his head toward me and peels open his eyes. "Something good or bad?"

"Come on," I tell him, dragging him out from under the covers.

Every dawn, any long silence or star-filled night, I thank fortune that Finley is by my side. It was hard saying goodbye to Rora after those first two months, so much so that I had had to bite my tongue in order to not call her back and beg her to stay the morning she took to the sky. Her presence had grounded me, a familiar, trusted face in a sea of lukewarm welcome. It made me braver. With Rora here, I didn't feel so alone.

Now she is gone, with a written promise to visit again in a couple of weeks; traveling alone, the journey is a two days' flight. It's an encouraging thought to cling to, but it's also not enough, because from here on out—or at least, for the foreseeable future—that's all her trips north will be. Visits. Temporary.

But Finley is still here. Fin, who keeps me sane, who helps me work through the problems I bring him, who slowly but surely learned the ins and outs of Oraes and charmed the castle staff. Finding the light, the way he does. Beautiful Fin, who kisses away the nightmares and the stress and pulls me out of bed in the middle of the night to dance in an empty ballroom.

Half an hour later, he and I are walking through the streets of a city just beginning to wake. Shop owners unlocking their doors and sweeping out front, bakers letting the scent of sweet breads waft through open windows. Finley tugs on his collar, but today I don't mind the late summer heat seeping through my tailored shirt. A flush of excitement dances across my skin.

"Was the early hour necessary?" he asks, though his gaze is sparkling, flitting like a hummingbird from shops to civilians to street corners. He senses my own anticipation, maybe, or perhaps it's just his usual need to move, the restless curiosity that seems to spur him on more strongly now than ever. I've begun to suspect his residual symptoms will always cycle back around—the headaches and the roaming pains, enough fatigue that he has to stop and rest more often than before. But Finley is learning to adjust. Not because he's brave, but because he must.

"Stop whining," I reply. "The fresh air will do you good."

Finley grins.

Now that I've made it ten months into my reign with no attempts on my life, the Royal Guard has agreed to widen its protective net enough to give me more space. This morning, they trail us a discreet twelve paces or so behind, which is better than the box they used to create. Most of the early workers we encounter watch us with varying degrees of interest. With every day that passes, I'm seeing less open hostility in their manner. To my relief, sometimes they even look friendly. Apparently Jol rarely went out into the city, and when he did, it was on horseback, never simply at eye level, on foot. My near-daily walks are something new, and they're not yet sure what to make of it.

When we reach the sprawling docks on Oraes's shoreline, Finley slows a little, glancing at me. "Another meeting with the fishing crews?" he asks.

I shrug, trying to force my traitorous face into an indecipherable palette. Inside, I'm jittery as a lightning bug in summer. "Not exactly."

The Royal Guard closes in as the broad streets narrow into wooden walkways. Finley and I weave through a maze of fishing vessels and civilian boats, the lapping waves nearly loud enough to drown out the sound of his walking stick snapping against the planks. There's a nervous energy about him, now. As if he senses something coming but can't tell whether it will be good or bad.

When we reach the shipyard, I halt us at the base of a work in progress. The vessel will be large, the length of a ballroom at least, with three masts and glorious gray-cut sails. But this morning it's only long stretches of mounted wood, just enough to begin curling up at the edges.

"What is it?" Finley asks, tilting back his head to try to see the top.

I shrug again, but I can no longer hold back the smile. "It's your ship."

For a long while, Finley doesn't react.

He just stares at the beginnings of the ship, motionless aside from the chest rising and falling a little quicker. Incrementally, he twists his head toward me. "What?"

Nothing about Finley has ever been quiet, or slow, but now his voice is hushed. Not brimming with his usual confidence, but hesitant. Uncertain.

"It's yours," I tell him, walking backward as I point out different aspects of the construction site. "Or at least, it will be. You'll have to give it a name. I didn't know which kind you wanted most, but I found a model in the castle that looked like the one on your mantel in Roanin, and, well, the architect told me it would work well enough."

Finley just watches me, unblinking. "Well enough for what?"

With a glance at the loitering guards, who have tactfully shifted their attention elsewhere, I return to his side and plant my hands on his shoulders. "To take you where you want to go. Anywhere. Down to Telyan, or out across the sea. It's yours, Fin. On one condition."

Still looking as if he can't quite believe this is real, he whispers, "What condition?"

I bend my head toward his, resting a hand on the back of his neck. "You have to always come back to me," I say. "However long you choose to be away."

It's true I need him by my side, this boy I love so much it steals the air from my lungs. This boy I now know, certain as breathing, I will ask to marry me one day, because he is the light that balances out the dark, the sudden break in the rain I will always run out to meet. But first, he needs to go. Finley has always longed for a life without bounds, always brought the sun. Now he needs to chase it, out of sight of the crown and the court, out toward an adventure that's entirely his, onto the vast horizon.

Finley shakes his head a little, his eyes sweeping my face. "You've always given too much of yourself to me."

But I want to give him more than me. I want to give him the world, because he can have it all—the adventures and the lingering pain, the unsteady gait I know still bothers him despite his cheerful face. The title he once resented and the feeling of flying, as far as he wants to go. "So what do you say?" I ask with a grin. "Do we have a deal?"

Finally, Finley smiles. It's a broad, brilliant smile that lights up his entire face, because this is real, the freedom he's always sought finally within his grasp. Because we're both here, the future stretched wide before us. A future we get to discover together, limitless as the open sea.

"Yes," he says, wrapping an arm around my waist. "From now on, my answer to you will always be yes."

RORA

After assessing a circle of obsidian stones which arose in the forest bordering Grovewood, finally, I am home.

My heart rises when Castle Roanin's high towers and spires color the horizon. Wings spread wide, I sweep over the sprawling estate and the oak-lined lawn four hundred paces deep that separates the castle from the complex's outer wall. This afternoon, groundskeepers tend to the gardens and grass in greater numbers than usual, scouring for damage following the morning's eager crowds.

It is exactly one year to the day since Finley and I walked the Old Forest, his unspoken gift to spare me from the Prediction's public reading. One year since I watched my friend collapse in the woods, tree limbs pointed toward him like a circle of swords. I woke this morning heavy with memories, as well as familiar apprehension for the hours to come. It turned out I had nothing to fear, because for the first time in eight strained years, the message that Violet read out to the assembled crowds was not, *Two shifters death*. With just nine words—nine liberating, untried words—the quill ended that chapter in Alemara's history, and my own.

An ending. A long-awaited beginning.

I fly through the open window in the eastern wing, my new-found freedom as curative as stardust.

For years, I lived in the one-room house situated near the stables and the complex's outer wall. Now my sleeping quarters are inside the castle, a luxury owed to my status as the sister of a distant king. *Princess*. Most days, it hardly feels real.

I shift to human and shut the window when I'm inside, opting for thin trousers and a breezy, short-sleeved blouse over the dresses I've been favoring of late. The summer sun won't set for a few hours yet, which means we should have plenty of time. Out in the halls, attendants nod politely as I pass, and if my royal title feels strange to me, the accompanying cordiality from people other than Helos and Finley feels stranger still.

Thoughts of my faraway brother elicit the usual strand of loneliness, but I maintain my pace, shoulders back.

Prediction Day, the seven hundredth and forty-eighth year since Fendolyn's unified realm divided into three. Also the fifth anniversary of the day Helos and I arrived in Roanin.

The first week here without Helos was the hardest. To go from seeing him almost every day to not at all, after a separation that was only meant to be temporary—at first, I missed the easy familiarity of his presence, and Finley's, so much it hurt. Fortune has been kind to me, though, because in the months since leaving them together in Oraes, the ache has softened to a distant hum. Still there, whispering its presence, but a little easier to ignore.

My footsteps muffled by the hanging tapestries and dark green runner underfoot, I round the corner and nearly collide with Wes, who appears to have been trying to read and walk at the same time.

He brightens when he sees me, the gesture a tiny beacon against the customary funereal black he and his sister both wear today. Beneath the tailored jacket, his collared shirt is mountain gray. "Looking for me, I hope."

"Mm," I murmur noncommittally, though of course, I was. I grasp the book and examine the spine—something dull about stonework. "Weren't you on a history of Beraila?" The closest continent south across the sea.

"I finished that."

"Show-off," I mutter, releasing the timeworn book with a smile.

In light of Weslyn's service in the war, Violet has granted him leave to move on from the army and begin shaping his next role.

Though he won't attend university like he once envisioned, already his days are more to his liking, reading and planning and advising with no sword in sight. The mix has provided the perfect distraction for Finley's absence, and recently he's added one more task to his queue, unprompted: convince Violet to open the ports and reestablish trade relations with other continents.

Today, however, he has different plans.

"Do you still want to do this?" I ask.

Wes sobers at that, running a hand along his trim beard, but nods all the same.

Prediction Day, and the anniversary of Helos's and my arrival in Roanin. Also the anniversary of Queen Raenen's death. It's Weslyn's hardest day, aside from the one additional anniversary still to come.

Though I'd like to take his hand, the castle is too public a space for that. So I simply gesture for him to lead the way, pausing on the threshold when he drops the book inside his private quarters. The high-ceilinged sitting parlor has been painted the same pale blue as Finley's, but Wes's bedroom is a darker hue, the duvet matching the sky between twilight and night proper.

These days, almost everywhere I go, the world shifts subtly around me. With the prison compound destroyed, magical wildlife roaming east of the river once more, and pockets of earth beginning to wake, magic seems to feel more secure in its capacity for survival. Most people afflicted with the Fallow Throes have found themselves cured of the worst, though as with Finley, they are not entirely without lasting effects; some remain unbalanced or unsteady on their feet, while others continue to experience pain, nausea, or fatigue. As for the other unwilling hosts, most who began the path to becoming a shifter, whisperer, or forest walker have lost their burgeoning abilities. Astra stopped trailing frost. My guess is, by the end, only those born with magic will retain it.

In Telyan, tensions between humans and forestborn have been slowly easing up; while Roanin remains an insular place, lately it feels less like a city in waiting and more like a city looking forward. Even the castle itself feels different. In place of arcing halls I used to navigate tense and alone, newly shared spaces take on better meanings. There's the library where Wes and I pass the time in companionable silence, and the wood-paneled dining room where we eat. The sprawling estate across which he goes for runs with Astra while I fly overhead, and the bedrooms where we, mostly, sleep. And though the absence of my two closest friends hits hard, new friendships are slowly blossoming in their wake, unfurling a little more with every passing day.

Ansley and Naethan seem to have accepted me as the fourth member of their group. The head groundskeeper hired a forest walker as an apprentice, and we've taken to keeping each other company on our days off. Down in Briarwend, I've told my friend Seraline my real name, and her little sister has stopped making the sign to ward off bad fortune whenever I draw near. Perhaps best of all, I've managed to see Peridon several times among his many visits to Roanin; he mainly comes to see the human girl with whom he's grown enamored.

Through all the changes, Wes remains the fixed point north.

I love him, I love him, I love him.

After ditching the book, he and I make our way outside and across the northern end of the estate, through the groves of red maples and hickory trees and past the old carriage house where Helos, Finley, and I used to meet. I feel their presence beside me like ghosts from the past, warm and comforting, when I lace my fingers through Weslyn's and lead him past the tree line.

The Old Forest sprawls heavy in full summer bloom, a vast canvas of bright green leaves glimmering in the afternoon sun. Underfoot, the ground slopes gently upward, squirrels hurrying from our path among the dirt-encrusted stones.

Wes keeps pace without complaint, but I can feel the tension settling over his shoulders. Not because a nightwing flew before us without warning, the small black fox doubtless too preoccupied with the aerial hunt to care much for our cumbersome presence. It's not because the trees are moving around us, bending a little out of our way as if in gratitude or respect for what we've done to reawaken them. That happens more and more these days, the land's magic rising steadily closer to the surface, and its inhabitants slowly learning to live with it again. Wilderness building toward its former state.

Aside from the first day of our journey to the Vale months ago, Wes hasn't walked these woods in more than four years, not since the day his mother died in them. Today, for the first time, he agreed to my suggestion to visit her grave.

The site is easy enough for me to find. Finley led me here more than once, and in any case, I've walked this forest so often I've practically learned it by heart. But today, the glade looks different than before. The worn granite headstone commemorating Queen Raenen is still here and dusted with wind-loosed leaves, but there's a new headstone to its left. The writing is crisp, the bordering floral design equally intricate. My heart pinches with regret. King Gerar, laid to rest beside his wife.

When we reach the sunlit clearing, Wes hesitates before stepping over the threshold. He doesn't speak, so neither do I. Instead, I follow his lead and sink onto the grass opposite the stones. We sit in silence for a time.

I have no headstones to mark my parents' graves. No graves to visit, anyway—after Father died, the forest reclaimed the land that was once our home, before those prison soldiers cut it down. Maybe by now, new growth has begun to blanket the site once more. I suppose it's a comforting thought.

"I wish—" Wes pauses, his honeyed gaze shifting to the quivering branches interlaced behind the headstones. Though he spoke softly, the words hang loud this deep into the woods.

"Yes?" I say, studying the headstones.

Wes's fingers toy with the grass. "I wish my father were here to see Finley recovered. He died without knowing."

Of course the wish would be for his father and his brother, not for himself. I press my shoulder against his, welcoming the warmth. "He died believing," I point out. "That has to count for something."

Weslyn nods thoughtfully, but he doesn't respond. Instead, we watch a cardinal perch atop his mother's headstone, ruffling its scarlet feathers, before continuing its flight.

"Wes."

He twists at the sound of his name. Once, I would have read nothing in his eyes save for the tightly controlled façade he uses in public, and the reservedness I mistook for severity. Now his expression is open, an offering, neither of us hiding from the other any longer. The mutual trust feels a little like a gift.

"I'm glad you let me bring you here," I tell him.

At that, he smiles and wraps an arm around my shoulders, resting his head on top of mine.

We stay like that a while longer. Holding each other, each healing in our own time. Sitting opposite the royal headstones, I can't help but wonder if Jol would have wished to be buried in the Holworth plot as he was, once they brought his body home. Whether it's really a coincidence that the Prediction he and Daymon so feared ultimately changed after his death.

I'm not sure it matters. Even if he *was* one of the shifters at its center, anyone could have been the second. Our mother, Helos. Me. Another shifter entirely. In the end, the Prediction's true impact came, not from the words themselves, but from the meaning humans assigned to them.

What matters is that with Eradain's surrender and Jol's downfall, Alemara found peace.

Far in the distance, the clock tower tolls the hour—low bells sweeping in on the breeze. An hour until Wes is expected to appear at tonight's feast, the meal which used to follow the annual Royal Fox Hunt, before Queen Raenen's death put an end to that particular event.

The spell broken, we push to our feet and pick our way down the hill. I'm glad to see that Wes's bearing has lightened a touch, but still I hesitate when we reach the Old Forest's edge.

"Okay?" he asks.

I nod. "I'll be back in time for the feast."

Wes, thankfully, doesn't question it. He just plants a quick kiss on my head before heading for home, while I turn back into the woods.

I can't say what exactly the future holds. As the land continues to awaken, the soil has grown richer, food more plentiful. Tensions between magical and nonmagical people have smoothed into a hard-won peace, but the road to recovery cannot mend entirely in so short a time. Healing is an ever-changing process without definitive end. I know that better than most.

Even so. If the last few months are any indication, whatever the years to come, I won't have to walk them alone. My feet are bound for a life of community, of friendship and love, with the wilderness crowding in around. Untamed. Unpredictable. Home. And after a lifetime of feeling stuck in the past, I'm ready to start looking forward.

First, though, there's a forest here that needs to be felt.

I run my fingertips along the rough bark, smiling a little. Handing my clothes to an outstretched branch for safekeeping, I shift to goshawk, spread my wings, and fly.

ACKNOWLEDGMENTS

I wrote *Wildbound* during a difficult time. Both personally and in the world around me, the last two years have been quite the cycle of ups and downs, a tumultuous blend of sadness and joy, anger and fear and hope. But that's the beauty of art, isn't it? That we can continue to create in times of hardship. The light and the dark—like Rora and Helos, I have found there's room inside for both.

Throughout this journey, I have been surrounded by an abundance of wonderful people. Lindsey Hall and Hillary Jacobson, my editor and agent, are twin flames of wisdom, advocacy, and support who understand, not only me, but also what I'm trying to do. Thank you for championing this story.

The folks at Tor Teen have ushered this duology into the world with invaluable support. Sarah Reidy and Giselle Gonzales are publicists of dreams, while Anthony Parisi, Isa Caban, and Eileen Lawrence are marketing legends. Andrew King, Sarah Pannenberg, and Rachel Bass are all essential players, and my production editor, Jeff LaSala, is an unsung hero. Lesley Worrell and Katie Ponder have once again turned this story's heart into beautiful cover art, while Ed Chapman copyedited both *Forestborn* and *Wildbound* with a deft hand. Farther up the chain, Devi Pillai and Lucille Rettino have enabled me to turn this writing dream of mine into published reality, and for that, I'm forever grateful.

On the personal side, my dad is probably the biggest advocate for this series there is, so I think I've got to give him this section's top billing. Dad, I hope you appreciate all the father love in this story—it's grounded in reality. Sorry I killed off King Gerar, though.

While on the subject of family, Mom—thank you for learning to incorporate words like "worldbuilding" into your lexicon. Proud of you. Sam—sorry I gave the bad guy your instrument, but at least I gave you the dedication. I love you and stuff. (Ugh, gross.)

AJ Stuhrenberg continues to provide emotional support along every step of the way. I'd say I could never repay them for it, but they'd only reply that I don't have to. Thank you, friend.

Hilary Mauro is a badass librarian and unflagging support system on this journey of highs and lows. Joanna Hathaway is one of my most trusted consultants for when the words just aren't coming out quite right, and for the long writerly chats over wine I value so much. My good friend, Dr. Amy Schettino, made sure I didn't embarrass myself by having Helos treat a patient with medically impossible methodology. (Aside from the occasional sprinkle of magic.) Thanks, you three!

To you, dear reader—thank you for believing in these characters and their stories. Your support means more to me than you know.

And finally, a word.

At its core, the Forestborn duology is a story of hope. Of learning to live in the balance, the good with the bad, the light with the dark. To come out of a difficult experience and find that strength remains, because you're still standing.

At the time of this novel's publication, and most certainly beyond, our planet could use some hope. Climate change is an ever-pressing crisis we must confront head-on. Rora, Helos, Weslyn, and Finley had magic to help re-wild their continent and restore a more natural, balanced state; we on Earth aren't so lucky. But we have voices, and we have our hands, and there is power in that.

It's not too late to make a difference. The Earth needs our help. Please do what you can to protect it.